I0687871

Kyle
The Apprentice
Warlock

By
M. J. Okawa

Published by

Warlocks In Space Publishing LLC
522 W. Riverside Ave, Ste N
Spokane, WA 99201

Original Copyright ©2019

Book cover design by K. R. Dalley

Dedicated to my awesome great-aunts who always tried to show me the magic in the world.

Chapter 1

It was a nice day, a nice morning. Clear, skies. It was also stupid-bright for this time of day and Kyle was shading his smartphone's screen, walking from the shade of one security golem to another as he tried to read.

"Cook!?" He whisper-screamed with irritation and a flare of magic enveloped him with a full body aurora of translucent dark blue flames filled with fuchsia sparkles as he expressed his displeasure. One of the dozens of security golems that lined the perimeter of the park turned its head to assess him as a threat. "Oh. Oops." The young man looked up startled. "Don't mind me. Just reading. Good golem. I'm not a threat. See?"

He groped for the lanyard around his neck and held up his tie instead of the identification card he'd been intending to. Large, blocky, and vaguely humanoid in shape, the dark granite security golem's supposedly emotionless stare began to seem terribly baleful at that moment.

Kyle realized he was holding up his tie and fumbled around his neck again before successfully holding up his ID badge. He stood very still as he was magically scanned because he was pretty sure that they did not like him. No siree.

In Kyle's, admittedly, biased opinion, those golems thought Kyle was shifty as heck. Were the other golems watching him out of the corners of their eyes? Were their heads turned ever so slightly to keep focus on him?

The surface of his badge flashed pearlescent as the magical security identifiers it was enchanted with activated at the golem's query. Satisfied, the golem returned to its assigned position, looking like nothing so much as a statue facing outward from the protected grounds of Central Park. The others in the row also shifted slightly as well, their heads returning to a neutral position.

"Pfft! I knew it." He crowed quietly. "They *are* watching me." After a second of squinting his eyes at them to make sure the golems had returned to their normal behavior, he let out a relieved breath and ran a hand through his short wavy hair giving it a quick tug of frustration.

"Whew! That was..." The young man scrubbed a hand over his face. "I've got to talk to the boss about lowering the sensitivity on their sensor enchantments. That is way too high." Grumbling, the young man returned to hurrying along while quietly cursing under his breath and scrolling on his phone.

"Cook. They said I'm a bloody cook? Damn this sun." Kyle squinted his eyes and shook his fist in the general direction of the sunrise as he continued with his distracted rant. "Anna gets a brilliant write-up, but me? Oh, he's just the family cook." His voice changed pitch and octave as he mocked what had been written about himself. "I can't believe...ah, hello." Noticing someone standing in his path, Kyle looked up to apologize and saw that it was just another golem.

This one was not the impeccable imposing dark stone edifice of the others. Nor was it one of the security golems that he swore held some kind of grudge against him. Instead, it was old, one might say ancient even. It had clearly been destroyed and reassembled.

The white marble of its weathered body was a crisscrossing tracery of golden lines welding the cracked stone together in a beautiful example of Kintsugi style art being used to restore an artifact. Of course, the regular type of lacquer used in pottery kintsugi wasn't strong enough to hold a marble golem together. This was enchanted.

Bright morning light reflected off the repairs where it hit them, but they shone with magical light where they were in shadow. And a series of enchantments and runes of restoration were carved into the stone body to reinforce the welds. They glowed softly on the parts of its body that were shaded from the sun. The magical carvings were not bright enough to glow in the sun, but in the lighted areas, the carvings of the runes could be seen faintly in the old stone.

It was the Apple Tree Golem, a favorite feature of the park and one of the many wonders curated by the museum. This golem was actually a New York City mascot, and its image was used heavily in tourism advertising. Visitors to the museum could buy miniature, non-functional versions of it in the museum gift shop.

The Apple Tree Golem carried a woven basket of golden apples over one arm. *They really do just look like solid lumps of apple-shaped gold.* Kyle mused at how they glinted in the morning light. As he paused on his trek to work, the golem took one golden apple from its basket and held it out to Kyle with its free hand. The apple glowed softly despite competing with the sun.

Magic apples. Magic apples the golem harvested from the tree it guarded and offered to parkgoers as they wandered by. A tree that was gifted to Central Park and The National Museum of Unnatural Science and History by Ladon, the guardian dragon of the Garden of Hesperides. These weren't *those* magic apples, the apples of immortality. Ladon would never give one of those trees out if he could even be persuaded to admit that they existed.

The tree had been a historic gift to celebrate the restoration of the ancient Golem which had been destroyed during a monster battle decades ago. It had protected the remains of its sacred grove until the very last. Ladon had been so moved by the story he'd felt the Golem deserved a new grove to protect and the tree he'd gifted was the first planted in the museum's Magical Tree Grove in Central Park.

It stood across from the entrance to The National Museum of Unnatural Science and History, golden apples glowing faintly nestled among the leaves of the tree. Kyle could see it over the golem's shoulder. Beyond that, the multi-story façade of the museum with its wide steps and pillars making it look like some ancient temple of the Gods sized for them to appear in their true forms. Already, the leaves of some trees in the orchard were beginning to change colors for the Fall season. That didn't matter though. The trees would fruit year-round.

"Thanks." Kyle took the proffered apple as the golem once again offered it to him. While it might not make him live forever, one of these a day, would keep the doctor away for most minor ailments.

It wouldn't work on anything a good elixir couldn't fix just as well or even better. Which was probably why no one fought over them or tried to steal them. And museum employees received an Apple Stipend as part of their benefits package. He shoved the apple into the deep pockets of his Warlock's robe, a rather modern design that resembled a dark trench coat with a hood but was enchanted to protect the wearer from magical and alchemical mishaps. Kyle hurried on, his robe swirling around his knees as his cell phone began to ring.

The ringtone was set to a song that amused him, and the Mountain King Mover's advertising jingle began playing. It was complete with lyrics set to the iconic *In the Hall of the Mountain King* music. The young man began to sing along as he squinted at his phone screen angling it away from the sunlight again to see who was calling.

"When you need to move your stuff,
Trust in us,
We are tough,
When you need to move your stuff,
We will get it done."

Kyle waited until the entire first verse had played before picking up the call.

Chapter 2

"Cooks R' Us." He smiled as he glanced at the caller ID, thought better of having fruit in his pocket, and pulled it out to tuck into his shoulder bag. If Samantha was calling for the reason he thought she was, she'd get the reference to his greeting, and he might as well beat her to the punch. Mock himself before she could.

"Kyle?" His sister hesitated slightly at his new greeting then plowed ahead with the conversation, ignoring the chance for friendly banter. "You wouldn't happen to know any memory-erasing spells, would you?" That was...not what he was expecting. He frowned and pulled the apple back out of his bag realizing he was a little peckish.

"I am legally required to say no". His glib reply was interrupted with a crunching bite into his golden apple. "However," the young man continued as he crunched annoyingly, "...if you tell me where the body is and who's involved, I can probably manage something for you." His chewing continued as silence came from the other end of the call. After a thoughtful pause, his sister finally spoke again.

"What!?" Kyle stifled a laugh that almost resulted in apple chunks up his nose.

"Ah... So, your government friends will take care of it. Gotcha." He sniggered at Sam's offended response as he swallowed.

"No! No one's dead, Kyle! Have you...read the article yet?" Yep. She'd called for the reason he thought she called. He'd been thinking she called to tease him about what the guy profiling their family for the PR campaign his mom was part of wrote about him, now he wondered...

"Working on it now. They did a nice bit on Anna. Too bad she's going to hate it. Just finished reading about me." A sigh of relief came over the line.

"So, you haven't seen the section on me yet? Good. I want you to erase everyone's memory of those stupid tissue commercials, so they don't haunt me until the end of time." *Oh, really?* That instantly piqued Kyle's interest. Did he smell more ammo for the sibling war?

"Haha, no! Sorry big sis. I'm afraid you're stuck with that." He'd turned his body to shield his phone from the sun and began looking for the section of the interview on his sister. "Give me a second to skim...Oh! Oh. That is hilarious." Somehow the writer had found...well, it wasn't that obscure. But that this, *this,* was what the author of the article focused on for Sam when she had such cooler aspects of her life to write about!

"What?" Samantha demanded hotly.

"I'm changing my ringtone to the jingle. Medicsayswhat!"

"Fuck you!" She called back. Kyle could just picture her face coloring with shame at the enduring nature of embarrassing stuff sticking around on the internet. The commercials she'd made for that business class project.

"Gesundheit." Kyle cackled with delight.

"You suck, Kyle" He had intended to stop, but this was a perfect opening for another shot.

"At least I didn't blow. Then I'd need a medic" Samantha smacking her hand into her head was loud enough to hear over the call.

"Normally, I'd have a good response to that, Kyle." Reasoned even tones that bordered on hysterical came to him. "Except for the fact that I've been receiving calls from people I haven't heard from since high school asking for a medic." It came out in an almost-sob. "I had deliberately made the ads as outrageous as possible specifically so that I wouldn't win the contest. I was trying to prevent my ideas from being featured in the Tissue Medic advertising campaign. Please help me make it go away?"

"Oh. I'm crying you a river. It's so deep I think I need a tissue...medic." His voice went up in pitch on his last mocking word.

"Yooouuuu...! I hate you! Ugh!" The call went quiet.

"Sam? Did – she just hang up on me?" He stared at the phone as the call counter beeped off. "She did. I'll call her back on break and apologize after she's cooled off a bit."

An incoming call from his younger sister started while he was dumbly looking at the just-ended call from his older sister. The new ringtone began playing. It was a jaunty jingle even if his sister had badly written the corny lyrics and Kyle chimed in with the catchy song.

"Dry your eyes.
Staunch blood flow.
Cheer you up,
on the go.
Body, heart, or mind,
enchanted Tissue Medic tissues
salve every wound from exes to skinned elbows."

The jingle began to repeat itself and Kyle interrupted it by answering the call.

"You have reached the cook's phone. He can't speak to you right now because he's busy slaving away over your favorite meals." The apprentice wizard was trying to cheer up his younger sister by making fun of himself because he knew she wasn't going to be happy. Not today of all days.

"Kyle, I think I'm going to do something my classmates will regret." While, intellectually, Kyle knew he shouldn't encourage it, he couldn't help himself chuckling. "You laugh but if *someone* messes with me today because I'm in the stupid news *again* I'm going to lose my cool." He sighed and put on his 'responsible-big brother pants'.

"If you lose your cool, just don't let anyone find it in the chest of one of your classmates." It was going to take a while to talk Anna down off the murder-everyone ledge and he realized with a sigh he was not, in fact, going to have time to get doughnuts before work. He stared longingly at the Enchantress Doughnuts food bike about half a mile past the museum.

"Cryomancer jokes. Ha, ha! Like that's not the same one you use every time." Usually, references to her magic cheered Anna up, however this was not looking like it was going to be a home run of cheering-up-kid-sis-by-the-big-bro kind of day. "Fine. I promise I won't get caught."

That was...better...than outright massacring people with no regard for getting caught, he supposed. Frankly, the thought of people bullying his little sister just boiled his bones and Kyle was more than willing to bring the pain on anyone who tried. However, Mom had left orders about how to deal with the inevitable article fallout. Keep her calm and de-escalate.

"Anna, it's just one little section of a PR puff piece meant to humanize Mom to the people who might be a little bit scared that she's the magical equivalent of a flying super soldier with nuclear laser lances and wing missiles of divine wrath." Halfway through that sentence, he noticed a few of the pedestrians walking in the opposite direction were eyeing him with concern.

"I shouldn't have had to participate," Anna grunted through the phone and seemed to be out of breath for a moment. She was doing something that made thumping sounds in the background, and he assumed that Anna was probably still getting ready for school. "I'm a minor. Aren't there laws about protecting my privacy and safety?" Inwardly, Kyle admitted it was a valid concern. The youngest member of the family was only fourteen and she went to a super prestigious private school full of spoiled children of the uber rich for a reason.

Bodyguards.

All the bodyguards and security on campus were the reason.

"I'm pretty sure you are the only eighth-grader on the planet who has a personal I owe you from the president of their country." This had been the plan that they'd worked out with Mom beforehand. Anna was inevitably going to be upset about whatever was written. She was a kid in a school with shitty spoiled-asshole classmates. The family *knew* beforehand that something, *something* would go down because of this. Their goal was to mitigate Anna's reaction to the bullies.

"You're right." Anna grudgingly admitted. "I do have that I Owe You from him." Kyle knew for a fact that it was framed on her dresser.

"Right next to the ones from three different Joint Chiefs of Staff." He reminded her of how she'd had to be bribed into participating so that Joe Q Public could have a chance to get to know their terrifying parent as the doting mother she was. Or at least, make them think she was. There were more IOUs, from various mom-related events over the years, and Kyle doubted that the individuals in debt would ever let her call them in... but if she ever did...

"It's a hobby." She admitted sheepishly as she tried to conquer her discontent. "Today's just going to suck." He could hear the resignation in her voice and his heart bled for her.

"I know." It wasn't hard to play the sympathetic older brother when he really was sympathetic to her plight. It wasn't that long since he'd been her age, and she had it rougher than any of her three elder siblings. She was the only one in the family who was visibly magic touched. She stood out with her waist-length white hair, dark eyes, and tan skin. "Hey. At least you got a nice bit about you that makes you seem really impressive while I'm *the cook* and everyone thinks Sam's in advertising."

"Yeah." Anna snorted and Kyle thought he may have heard a snot bubble pop. *Someone needs a medic, a tissue medic.* He couldn't help the thought whispering in his head though he wisely kept it to himself so that he didn't aggravate his baby sister further. "They made me out to be like I was *so* powerful and maybe the heir to mom's magic and position."

That? That had been bad. Kyle had thought it was a bad move while he was reading it. That should never have been okay to publish, and it was a damn good thing that Anna attended a school with security up the wazoo already otherwise they'd have to pack her off to some obscure boarding school built like a medieval fortress for her own safety. The crazies would be out in force for her after this.

"It wasn't as bad as all that." Kyle soothed while lying through his teeth. The golden apple clutched forgotten at his side.

"The writer called me the next Harbinger and said that I 'Light Up the Dawn with my magic'." She scoffed. Kyle was nearing the museum where he worked and paused in a shaded spot near the steps so he could keep talking uninterrupted. He heard the beep of an incoming call and pulled the phone away from his face to see who was calling now. It was, not surprisingly, his mother this time. He sighed with resignation.

"Just don't worry about it, kid. Go to school. Have the best damn day you can. And spit icicles in the face of anyone who gives you grief." It was not the most responsible thing he could say, it was however the most big-brotherly thing to say. "Look. I gotta go. Mom's calling. Probably to tell me not to encourage you to do anything rash and to stop making fun of Samantha."

"Kay. Bye, Kyle. Love you." Her morose response gutted Kyle a bit, if he thought he could get away with it he'd play Hookey and hang out with Anna all day. Unfortunately, he had to adult, and they'd get caught when the school notified his parents that Anna wasn't there.

"Love you, too, Snow Cone."

Chapter 3

Kyle glared at the screen of his phone as the incoming call from his mother took over the place the one from Anna had just held. Whereas Anna's image was a cute little cartoonish picture of a snow cone, his mother's well, it was one of the more incredible shots of her that someone had taken. He wasn't sure if it was a captured image from video footage or if someone somehow happened to be that lucky. The picture was just about one of the most epic things he'd ever seen in his life.

The image of his mother that Kyle used in his phone book was one of her in her full-powered exoskeleton armor. Her magical wings spread behind her with her lance raised and ready to fire. She was ringed with power in all the glory of divine wrath that her patron gifted her with. His mother looked like the most badass anime warrior goddess come to life. His mother, a warlock of the Archangel Michael. Known throughout the world as one of the most devastating forces in existence.

A warrior patron for a warrior woman.

Normally, Kyle was so proud when he looked at that photo. Because his mother was amazing. Today the image of her mid-attack represented the darker side of being one of her children. The expectations that everyone else placed on them to live up to her greatness.

And the teeny tiny size of the picture on the screen did it no justice at all. He scoffed, not bothering to sing along with the song playing as his ringtone. It was no longer amusing him. His mom had messed up. Fine. He'd have to talk to her eventually. So, he slid his finger over the button to answer his phone for the third time that morning.

"You promised." That was how he answered the call. The cold flat tone of his voice trembled with anger, and he had to stop before he said anything he'd regret. On the other end of the line, Camina Watkins, The Harbinger of Dawn, The Light Bringer, The Morning Star, THE Valkyrie, The Last Sight You'd Ever See, The Last Resort, The Last Line, sighed as she heard her son's tone of voice.

"So, that's how it's going to go." It was more statement than question.

"You promised they were going to lay off of Anna." The young man continued doggedly. If it had been himself, he might have capitulated and let himself be pressured, for his little sister...NO!

"You promised that they were going to stop pressuring her to take Michael's pact. You promised she'd be allowed to choose her own patron if she ever chose to become a warlock. She doesn't need to take a patron. Anna's got enough natural magic that she doesn't need a pact to be a magic user."

He kept his voice to a low growl and glared off into the park, watching pedestrians on their way while he took the time to have the inevitable conversation. He knew he was the only one who would do it, too. Once again, he heard his mother's sigh. However, her voice, when it came, was steel.

"First of all, what went to print wasn't what I was shown and approved of. Secondly, I'm just a soldier. I couldn't have prevented this even if I had known they'd gone this way with it. And thirdly, *everyone*, and I literally mean every person on the entire planet *knows* that Anna has been offered a divine patron." Her voice dripped with scorn at the obvious.

"The angels put a God damned star in the sky over the hospital when she was born. It doesn't have to be Michael or even one of the angels, but that doesn't change the fact that the offer stands. That the offer will always stand. I can't change that!"

"You could remind people that she's just a kid and she's not ready –" Kyle never got to finish his sentence.

"Not ready? Not ready?" For the first time in the conversation, Camina's voice began to rise with anger. "Samantha entered her pact at thirteen. You? Not much older. *I* was burning monsters with the power of an archangel when I was ten. My entire family has been powerful military assets for centuries. Centuries Kyle. I'm literally called The Last *fucking* Line! You know what that's of?" Kyle wanted to turn around and throw his phone at the wall he was leaning against, instead, he let the word come from between his gritted teeth as his mother spoke at the same time.

"Defense." The word was sullen as he said it, but fiery in his mother's tirade.

"Defense!" She paused and lowered her voice. "My superiors, they look at the history of our family, they look at me aging, and they are freaking out. Have you ever seen a four-star general have a panic attack and an existential crisis because *I* don't have an 'heir'? There is no one in our country at my level to replace me. Not one of my older children has chosen to be an actual *War*lock despite taking warlock pacts with fairly powerful patrons."

Here Kyle thought he might be able to argue, but his mother wouldn't let him. They both knew why she didn't have a proverbial heir.

"I know Kyle. I *know* that Samantha isn't cut out for it and her pact item is too unstable and her patron too bloodthirsty even if she were willing. I *know* your brother has a peaceful patron even if Asclepius is powerful. *I know!* I also know that you are capable of so much more even if no one else does. But I also *know* that, Anna. Is. Special. New-stars-in-the-heavens kind of special. And the whole world knows that too. There's only so much interference I can run, and I *know* that I'm failing her as a mother. *I know.* And I *am* sorry for that."

She finally stopped long enough for Kyle to get a word in edgewise. She'd already said out loud the thing he was going to imply quietly without ever outright saying. She was failing Anna as a mother. Camina Watkins was a soldier first, a warlock second, a wife third, and a mother last.

That was a quote from her official biography. She didn't say that about herself. It was something the author had said. Kyle pushed down the lump that had been forming in his throat as his mother waited patiently for his response. Finally, he spoke, and his voice was only slightly hoarse.

"Will..." He coughed to clear his throat and continued quickly. "Will you just make sure you tell Anna that?" He pleaded. "Not all the other bits that will make her feel guilty and pressured, just the part about being sorry."

"Yeah." Camina gave a rueful laugh. "I think I can do that."

"In person." Kyle admonished, as he rubbed something from his eyes. "Not a text. At least a voice call."

"Yes. I pro –" Kyle cut her off before she could finish her sentence.

"*Don't* promise!" He felt like a jerk, yet it was a well-known fact in their family that their mother couldn't be relied upon to keep some promises. "Just do it."

"Alright." She was quiet; ashamed with the knowledge of shared history as to why he spoke that way. "I better let you get to work before you're late. Lots of love baby boy." With that, she hung up and Kyle puffed out his cheeks with a huge sigh of relief. He loved his mom, however these conversations...sometimes she made him feel like he was the parent.

He made sure the call had disconnected and locked the screen on his phone before shoving it into a pocket of his robes. Kyle looked down at himself with that same assessing self-loathing he felt whenever someone tried to 'guide' Anna into being their mom's replacement. It didn't matter that as a warlock of an archangel Camina Watkins was going to live and be a viable military asset for a good long while yet. It mattered because if Kyle had chosen a different path, maybe Anna wouldn't have had to deal with those fools at all.

Yeah. When other people looked at Kyle, they saw an academic warlock. Someone who took a patron to help them gain knowledge more than magic. But what if...No! The young man shook his head and straightened the strap of his messenger bag over his shoulder. No. He'd chosen the Archivist and knowledge, and magic for magic's sake. Knowledge was power after all.

Another ringtone came from the phone in his pocket, and he pulled it out again. It was just his alarm, telling him work started in fifteen minutes. His shoulders slumped as he trudged out of the shadows. Sunlight glinting off the natural blonde highlights in his light brown hair. He was just an average apprentice warlock – not even a full warlock like his older siblings – working an average job as a museum intern.

Nothing more. Nothing less.

Well, a little more. He also had some wizard powers.

Not nearly as spectacular as all the other members of his family.

Chapter 4

10:00 AM September 13th, 2026
New York Preparatory Academy, New York, NY

It started out a nice day. Except for that stupid article. But the weather was nice. Really nice. Like most days that change the course of history, they are stereotypically either really nice weather or very terrible weather. It's never just an average blah kind of day. Today it was an absolutely gorgeous Fall morning.

The leaves had just started turning colors, the sky was an unbelievably deep blue for that time of year, and it contrasted incredibly with the red brick buildings of the grounds for the New York Preparatory Academy for the absurdly rich and spoiled. That last part about the absurdly rich and spoiled wasn't actually part of the school's name. That was just something Anna's big brother, Kyle, would say to cheer Anna up about going there.

It was a really beautiful campus. Austere red brick facades on emerald-green manicured lawns, obsessively landscaped formal gardens, shingled rooftops, and fall leaves. That was why Anna Watkins was deep in concentration, working on a watercolor pencil landscape sketch when Sara White approached unnoticed and kicked her sketchbook out of her hands.

Confused and startled, Anna shrieked in surprise and jerked her head up to see who had interrupted her while she was in the zone. Seeing it was the most popular – which everyone knew meant richest – girl in school, Anna contained her sudden urge to destroy the first person she saw. Her nostrils flared, and she pushed the few strands of hair that had escaped her bun back over her ears in a nervous habit.

"What the fuck Sara?" So, what that they weren't allowed to swear at school. Sara's behavior was bullshit.

"You think Liam Ecclestone would ever be interested in a freak like you?" The brat's golden curls jiggled around her porcelain face as perfectly painted glossy red lips spat scorn at the girl sitting on the ground.

"Um, nooooo…" Anna arched one pale eyebrow unsure of what had spawned the current confrontation. "I'm not even sure who that is?" Unable to scoot back as she was leaning against a tree, Anna rose in one smooth graceful movement. That only seemed to infuriate her opponent more as Anna towered a full five inches over the other girl once standing.

"Stop pretending you aren't into him. Gina saw you say 'Hi' to him before school this morning." In a moment of clarity that made even less sense, Anna was able to place the interaction that seemed to have garnered her this unwanted attention.

"Look, I was just being polite to someone who was polite to me. He said 'Hi' so I said 'Hi' back. There's *no* interest between us from either party." Remembering her mother's words that it's harder to de-escalate a confrontation than to escalate it and that no one really wins in a fight, she tried to reassure Sara that she was *not* 'competition'.

Anna had noticed that Sara had shown up with her little clique of bullies. Not that they were there for intimidation or anything, just that the five of them went everywhere together. Sara's shrill accusation that Anna was 'into' someone had drawn kids from around the school grounds. There hadn't been a real knock-down drag-out fight yet as the school year had only started that week and everyone was aching for some drama and gossip. A crowd was forming, and Sara had noticed she now had an audience.

"Well, good! Wouldn't want a freak like you who bleaches her hair white for attention thinking she was good enough for a man like that." It was all verbal poison and vitriol from Sara who didn't seem to want to de-escalate anything. A sigh escaped Anna that she couldn't quite suppress. Her hair was naturally white, all of her hair. This made for a striking contrast against her dark tan skin. It was eye-catching. And who the fuck called a teenage boy a man? The dumb bitch trying to let him know she was willing to let him in her pants, that's who.

"It's naturally white. I asked my parents if I could dye my hair dark to look more natural, but they said that they weren't going to let me change the way I look just because an insecure little cunt like Sara White is afraid a shallow boy that only cares about looks will like me more than her."

It was wrong. Everything her parents preached was for her to stay out of fights and avoid conflict. Yet she was done tiptoeing around the girl who had made the lives of half the students at school miserable for years. If the spoiled little princess wanted to throwdown with 'the next Harbinger', Anna was more than capable of beating some sense into Sara of all people. She was having that kind of day and in that kind of mood.

"You expect us to believe that you have skin that dark with hair that white. Puh-lease!" Sara scoffed and glanced at her gaggle of girls who laughed along with her. "That's complete and utter bullshit."

"I come from a magical family. Sometimes magical abilities affect the way a person looks." She paused for a moment to let that sink in with the crowd. It couldn't hurt to remind Sara where she came from and what picking a fight with her really meant. "You would know that if you had been smart enough to pass any grade and not just had your parents bribe the school into advancing you so you could still play with your friends."

"You bitch!" The shorter girl gasped.

"At least bitches don't get known for being easy like you, skank!" Anna shot back unconcerned as Sara dropped her bag and handed her coat to one of her friends in preparation for the fight she'd been looking for.

"I'm going to kick your freak ass." The crowd let out a collective 'ooOOOOhoooo' of appreciation.

"You sure you want to do that?" She was more than willing to fight and deal with the consequences. It would be her first offense, she was a decent student, and her parents would support her decision even if it was against what they would encourage. Okay. Her dad, the pacifist, would be hella disappointed. Her mom would one hundred percent approve of Anna's choice to beat the ever-living hell out of this obnoxious immature little shit. Maybe. "You know who I am."

"You can't hide behind mommy's skirts forever. Eventually, you're gonna have to take your medicine like the upstart piece of trash you are." For a moment, Anna couldn't believe she had just heard what she'd heard. Did Sara White, the girl who called on her daddy's wealth and power to threaten, bribe, and coerce everyone from classmates to teachers, to school officials really just accuse Anna of hiding behind who her mother was?

"Bwahahahaha!" Laughter erupted out of her, and the pale-haired girl doubled over with uncontrollable amusement. The crowd watched in stunned awkward silence. Then a few chuckled while others smirked. "See?" Anna straightened as she caught her breath. "They get it." She gestured broadly at the giggling teens around them.

"Get what?" Bewildered disgust twisted Sara's face and Anna took pity enough on her to explain.

"That was funny. That you, who only have anything because everyone is afraid of her father, accused someone else of hiding behind their parents." Unable to stop herself, Anna giggled again. "It's funny."

Sara had been glancing around at the crowd whom she had thought were on her side. Now she realized that maybe they were not rooting for her but laughing at her. She balled up her fists and lunged for Anna only to stop short when Anna pulled her hands up to a ready fighting position and each fist flared with balls of cool white light. A crisp chill wave blasted out from the white-haired girl and her hands frosted over with ice.

"Oh, what the heck. Kicking your ass without magic is going to be so much more fun." She shook her hands and dissipated the spell. Where the balls of summoned ice had been moments before were just bare knuckles now. Then she swung a hard uppercut into Sara's stomach driving her fist through the girl's diaphragm.

The teens around her screamed with delight as the biggest bully in school doubled over gasping. 'Fight! Fight! Fight! Fight!'

"Oh, for fucks sake!" Anna muttered under her breath. "Why do teenagers have to be such animals."

"That's not fair!" Shrieked one of Sara's clique, "You're bigger than her." The girl threw a bookbag at Anna.

"And there's five of you who wanted to fight over some boy whose name I don't even know." Snatching the bookbag out of the air, Anna hurled it back with superhuman strength at the girl who had interfered, sending her sprawling on her back several feet away.

Meanwhile, Sara had caught her breath and rushed Anna. Which was a mistake. With a general air of unconcern, Anna backhanded Sara across the face. Her head jerked to the side with a split lip before she fell.

"Anyone else want a piece of me?" It looked like one of the three girls from Sara's clique that were left standing might have been about to step forward when an adult could be heard shouting. The group who'd been chanting 'fight, fight, fight' let out a collective 'ahh' and a few 'boo's', as it parted to let a teacher and several security staff through.

"Anna Watkins? Fighting with magic? What would your mother say?" The teacher tisked her disapproval.

"Hit hard, hit fast, make sure they don't get up." The teacher scowled at Anna as she quipped the famous Camina Wattkins quote almost automatically. "Hey, I didn't use magic to fight. Just to try to convince her she didn't want to fight." Shrugging, Anna pointed a finger briefly at Sara then collected her belongings while trying not to scoff at the girls who were now worried about getting in trouble. "Besides, Mom says it is the moral obligation of the strong to stop bullies and protect the weak. Didn't we just cover that quote from her in modern history class?"

"Get out of here everyone." The teacher frowned, her face looking like she had a bad taste in her mouth as she made expansive shooing gestures with her hands to send the gathered teens off. "Not you five." She whirled and pointed a finger at the three trying to help their two fallen comrades slink away quietly with the disbursing crowd. "You are going to the dean's office with Miss Watkins. We need to have a chat with your parents."

And the day was still gorgeous. Multicolor leaves rustling in a brisk breeze under a sunny azure sky. Anna sighed up at the heavens in resignation. Was this really what Michael and the angels had in mind when they chose her?

Chapter 5

10:45 AM September 13th, 2026
35,000ft Altitude between New York City and Washington DC

A statuesque brunet rested her head against the window frame watching the landscape and fluffy clouds slide by beneath her. She let the vibrations of the passenger jet soothe her while she tried not to offend the young gentleman sitting next to her. He had already requested her autograph while jabbering on about what a big 'fan' he was of her work.

"Really, the way you took out those monsters during the last Appalachian magic surge…" He shook his head and exhaled with what appeared to be something between a sigh and a moan."…It was pure artistry. I watched the whole operation. Everything that the embedded journalists filmed." His gushing was annoying, to say the least.

"Embedded journalists can't film everything in high magic areas. High enough levels of magic can cause even magically hardened electronics to fail. So, the monster battles that were filmed and broadcast to the public were only a small portion of the cleanup that actually happened."

The correction was almost automatic now and she tried not to groan in frustration. This was why she hated traveling on civilian airlines even if the seats were slightly more comfortable. And quiet. Was it weird that she was more relaxed flying in some giant military cargo plane with the rattling and the roar of the engines getting ready to do a high altitude jump into an untamed magic zone overrun with monsters than sitting in relative comfort next to a... fan?

But, if the public continued to believe that the dangers out there were all known and easily dealt with, they wouldn't take funding the military seriously. And that's the problem she was having with the Senate Appropriations Committee. Somehow, the fact that known dangers had been successfully eliminated or removed meant to the politicians that the military didn't need as much money as they had been giving it. So, she said the words that needed saying.

"Really?" Her seatmate brightened at her words. "So, there was stuff that you saw that wasn't broadcast?" Placing one tanned hand to her face the woman rubbed the bridge of her nose in a failing attempt to ward off the migraine she knew would soon follow. "I'd love to hear all about it?"

Before she could think of anything to say to avoid this part of the conversation, her phone rang. Her shoulders sagged with relief as she jumped at the excuse to avoid talking to yet another Gore Groupie about disemboweling monsters. The number wasn't one she recognized yet she was determined to take the call anyway.

"Excuse me. She interrupted the young man. "I need to take this." Seeing the flight attendant on their way down the aisle, she paused for a second before answering the call and whispered hurriedly to her seatmate, "If I'm still on the phone when the flight attendants reach us, tell them I want coffee with two sugars and one cream." Then she quickly answered the call.

"This is Camina speaking." Camina hadn't recognized the number, but anything had to be better than talking about work on her day off while traveling *for* work. Right? The young man next to her narrowed his eyes in suspicion and casually tilted his head as he nonchalantly strained to listen in on her conversation.

"Hello, is this the parent of Anna Watkins?" The voice was brusque and tinged with a level of disgust Camina had never before heard directed at her by someone she didn't know.

"Yes. This is her mother, Camina Watkins. How can I help you?" For a few breathless moments, Camina was worried that something had happened to her daughter, and she pursed her lips together expectantly.

"This is Dean George from New York Preparatory Academy. I'm calling because Anna has been suspended for fighting and a parent or designated guardian needs to pick her up. I've been unable to reach Mister Watkins." A frown creased Camina's forehead, and the corners of her full, expressive lips turned down.

"Suspended for fighting? Well, certainly I hope it was the bully that keeps breaking her stuff because I told Anna I'm not replacing anything else that Miss White breaks anymore." Silence from the other end of the call strung out long enough that Anna's mother thought the line had disconnected. "Are you still there, Dean George?"

"Ahem. Yes." Hearing the discomfort in the Dean's voice, Camina's frown curved up into a smile. "Be that as it may, your daughter participated in a fight and has therefore been suspended along with all the girls she had been fighting with. When can we expect someone to pick her up from school."

"I'm currently on a flight heading toward New York, but I'll be landing within the hour. I could probably pick Anna up within two hours if there aren't any delays on landing. You could just release her and let her walk home. We don't live far from the school." She'd tried to sound as cheerful as possible but let some aggravation into her voice.

"Umm…Unfortunately, school policy does require that a parent, guardian, or an adult designated by a parent or guardian pick the child up when they've been suspended." The Dean had been taken aback by Camina's suggestion that her child be released to walk home.

"Then I'll be there as soon as I can." She paused artfully knowing full well that she would be annoying the heck out of the Dean. "Probably around 1:00 PM but maybe not until after 2:00 PM. I really can't speed up the plane. That's a bit beyond my control."

The young man beside her stifled a giggle as a flight attendant handed him a hot coffee, two sugar packets, and a creamer. Glancing over her shoulder Camina winked at him as he handed her the coffee and condiments, and she mouthed 'Thank you!'

"Umm hmmm." Her mouth occupied with a hot sip of beverage; Camina agreed absently to something she didn't quite hear. "See you then. Ba-bye, Dean."

"Ba-bye?" The young man next to her sniggered as the call clicked off.

"I'm allowed to say ba-bye." She blinked innocently at her neighbor. "Thanks for grabbing my coffee for me." The cool air of the plane made a pleasing contrast on her face as the steam from her cup caressed her cheeks while she took another sip. "I haven't had a chance to have any yet today and I've been craving it."

18

She fumbled with the knob to release the seat back tray in front of her. One hand held her coffee, and the other, her sugar, creamer, and the snap-on lid to her cup. Juggling the way she held her condiments, she easily opened the tray and lowered it to set her things on.

"Trouble at home?" Camina's erstwhile traveling companion asked with a look of intrusive concern that bordered on glee.

"No, not really." Her smiled reassurance was more than just an act. She was sure that her husband had just been busy with a patient and that he would be picking up their daughter soon. As the gears in her mind spun up back into 'mom mode' after the time she'd spent away, Camina absently doctored up her cup of joe the way she liked it before taking a thoughtful sip. "Mmmm…" Tension poured out of her body with the taste of her caffeinated savior. Her shoulders sagged gratefully. "So, good. Thank you, again."

Gesturing with her cup, the woman indicated what she was thanking her neighbor for. Then she opened the contacts list on her phone and scrolled through. Finding the name she was looking for, she dialed. The phone rang, and rang, and continued ringing several more times before eventually going to a generic voicemail box prompt asking her to leave a message.

"Hey, honey. It's me. The school called and needs someone to pick up Anna. I'm on a flight back to New York now and *should* be landing in less than an hour. I came back early to surprise you. So…surprise! If you get this message before I pick up Anna, let me know if you are planning on doing it."

She hung up. There wasn't any reason to be concerned that her husband wasn't answering the phone. He was sure to have patients today, and he'd check messages between them. It was almost guaranteed that he would be calling her before she landed.

Chapter 6

Backstage was bustling as sound and light crews jogged and speed-walked through the final preparations for the show. Backup dancers, showboating rockstars, and the puffed-up wannabes who were going on before the main lineup made for colorful and flamboyant obstacles as they ducked in and out of dressing rooms calling for makeup artists, hairdressers, and last-minute costume alterations.

Of course, there were the inevitable groupies too. Wearing outfits that were too tight and consisting of too little material to justify the outrageous prices of designer clothes. One particular groupie in a loud purple jacket and jean shorts, with back pockets hanging out a hem that might as well have belonged to a bikini, caught Deveraux's attention. His long blonde hair swirled loosely around his shoulders as he spun to watch her go by.

He wasn't checking her out. No. But her aura was out of control. Angry and swirled up with hints of vengeance and rage. In the dressing room she had just walked out of the band was gathered around a pre-concert snack table filled with baked goods.

There was a small tingle of magic surrounding the food. Not enough to set off the security monitors or affect the electronics of the building; but enough to be no good if the dark spell coiled through the cookies was anything to judge by. Deveraux considered going in to warn the main attraction yet was discouraged by the dour-faced security guard at the door.

"You might want to warn the band to not eat any of the…whelp…never mind…" He had tried, but the leather-clad young men had already started stuffing treats into their mouths.

"They wouldn't have listened anyways. Not when there are 'magic cookies' to eat." The security guard harrumphed with disdain. The way he had made air quotes when speaking the words 'magic cookies' implied that the band was expecting something recreational.

"OH…" The long-haired hippie…or maybe he was a hipster douchebag…sucked in a sympathetic breath through his teeth. "It's not the kind of magic they think it is this time. The girl who just left was *very* upset." He shook his head and shrugged as the security guard laughed before heading into the room to wrangle some discipline into his charges.

The show would be starting any moment now and Deveraux wanted to get a last look at his makeup before heading up on stage. He ducked into his dressing room and pulled his cell phone from his back pocket. Checking it for messages and then setting it to silent, he chucked his phone into his bag.

Wouldn't do for it to go off while he was performing and distract him. Or worse, for it to be picked up on a microphone. Or…worst of all, for him to lose it. The thought made him pale, and he blanched at himself in the mirror while he was giving his makeup a cursory final glance.

He looked good. He knew he looked good. Muscular? Toned? Long sexy hair? Check. Check. And check! Jeans that made his butt pop? Check. He headed up to the stage prepared to face the biggest audience he had ever Deejayed for.

While the sound crew next to the stage fitted him with his wireless mic, he could hear the announcer introducing him. He blushed and grinned when the crowd cheered for DJ Deveraux as he jogged and jumped out on stage. Raising his hands like a prizefighter for the crowd to cheer.

They weren't really cheering for him. They were cheering for the main act that would be coming out later on, but DJ Deveraux didn't mind one bit riding the high their response gave him. After all, how often did he get to shed his normal persona of a responsible husband and father to indulge in his craving for praise and use his talents in Technomagery the way he loved most? Back in his changing room, his phone in his bag was ringing with a call he was missing from his wife.

Two individuals in black padded motorcycle gear with molded black body armor sped through the streets of New York City without a care for the flow of traffic. They weaved and dodged expertly among the sparse vehicles in an industrial part of town as they headed toward their quarry.

Their target was an innocuous everyday average moving truck. It moved placidly along at the average speed of traffic. There wasn't anything to call attention to it, aside from the fact that maybe it was unusual for it to be in this part of town. Though not out of the question.

It was the kind of moving truck anyone could rent for about fifty bucks a day. It was shades of blue and white with the Mountain King Mover's logo of ice-capped mountains under their name in gold. A company that reliably had franchise locations in every large city and small town in America.

Not until the driver of the truck heard the two cyclists and glanced in his side view mirrors to see them pulling up behind him did the moving truck have anything about it which would draw attention to it. Once the driver realized he was being pursued, his behavior changed drastically. The truck accelerated and passed the vehicles ahead of it, narrowly avoiding a head-on collision with an oncoming flat-bed semi, laden with small crates.

The semi swerved off the side of the road. Water exploded from barrier barrels as it impacted. Restraints securing its precariously stacked boxes snapped and the crates toppled from the flatbed and spilled across the road. The two individuals in pursuit dodged the rolling boxes.

One motorcycle nearly crashed, the armor on the rider's kneepad sparking on the pavement as the vehicle slid onto its side. The rider released the handlebars with the hand closest to the ground and punched the pavement, launching themselves and their vehicle back upright with a visible shockwave of magical force.

A chase was on, and the pursuing motorcyclists gunned their engines as they followed determinedly. Behind the speeding vehicles, a crack split the road where the fallen rider had righted themselves. Traffic in both directions was stopped by the widening rift in the ground.

Chapter 7

10:52 AM September 13th, 2026
Industrial Park District Near the Port of New York

Inside the back of the Mountain King Movers truck, four security guards uniformed in armor and covered with weapons huddled uncomfortably around a locked steel crate. They looked like a typical group of Hollywood-ugly heroes from an action movie who were about to launch a four-man war against the Bad Guy. In reality, they were…maybe not *the* Bad Guys, but they definitely weren't Good Guys either.

They were guarding the locked steel crate and a man in a lab coat. None of the guards liked the balding, middle-aged, arrogant asshole who pretended to be cocky and confident, but who clutched his briefcase too tightly to his chest to be anything other than terrified. His nervous habit of pushing his spectacles up his nose gave him away further. He'd push them up even when they did not need to be, then had to adjust them back down to see properly.

When they felt their vehicle's speed increase, the four guards glanced at each other with only mild interest. One raised an eyebrow and another shrugged back at him. When they were jostled to almost fall over as the truck swerved to miss the semi, that's when the lead guard became concerned. He frowned and grabbed the radio clipped to his uniform chest.

"Check in." His voice was steely, calm. Then the vehicle swerved again, zigzagging through traffic wildly. "Hey, I said check in." There was no answer. The radio clicked. It whined. The radios of each of the guards began to whine, a low buzzing at first that ran steadily up through the octaves.

"Shit!" One of them exclaimed, unclipping his radio and staring at it horrified.

"High-level magical interference. Radios off. Eject the batteries before they blow." Their leader was still calm, but his voice had an edge to it. "Don't worry. The truck is hardened against magical activity so we'll keep moving and the collector will maintain ambient magic below toxic levels." He'd been removing the battery from his radio as he spoke, and his subordinates followed suit. "Just be ready. There's something out there."

10:52 AM September 13th, 2026
Radio Empire Concert Hall New York, NY

Deveraux finished his set to so many cheers. The crowds were screaming. He couldn't see them really, just a seething mass of bodies in the dark, his eyes blinded by the stage lights. He didn't care.

His heart was pumping, racing so fast. It was so gratifying. So, exhilarating. Sooo intoxicating. He could sense the emotions riding high and he'd been able to use his magic to accentuate it with the tones and rhythms of the songs he had played. They were ready for the main act. But the main act was probably not going to be ready for them.

There were a few more openers before the band was scheduled. Maybe they had time to get themselves un-hexed before the show was on.

"Thank you, New York." Deveraux grabbed the bottle of water a stagehand had set aside for him. He took a long gulping drink letting some of it run down his throat and front. Making magic was hard work and he was dripping with sweat, but this was part of his act...and some of the ladies, and lads, loved it. The water made his tight shirt stick to him and transparent where it was wet.

Then he grabbed the single red rose laying on the same side table where the water had been. He swaggered jauntily to the front of the stage and tossed the rose as far out into the audience as he could. Deveraux didn't wait to see where it landed. He swiftly exited the stage as the screaming fans surged to even greater excitement. Overhead the announcer's voice gave him an outro.

"That was DJ Deveraux. He makes music that the heart *always* knows." There was a suggestively lewd lilt to the announcer's voice but that was show biz. Sex sold. And Deveraux was sexy, if he did think so himself. At least, his fans told him he was sexy. "Now where is the lucky audience member who caught that rose. What's that? You're sharing it with your friend? Well, congratulations ladies. You have just won yourselves a backstage pass to meet Maiden's Voyage after the show tonight. Say, thank you, to DJ Deveraux."

Even more wild screaming followed the DJ, and he smiled broadly all the way back to his dressing room. He continued smiling until he saw the missed call from his wife. By the end of the voice mail, Deveraux was frowning with disappointment.

Now his plans for rubbing elbows at the afterparty and spreading his name for more gigs was going up in smoke. Or maybe that should be frost, considering it was his icy frost queen of a daughter who had messed things up. No. That wasn't fair. She'd been complaining about that bully for a long time. It was bound to happen if the school didn't take action.

This just...

It wasn't fair. None of his other kids had ever.... No. That wasn't true. Samantha..., Samantha was a statistical outlier and while she'd never started fights, she made sure she finished them. In a way that prevented the loser from ever wanting to fight her again.

What had Kyle called her? Oh yes. The Prodigy of Pain. Remembering that bit of his oldest daughter's hellion years made Deveraux feel a bit better. And remembering that his son Kyle was now old enough to pick Anna up from school made Deveraux smile with guilty but unrepressed glee.

Just this once.

He sent the text.

'*Kyle. Need you to pick up Anna from school. She got suspended I've got a busy schedule today. Your mom took an early flight but she's still not back. You can just drop her off at home. Thanks, Dad.*'

Chapter 8

10:53 AM September 13th, 2026
Radio Empire Concert Hall New York, NY

DJ Deveraux was just packing up to get a head start on the afterparty when he heard the call. The drummer and the second bassist of Maiden's Voyage were out of commission and the lead singer was desperately calling for anyone who could fill in from the openers. Before he could muster the arrogance to volunteer himself, someone else chimed in that 'DJ Deveraux is a technomage, he could cover both parts".

"Really?" The leather-clad singer grasped at the statement with desperation and relief. "Where is he? He hasn't left yet, has he?" Swallowing the crow of joy that threatened to leap from his throat, Devereaux sauntered up to the frantic frontliner as he turned to look for the technomage.

"I'm right here." Devereaux gave the other musician a big friendly grin even though he knew the star would never have given him the time of day in any other circumstances.

"Did you hear? Are you willing to stand in? There are thousands of tickets we'd have to refund if…" The man trailed off as Devereaux held up a hand graciously. One might even say he did it calmly. This was it. This was his chance. This was his one shot at being famous for his music. He was shocked that his hand didn't quiver even the slightest and his voice was clear and firm, reassuring even.

"I'd be honored and delighted."

As if the entire backstage had been holding its collective breath for a frozen second, unsure if he would accept, some hoping he wouldn't so that they might have a chance, then the spell broke, and everyone sprang into action.

"Alright, come on." The singer had an accent that Devereaux hadn't noticed at first. Now it came out strongly. Though the technomage could not place it. "I got George's bass on stage. Hey, you, roadie," he called out to one of the technicians dressed all in black that were all over the backstage and most definitely weren't all part of this particular band's personal roadie group. "Set up the bass for hands-free operation."

"Don't forget the drums," Devereaux added.

"The drums too?" The technician called back uncertainly.

"They're electric, aren't they?" He turned to the singer from Maiden's Voyage who nodded.

"Yeah?" His tone was voice made it clear that he didn't think they could be used that way.

"Then I can operate those hands-free also, I can switch back and forth between the two if you like. The grin of delight that met his words was immensely gratifying.

"I do like." He clapped the DJ on a shoulder as they walked to their locations on the stage. "I would like that very much."

Before he knew it, the curtains were going back up and he was reading sheet music someone had discreetly placed for him. It was cleverly lit with one of the lights that were on him. But it wasn't necessary. He recognized the song from the radio, and he was playing it mostly from memory.

They'd started out quietly and the announcer was letting everyone know that Technomage DJ Devereaux was guest appearing with the band. Like no one was going to notice that he was covering for two missing members. That was fine.

His magic was humming through the drums and the bass as he sat down and started playing by hand. The singer and the backup were belting out the lyrics, but they were *not* looking good. They were looking quite bad actually. Sweating and swaying like they were about to topple over.

The lead singer lost it first as he ran for the side curtain. He barely made it past the sight of the crowd before tossing his cookies all over the stagehand who had rushed to bring him a bottled water and a bucket. There was a faltering in the cheering of the crowd before DJ Devereaux started a crazy drum riff.

He rolled out the snare into a fast complicated rhythm on the toms that wasn't part of the song but that he knew would punch it up a bit. After laying into the hi-hat with a crash for good measure, Devereaux chucked the drumsticks out into the crowd. Then he pointed at the lead singer's abandoned guitar lying on the stage and made that baby stand up and walk into place as it rejoined the song.

The lead guitarist waved at the technomage to get his attention and clutched at his abdomen. Devereaux nodded and gestured for the guitarist to toss his instrument at him. With a doubtful cock of his head, the musician complied. The audience lost their minds.

And Devereaux flicked out one hand and caught the guitar with his magic only to set it playing immediately. With a quick gesture of his other hand, one of the abandoned microphones leaped into his fingers. Coordinating so many instruments at once was only a light strain for him. He'd practiced this kind of thing for years. Now, he began to sing, finishing up the song he'd started.

Three songs later, the lights went out as every piece of electronics in the Concert Hall not hardened against magical overload whined with a piercing crescendo. Cell phone batteries exploded in people's pockets while cameras burst into flames, taking a few hands with them. Plastic cases started melting and the music stopped.

It wasn't Devereaux's doing.

The two motorcyclists chasing the Mountain King Movers van approached quickly. Though the van was now speeding through the streets, its driver was unable to shake the more mobile bikes behind it. Knowing there is nowhere for their quarry to go, the duo closed on the vehicle quickly. Their expertise allowed them to avoid falling or crashing despite the less-than-ideal road conditions in this part of town.

Dodging cracks and potholes as they swerve around corners, the bikers are undeterred even with freeway overpass pylons flashing by. Closer and closer they creep until one is able to reach out with their left hand and touch the handles on the back gate of the truck. The other cyclist grabbed the left handlebar of the first cyclist's bike as the first biker grabbed the truck.

Smooth as silk, the transition. The first cyclist jumped over the handlebars of his bike onto the back bumper of the truck as their partner took control of their bike and pulled it along with them. They used their grip on the handle to pull themselves forward and up. It was a maneuver intended to protect the vehicle rather than let it fall to the ground and be damaged. They wanted a fast getaway.

After taking a moment to stabilize their position the grim bandit shoved one hand through the solid metal rear gate of the moving truck. The metal tore with a screech. Once they had the more secure handhold of the deformed gate, the attacker took their other hand off the handle and used it to help push the opening they'd made even further open. Little by little, they forced their way inside.

Staccato gunfire echoed around the intruder, ricocheting off their head and shoulders. From inside one of the defenders shouted.

"Either they've got the mother of all defensive magic or they're not human." His words are followed by curses. "Barrier up." The hum of a spell activating chimed loud enough to be heard even over the gunfire.

Behind the barrier and the armed men was the one unarmed man and his metal box. He cowered with terror and seemed to try flinching with the sound of each shot fired. Upon hearing the guard's shouted warning about the attacker's defensive magic, he began frantically working to open his box.

"What are you doing?" One of the two guards who was inside the barrier with him called out angrily. The man they were guarding had distracted the guard at a critical time and it might…it did. One of the two guards outside the barrier was pummeled with a crushing blow from the unknown attacker.

"This artifact will disable any magical protections he has." He was fumbling hastily with unlocking the box when a gurgling scream drew his eyes up from his task. The scientist, or whatever he was, stared in horror as the second guard outside the magical barrier was chucked out of the mangled rear of the truck to bounce sickeningly off the pavement. It was then that he remembered that there was not one, but two such terrors to worry about as the second motorcycle rider dodged the rolling body with both bikes, keeping pace with their fleeing vehicle easily.

Now nothing stood between them and the thin but sturdy barrier protecting the thing they wanted. The tall humanoid shape disguised in thick motorcycling gear stalked toward the group and began smashing down their barricade.

"What are you doing?" The keeper of the box screamed hysterically. "Shoot them!" He'd paused only briefly in his fumbling to open the box as layer after layer of protective insulation was ripped off in his haste.

"If we fire before he takes down the barrier the bullets will just bounce around inside it and hit one of us." The leader shouted back. This was not how today was supposed to go. It was supposed to be a simple relocation job.

With a whoosh, the barrier came down and the two remaining guards began to fire. They only stopped when they had to reload but there wasn't any point. They were going to die. Then the civilian shrieked in triumph.

"Yes! Take this, whatever kind of monster you are!" There was a high-pitched whine, like the sound batteries made before they exploded from magical overload. The protective barrier was trying to sputter back to life, but it didn't matter because the person-sized attacker went down like a thousand-pound sack of flesh, hitting the floor with a clang. Behind the van, the remaining motorcyclist following them lost control of both motorcycles and rolled away in a devastating flipping disaster.

Then the whining sound was followed by a whump that shook the whole van as it moved. A few seconds later there was a small compressive explosion inside the van, and everyone ceased moving. That might have been the end of it, but the cause of that small explosion was an enormous surge of magical energy. A devastating shockwave of arcane power spread from the scene of the event.

Luckily the city was built to harvest and direct harmful quantities of magic. The infrastructure built into the roads directed the wave of power into the conduits that fed the city's magic collectors. The magic collectors, miraculous workings of science and magic that protected all of New York City, in turn, made a similar high-pitched whining sound albeit magnified a thousand times before they too were overloaded by the massive influx of magic.

Across the city, batteries exploded, plastic melted, and Prometheus-brand emergency flares went off, their color-coded light, notifying residents of how much magic they were currently exposed to.

Chapter 9

10:55 AM September 13th, 2026
New York Preparatory Academy, New York, NY

After three hours sitting in the office Anna's butt was getting sore. She'd tried to get up and stretch her legs, but the Assistant Dean had snatched up a yardstick from next to his desk and menacingly smacked it on the edge of his desk before pointing at her threateningly then back at her just vacated seat. Geez, that guy was so over the top. He might as well have been pointing two fingers at his eyes and then at her to indicate that he was watching her.

Where did he get that stick from anyways? From her position, she should have been able to see the object. Yet when she observed him putting it away, the thing just kind of disappeared. As if it had been subsumed into the material of his desk. Maybe it was a warlock pact item from his patron –

Did he have a patron? Was he a warlock? She didn't know. Until this morning Anna had never spent this much time with the school's administration. She wasn't even sure if she'd ever been in the office. Sure, she'd walked past it literally hundreds of times. But inside?

And now she'd been here for hours.

Hours!

So many hours!

Hours, and hours, and hours, and hours.

Next to the stuck-up, spoiled little shit-for-brains, cunty bitches – No. Stop. She had to stop. If she got riled up, she might start oozing cold. Once she got too upset, she was going to become a hazard to others. So…calm. She had to be calm.

While sitting on this hard, hard, wooden torture device of a chair. Seriously! *Who still uses wooden chairs in schools?* It wasn't even enchanted for comfort. Nor was it one of those creepy ones carved into the ergonomic shape of an ass for, you know, comfort.

Over the course of the *three hours* since she'd gotten the worst grilling of her life, two of the girls had been picked up. Their parents had sent chauffeurs and family limos for them. Ironically, Sara's parents couldn't be inconvenienced to even notify the help to get their daughter early. Anna might, *might* have gotten caught sniggering when she overheard that conversation. She'd received stern looks of disapproval from both the Dean and Assistant Dean. But the glares of hatred from Sara and her cronies? Priceless!

She fidgeted uncomfortably. There was something seriously wrong with her chair. From the corner of her awareness, she noticed that Sara and her two remaining cohorts were fidgeting also. They seemed to be experiencing the same discomfort that she was. The young cryomancer was almost of the opinion that it wasn't possible to make a more uncomfortable chair even if it had been enchanted…

Wait a minute! Anna straightened in sudden suspicion. Everywhere else in this hoity-toity school is filled with state-of-the-art ergonomic bliss. But in the school's office, the chairs where students had to sit were the epitome of gluteus abuse? Now that she thought it out, it was clear that this was a subtle form of punishment.

Her eyes narrowed and her expression turned flat. Of course. That was the kind of thing mister I've-got-a-magic-stick man over there would do. For the first time since she had been filed in here with the other fighters, Anna turned her ire on the administration. Then she sighed and forced herself to relax.

She'd done the crime and now she was doing the time. Things would only get worse if she lost the strict control she had to keep over her magic, and her 'cool' ended up being even the slightest bit noticeable by someone else. The only thing for it was to accept it and remain calm. Besides, it wasn't all bad.

There was television. It had been on the twenty-four-hour news channel the whole time. But still…good and proper brain rot to zone out on and distract her from her desire to cause other people serious bodily harm. Anna leaned her head back against the wall behind her in resignation and returned her focus to the droning of the news anchor.

"In preparation for the expected arrow swarm intersection over Southern Lake Michigan, Chicago has reinforced its defensive grid while the recently emptied magic collectors have been set to the highest absorption capacity. The Governor of Illinois has activated the Magicorps division of the National Guard to aid in diverting this natural disaster. Experts say that the empty magic collectors will siphon off enough magical energy from the enchanted arrow swarms that the city defense grid combined with the efforts of aeromancers from the National Guard will be able to divert both swarms as they intersect."

"That's right, Bob." The second anchorperson added, butting in helpfully. Probably following a script written on some teleprompter. Now that they'd done the grave reporting, they would put a positive spin on the potential danger and follow the segment up with some light-hearted puff piece. Was she getting jaded already? It must be Kyle's fault. And she nodded in satisfaction as the commentator continued.

"Enchanted arrow swarms are volleys of enchanted arrows from ancient wars that are still flying and traveling the world today because they were made to draw on ambient magic to power their speed and flight enchantments. These swarms may have started as man-made phenomena, but they have been around so long they are now basically considered a natural disaster. Which swarms are we watching today, Bob?"

Anna resisted the urge to snort. Everyone knew what a magic arrow swarm was. It was stupid that the news reiterated their definition every time one intersected near a large city. After all, nobody went over the definition of a hurricane every time Florida flooded.

"We've got the Trojan Six swarm, the swarm generated during the sixth Battle of Troy, and the Punic War swarm intersecting ten miles North of Chicago. It's uncertain how their enchantments will interact as there are no historical records of these two swarms intersecting before. It's possible that they will join together, forming a larger more powerful swarm. Or their enchantments may negatively react causing both swarms to self-destruct."

"Don't forget the third option, Bob." The second anchorman added continuing the friendly but mildly concerned banter bit.

"What's that George?" Bob was getting irritated with George. There was a bit of a bite in his tone. Anna was right there with Bob; George was an

irritating a-hole. Just look at him, he was so polished and suave that he had to secretly be a serial killer.

"There's the possibility that there will be no synergy or reaction between the enchantments and the swarms will pass through each other with nothing more than a few light collisions." Bob rolled his eyes at the same time as Anna because, when in the entire history of the world had that actually happened?

"Whatever the case may be, stay tuned to find out." Bob continued smoothly, busying his hands with a few prop documents on the desk before him. "We've got a countdown clock at the bottom of the screen there below the streaming updates."

"Yes, Bob. Stay tuned to find out in just under four hours. But on a lighter note, a new article profiling Camina Wattkins, The Harbinger of Dawn has shown the world the lighter side of divine wrath as a homemaker and mother. The writer interviewed all of her children as well as her husband and painted a picture of life at home with a Holy Warrior. Your thoughts, Bob?"

"Well, George, I loved the article. Mrs., Wattkins is probably one of, if not, the most famous Warlock in modern history. I have to admit I've been a fan since high school and even then, she was already finding her way into our history books. I'm sure that everyone who has been following her meteoric career was thrilled to see this more personal side of her."

Anna had stiffened slightly from her repose of negligent boredom when the segment started but she relaxed as she saw they were focusing on her mother, as they should be. Then that asshat, George, started talking and she stiffened right back up again.

"The profile of her youngest, Anna Wattkins, was particularly intriguing."

"Oh, for fuck's sake. It's everywhere." She'd half risen out of her chair when the Assistant Dean looked up from typing industriously to glare at her in reprimand. The yardstick appeared in his hand and the teen slammed herself back down with her arms folded angrily. She went back to watching the discussion with far less equanimity as the school's fluorescent lights flickered with a dangerous rising hum.

"I'm warning you, young lady." Yardstick guy pointed at the lights and then back to Anna, brandishing his yardstick like it was a wand.

"It's not me. I've got my powers locked down. It's the AMD rising." The hum in the lights continued rising in octaves and she glanced at it nervously. The ambient magic density of the air was rising far higher than it should in a city with magic collectors as big as New York's. The offending news segment continued under the increasing noise.

"Everyone's speculating on her potential. Perhaps we'll be seeing another young Warlock enlisting in the Magicor –" The television the lights, and every electronic device in the room blew out at once.

Two teenage girls shrieked as the cellphones in their pockets – which should have been powered off in their chic white leather backpacks – burst when the batteries overloaded. Anna, who had been expecting something like this, lifted her sturdy messenger bag over her head and used her textbooks to protect her head from falling glass. There was no explosion from her bag.

"Down!" Her reaction was instinctual, knee jerk really. "Down now!" The fact that she actively loathed the girls beside her didn't matter. What did matter was that the school used backup batteries on all the important computers, the building was loaded with electronics, and clearly, the board hadn't used the generous donations and the absurdly high tuition to retrofit the buildings with magical shielding.

She threw herself on the floor and two of the girls followed her. The third must have been wearing a watch, she was scream-crying and holding a bleeding wrist in her other hand. Anna pulled the girl down with the other two. Not bothering to see who was who, she summoned a barrier shield to protect the four of them until all the secondary explosions were over.

Chapter 10

10:50 AM September 13th, 2026

Inside The National Museum of Unnatural Science and History

"Miss, you dropped your phone." A woman in an 'I love NY' T-shirt where the 'love' was replaced with a doodled heart paused in her return to the tour group and groaned. She'd waited as long as she could before making a break for the bathroom because she hadn't wanted to miss any of the tour. It wasn't every day that your tour guide looked like the son of the famous Harbinger of Dawn, but this guy wasn't a cook so it couldn't be him. Still, if she got him to take a selfie with her no one would have to know he was just a lookalike.

So, she'd held it waiting for an opportunity to ask which had never come. Eventually, she'd had to give in to the call of nature and it had been the most explosive – she'd been quick. So quick, that she hadn't shoved her phone deep enough into the stupid mini pockets that cursed her stupid pants. And she hadn't even heard her phone drop.

Suspecting that it was just some bozo trying for an excuse to strike up a conversation she ran her hands over her ass, double-checking her pockets to make sure the phone was really gone even as she turned to the speaker. Yep. Her phone was missing. That was probably her phone. She was already plastering a grateful smile on her face before she'd turned far enough to see the individual speaking.

The hallway was dark too. Unnaturally dark despite the dim lights glowing overhead. Yet not so dark as to be unnavigable. She had to squint at first to get a good look at the person calling her and when she saw the man, her face fell. The was no head where she expected one to be. Only a broad chest. With a museum identification card on a lanyard. He was still off away, but he was huge.

She slowly trailed her eyes upward and saw a large man with thick straight blonde hair that came down over his shoulders. Light-skinned, he was too far away and too dark in this hallway for her to tell what color eyes he had but he looked like the discount version of a hot Viking. The distinct lack of obvious muscles and the chef's whites is what made him the discount version.

Too tall. Shoulders aren't broad enough. No muscles. She thought crassly as she headed toward the cell phone in his outstretched hand. Then she noticed the stains on his white clothing. They weren't large. But they weren't old. Fresh.

Bright red blood.

On his hands. On his knee. And a bit on his collar. A small dabble near the large knife in the sheath on his belt.

"Good thing I caught you." He grinned and she saw more blood on his face. Was it dripping from his mouth? She slowed. Stopped. Then began backing away.

Seeing her hesitation and movement away from him, the giant of a man sped up his walking trying to get close to her faster. This only unnerved the woman more and she turned and fled.

"That's okay." She called over her shoulder. "Just remembered that someone is waiting for me. Drop it off with the security desk and I'll pick it up later." She was in full retreat sprinting down the hallway back to the tour group before she had finished shouting her excuse.

The man stopped, sighed sadly, and trudged back the way he had come. Kyle met him coming from the opposite direction. He stumbled, caught himself, and continued on.

"Hey bro." He called out to the Viking looking chef. "Do you know when the director is going to do something about the lighting in this hallway? It has got to be an OSHA violation. A damned hazard at the very least."

Kyle was friendly and cheerful, having just finished the last of the dreaded, guided tours that he hated giving for the day. Knowing he wasn't on tour duty for a few more days always put a spring in his step. But his smile dropped a bit when he saw the frown on his coworker's face and the sparkly pink phone in his hand.

"Ah, man. Did it happen again?" The chef nodded and neither had to specify what *it* was. "Well, you get cleaned up, I'll hit the John, and we'll drop it at the lost and found when we head out on break." The Viking chef nodded, and they walked into the men's room together.

A few minutes later they emerged, the tall chef looking decidedly less like he'd just finished eating his latest serial murder victim. After a brief stop to drop off the lost phone, they strolled out the front doors of the museum and onto its giant Greek temple-esque steps talking animatedly like the good friends they were.

"The look on her face, Kyle. It was bad." He scrubbed a now clean hand through his hair and continued his self-castigation. "I feel like I'm cursed with this height."

"Nah, bro." The apprentice warlock assured his friend with a good-natured laugh. "If I had walked down that hallway looking like a cannibal serial killer, she would have probably reacted the same way. At least with your height, when you freak people out they choose to run away instead of deciding that you are small enough they actually can take you if they 'defend' themselves." Kyle made air quotes to emphasize his point. "And look on the bright side, with a vampire for a boss, it's not like you are going to get in trouble for wearing a little blood around from the kitchen."

"Ha, ha." His friend responded with only mild sarcasm before smiling and agreeing. "Yeah. It would suck if people tried to fight me every time I weirded them out. Okay," He clapped his hands together then flung them wide and took a deep breath as they descended the stairs. "You know how my morning went. How was yours?"

"Will you look at the time? I guess we won't be able to discuss that particular topic." Kyle jokingly made to run off before his friend made a grab at him with a face. "Actually, shoots, no! I can't look at the time. I forgot my phone." He glanced back up the stairs then waved a dismissive hand. "I don't need it. We're just going for doughnuts."

"Yeah. It's just doughnuts. Not like there's going to be a catas –" It was said nonchalantly but Kyle gave his friend the evil-side-eye as he joked.

"Don't even joke. You'll jinx us." Kyle scolded as his friend shoved his hands in his pockets on their morning stroll. It was still a gorgeous day. The sky was very blue, the leaves were just changing.

"Oh, look, the cloud hopper rabbits are eating cherries from the Alchemist Tree." His friend interrupted. "We should stop by it on the way back, I promised Sam a photo next time she came by your place."

"Uh, huh." Kyle gave his friend the side-eye again, this time deeply suspicious and far less evil…for now. "You could just text it to her." The apprentice warlock volunteered, not sure if he was thrilled by the idea of his slightly older friend sharing numbers with his sister.

"Oh, I don't have Sam's number." He commented, studiously *not* looking at Kyle as he said it. "I figure that if she wanted me to have it, she'd give it to me." The wistful sigh – was that a wistful sigh, it better not have been a wistful sigh – that escaped the proverbial giant of a man would have garnered Kyle's sympathy if they'd been talking about any woman in the world that wasn't related to him. Because it was his sister, Kyle decided to update his how-to-dispose-of-bodies plans in the near future. Friend the chef may be, dating his sister he would not.

"Come on, you keep changing the subject. How did the morning go…" He paused and grinned slyly at Kyle "…my fellow cook." Kyle stopped and stared up at the heavens shaking his fists at the sky with both rage and entreaty.

"You read the article." Came his flat reply after his moment of self-indulgence.

"And saw three news segments discussing it." The chef nodded happily while providing more fodder to upset the weary Kyle. "They even played some of those Tissue Medic ads that Sam wrote back when she thought she wanted to be a business major.

"Oh, Sam and Anna are not going to be pleased about that." Cackling with glee, Kyle pulled out his wallet and began checking how much cash he had. "If you've got links text them to me. I'm making a long edit of all the coverage for grandma…" Then laughed evilly and added conspiratorially, "And I'm collecting all of Sam's commercials as ammo for later."

"You two have issues." The other laughed, "My siblings and I were never so…whatever you and Sam are. Before the…incident…we all got along all the time."

"Yeah." Both sobered quickly but the chef chimed up with a question before they could become morose.

Chapter 11

10:55 AM September 13th, 2026
Central Park, NY, Outside the National Museum of Unnatural Science and History

"What was that bit about doughnuts, though? You don't really think that they are the greatest food on Earth, do you?" His incredulity was offensive to Kyle as they passed by the Magic Tree Grove and the golem that guarded it. It was still passing out apples to passersby and that, as well as the question, made Kyle smile bigger.

"Doughnuts *are* the best food on Earth, and everyone knows it," Kyle assured his friend with a swagger and all the bravado he could muster.

"No, they aren't." The chef argued back. And I'm pretty sure that there are many people who do not even like doughnuts."

"Get stuff!" Kyle cried out in mock rage. "Everyone loves doughnuts, and if they don't, they haven't had the right doughnuts. Because Enchantress Doughnuts are bewitchingly good. Magic doughnuts, enchanted to be delicious. You know that no one can dislike them once they've tasted them." As Kyle repeated both the slogan of his favorite doughnut chain and the urban myth behind them the chef shook his head in amusement.

"I'm pretty sure that's illegal." He admonished.

"Nope. Not illegal to make it taste better, only to make it addictive." Kyle assured his friend, replacing his wallet and frowning as he felt something else in his pocket. Taking it out he saw that it was the unfinished apple from this morning, he picked a bit of lint off it and gave it another bite.

"Oh, man." His friend looked away in disgust. "You are a bachelor."

"What's that supposed to mean?" Kyle protested with a full mouth, spraying a few bits of apple flesh as he spoke.

"Old half-eaten apple and doughnuts for breakfast?" He shook his head with disappointment this time. "Nobody likes doughnuts. It's a fringe food. That's why I'm the only one who will go with you to get doughnuts on break."

"You take that back." Affronted, Kyle paused in his walking and took a step back from his friend. "Doughnuts are gifts from the Gods and no one else comes with me because they just don't have enough self-awareness to understand that it's okay to indulge in your inner child and have doughnuts as an adult. They have to wait for someone with a more highly developed pallet and magnanimity to bring doughnuts into the breakroom for them. I just choose to have you come with me because I like you best and want to share the blessing with you directly."

"Right," Chef scoffed with a raise of his eyebrows. "If doughnuts are so great, I bet you couldn't even give one away to a stranger on the street let alone talk someone who wasn't me into going to get one with you."

"I could get anyone to come buy doughnuts with me." Kyle exclaimed. "Challenge accepted." Before the chef could blink, Kyle had strode off on a tangent and was approaching a woman pushing a stroller and wearing exercise clothing. She took out her earbuds and Kyle began animated gesturing as he was talking to her. Chef could not hear what he was saying but she shook her head, laughed, put her earbuds back in, and jogged off while Kyle was midsentence.

Undismayed, the apprentice warlock hurried up to the next closest person. The chef checked the time on his watch and began strolling after him. They had time. And this would be amusing.

Kyle was on his third person by the time the chef had caught up with him. A balding middle-aged man, who still had more hair than not, was listening avidly to Kyle's lurid and graphic descriptions of the doughnuts at Enchantress doughnuts. And Kyle was deftly luring him in the direction of the doughnut stand at a slow distracted amble.

"Even though they are plain glazed doughnuts, they are delectable. The sight of the creamy glaze dripping down through the hole of a fresh warm doughnut. Glistening with sweet sauce. You've never tasted anything so light and creamy. Sometimes I like to lick it off—"

Kyle paused in his monologue as his robe jumped. The man backed away from his startled.

"What the?" he exclaimed "What is that? Kyle's robe jumped again, and he raised his arm as a plain leather notebook jumped out of it to float in the air before him. He was backing away with distrust, but Kyle wasn't paying attention to that anymore. He'd noticed a sudden change in the ambient magical density, and it was not good.

"That's not normal." The chef commented as he watched mesmerized over Kyle's shoulder.

"No. It's not." Kyle agreed. The notebook was his warlock pact item, a gift from his patron to channel the power it shared with him. As he watched, it opened itself to a page and letters began writing themselves into existence.

His patron, the Archivist, was an intellectual. As a collector of knowledge, the Archivist's pact item had been a book from which Kyle could access any knowledge that the Archivist had collected, and which Kyle would use to transfer new knowledge to his patron. It didn't generally move around on its own like that. It wasn't that kind of item.

Kyle carried it around in a concealed magic book holster under his robe to keep it close and prevent it from being stolen or lost. Or to avoid not having it when he might need it. There were any number of reasons, really, for going through the trouble of getting a concealed carry license for a magical tome.

It wasn't a security book. He wasn't being weird, *Samantha*. It was practical. But now his pact item was doing something he'd never seen it do but was aware was possible, it was warning its holder of danger to his life. His look of concern grew with each letter that appeared in bold text at the bottom of the open page.

Ambient magic density has reached dangerous levels.

"Holy shit." The chef breathed in disbelief. He glanced around at the perfect weather, the blue skies dotted with occasional light puffy clouds. There were people playing throughout the expansive manicured lawns of the park without concern. "It can't be right. Look at…" He struggled for the words and gestured helplessly around, "…everything."

"Magical density doesn't have to affect the weather," Kyle murmured quietly as he grabbed the book hesitantly and closed it. "Check the danger level indicator on your ID badge." Kyle was reaching for his badge with one hand as he was returning his book to the holster with the other.

"Yeah. Of course." The chef replied, remembering that bit of trivia. Only the employees who actively worked with the artifacts usually had to worry about magic levels. Dangerous artifacts were contained and stored. But all museum employees had an ambient magic density indicator on their badges, just like people who worked around radiation had radiation indicators on their badges.

"It's purple," he whispered to Kyle.

"Mine too," Kyle replied quietly.

"Were we exposed in the museum? Or is it out here?" That was the question, wasn't it? If it was out here, they should get to the museum and take as many people as possible. If it was something inside the museum, they should get as far away from it as possible.

"I don't know." Uncertainty had him waffling between the two choices. Run, or go back. Then he realized something. "Wait. None of the indicators in the park have gone off. It must be inside. Come on." Kyle gestured for his friend to follow him, and they began trekking across the lawn of Central Park to get as far away from the museum as possible. "Call the boss and tell him we got the notification. They'll start evacuating any second now."

Then every security golem in and around the park activated at once. Statues hopped off of pedestals, splashed out of fountains, or stood from their repose to join the dedicated security golems that lined the periphery of Central Park. They began the trek to form a protective ring completely encircling the perimeter of the park, feet stomping in time with military precision.

A few seconds later the magical streetlamps in the park turned on and flared purple. Prometheus ambient magic density indicator flares placed regularly throughout the park blazed into life with a flickering purple flash. Kyle knew they were color-coded to indicate the level of magical danger. Purple meant that the ambient magic level was high enough to generate monsters from inanimate objects as well as mutate non-magical animals into monsters.

From the museum, the external and internal alarms began sounding and a speaker broadcasting an automated voice began a prerecorded message.

"Warning. Ambient magic density has reached dangerous levels. Monster formation is imminent. Seek shelter immediately. The Museum is a safe zone and possesses a magical insulation barrier. If you cannot evacuate the vicinity, you may seek shelter within."

Kyle and his friend looked at one another briefly, then began running back the way they had come to the shelter of their workplace.

Chapter 12

Camina laughed, really laughed, at the snarky comment her seat partner made. He'd been regaling her with stories about his own high school indiscretions, and it made her issues with Anna pale by comparison. Though...Samantha...Samantha and her patron gift Gleipnir gave Camina ulcers on a regular basis still.

"I can't believe it." She shook her head at the young man who'd been so eager to cheer her up.

"Swear on a stack of Bibles." The young man held out a hand in front of his face to emphasize the height of the stack he would swear on. "We turned her desk transparent, and she was feeding a nest...an entire freaking nest...of micro-sparrows in her drawer."

"Oh, wow." The woman chuckled and shook her head appreciatively. "Thanks so much for sharing some of your misadventures with me. I feel less worried about the one and only fight that Anna's been in."

"Anytime." The young man smiled hugely almost shy for a second. "I mean, come on. How often does a guy get to say that he cheered up his hero with embarrassing stories of his childhood?" He ran a hand through his hair nervously.

"True." The woman nodded in agreement. "That's true. But I can't possibly be your hero."

"No. No. I mean. Yes." He laughed and corrected himself. "Camina Watkins. You are my hero. And probably a lot of other people's hero also. But I want to be, I'm trying to be, an embedded journalist...."

"Really?!" Camin felt briefly guilty for thinking earlier that his interest had been purely because he had been a Gore Groupie, someone who liked watching monster battles simply because of the blood and guts.

"Yes, really. And people like me can't do what they do without people like you to protect us." He had that determined look in his eyes that said he wasn't going to cry even if his hero said something shitty that might squash his dreams.

"Oh. You are going to do wonderfully if you keep thinking like that. Just remember that warriors and adventurers can fail and that you will be in danger." The young man had been so honest and vulnerable that she smiled kindly at him. "I hope you have some basic self-defense abilities?"

"Yes. I've had my Tier Four license for a few years now. Though I had to leave my wand at home since you can't get a license to bring a wand or magical item on a plane until –"

"Tier Six." Carmina volunteered. This was something she was familiar with. Magical law and restrictions. "Something that drives any frequent flier warlock batty, are the security protocols around the transport of magical conductors on passenger transports. It's one of the reasons I hate traveling as a civilian." The young man nodded emphatically.

"While I've never flown as anything but a civilian," he started "I've got nothing to compare it to. But I hate the lines, the waiting, never knowing who you will sit next to. It's a complete lottery unless you're traveling in a party. And arrival and departure times are not guaranteed."

As he finished distractedly, he looked out the window now that something dawned on him. He craned his neck and angled his head to get a better look out the window. He'd finally noticed the change, and Camina waited for him to comment on it as he checked the time on his phone.

"You know, I've been so distracted talking to you, I didn't notice that we were supposed to have landed by now." He scratched at his head with confusion. "I could have sworn I felt us turning in preparation for landing a little bit ago."

"Don't be loud about it." Camina smiled and kept her voice conversationally low. "I noticed us changing direction several minutes ago. We seem to have been redirected to another airport and the captain has chosen not to tell us passengers. Why do you suppose that might be?" The young man thought about it for a few seconds before his eyes went round.

"Well, shit!" He exclaimed quietly and dropped his hands into his lap. "That's bad." Camina chuckled at his calm response. He'd do well as an embedded journalist with the Magicorps. She'd had to work with people who wouldn't have reacted with even half as much aplomb as this young man.

"Eh. It's not good, but it's not necessarily awful." Camina amended. "We know it's not really bad yet." She commented cheerily and he gave her a twisted look of doubt.

"How could we possibly know that?" He was skeptical, but Camina was prepared and held up her phone with a grin.

"No one's called for me yet." But her grin only lasted for a few seconds before her seatmate shot back.

"You're assuming there's anyone left to call you." She'd just been playing around, trying to cheer up and reassure the young man who was undoubtedly going to be upset about their flight being redirected. A catastrophe of that level never even crossed her mind. For a moment she was stunned, then shook her head in disbelief.

"No." She paused, then repeated the word again as if to dispel any chance of such a reality. "No. My patron would have let me know if it was something like that." Pausing, Camina frowned. "You know, I'm sorry, I just realized that I forgot to ask your name."

"Oh." The aspiring journalist exclaimed. "I'm sorry. My bad. I was so star-struck I totally forgot to introduce myself." He wiped peanut salt off his hand on the front of his worn lightweight jacket.

She noticed for the first time, the many-pocketed vest showing beneath. A vest like the kind all her embedded journalists wore when they followed her on a campaign. The pockets bulged with camera equipment that was probably a pain to get through airport security. Camina hesitated as she absorbed more about this young man, dedicated to his career even when off the job. Finally, she smiled and took the proffered hand.

"It's a pleasure to meet you. I'm Camina Wattkins." They shook as the young man finally provided his name.

"Hi, Camina. I'm Jim Thafesh, aspiring embedded journalist for the Magicorps. And I'm your biggest fan." He shook her hand enthusiastically for probably longer than he should have then winced sheepishly through the grin that was splitting his face before finally letting go. "It's an honor to meet you."

"Well, Mister Thafesh, the Magicorps is always on the lookout for talented people. Why don't you show me some of your work? If you have any yet that is?" She hadn't thought Jim's grin could get any bigger, yet somehow it did.

"It's mostly just projects for school. I'm at NYU, just heading back after an internship in DC over the Summer. But, yeah, sure. I'd love to. Please don't be too harsh?"

The last bit was a little pleading and Camina smiled with indulgent reassurance. This charming young man reminded her of her son Kyle. Chronologically, he was probably a few years younger. Practically, Kyle hadn't really ever been young. Always a level of maturity and cautiousness that Jim didn't exude at all.

"I promise I will not judge the work of a student harshly." And she didn't. He did good stable camera work. The exposures on his photos were great. The video was in focus and not shaky. He didn't use any obnoxious filters. And his articles were factual, and non-biased while hitting all the right emotional buttons. Most importantly, he was already a level four magical license holder at the young age of twenty with an extreme sports enthusiast's nerves of steel and adrenaline addiction.

A plan began to form in her mind. A plan that she was not proud of herself for having. No. It wasn't even coherent enough to be called a plan. Just a sense of knowing that this young man was the kind of person her superiors wished her children had been.

I can work with this. Camina thought a little selfishly. This one can be molded for greatness.

Chapter 13

11:15 AM September 13ᵗʰ, 2026
The National Museum of Unnatural Science and History

The screaming and panic had finally died down a bit as he ushered people seeking safety deeper into the museum. He and his friend had rushed to the museum with all the other people fleeing the danger of potential monsters. Unlike those panicked patrons, Kyle had known that he needed to report in and start helping coordinate the evacuees from the park.

They'd fill the lecture halls first. Then the loading dock. After that, they'd started siphoning people into the onsite restaurant where a certain Viking-looking chef who couldn't keep the blood off himself worked.

It had been a sketchy for a few minutes there as he was fighting his way through the sea of bodies trying to help sort order out of the chaos of the crowd. But they'd trained for this. Their boss had made sure everyone drilled on safety procedures. Kyle had begrudgingly come in on days the museum was closed for the boring emergency drills that made him feel dumb pretending that he was shouting at a swarm of panicked people represented in the drill by his vampire boss doing his best impression of a stereotypical yokel. Which felt suspiciously like the vampire being racist against humans…. Yet, he couldn't help but admit the training had paid off. Every employee who had participated in one knew what they were supposed to be doing.

Now that things had settled down, Kyle wiped the sweat from his forehead and leaned against one of the walls for support. After a moment, he decided that the adrenaline rush leaving his body had been too exhausting and he slid down the wall to rest and collect his thoughts for a bit. He'd go and report to the director that everyone had been settled soon enough.

No sooner had he taken a second to relax, than did one of the security guards come trotting up. She looked official and badass in her bulletproof vest with a radio clipped to it and her crisply pressed uniform. A gun was holstered on one hip, a wand on the other, as she came to a parade rest in front of him with her hands clasped behind her back.

She didn't look at him, instead looking into the middle distance straight in front of her, which was somewhere through the wall above his head. Kyle had a great view of her set jaw as the perfect bun that stuck out under the back of her beret kept her hair from obscuring any part of her face. Yeah. She *looked* impressive as hell.

But Kyle happened to know that she was scared shitless of a certain bloody coworker.

"Mister Wattkins. I have been ordered to relieve you. The director has requested your presence." Kyle tried not to chuckle. All the security guards in the museum were military personnel. They were here because magic was 'dangerous'. And because if an artifact that the museum restored had military potential, then the military took it, and it wouldn't do for it to go missing before they had been informed it existed.

But the smart ones knew who Kyle was in relation to a certain famous Wattkins. This either meant that they were very respectful as they didn't want to get known as that dumbass who fucked with the Harbinger's kid and pissed her off. Or they sneered because they were disgusted that he hadn't followed in his mother's footsteps.

The profile article with its highly inaccurate description of Kyle's actual career combined with the fact that it did not mention *at all* his position in the museum, had changed that somewhat. How it had done that and what they were thinking, Kyle didn't know, but all morning long he'd been addressed as if he were a superior officer or a high-ranking civilian official. He wasn't sure if he was being punked, or what.

"All right." He stood with a groan. "He's in his office?" The Magicorps soldier still wouldn't meet Kyle's eyes as he stood up in front of her. But she responded with the same precise and respectful tone that she and the others had been addressing him with all day. Which was, of course, the complete opposite reaction of every civilian who worked at the museum.

"He's waiting for you in the foyer…Sir." Oh, it had been slick the way she'd said it. If he hadn't been sensitized to the way the lot of them had been behaving all day, he wouldn't have noticed the slightly too-long pause that turned the 's' in sir from lower to upper case.

"Err. Thank you," he acknowledged, and began to walk away. She didn't drop her formality but completed a precise about-face and took over observing the milling evacuees. This day.

What the hell was happening?

Kyle trudged wearily down the hall and back up into the foyer. It was darker than normal lit only by the yellow emergency magic-powered lights inside the building. The big glass windows that lined the Greek-temple-esque front of the museum had been blocked when the heavy-duty metal security shutters had come down. Glowing runes and enchantment etchings in gold and blue-green glowed softly on the metal of the many jointed rolling shutters.

The foyer was still in a slight state of semi-chaos, but the military security personnel were directing traffic. They'd managed to enforce order quite effectively under Mister Arcas' instruction. Maybe it was just the weird lighting combination of the emergency lights and the magical reinforcement on the doors, but Adrian Arcas almost looked excited by events. The vampire's burnt umber eyes glowed more brightly than normal. As if he was on the hunt.

It's probably just because of the higher ambient magic density. Kyle reassured himself. But the slight twist of sardonic smile he always wore combined with the gleam of his eyes made the pale-skinned director of the museum seem uncannily as if he was enjoying himself. It didn't help at all that the smoothly fluidic stalk of his normal walk looked like a hunter about to pounce at all times.

"Director Arcas." Kyle called out to get the director's attention over the hubbub of voices. The director's keen pointed ears could pick out someone's location in a crowd without error just by the sound of their voice. His head snapped around and his eyes laser-focused on Kyle, that slight twist of a smile cracking into a bright fanged grin.

"Ah, Kyle." His accent was vaguely Eastern European but not distinctive enough for Kyle to ever place. *But that was probably an effect of living so long and speaking so many different languages. Right?* The apprentice warlock reflected as he edged along the wall while skirting the incoming evacuees. The director turned to one of the soldiers to give a few instructions before finding his own way to join Kyle.

"You have new instructions for me?" Kyle asked when they finally met. The director was still smiling, this time a bit sheepishly as he ran a hand through his jet-black hair.

"First, I wanted to let you know what happened. An unidentified source overloaded the city's magic collectors." He paused to let that sink in, his glowing eyes assessing Kyle's response carefully.

"Overloaded the collectors? The city's collectors?" That was…That was unheard of. "It would take a monumental magical event to cause that."

"Yes. I've received a message scroll communication from the FBI's Magic Crimes Division, and they have identified the location of the event." Kyle nodded as he heard that. The Magic Crimes Division was good. They would be on top of any situation like that.

"Good. Good." Briefly, he thought about his older sister. Everyone in the New York office was probably working on this.

"You are either going to be very pleased with or very upset with what I'm about to tell you next." The vampire sighed, clearly pausing for time as he thought of the best way to present whatever he had to say. Kyle's heart rate, which had finally calmed down after the initial emergency alarm, skyrocketed back up again as his system experienced an adrenaline dump.

"What is it, Director?" His hands were trembling, and he tightened them into fists nervously. Had something happened to Samantha? No. Clearly, it wasn't news of a death, or his boss wouldn't think he'd be happy.

"They are requesting a curator from the museum meet them at the scene and provide expertise when they approach the epicenter." *Okay.* Kyle thought distractedly. *That's normal.* The director and other senior staff often provided consultation services on various magical phenomena and artifacts.

"All right. What are your instructions for your absence?" It was a logical question. "Or will one of the other senior staff members be taking this request?" The director's grin widened in a way that almost looked painful. Kyle was sure it would pain him if his teeth pressed into his lips the way the vampire's fangs indented his lips.

"I'm afraid that protocol dictates that in the case of an emergency, all senior staff on hand are to remain on premises until relieved by an appropriate security force." He winced before continuing. "But, because of the unprecedented nature of the event, they've requested a consultation with the Archivist." That was understandable. Arcas ran a pale hand through his dark hair yet again. It might have been a nervous tick?

"But I'm the only Warlock of the Archivist at the museum," Kyle stated lamely. Once again, his lack of full Warlock Status was going to hold him back. They'd send the request to another location for consultation in favor of getting a fully licensed Warlock.

Disappointment flooded him and his shoulders slumped. He wanted to sink to the floor in despair and have a good, 'I'm not crying there's something in my eyes' moment. The apprentice warlock didn't get that opportunity though because the director started speaking again.

"And I told them that. But they aren't going to wait for the next closest Warlock of the Archivist to arrive. They can't wait that long. So, grab your stuff. You're about to handle your first solo artifact acquisition."

Kyle's mouth dropped open in shock before morphing into a face-splitting grin. His heart soared, both with excitement and trepidation. This was it. This was his chance. This was the day he became part of history instead of just studying it.

Chapter 14

11:42 AM September 13th, 2026
Industrial Park District Near the Port of New York

Oh, this day was going down in history alright! Samantha Wattkins fumed as she carefully navigated her way through the wreckage of roads that remained in the industrial district. All she had wanted to do was work her way through the fucking mountain of paperwork on her desk. She'd been taking the jokes from all the boys in good humor and pretending that she wasn't bothered at all so that she could trick the coworkers who'd been teasing her about the Tissue Medic commercials into a couple of practice bouts in the training rooms.

"Come on, Samantha." Agent Alex Parker wheedled from the passenger seat. She was pressed against the door trying to avoid the sharp edges of Sam and her pact item, Gleipnir's combined auras. "Cheer up." Sam turned her head to glare flatly at Alex and Alex shrank back against the passenger door of the bureau sedan.

She looked to Gleipnir for help, but his normal friendly glow had transmuted to a disapproving dark shadow. Gleipnir, the ribbon – or chain, depending on which translations of the myth one read - which had been used to restrain *the* Fenrir of ancient days, had been gifted to Sam by her patron Frigg. He, Gleipnir might have been a genderless transforming sentient magical item, but he *identified* as male, had changed himself into a large needle-like sword shape trailing several feet of a fine razer-sharp braided chain whip from the handle, and hovered protectively in the back seat between Alex and Sam.

"*Sam*antha," Gleipnir emphasized the first syllable of her name when he addressed Alex, as Sam preferred to be called, Sam. "…is not speaking to you." Alex gave an annoyed look at Gleipnir. She hated speaking to sentient artifacts. And this particular magical artifact did not like her. It really wasn't her fault that she'd been called 'The Next Sam' and 'The New Sam' when she first came through the training programs at the bureau. It wasn't her fault that 'Sam' Wattkins thought she was better than everyone just because she was the daughter of a famous Warlock.

Alex crossed her arms in frustration. Both humans fumed in silence for a few minutes. Gleipnir hovered menacingly making a low-pitched growl or buzz. *I hate being partnered with this stuck-up bitch.* But Sam Wattkins was undisputedly acknowledged as The Best magical engineer in their office.

So, new agents vied for the chance to be paired with her. Except, she'd somehow managed to strong-arm her way into not being partnered with men anymore. Stupid Gleipnir kept stabbing them for coming on to Sam. The thing was a menace to society.

"You were trying to trick the guys into thinking you weren't mad at them so you could hurt them while sparing!" The sentence just blurted itself out of Alex's mouth as if she had no control over it. "So, I volunteered us for this assignment." She covered her mouth with a gasp as if surprised that she had said it. Alex suspected that it was a skill or effect that Samantha or Gleipnir could cast on others. "Not as if we wouldn't have been sent anyways with something this big." She mumbled gloomily.

She and Sam might not get along because Sam was stuck up and Gleipnir felt like Alex's talent was a threat to *his* Sam's position, but Alex needed things to go if not smoothly, then at least without animosity and conflict while she was partnered with Sam. As soon as she could, she'd get transferred somewhere else and she'd have the prestige of having been mentored by The Samantha Wattkins on her record. The two of them just didn't make it easy.

"I wasn't going to hurt them…" She looked over to glare at Alex again, but the younger woman just gazed back incredulously. "Not irreparably." Sam amended indignantly. They went back to silence for a few moments before Gleipnir spoke up again.

"Oh, your God!" He exclaimed ridiculously. *Yes. We get it. You were made by multiple Gods. There is empirical evidence that there is more than one God.* The junior agent also hated the way that Gleipnir seemed to flaunt his divine origins. "Look at that mess. I think we should park here and hike in."

"Yeah. I think you're right Gleip." Sam replied distractedly. "It will be hella hard to turn around if we need to flee in a hurry." She navigated over to the other vans, sedans, and armored vehicles, some unmarked and some with the FBI Magic Crimes Division emblem on them. She turned around and parked facing out.

"Should we do something to make sure we aren't boxed in by latecomers?" Alex piped up petulantly. Sam paused getting out of the vehicle.

"Alex," She looked at her supposed protégé with confused disgust. "We are non-combatant technicians and engineers. We *are* the latecomers, and we *never* block anyone's route of egress. Do you understand?" Alex gulped and nodded nervously. She'd known that. Hadn't she known that? "Answer me. Do you understand?"

"Ye...yes." Then she grabbed the door handle and bailed out of the vehicle as quickly as she could.

"Always giving me the greenhorns fresh out of training." Sam was muttering as she stood and waited for Gleipnir to exit the car behind her. The older agent looked up as she closed her door and met Alex's eyes. She was entirely unrepentant about the fact that Alex had heard her. "Did I say something untrue?"

"No." It was shot back defiantly with Alex's regular disdain for the Warlock she thought of as a snob.

"Ohhh, whatever." Rolling her eyes and shaking her head, Sam held her hands out to the side and spoke to Gleipnir. "Hey Gleip, wanna ride?"

"Don't mind if I do, Sam." His tone of voice brightened considerably when chatting with his warlock and he wound his whip chain around Sam's waist to hang himself from her hip like a sword on a belt. Somehow, the razor-sharp links that would have sliced Alex's hand off if she touched them, didn't harm Sam – or her clothing – in the slightest.

Tendrils of envy tried to worm their way into Alex's irritation with her partner, so she looked around at the scene as a distraction. Focusing on work was probably the way to avoid being irritated with Miss Fancy Pants. The road was damaged, and the buildings that were a ways into the distance across vast industrial parking lots were cracking with a hole in the wall of at least one.

Even some of the supports for freeway overpasses looked precariously close to collapsing. She scooched about fifteen feet to the right as Samantha rummaged around in the trunk of her assigned vehicle for the tools of their trade. It was still a bright beautiful early fall day. The event had not changed the weather at all from the brilliant clear skies of this morning.

Sam stepped up next to her and began assessing the situation and gestured to Alex to follow her up to the senior agent on the scene. She ran a commentary as she walked, sharing her assessment. However, Alex suspected it was more for Gleipnir's benefit than for hers.

"Crime scene barrier tape surrounding that vehicle." The magical engineer glared hard at the mangled van in the center of the tape circle. "Hmm. The magic is active on it. The runes are very bright. Too bright. Like the ambient magic density hasn't disbursed yet." She stopped musing as she shifted her gear from one arm to another.

"Hi, Frank." She pulled the name she needed from her memory. "Sam Wattkins, Magical Engineering Technician, reporting in." Sam didn't smile but her face wasn't unfriendly beneath her businesslike expression. The Senior Agent on the scene was someone she'd worked with before. He was likable and smart enough to admit when he didn't know what was what and defer to the technicians. "What are we looking at?"

"Sam," The agent grabbed her hand and shook it. He was middle-aged, with laugh lines and crow's feet that gave him character which was a better look than if he'd been conventionally handsome. "Thank fucking God you are here. I have no idea what I'm looking at."

"Tell me what data you've got. I see from the runes on the barrier tape that the AMD is still up in this area." Frank shook his head in frank bewilderment.

"Yes. The tape is as close as we could safely get to that vehicle at the epicenter when we arrived." He pointed to the mangled vehicle which she could see now was some kind of large van or delivery truck. The branding colors looked familiar, but she couldn't make out any images or writing from this far out. "AMD levels were in the Pink."

"Pink?!" Alex gave a gasp of disbelieving horror. "We're too close. We could die." Gleipnir chuckled as Sam and Frank rolled their eyes.

"Newbie," He patiently explained to Alex, "we've got mobile magic collectors bringing down the ambient magic levels." But he didn't waste time seeing if she was mollified by that or not and got right back to business with Sam. "The vehicle, or something in it, is emanating high levels of magic. Whatever it is must be incredibly powerful because arcanes are sustaining at purple on the Prometheus scale even with the magic collectors working at full intake capacity."

"Oh, shit!" Sam's exclamation was mild as she examined the vehicle with intellectual fascination.

"Yeah. I've requested a curator from the Museum." Sam nodded thoughtfully.

"That was a good call." There wasn't a need to say which museum. Everyone knew which museum you called for something like this. "We'll go in when the curator gets here."

They needed an expert for something like this. So much power. She could feel the magic radiating from the vehicle even from here. It was a rich, pure magic. The kind a magic user could be tempted to drink into their pores and hold for workings. It was tempting, but it was too much magic. It would twist a person, taint them, and kill them eventually.

"At purple?" Once again Alex squeaked out her surprise and both older agents gave her a flat look."

"If arcanes are high enough for AMD to hold at purple even with magic collectors, we have to go in." Sam tried to keep her annoyance in check, but this kid was really trying her patience. "We need to find out what it is and how to contain it before we run out of mobile collection units." She went back to watching the still vehicle and sensed the ripples and currents of magic coming from it seeking things to join with. "Did you order up a contingent of defense specialist mages? We're going to have monster formation soon."

"All my agents are certified to fight monsters," Frank assured her with his Southern drawl.

"Not like this, Frank." Sam winced as she heard a siren going off in the distance. At first, she thought it was first responders dealing with the aftermath of a city-wide blackout or under-trained and ill-equipped law enforcement trying to deal with the first of many monsters that they should expect from this event. Instead, the siren grew closer and closer to them, and a horrible realization dawned on her.

"Why does that vehicle have sirens on?" Frank grumbled as an armored vehicle with flashing lights pulled up, the emblem of the Museum was on its doors. "Is that the curator? You'd think they'd know better. They'll have any monsters in hearing range converging on us."

"I think that was the point." Alex watched the strange rueful-perturbed look on Sam's face as it mottled with conflicting emotions. Then she looked at the incoming vehicle speeding over the bumps, cracks, and folded bits of asphalt that they had navigated so painfully slow around on their way here bumping and jumping over those obstacles with ease.

The armored vehicle skidded to a halt and the sirens and lights quit abruptly. Sam was glaring with extreme distaste at the young man who hopped gleefully out of the driver's seat. He was grinning, a wild gleam in his eyes.

Short brown hair with sun-bleached golden tips, tannish, average looking, in a warlock's robe that looked like a stylish dark-colored men's long coat. Maybe kind of cute? He looked good in nice clothes, a pair of slacks, a dress shirt, jacket, and a vest with a long tie and dress shoes. It was like a fictional academic warlock character had leaped out of a TV show and swaggered into real life.

"Hey, Kyle." Sam waved and smirked at him. She clearly knew him. He stopped in absolute horror. The look of shocked betrayal and disappointment he gave Samantha Wattkins was not lost on any of the agents whose attention had been grabbed by his flashy arrival.

"No. No way." One slim finger pointed accusingly at Sam. Alex smirked. It looked like she wasn't the only one to see through her partner's bullshit. "You cannot be here." He looked to the gorgeous autumn sky and shook a fist admonishingly the shouted. "I will not work with her!"

Then he got back in his vehicle and rested his head on the steering wheel in defeat.

Chapter 15

11:47 AM September 13th, 2026
Industrial Park District Near the Port of New York

"When you asked for a curator…?" Sam turned to Frank with a grimace, "What exactly did you request?" Frank raised inquisitive eyebrows as he glanced between the dejected young warlock and Agent Wattkins' thinly disguised attempt to maintain her professionalism.

"I requested a Warlock of the Archivist —" He started, and Sam's head drooped as she spoke over him.

"Of course, you did." She sighed as he continued the sentence she had spoken over.

"— in case the cause of the event was a known phenomenon or item." Sighing, Sam rubbed the bridge of her nose and felt the familiar pain of 'dealing with Kyle's shenanigans' beginning behind her eyes. Rubbing her eyes lightly for good measure while her hand was up there anyway, Sam Squared her shoulders and spoke. "Get ready. We'll be going in momentarily."

Kyle raised his head from the steering wheel when he felt his sister's aura approaching him. He knew he was being childish, but it honestly hadn't occurred to him that his sister would be here. Having his older sister as one of the agents on the scene when he had his first solo acquisition? Nah. That wasn't – that was going to seem like so much nepotism. It wasn't a good look for his career.

"Hey, Shrimp." Her voice was quiet enough that the other agents couldn't hear. He hadn't thought his shoulders could droop any further, but then she brought up her derogatory nickname for him.

"Could we not make fun of my being shorter than everyone in the family but Dad in front of all the other agents?" It was an old conflict. One she relished and rubbed in any chance she got. "You're just going to be calling attention to how freakishly tall you are."

"I'm sorry." His sister amended softly. "That wasn't professional of me." With a groan, Kyle got out of the armored vehicle as the Magicorps soldier escorting him looked up from rummaging through the gear in the back of the vehicle pretending not to listen in and failing horribly. The two siblings shared a suppressed smile.

"You shouldn't be here Sam." Kyle soberly scolded as he walked briskly around to the rear hatch to help sort through gear. "These kinds of arcane levels have to be from an artifact or an organic source. It's too dangerous." He didn't add the words 'for you' to his sentence. They were implied.

"Yeah. It's unlikely it's from technology. But the suddenness with which the release happened smacks of technology." The older sibling studiously ignored her younger brother's attempt to be protective of her while Gleipnir bristled silently at her waist. "Hush, Gleipnir. Kyle's just being a brother, he's not insulting yours or my abilities."

"Well, he was rude even if that wasn't his intention." Gleipnir's words had the usual effect when he spoke, and Kyle rolled his eyes at the ancient magic sentient item who always took his role as Sam's protector too seriously.

"Stop." It was a sudden crisp order he gave to the soldier pulling gear out of the armored vehicle's rear storage. "Err...Private? No, Lieutenant Jones." The soldier halted with a pained look on his face.

"Sir?" The soldier's face blanked at the address.

"Oh, for fuck's sake Kyle, he's a Specialist. And quit fucking with them by pretending you don't know their ranks." She turned to Specialist Jones and pointed at the pile of gear he was organizing. "What my brother was about to tell you is that we don't need most of that stuff."

"Yeah." Kyle scruffed his hair with another wince. "Leave the bulky containment equipment in the car until we ascertain what we're dealing with. I can guarantee that we'll need something bigger than what we've brought to transport it anyway. I mean, just look at the size of the vehicle they were transporting it in and how it has deformed the walls of the cargo compartment."

"Oh. Yes, Sir." The soldier replied and obediently looked at the truck hundreds of feet away. He began putting the gear away.

"Leave out the portable magic collectors. Activate a spare one in the vehicle in addition to the onboard one, we don't want our ride transmuting into a monster on us. And toss us the personal shield collectors. Put one on yourself too." Kyle was knowledgeable enough and had ridden along enough on consultations and artifact collections that he knew what he was doing.

"Good call Kyle." Sam offered a rare compliment to her baby brother as she caught the shielding device and strapped it on one wrist. Her brother and the soldier did the same. "Don't activate these until we're closer. It will prolong their use."

"I know that, *Mom*." Snark. It was Kyle's native language.

"Yeah. But Specialist Jones didn't." She added peeved. They were already getting on each other's nerves. "Make sure you activate the sensor but not the collector until Kyle or I tell you. They'll interfere with our readings once they're on. Ignis Promethi."

Sam activated the Prometheus sensors on the techno-magic devices by placing two fingers on the half-heart-shaped arrow that was the symbol of Prometheus and spoke the activation spell. The enchantment flared to life and the large clear crystal glowed purple within. Her words were echoed by the two men with her. Kyle frowned as he grabbed a fourth personal collector and offered it to Sam.

"For your partner?" She gave an 'Ugh' and nodded. He tossed it to her.

"I'd rather let her use the FBI standard-issue gear." She snorted derisively. "But the museum's work better in high AMD areas." They turned and began heading back to the group of waiting agents. There was a cluster of them around Alex and Frank. Their bearing and the conspiratorial looks on their faces combined with the way they were speaking to each other behind the occasional hand seemed...Sam narrowed her eyes as she saw what was going on.

"Well," Specialist Jones commented, "Those people are clearly gossiping about you two."

"Yes," Kyle answered with a thoughtful smile. "I guess we shouldn't disappoint them." He turned to his sister and for the first time since she read that article this morning, her mood lifted. Maybe she couldn't beat some kindness into her coworkers, but as much as her brother might annoy her, he always had her back.

Samantha Wattkins grinned evilly.

Chapter 16

11:50 AM September 13th, 2026
Industrial Park District Near the Port of New York

Frank liked Samantha Wattkins. He really did. She was competent, polite professional, and worked hard. Which was a lot more than he could say about a lot of people he'd worked with over the years.

Sure, there were people who had issues with her…if they were insecure jackasses who thought she only got her job because of favoritism. Or if they mistook her professionalism and competence for arrogance and standoffishness. Then, of course, there was Gleipnir, who was both arrogant and was an absolute void of professionalism.

So, it was normal for Frank to initially assume this was someone Sam and Gleipnir had just rubbed the wrong way. After the two began speaking, however, it started to seem as if there was something else going on. He sidled over to the junior agent who had arrived with Sam Wattkins.

"You Wattkins partner?" His question was pitched low, but Alex was also so distracted watching this interesting interaction that she didn't notice the conspiratorial nature of the question.

"Uh. Huh?" The young woman spared only the briefest glance at her addresser. "Um, yes." Her head snapped back to watching Sam and the kind of cute curator from the museum.

"I know I shouldn't ask but," Frank hesitated because he'd never really participated in gossip before. "What's the story with those two?" He nodded at the pair off in the distance and the poor Magicorps soldier awkwardly trying to avoid being noticed. "Like, is this a work thing or a…personal thing?"

"I…I…" The junior agent stuttered absorbed in the distant drama. "I have no idea. Whatever this is, was before my time." They watched in speculative silence as Sam coaxed the younger man out of the vehicle.

"Five bucks says it's an ex." A third agent added as they walked up. Frank frowned but couldn't stop watching the train wreck in action. Inexorably his eyes would be drawn back every time he tried to jerk them away.

"I'll take that." Alex chimed in. "Five dollars says he dislikes her because they've worked together."

"I mean," Frank added thoughtfully, "Those two situations aren't mutually exclusive." Then he blushed and ducked his head before glancing back at the vehicle. The two junior agents turned their heads slowly to stare at him in awe for suggesting to them a scandal that neither would have attributed to Sam on their own.

Everything seemed to be moving along, and the possible former couple were smiling when Sam suddenly stopped, turned on the curator, and slapped him viciously across the face. He staggered back with a look of disbelief. The watching agents gasped. It wasn't all the agents, just the few who weren't actively patrolling the perimeter of the quarantined area.

"Don't pretend you don't know what that's for." Sam's shout of pent-up betrayal almost sounded like a sob. "Now let's just get this done so I don't have to spend another second in your presence.

"Fine by me." The young man cupped a cheek and rubbed it wincingly as they started walking again. The soldier with them covered his mouth as his eyes bulged in surprise. He slapped his other hand to his thigh and took a second to recover from his shock. His hand was still covering the lower half of his face as they approached the cluster of senior agents.

"Alex, catch!" Sam tossed a personal magic collector and arcane sensor to her partner without bothering to see if the woman caught it. "Gear up. The faster we're done with this the faster our curator can leave." The three veered toward the barrier and made a beeline for the waiting mystery within.

"Oh. My. *GOD!*" Alex whisper-screamed to herself as she put on the magic collector and activated the sensor. Then mouthed it a second time. Frank gave a shake of his head and turned after the trio.

"Okay, people!" He gave a bellow aided with magic to make it loud enough for all the agents on site to hear. "We're sending the museum curator and the magic technicians into the perimeter."

Alex hurried to catch up, wary of getting caught in other people's drama. Without looking at her the curator snapped.

"Turn off your collector until we finish our readings." How did he know? Alex couldn't sense that much difference in the magical currents. The place was flooded with magic. She obeyed quietly.

For once, Sam seemed to be behaving humbly, letting the curator take the lead even if she had slapped him only a few minutes ago. So, Alex turned her attention to the curator. Despite his potential cuteness, the Warlock of the Archivist was haughty. His gaze was intensely serious, and his jaw set with determination as he took measurements around the open area of devastation around the vehicle.

The asphalt, sidewalk, and parking lots nearby were ruptured and crumpled like demented accordions. Some large pieces were completely vertical with the gravel and earth beneath exposed. Water pipes and other infrastructure poked through the surface periodically.

"Okay," Kyle exclaimed after a hike around the wasteland. "...I've gotten all the readings I can. Turn on your magic collectors and stay behind me and Sam. Gleip, I need you to do your thing."

"What thing?" Sam questioned, though she suspected she didn't want to know.

"That thing where I drag you to safety at the slightest sign of danger whether you want me to or not," Gleipnir responded smugly as he unwrapped his chain from his warlock's waist.

"That's right, my man read my mind." Kyle held out a hand and got a high five from the tail of Gleipnir's chain before it rewrapped itself around Samantha protectively. Both chuckled as Samantha glowered.

She tried to brush a lock of her light brown hair back in irritation, but it was already securely restrained in a ponytail so she smoothed any that might have come loose instead. Then she activated the magic collector on her wrist and tried to focus on their destination. The closer she got, the more familiar the vehicle and its branding became. Was that a giant with a crown missing a chunk out of its side standing over…

"Oh, my gosh." Finally, the information that had been tingling in the back of her head popped into her awareness. "Kyle, the company branding. Is that Mountain King Movers?" Kyle narrowed his eyes and blocked the sun with one hand as he tried filling in the missing imagery with his imagination. Then his eyes widened, and he turned to his sister in excitement as he came to the same conclusion.

"I do believe you are right." His gleeful exclamation was echoed by Gleipnir's own crowing.

"Ha, ha. Yes, it is my darling Samantha. On the count of three. One, two, three…," The sentient magic item counted down as Alex and Specialist Jones gave each other dubious looks behind Sam and Kyle's backs. Then the two siblings and Gleipnir broke into the song from the company's commercial set to the tune of *In the Hall of the Mountain King*.

"When you need to move your stuff,

Trust in us,

We are tough,

When you need to move your stuff,

We will get it done."

Their impromptu serenade ended on laughter and the three paused for a moment then exclaimed in unison "Jinx."

"Da fuck?" Specialist Jones murmured under his breath. "I think I'm going to hate my job when those two work together." He added thoughtfully, lost in imaginings of what other horrors they might drag him into. He was already dreading what would happen if someone reported the whole slapping incident to the museum director and word got back to his boss.

"I think I like that guy," Alex exclaimed with a smile.

Chapter 17

The vehicle that seemed to be the epicenter of the magic emanations was in a depression on the ground. Kyle picked his way over and around the broken crumpled asphalt cautiously. Out of corner of his eye, he kept checking on Samantha's progress. Not that she couldn't handle herself, but old habits died hard. Their big brother, Davelor, had always ground it into his head that they were supposed to look out for Sam.

School had been rough for Sam. And after Gleipnir became a part of her life, things had gotten more complicated. The pact item had been both her new best friend and defender, and the cause of so very many calls from the principal. Even if it was only because he was adamantly defending his partner.

"Wait a second." Gleipnir called out. "I'm sensing a changed in the magical currents. Is anyone picking that up?" Everyone stopped in their advance and Kyle took some more readings.

"Yes." He confirmed, his brow furrowing at the meter. "I'm reading two sources now. One's coming from…" Looking up at the damaged building that had been incorporated into the quarantine zone, he pointed toward the highly suspicious hole in the wall before glancing at his sister again.

"Hey, Sam." She quirked her eyebrow at him inquisitively.

"Yes, Kyle?" Sam's obvious wariness was not lost on her partner who tried not to snort in amusement.

"You requested defense specialist mages to back us up, didn't you?" Kyle was kicking himself now for not remembering to ask for them himself. He'd let himself get distracted like the young impetuous man everyone older than him thought he was.

"I sure did." She assured her brother. "I don't know why they weren't out here already. I mean, it's a Purple Alert. How are we supposed to do our jobs if we get attacked by monsters while we're out here." The diatribe wasn't one she'd intended on, and she blushed slightly. Working with her brother was making her act too familiar in this serious situation.

"We've got two major sources of magical emanation. One is from whatever is in the truck and the other is from the thing in that…is that a warehouse," Kyle squinted against the sun again. There was just no avoiding it in his eyes today, "…well, whatever that building is over there. He waved a hand, and the loose sleeve of his warlock's robe flopped around his wrist as he did.

"What's your verdict then?" Sam asked affably. "You're in charge baby brother." Kyle's shoulders dropped and he gave her a flat look of disgust. "What now?" The technician really wasn't sure how she had offended her kid brother this time.

"You just blew our charade." He gestured to Sam's partner, Alex, who was choking on air as she processed the trick the siblings had played on everyone. "Oh, fuck it!" He gave up and moved on to more pressing matters.

"I'm fairly certain that what we're looking at is one dead magical creature that released most of its magic at once, which is what overloaded the magic collectors. The dead body and whatever the second source is, are still leaching magic into the vicinity. And…" he gestured at the hole in the side of the building, "I'm not entirely sure that second one is dead. Let's get the first thing identified before the second wakes up, yeah?"

"Heck yes." Specialist Jones spoke up in emphatic agreement. "I have orders to remove you from the area if it's dangerous. How dangerous is it, Sir." Unsure why the soldier was treating her brother like he was a superior officer and not just a civilian he was guarding; Sam gave the pair a quizzical look.

"Agreed. Let's get a closer look at what's in the truck." They began moving again in the direction of the Mountain King Mover's vehicle. All the while Specialist Jones kept a hand on his weapon and alternated his watch between the vehicle and the ominous hole leading into the dark interior of the warehouse.

As they drew closer, it was plain to see that something hadn't exploded inside the truck. Instead, it seemed as if something that was small, had suddenly gotten too large.

"Someone's shrinking spell wore off, you think?" Sam offered to Kyle who nodded grimly to her.

"That or a shapeshifter that reverted back to its full size after death." The younger brother chimed in, sharing his theory. "I think I see flesh."

"And blood." Sam confirmed pointing at the red that had flowed out of various tears in the sides of the vehicle to dribble and pool congealing beneath it.

"I see scales." Alex proffered unprompted when they'd finally gotten close enough to focus on what she could clearly confirm was damaged flesh. From his place on Sam's hip, Gleipnir sniffed. Then he growled and snarled in a low offended voice.

"I. Smell. Dragon." The whole group stopped at that. Kyle and Sam because…well…dragons! But the two with them gave pause for another reason.

"How the hell can you smell anything, Gleipnir?" Alex rounded on Sam and glared at the shining surface of Gleipnir's current needle-sword-whip combination. "You don't have a nose."

"Ugh!" He complained angrily. "Must you humans always question my ability to sense things. I'm alive. I can see without eyes. I can hear without ears. I can feel with, well, I do touch things. Why wouldn't I be able to *smell*? Good grief." He settled down after his spiel to just grumbling about how insensitive some *humans* were, and Kyle had to interrupt them before Alex got pulled into one of the Gleipnir debates that the pact item was famous for in their family.

"I see scales too." Kyle verified what Alex had said and pulled his notebook out of its holster. He set it in place, hovering in the air, and flipped it open to a random blank page.

"Archive query." He commanded. "Scale patterns of magical creatures that emit high levels of arcanes after death." He watched images appearing in the notebook, hmming as he compared and discarding the ones that didn't match what he was seeing before him. "Too many close matches. I need more information to go on."

Chapter 18

12:00 PM September 13ᵗʰ, 12026
Industrial Park District Near the Port of New York

"I can see a claw from over here." Specialist Jones called out, and Kyle jogged carefully over the disrupted ground to him.

"Oh. Good. Good." Kyle murmured as he held up the notebook to the claw over twenty feet away as if he were taking a photo. "But still need more to narrow it down."

"Just ask about dragons." Gleipnir cried out from where Sam was poking at one of the large cylinders of flesh poking out the side of the truck. "Eastern dragons." He grumbled with clear frustration that Kyle hadn't listened to him the first time. His sister glared at him in solidarity with Gleipnir but said nothing as she literally poked the huge, scaled hide with a stick she'd picked up somewhere.

"WTF Sam.?" Kyle scolded, "Get back. It's dangerous." before crossing his arms and doing as he'd been asked. "Archive query." Kyle stated again in exasperation. "Compare scale patterns and claw shape to dragons." The young warlock gave his sister a 'so-there-are-you-happy look. "Will you back away from the dangerous source of magical radiation now?"

"Yep!" Jones stated quietly from much further back than either of the Wattkins siblings. "I'mma gonna die." Alex looked over at him dubiously.

"It's not *that* bad." Then she looked back at Sam and Gleipnir quietly arguing over whose turn it was to poke *it* with a stick and whether or not it was cheating for her to be using a stick instead of him. Eventually, they agreed that if Gleipnir could use the stick also, then it was not warlock infidelity of the pact item.

"Yeah, it is." Jones confirmed. "When the Harbinger finds out I let *two* of her kids get within stick-poking distance of a possible dragon corpse, she's going to kill me." He gestured at the two Wattkins, but mostly Sam, for emphasis. Alex snorted and covered her laugh.

"Oh yeah. You're going to die. But it's not all bad." She offered the soldier a ray of hope before dashing it to smithereens. "It's my job to just follow where Sam and Gleipnir lead, so she won't have any reason to kill me." It was Alex's turn to receive a flat betrayed look from Jones.

"Ha. Ha. I'm so comforted." He replied drily.

"Alright," Kyle shouted to get the attention of his three companions. "The archive confirms it. Gleipnir was fucking right." Then he added in an aggrieved aside "For once."

"What's that whipper snapper?" Gleipnir called out surprising Alex and Jones that he'd been able to hear something that quiet. "You got something to say, say it to my face."

"You don't have a face!" Kyle shot back petulantly.

"You speciest little pric –" The magical item had unwound his whip end from Sam's waist and made as if to come after Kyle. "Hold me back, Sam." He ordered his warlock. "Otherwise, I'm gonna lay the hurt down on your brother." Rolling her eyes and smiling fondly at Gleipnir, she gave Kyle a sardonic shake of her head.

"You just had to?" Her question made Kyle look down at his feet in shame. He and Gleipnir had…issues.

"Let's head back to safety. We've only got a few more minutes on our collector shields." The four made the slow arduous way back to the waiting agent in charge and Sam and Kyle gave their reports.

"Frank," Sam began. "I won't be able to determine if there was any magi-tech involved until after we've gotten the vehicle to a secure lab site and properly quarantined." She felt her phone vibrating and looked down at it. That person shouldn't have been calling her right now, so it was probably important. Gesturing to Kyle she explained "Kyle can tell you why that is. I have to take this." Then she peeled away to answer her call in semi-privacy.

"We are looking at the corpse of an Eastern Serpent Form Dragon with shapeshifting abilities. We won't be able to see if there is anything else in the truck until the dragon is removed." Frank's eyes bulged momentarily before he rubbed an eyebrow in thought.

"When will the AMD level go back down to safe levels?" He questioned distractedly; already lost in the political quagmire this was going to be. The dragons did not like it when other species had access to their remains.

There were people who still hunted dragons for their magical properties. And yes, every nation in the world 'officially' recognized dragons as people, but that didn't mean that they were *treated* as people. Nor did it mean that dragon hunters were actually prosecuted in every country where it was 'illegal' in the nod and a wink kind of way. The number of magical artifacts and potions that could be created from one corpse was staggering. *BIG bucks!* This was going to be an incident, that was for sure.

"They won't. Not until the remains are contained. And there is possibly another live magical creature or the corpse of one in that building over there." Kyle pointed in the direction of the damaged wall with the hole in it. "Seeing as how whatever it is smashed a hole in the wall, I didn't want to go check it out in case it was still alive."

"Ho-ly sheeit!" Frank rubbed more furiously at his eyebrow. "Two sources?" Kyle nodded.

"You need the largest containment vehicles you can get, and a refrigerated warehouse with not just magical shielding but with exchangeable magic collectors that can be replaced when they near capacity." Kyle was explaining while he spoke, much in the same way he did while giving a lecture to museum visitors. Using engaging facial expressions and gesturing larger than was strictly necessary.

"Dragon corpses continuously give off arcanes as they decompose. Dragon bones and hides will retain magic for centuries. Millenia even. If we leave this carcass here, New York would be a purple zone for at least a hundred years. Maybe longer." He was just getting into the swing of his lecture when the senior agent interrupted.

"And there might be a living one, possibly injured, and needing help, in the warehouse?" That brought Kyle up short. He hadn't thought of the magical source in the warehouse as being anything other than a dangerous threat. But perhaps, it could be a wounded sentient being in need of help.

"Err, um. Maybe." He gulped down a squeaked reply. "I can't say for sure what it is. Only that it put a hole in that warehouse and has a similar magical strength to the deceased dragon in the Mountain King Movers van.

"Oh. This day just gets better and better." Groaning, Frank waved over to one of the agents who was holding their communications scroll. They were reading the lines of messages as they formed keeping them updated about recovery and patrol efforts all over town.

"Get on the scroll, Embry. We might have an injured magical creature on our hands, possibly an Eastern Dragon. So, we need a containment team and healers. We'll also need more forensic specialists; this is possibly an assassination or a murder. Maybe dragon hunters. And ask them again where the hell our defensive combat specialists are."

"Someone killed a dragon?" Embry exclaimed in disbelief before unrolling the communications scroll to the clean spot under all the previous communications.

That wasn't good news, Kyle thought. The combat specialist mages not showing up yet, that was. Kyle had passed quite a few places where first responders had needed to help people on his way over from the museum. A magical overload destroyed a lot of electronics, and a lot of people had found out that morning why it was important to use the appropriate magically safe equipment. None of those cheap knockoffs from questionable factories. The emergency lanes down the center of every street had been empty for him, but he wondered if it had been so orderly everywhere else. Why else would backup not have arrived yet.

"Hey, Frank." Kyle grabbed the senior agent's attention when he'd finished shouting. "Why do you have so few agents? This…" He gestured around at everything. "…this is huge. This is the biggest magical disaster to happen in America in hundreds of years." Frank shook his head at Kyle, a look of clear confusion on his sweaty face.

"I don't know."

"What?!" Sam's screamed cry of outrage reached them, and both turned to her in surprise. "What do you mean he never showed up? I'm coming to get you. I'll be right – fuck!" She stopped in her panicked flight back to her car. "Hold tight Anna, Kyle's with me. I'm sending him to get you now."

"Anna?" Fear gripped Kyle when he heard his little sister's name. She would have been at school. She would have been at school when magic collectors blew. Their mom was out of town. *But dad would have gotten her surely!* He thought frantically.

"Kyle." Sam was wide-eyed and white faced with terror. It was a stark awful look, and a pit of horror began to open in Kyle's stomach as he thought of all the things that could have gone wrong.

"Sam," The warlock forced the words out calmly, through gritted teeth as he clenched his hands until his short, trimmed nails cut his palms and made him bleed. "What's happened to Anna?"

Chapter 19

12:05 September 13th, 2026
New York Preparatory Academy, New York, NY

"Okay." Anna calmly ended the call and closed her phone while taking long deep even breaths. She repeated a word with each exhale. "Okay. Okay. It's…going…to…be…okay…" Things were not *okay*!

But Anna shook her head to dispel that thought and moved with what felt like a preprogrammed deliberation as she removed the battery from her phone and returned it to the magically hardened case that she kept the charged spare in. Then she carefully peeked her head up over the desk she was hiding behind with Sara, Dean George, one of Sara's friends who hadn't been picked up yet, and three of the school's security guards.

It had been going so well after the event. Ridiculously well.

Now it wasn't.

How had things gotten to this point?

How…?

This is how:

To say that things had been hectic after everything blew would be an understatement.

Dean George had stepped up and handled it admirably well. She also had some really choice words for the contractor that the school's board had used to 'update' the safety infrastructure. Seriously, Anna had heard words she'd never even known existed and had stared in awe with the other three suspended students as Dean George cursed a river of vitriol that would go down in her mind as one of the most important moments of history.

The Assistant Dean would live, thanks to Dean George's quick thinking and the school nurse also being a level eight licensed healer. She'd come running from the nurse's office when Anna had breathlessly come running in for help. The woman had already had her potions and med-kit in hand and was about to make the rounds when Anna had arrived, too out of breath to even speak. Instead, the nurse had told her to just lead the way.

Once the wounds the Vice Dean had received from his computer exploding into him had been stabilized, Dean George had rallied the security team and sent them with the head nurse to assess injuries. Then she'd made sure that the assistant nurse was staying put in the nurse's office to receive any patients that came looking for help. And once she was alone in the administrative office and everyone else had been shuffled off to carry out her orders, then Dean George had walked into her personal office, shut the door behind her, and screamed her fury for a full two minutes.

It was glorious!

Afterward, she'd walked out of her office into the main administrative office, calmly straightened her suit jacket and skirt, then held out her hand to Anna.

"Miss Wattkins," Her voice was smooth, even, prim like always and ever so polite and matter of fact. "The Academy would be extremely grateful if you would allow the administration to borrow your phone during this emergency."

The Assistant Dean was still staring at his superior mouth agape. Sara and her cronies turned to Anna in suspicion, and Anna's jaw dropped.

"How…how did you know that I would have a working phone?" There were so many other things she could have said at that moment like; 'that was amazing, I don't even know what half those words mean', or 'you are the coolest dean ever'. Instead, she'd chosen; how did you know I have a working phone? *It's official. I am not cool.* She shook her head internally.

"Anna," the dean glanced away with an embarrassed sigh and tucked a loose strand of hair behind an ear before continuing. "It's my job as dean, to know my students, their potential, their weaknesses, and any danger they may pose to their fellow students. Your magical capacity is high enough that if you lost control, you would…damage electronics. So, I assume you either have a magically hardened phone, or a backup battery in a magically hardened case to protect it. It's standard military procedure anyways. So…?"

She cocked her head to one side, looking at Anna expectantly. And Anna had shrugged and gotten out her phone and the battery in its case. Then she handed it over.

"Right. You four are going to be my assistants." Dean George continued brusquely. "And if you don't tell anyone about my little meltdown, I will teach you what the words you didn't recognize meant." *Ooohhhh!* Anna hadn't been planning on telling…no scratch that. She'd been planning on telling *everyone* because it had been so fucking epic.

"What do you need us to do boss?" Anna had smiled up at the dean who looked at the other girls waiting for their response. They'd smiled their evil little smiles, traded glances among each other, then shrugged and agreed. For now.

Then the dean called nine-one-one for assistance. Students and faculty all over the campus had received injuries. Some minor, some not so minor. The security guards had locked down the campus and made sure no students wandered off.

That was how Anna found herself helping to coordinate the evacuation of the school with her mortal enemy. It wasn't fun per se, but she got to wear a bright neon yellow-green emergency vest as she ushered the first responders to various locations throughout the campus or escorted students to the front doors when a family member, or representative came to pick them up.

It kept Anna occupied so she wasn't straight up freaking out. But it also made her worried about her dad. He hadn't come for her. It had been literally hours since the dean called him, and he hadn't come.

Mom was out of town. Yeah. So, she couldn't expect her mom to come get her. But her dad? He had his own practice. He could have rescheduled an appointment. Or called the school between appointments to let them know when he'd be able to come get her. He could have even had one of her older siblings come get her.

But nothing?

That wasn't normal.

Was it?

They had to evacuate. It was clear that the school didn't have the appropriate magical shielding or protections. With arcane AMD levels at

Prometheus Purple, they needed to evacuate quickly. Not even the dorms for the international students were considered safe. And since the dorms had originally been built with protections, it was clear that the renovations that had updated the school had also stolen a lot of valuable material from it.

The dean had managed to secure a large, shielded room at a conference center not far from the school. She'd pulled strings and gotten a bus company to send out magically hardened buses and there was a steady stream of luxury tour busses ferrying students to the relative safety of the conference center. Many kids had actually been picked up by parents, chauffeurs, family security, in limos, armored luxury vehicles, and even a couple of helicopters that nearly collided over the lawn.

Chapter 20

As the students and faculty were evacuated, so was the very expensive private security that the academy employed. More than half the students had left with about half the faculty and security. And Anna admitted to herself as she ran from one classroom to another notifying teachers of when there was a bus ready for them and their students, things had been going well.

Too well.

It was Prometheus Purple out there.

Where were the monsters?

That's what some of the other kids were grumbling about. The city kids. The students from the U.S.A. They didn't know.

America had magic collectors and defensive perimeters around their cities. America had an entire branch of the military dedicated to monster defense. That was in addition to every branch of the military and law enforcement organization being required to have at least twenty-five percent of their service members qualified as level eight magic license mages.

There hadn't been a city-wide monster incursion in decades. Because the colonists of this great nation had learned. They had learned from Roanoke what happened when you ignored the warnings the natives gave about the things magic did to people here. They had learned from Salem the depravity of demons who preyed upon young warlocks. They had learned that the only way to live here was to conquer magic, reduce ambient levels in population centers by capturing it, and incorporate its use into their lives.

So…where were the monsters?

They were coming. Anna didn't know when, or how, or what form they would take, but Anna knew it was inevitable. She redoubled her speed as she sprinted down the hallway to the next teacher in line. They'd started with classes furthest from the front gate so now, with only half of the student body left, she only had half the distance to run.

It was still taxing. Her legs were starting to get a burn in them from the constant relay back and forth. Sara and one of her friends had kept up, not surprising as they were cheerleaders and the school's team trained competitively. One member of the group was on the swim team and she did not fare well. Her legs were trained for a different kind of athleticism.

Honestly, Anna had been surprised that she was as fast as the others. Sure, she wasn't out of shape. But she wasn't in sports. She ran with her mom, participated in mom's mandatory physical fitness training, and self-defense instruction with Sam, because her mom hit too hard even when she pulled her punches. Yet, she honestly hadn't considered herself to be genuinely athletic.

"Mrs. Deville?" Anna called out as she slid to a stop in front of the ninth-grade history teacher's classroom. "The buses are on their way back, they're ready for your class at the front office."

The nervous woman, turned from her fretful watching out the window and smiled with relief. It always struck Anna as odd that someone so stunningly beautiful – even oblivious Anna could tell that Mrs. Deville was more than supermodel gorgeous – had chosen teaching as their profession. Many of the petty girls whispered that she'd used magical enhancements to make herself prettier, as if those same girls didn't do the same.

"Oh. Excellent. Class..." She clapped her hands together several times, making the flowing sleeves of her dress flutter. "Like we practiced in drills. Line up and follow Miss Wattkins to the front."

"You're not coming with?" Anna asked with alarm when she realized that the teacher was not ready to leave campus. She lived in the on-campus housing with her husband and they each supervised one of the dormitories for the international students. The resident faculty had been instructed to prepare for evacuation along with the students they supervised. "You don't have anything to take with you?"

"I'll escort the students part way." She assured Anna, nervously pushing a strand of brown hair with tints of green in it out of the way. "I'm not leaving without my husband. The dean knows."

It always felt to Anna, like Mrs. Deville was extremely young. Though rumor was she'd been around for years. The woman blushed when she mentioned her husband and her voice got a little shy. Like was that just what happened to someone who was madly deeply in love with someone else? Because that was not even a little bit how her parents acted. Though, to be fair, Anna didn't think that anything could make her mother blush.

"I'm right here." Marax Deville called from down the hallway. He was hurrying up, his massive bodybuilder–esque frame trailing a grey cloak or cape – Anna could never decide which it was – from the epaulettes of his jacket. His cloak-cape seemed to change shape and style as necessary. It was yet another thing the students whispered about.

The huge man dressed like nineteenth-century royalty in military dress. Without the ribbons and symbols of rank of course. He could have stepped right out of a history book with his deep blue and dark grey heavily starched uniform and heavy epaulettes and gold braids. And he had this musty sulfur smell to him – magically, he didn't actually stink – of hot stones and metal that always made Anna suspect him of sketchy magic. You know, the kind that was outlawed and resulted in priests and paladins showing up.

Wherever the case may be, his wife smiled a huge blossoming smile that made her already supernaturally beautiful face even more radiant. If one were to ignore their suspicions about Mister Deville, one could grudgingly admit that the couple were adorable. And maybe even have shipped them before they started dating.

"Right. Then since everyone's here, let's go." Anna spun around just as the shattering of glass was followed by the crash of desks being overturned...and shrieking. Of course, there was shrieking.

"I was afraid that this was going to happen." Eik Deville sighed like a monster crashing through the wall of her classroom was a normal everyday kind of inconvenience. "The arcanes have been twisting up pretty badly over there. I suspect this is just the first of a herd formation."

Chapter 21

Not all the students had finished evacuating the class and Mrs. Deville acted quickly to protect the ones still inside it. Raising her hands, she cast the wildest, rawest, purest nature magic that Anna had ever sensed. The perfectly manicured lawn and the flowers outside of her classroom window experienced a massive growth spurt. Whips of grass sprang up over a dozen feet in length to snap around the stubby rubber legs of the transformed motorcycle that had been parked in the faculty parking lot until a few minutes' prior.

"We'll hold this breach." Marax chimed in chipperly with his proper British accent. He even sounded like royalty. He ran a large hand through his dark hair and winked one of his dark eyes reassuringly at the students as they fled past him to join Anna. The motorcycle monster was gnashing its teeth and struggling to get free from his wife's magical grip.

"Honey. Could you hurry?" She called out sweetly, clearly trying to hide the edge in her voice from the students. "There's only so much one can do with grass and shrubbery against metal and teeth."

"Of course, my love." He blew his wife a kiss suavely and his eyes began to glow red. His long head transformed into that of a bull as if he'd suddenly become a minotaur. Or had the image just superimposed itself over his face. Anna couldn't tell. It happened so quickly and smoothly.

Practice. This is why practice is important. Even in this time of crisis, Anna could imagine exactly what her mother would say. Or maybe it was just what she herself thought about any skill. If you want it to work right when you need it, then practice it when you don't.

"Run child." Marax Deville called over his shoulder as he blasted a good old-fashioned fireball spell at the creature and was immediately accosted by another coming in through the broken windows. "The herd is manifesting." Anna's shock stilled her for a few seconds longer before she shouted at her terrified schoolmates.

"Go. Go. Go." She waved them past her down the hallway back the way she had come. "To the front entrance." Screams and crashes of glass were coming from the other classrooms as other monster-formed vehicles from the parking lot found the un-evacuated classrooms along the route to the front of the school. "Oh. Shit!"

It was murmured quietly as she began running after the others, bringing up the rear. Then she stopped short. The hallway began to fill as more students and teachers streamed into it from the compromised classrooms. But only the classrooms on one side of the hallway. She stopped short at the first one and waved the students out.

"Evacuate to the front office." Anna shouted at the students as she waved them down the hallway preventing them from fleeing in the wrong direction. Peering over the heads of the older students he could see Miss Callahan, a non-magic user heroically trying to fend off the metal and rubber beast that had invaded her classroom.

The petite Asian woman, Anna had never found out which actual nationality she was, was holding a tall metal stool by the seat and brandishing the long legs at the creature sobbing defiant invectives at the monsters in a desperate last stand. The small woman, smaller than Anna herself was, was cornered. If she fled, there would be nothing between herself and the students. If she didn't flee, she'd be overrun. As Anna watched horrified, one of the jocks in back of the crush of bodies caught the look on her face. He followed her helpless fatalistic gaze and noticed their teacher's plight.

"Miss Callahan!" Anna vaguely recognized one of the few lower classmen who were taller than she as he shouted in alarm. *No, you idiot!* While it was brave of the boy to try, Anna had to groan internally at the fact that any actions he took would just divert the attention from the doomed teacher onto the students. And without magic, he wasn't going to make a positive difference.

Or maybe not. The blonde boy picked up a whole desk like it was no heavier than the light stool that the monsters were gradually eating the legs off of to Miss Callahan's absolute despair. Wielding it as both a defensive shield and a weapon, the boy set his shoulders determinedly and called out to the motorcycle monsters.

"Come pick on someone your own size." A shocked short laugh of incredulity burst out of Anna. *Really? Did, did I really just live that trope? He just said that? When he's about to feed himself to monsters?* One of the monsters turned. It was hundreds of pounds. They were all over a hundred pounds. The only thing allowing the students time to flee is that the heavier motorcycle-form monsters weren't strong enough to break through the wall beneath the windows and were too heavy on their new stubby rubber legs to climb over the wall.

But the car-forms were coming.

One of blondie's friends saw him taking a stand and frantically tapped a few others to try and help. Only two chose to stay behind, lifting chairs or desks of their own, and Anna started trying to shove her way into the room against the tide of exiting students. True, it had only been seconds, but it felt like forever.

Finally, the line of students was past her and running in the direction she'd shouted at them. Anna rushed into the nearly vacant classroom except for the four moped and motorcycle-form monsters. Then she stopped. Because…what the hell was her plan? She couldn't just run into the chaos. Fighting with chairs was stupid against large heavy creatures.

And past the empty window frames, across the manicured lawn, the larger vehicles in the parking lot were stirring. Their dead headlights lit up with eerie glows. Wheels lost their roundness, becoming short stubby legs. Grills and windshields turned into gaping maws, some with glass for teeth and some with metal teeth. Death in aluminum and steel lumping toward the school.

"Right." Nodding, Anna knew what she needed to do and pulled her hair back from her face. The loose strands were distracting her. "Time to seal the breach." Maybe she shouldn't have done it the way she did, but this was the first time Anna would ever use her magic in a life-or-death situation. This was fine. She could do this. She just needed to take the time to do it right.

80

Chapter 22

Anna took a bracing stance and squared her shoulders. Then she took a few deep even breaths summoning her magic. Something that had never been hard. It was always there, swirling under the surface of her consciousness, looking for an opportunity to break free of her control. Now was no exception. Her power surged like a wild animal trying to bolt from her body in any haphazard way.

No! She thought at her magic, talking to it in her head as if it were a separate entity. *Not like that. Not all at once. Measured. Directed.* Anna was willing to swear to any being in existence that her magic really did have a mind of its own. It was something she had to coax into cooperating with her sometimes.

The room chilled, the air temperature dropping swiftly. Then the frost came. It didn't creep as it radiated out from her feet across the floor and up the walls. Crystals of ice forming and coalescing into icicles hanging from the chairs and desks. The American flag over the blackboard became too heavy for the mount attaching it to the wall. It cracked from where it was and crackled with the tinkling of ice when it hit the floor.

Everyone trying to fight monsters had noticed when the floor suddenly slicked. Though the monsters had rubber feet, their ungainly forms led them to lose their balances as they slipped on the new surface. One of the boys turned wildly to see what was happening, something he was only able to do because of the opening the change in the battle had given him.

"Anna?" Anna recognized the voice, but she couldn't place it. Her dark brown eyes had closed as she concentrated on reigning in the seemingly endless well of elemental power within her before it could become a raging torrent. The sounds of receding screams and other desperate battles in the adjoining classrooms faded from her hearing.

Time slowed as she lifted her hands to direct the flow of her magic.

When she opened her eyes to aim, they were no longer their normal dark brown, nearly black. Her eyes glowed an icy bluish white. Magic-touched in the use of her element like her white hair showed the world her ice affinity.

"Move." She commanded the group of boys she now recognized as being from the football team. "Help Miss Callahan and get behind me." They scrambled carefully to help the petrified teacher. Only one of the monstrosities she had been fighting was still after her and it was having enough trouble maintaining its footing that she had managed to flee on top of her desk and was throwing staplers, erasers, and other office supplies at it.

Miss Callahan shrieked as the tall blonde boy grabbed her from behind and hauled her away from the creature trying to eat its way through the desk she sat upon. At first, she struggled, thinking she had been attacked by something that had snuck up on her. He spoke to her soothingly as he wrestled her behind Anna and toward the door.

"It's Liam. Miss Callahan. It's Liam Ecclestone. We're leaving. Come on." She'd sagged in relief for a second until he said that they were leaving.

"But there's still a student." The petite math teacher protested. "I can't leave a student." One small hand pointed at Anna.

"Get out of here," Anna shouted at the teacher even as she herself was backing carefully away from the monsters who were getting used to the mechanics of moving on the icy floor. They were scrabbling frantically towards her, and she didn't like how close they were getting. "I don't have enough control to use my magic while you are still in the room. Not for the amount I need to use for this."

Her eyes left the immediate danger to check the progress of the herd. There were much larger creatures coming now. Sports cars and sport utility vehicles were bad enough. Dangerous in and of themselves. But there was a limo-form monster that seemed to have crossed with a centipede or a millipede and become a Lovecraftian horror worthy of the Eldritch classics.

Nope. She was done. Anna was *not* going to fight that. She would yeet herself right the fuck out of there like a coward. It had rows of gnashing teeth in a maw half the length of its body. Those teeth were backed by a thready baleen looking kind of organ which as she watched shredded a smaller slow to waken moped-form monster. It cried piteous honking cries as it was sawed by the vibrating razers of the baleen until it gurgled black oil blood in death.

"Oh, the hell with this." The young elementalist's voice shivered with her emotions. She didn't wait to see if the room had been evacuated like she'd instructed but released her hold on her magic. Just enough. Just enough to let it out and form the far-reaching effect she needed for the construct she was building.

It was simple. Just an ice wall. But it was fast and dirty and stretching not only the length of the windows in the classroom but along that entire side of the building. She was following the flow of her power as it greedily gobbled up territory. As an elementalist, forming the ice wall wasn't a spell like it would be for other magic users. It was just the form of power she had. The school was large and the row of glass windows that provided literally no protection from the approaching monsters stretched…

For the first time Anna was grateful that she had more untapped magic than she had ever wanted or needed. Her magic power was something she had always been angry about. Who could possibly ever need this much ice magic? Ice. Element. Magic.

But she did. Anna needed it now. She needed to have the ability to sense the course of the ice as it traveled over unbroken windows. Her affinity for the ice told Anna when her wall construct needed to create a bridge and cover gaps in broken architecture. It told her when she needed to leave a hole because a student two classes down was being pulled out the window by a retreating monster and his classmates helping him needed a few more moments to pull him back into the room after a spike of ice punch out from the wall to skewer the monster trying to eat him.

Then it was done. The breaches were sealed. For now. But it didn't do anything about the monsters already in the building. There were…a few. Dozens.

"Holy shit, Anna." Someone exclaimed behind her. Turning, Anna realized that it was the blonde boy. He looked familiar. What had he said his name was? Crap. Liam? Anna's eyes narrowed unfriendlily at him.

This was the kid Sara had the hots for? The guy that just got me suspended? While it wasn't technically his fault, Anna couldn't help but be irritated at him for the mere fact that he had unintentionally made her the object of more of Sara's ire. It may have affected the next words that ran through her mind. *Come on girl. Could this guy be any more generic?*

Which… Anna admitted was an unfair evaluation of the boy. He was clearly brave, stupidly so. And he was conscious enough to know her name even if they weren't in the same class. Though, to be entirely honest, there weren't a whole lot of people in the city who didn't know her name. So….

Why was she standing around glaring when she should be running?

Right!

Chapter 23

Not waiting for anyone else in the little group to come to the same conclusion she'd come to, Anna peeled out of the classroom stumbling and sliding into the hall only to be stopped short when the texture of the floor surface changed suddenly in the dark-un-frozen hallway. Though she'd managed to encase many of the smaller monsters in ice, there was still the sound of battle coming from Mrs. Deville's classroom where she knew a car-form had challenged the couple there.

It actually sounded like Mister Deville was having fun despite the noise as he was shouting things like, "Come to daddy." and "Take that you fowl beast." But when he called out, "Babe, watch this and toss me some of the condoms from your purse because this bastard is about to get fuc – "

The words were drowned out by a clearly pained roar or grinding metal-organic gears. It cut short suddenly, which meant it was probably dead, and Anna grimaced at the weirdness of adults as she shook off the sound of Mrs. Deville exclaiming breathlessly to her husband.

"Oh, Marax, that was amazing." She giggled. Giggled. And the white-haired teen turned to the boys and the teacher behind her as she shuddered before gesturing for them to go.

"That ice isn't going to last long against the big thing out there. It's just hiding us from it for now. Go. Go to the main entrance where the busses are coming in." Two of the boys ushered their teacher between them and Liam came up to Anna.

"What about you?" He questioned intently. "What are you doing?" Anna didn't have an exact answer for him, but she had the vague outlines of a plan.

"I'm going to try and help anyone who needs it and make it as difficult as possible for anything that gets in here to follow."

"An excellent plan, Anna." Marax Deville walked up with his wife linked arm in arm. Liam gave a shout of fear when he saw the professor's bull-head. It must have been a transformation because some of his wife's lipstick was smeared across the lips of his bull form to disappear into the fur of his muzzle. The lipstick wouldn't have been visible on an illusion. "Buck up boy," he dusted some frost off Liam's shoulder. "It's just me." Liam leaned back a bit, but he didn't flinch much at the professor's touch.

"Thank you, Mister Deville." As she said the name, Anna watched Liam begin repeatedly mouthing it questioningly at Anna behind Marax's back, pointing at what appeared to be a tall demon in what was clearly an imperial style military uniform. The boy was distracting her from what the teacher was saying.

"Anna, with me. We'll clear this corridor room by room sending any surviving stragglers ahead to evacuate." He cocked his head at Anna quizzically as she alternated nodding at the instructions that the powerful minotaur was giving her and shaking her head at Liam to stop. "Are you paying attention, Anna?"

The minotaur narrowed his eyes at her then glanced over his shoulder to Liam who shrank back as Anna mouthed, *'Shut up!'* at him. Mrs. Deville giggled at the interplay between the trio. Liam sidled over to stand beside Anna, maybe slightly behind her. The minotaur's narrowed eyes followed the boy suspiciously.

"I'm ready, Sir." Anna volunteered to get his attention off of Liam who was not nearly as brave in the presence of a friendly teacher who looked slightly different than normal, as he had been in front of mindless monster machines. "I wanted to seal the hallway with an ice wall after each classroom to cover our retreat."

"Ughm." That caught the teacher off guard as he made a disappointed sound somewhere between a cough and an 'um'. Anna didn't know what his problem was, but she didn't want to keep standing around talking. She could sense the ice wall slowly losing structural integrity from the monsters assaulting it. There were still people shouting in some of the populated rooms.

"I'd like to leave a route open back to this location." The demon minotaur exclaimed in his deep bestial voice with an incongruous British accent. "Eik," He gestured to his wife holding his arm and leaning her head against his shoulder. "She's going to stay here and guard our rear. I will come back to help her after everyone evacuates."

"Riiight." Anna glanced at the absurdly beautiful young teacher, not entirely believing that she really wanted to stay behind. Anna had seen with her own eyes just how powerful the woman was and that she had not been strong enough to face down the monsters on her own. Liam began to speak up, something that would have been stupid anyways and Anna elbowed him to keep his mouth shut. "If that's what you want to do, Mrs. Deville?"

"It is." The teacher smiled brilliantly. "I have means of protecting myself that I can't use around others." She explained in her kind and gentle way, alleviating almost all of Anna's concerns. "I'm the best choice to hold the rear."

"Okay." That was fine. That, actually, made a lot of sense.

"Liam, you be ready to escort any survivors to safety, Mr. Deville instructed. "Anna, you'll be my defensive support. Raise shields in front of me while you stay in position behind me and to my right. I'll enter each room first. Once the entrance is clear to the right, I'll enter and go to the left and you will enter to the right. Hold and clear that corner while providing supporting cover fire with ice spikes and creating ice wall barriers as necessary."

"Yes, Sir." Her heart was pounding. Part of Anna was frightened of what they would find. But part of her, was rejoicing just a little bit that she was going to be using more of her magic.

"Have you done this before, Anna?" Liam hissed a bit loudly as she followed Mr. Marax dutifully.

"Yes."

"Yes?" It came out as a high-pitched yelp.

"I assumed you had gotten at least some basic training from your mother." Marax commented a little self-satisfied that his assessment had been correct.

"Never with monsters this large before. Never without my mom and sister there leading me." It was whispered thoughtfully. Marax just nodded amiably.

"This will be the same. But we may be too late to save everyone."

Chapter 24

Another group of students ran past Anna, helping the injured as they went. They'd cleared eleven classrooms. No dead yet. No dead *people*. At least, none that they saw.

There had been monsters. Dead or dying. Mr. Deville used an obsidian battle axe he'd summoned from somewhere that glistened with dripping liquid flames. Crimson, like blood, the flames splattered as he'd swung his heavy blade with its stout hilt. Each drop of fire elicited howls of pain from any monster it touched.

The blood flames – as Anna had come to think of the flaming substance on Mr. Deville's axe – soaked into the metallic flesh of the monsters to rising wisps of steam. It smoked like it burned them where it touched but merely sputtered out wherever it fell on non-living matter. He'd used it to decapitate the smaller monsters, killing them with swift, efficient, sizzling strokes.

When the transformed teacher had pulled a weapon as black and glisteningly deadly slick as the enormous horns on his bovine head out of nowhere, it had pretty much confirmed to Anna her suspicion that maybe he wasn't entirely on the up and up with his magic. Because it was dark. He'd performed spells on some of the larger monsters that Anna was certain were against the Covenants.

They'd also found blood…in the classrooms.

There was some blood, and Anna couldn't help wondering if the people it belonged to had survived. Was it students? Teachers protecting their students? Or was it the security contractors that got paid truckloads of cash to protect the children of the uber wealthy?

The private security contractors still on campus had been doing their jobs protecting students and ferrying them to safer areas of the building. But many of the students and teachers in this wing had broken and ran when the monsters attacked. And that was okay. They weren't trained for this kind of thing. Running had probably saved a lot of them.

However, it made it a bitch of a time trying to determine if any of them had been dragged away and eaten.

Mr. Deville crept up to the door of the next room with his new protégé attempting to be stealthy behind him. It was getting less awkward, and honestly, less scary with each room. This next class, however, brought Anna's anxiety levels back up to at least eighty percent. Anna could sense her ice had frozen a monster in place partway into the room with its rear suspended outside of the building. It had been an imperfect catch, and the nasty creature was working itself free.

So, at the very least, there was one monster who she and Mr. Deville needed to worry about possibly dealing with. She resolved to bury it in ice as soon as she had a clear shot. But for now, she focused on watching the silent hand signals that the minotaur was giving her after his first peek through the window on the classroom door. Three fingers, then pointing to the left. Two fingers, then he pointed to the right. Monsters or monster bodies is what it meant. Three to the left and two to the fight. A hand flat, palm down, people may be alive.

Anna's eyes widened with questions that Mr. Deville stopped with tilt of his head, some raised eyebrows, and a stern shake of one admonishing finger. *Right!* The teen elementalist nodded agreement. *Later. When they were sure it was safe to talk.*

Then the door had been opened, and the minotaur was hurling fireballs and a spell that made a wounded monster that had corned three people screech with a dizzying resonance. Swallowing, Anna gulped down her fear and followed the teacher into the room before turning to her responsibilities on the right. Anna hadn't been carrying a weapon anywhere on her when the emergency started so she'd created a shield out of ice to cover one arm and protect herself. For killing monsters, the elementalist had manifest a shaft of ice that she could reform into a sword, a spear, or a mace as needed. So far, she hadn't actually needed to use her armaments.

That didn't last long.

There were two barricades in this room. On separate sides of the room. The room was dim and the light filtering through the ice wall was mellow and tinted ever so slightly blue.

This was fine. But the monsters were alive and though they'd been distracted, working their way through a mountain of desks and chairs toward what may or may not have been living people. Okay. She could do this.

Anna stayed far back from the monsters that were easily twice the size of a school desk and many times the weight of one. They were still not moving all that nimbly on their stubby rubber legs. One even seemed to have 'flat tires', and its feet flapped flatly as it hopped like a happy dog expecting treats and pats toward her. Except that Anna was the treat it wanted to eat.

Anna had kept her elemental magic near the surface, and she focused it through the makeshift sword, aiming it at the creature coming toward her. For a second, just a second, she hesitated. The monster had a lolling tongue and what had once been handlebars flopped on either side of its one-eyed head like ears. A floppy eared cyclops motorcycle monster, that flapped on its feet as it happily struggled toward her. Like an oversized excited puppy, or a demented metal and rubber seal.

It was cute. And it liked her.

That was why she hesitated. Frozen with the inability to bring herself to kill someone so sweetly innocent looking, she almost hesitated too long. Then she saw the monster slip in a pool of blood. Saw the blood on its teeth. And she remembered.

It wasn't cute.

It didn't like her.

It just wanted to eat and kill.

So, she shot it. First it was just an ice spike that flowed like a flash of light from the tip of her sword. Then it was a steady stream coating the monster's entire body, weighing it down. It slowed but not quickly enough, getting uncomfortably close before it was completely encased in ice and unmoving.

Anna sighed with relief then shrieked as another monster came from her right. Raising her sword, she was just barely in time for the thing to impale itself on the lightweight weapon. But it was big and heavy.

"Crap, crap, crap, crap, crap." She fed ice magic through the sword and into the monster, scrabbling backward in panic.

Chapter 25

When trying to freeze the monster from the inside didn't work, Anna started to panic. So, she hit it. With her shield. The ice shield. The first few bashes with her shield didn't do much at all, so she focused her power and sharpened the edge of the shield to hack at the back of the monster' neck.

Oily blood splattered her face along with flakes of ice shattering from her shield. Grinning at her success, the teen redoubled her efforts and adjusted the thickness of her sword lodged in it. The blade widened and bit gradually into the metal flesh of the monster's chest even as she hacked its neck apart from above. Then, with a push of the magic that struggled to escape her, she sliced the beast in half from the center outward.

Her blood was rushing her through her fourth or fifth adrenaline high of the day. It was amazing. She'd done that. She'd fought monsters.

"Nice work." Mr. Deville called over his shoulder as he pulled down a barricade to get at the bodies behind it. "How much more of that do you have left?"

"Of what, Sir?" Anna was making her own way toward the barricade on this side of the room checking if the people behind it were alright.

"Stamina." The teacher clarified. "How long can you modulate your magical control." She slowed as she began pushing pieces of desks and chairs out of her way, wading through the mess to reach what she hoped was a living person.

"Oh. Four hours without a break. Ow. Stupid metal shards." She cursed as she stubbed her toe through her shoe.

"Hmmmmm…?" The thoughtful tone from the teacher made her eyebrow rise as she turned to glance at the minotaur over her shoulder. "Good." They worked without speaking then. "Got a body." She called out hesitantly before a groan made her amend her statement. "Oh. This one's alive."

It was one of the security contractors, half buried under the barricade. It looked like when the students had scrambled out that the pile of furniture had fallen on him. He didn't look seriously harmed, but that didn't mean he wasn't.

"I've got two over here." The teacher added. "Do you know any healing magic? Can you get him up and moving?" That made Anna hesitate…because of the caveat.

"Erm…I could…" The girl started as she continued moving furniture. "But then I wouldn't be able to do anything else."

"Right." From the other side of the room, she heard a pause in the moving of metal and the distinct smacking of a large hand into a fury horned head. "Elementalists lose magical efficacy in magics that aren't affiliated with their element." Anna had thought that was the end of it before the teacher continued. "We'll need to work on that. But another time. Not today. You need your full strength today."

His words made her shudder with a dread chill, and Anna was terrified wondering what else the teacher could sense beyond the ice wall that she couldn't with her limited affinity. Another sound drew her attention to the ice wall, and she saw the monster she had trapped there struggling to get free. *Oh yeah. I forgot about that one while I was dealing with the other two.*

With a distracted nonchalance Anna raised one hand and froze the monster in the wall all the way over. Through the new stream of magic, she reconnected with the existing ice construct and extended it around the back of the monster also. She made adjustments to her control and continued uncovering the security guard while strengthening the ice wall construct.

Before long, two security guards had been revived by the minotaur, and he resuscitated the man Anna had uncovered. They continued their room-clearing retreat and Anna sealed the room behind them. That was the last room they found that had been breached and the rest of the classes had been evacuated.

That didn't matter though. The limousine-form-centipede monster was making its way through the outbuildings. Mr. Deville passed Anna off to Dean George before heading back down the dark hallway to his wife. Anna was soon distracted.

"Dean George," the school's head of security spoke like he was reporting to a superior officer in the military. He had that look about him, Anna had noticed, and she wondered if he was from one of those civilian contractor firms that her mom was always bitching about. "The majority of faculty and students have been evacuated to a hospital or to the alternate location. It's just the last two busloads waiting to leave."

That was good to know. Anna was ready to go. She'd had enough of a monster experience for this emergency, and she wanted to sit down and relax for a bit.

"Good." The dean nodded acknowledgement dabbing away some perspiration from her face. "Are we ready to go?" The security chief checked an enchanted gauntlet he had strapped to his arm where a mini message scroll was keeping him apprised of his men's movements.

"Yes." His brow furrowed with concern a moment before his head snapped up. "Ma'am. Primary target is approaching the main building. The busses won't return to evacuate the remaining staff and students before intercept."

"Ah." The dean's shoulders slumped, and she rubbed the bridge of her nose in resignation. "I see. Pull back and create a defensive line for retreat." The dean ordered with a sigh before turning to Anna who had been slumped against a wall giving her legs a rest. "Anna?"

"Yes?" She called out unsure how she could help or what she was going to be asked to do.

"I need you to call your mother." The dean was holding Anna's phone to her and Anna felt the bottom falling out of her stomach as the remaining students and faculty susurrated in sadness.

"Oh." You didn't call Camina Wattkins when you thought the odds were in your favor. She turned the phone back on and dialed. But the call didn't go through. It went to voicemail.

"She's not answering."

"Shoot." Dean George snapped her fingers in recollection. "She was on a plane when I called her earlier. They would have been redirected away from here and she might be too high up to get reception."

"I might be able to call someone else." Anna volunteered hopefully. When the words had left her mouth, she'd been thinking of calling in some of her IOU's, but she quickly remembered that she didn't have phone numbers for any of the joint chiefs' of staff. *Okay. Then Kyle?*

Dialing his number, Anna turned and fidgeted to avoid showing anyone how nervous her face was right then. Voicemail again. Fine. She knew she couldn't get ahold of her dad and his magic would be useless with all the power out anyways. So, there was only one option.

Before she could dial, a group of five men with weapons and wands drawn came running through the front door of the school. The huge limousine monster leapt into view from around a corner and suddenly it was screams and panic again. The monster fell sideways with a lunge, its pincers gnashing.

"Retreat." The head of security shouted. "Retreat to the second floor." A pair of guards lead the way up the double stairway of the main hall, somehow their uniforms looked surprisingly reassuring suddenly. Anna, along with everyone else ran. The guards took up defensive positions on the staircase to cover their charges' retreat.

Panting up the stairs, Anna made her last call.

"Please pick up Sam."

Chapter 26

12:32 PM September 13ᵗʰ, 2026
Heading from the Industrial Park District near the Port of New York to New York Preparatory Academy

“Hang on.” Kyle shouted as he rounded yet another corner on two wheels. Jones felt his body slam against the passenger door as they took the hard left turn then rebounded off it as their armored vehicle lost traction. They slid into a line of vehicles that had been abandoned in the street when the magic collectors had blown.

“Oh, shit.” Jones shouted as one of the vehicles they had sideswiped began lumbering awake in a monster manifestation process. Then he ducked as a traffic light post bent down to try and grab them. Kyle hit the gas to accelerate their vehicle out of the newly manifested monster’s reach. “KIDS!”

Jones pointed to the group of thirteen or so young people, not actually children, but young adults who had shot out into the street fleeing something. They were carrying a collection of various weapons like baseball bats, hatchets – that they had probably liberated from the outdoor store they were exiting – pool sticks, and at least one had a loaded rifle. But some were carrying things like new fishing rods, televisions, and laptops. The vehicle swerved yet again to avoid killing anyone and ended up on the two opposite wheels from before. Several of the ‘kids’ swore at them; one threw a hatchet that bounced off Jones’ bulletproof window.

“You mean looters.” Kyle growled at his passenger before rolling down his window and shouting at the receding gang, “You’re welcome, you ungrateful hooligans.” He rolled the window up and grumbled to himself. “Magic collectors blow out all the shitty electronics and their bright idea is to steal more electronics instead of hiding from the bloody monsters?”

“Real geniuses!” Jones volunteered dryly in an attempt to disguise his absolute terror of just everything in the last few minutes, from the wild ride to the multiple near misses. “They might as well be rolling down their bullet proof windows to shout at idiots throwing hatchets and toting guns.”

“Point taken.” The younger man snorted as he slowed to take another corner and then slammed the breaks on when he saw what the street looked like. There was a herd of vehicle-form monsters. A group of swat vehicles had formed a barricade while heavily armed NYPD officers in body armor were trying to down creatures the size of sport utility vehicles with plain old gunpowder projectile and melee weapons. Yes, they had magic users, but…

“For the love of…” Kyle cut off the oath as he slammed the armored vehicle into park. “They don’t even have adequate cover or a ranged specialist.” Before Jones could inquire about or suggest a plan to go around the herd, Kyle had unbuckled his seat belt and was hopping out of the safety of the vehicle.

“No. No, no, no, no, no. Kyle. You need to get back in the vehicle.” Jones scrambled to retrieve his charge. But the headstrong young man wasn’t hearing any of it. He strode confidently up behind the officers that were cowering behind their luckily un-monsterfied as of yet vehicles taking ineffectual pot shots at an overwhelming force of monster manifestations.

"Hey." He called out, strolling toward danger with a big friendly smile on his face while reaching for the lanyard around his neck. "Hello. Who is in charge here?" It was such a change in Kyle's normal self-effacing demeanor that Jones, for a moment, wondered if the conspiracy theory that had been floating around the other military personnel guarding the museum was true. Maybe Kyle really was – Nah! He was just a really dedicated big brother.

"Get back." Only four of the harried officers risked turning their backs on the approaching throng to see what new hell they had to deal with. "Stay back." A middle-aged man who looked like he was probably in charge. "We've got a massive herd formation heading this way with class ones, class twos, and multiple class three monster manifestations."

"I know." Kyle called back, though he'd stopped when he was told to without provoking anyone into aiming a weapon at him. "I'm a curator from the museum." He jiggled the identification badge that he was holding by the lanyard in the direction of the man who had spoken. Then he gestured to the armored vehicle they had vacated with the National Museum of Unnatural Science and History logo emblazoned brightly on its side.

The officer seemed skeptical until he glanced in the direction that Kyle was gesturing. The familiar emblem brought a surge of relief to him, and his shoulders sagged as the implications sank in.

"Thank, fucking God." He breathed almost reverently. "We've lost communications. Get over here." He gestured for Kyle and Jones to advance before calling out to his men. "Museum curator on site." His holler as met with a chorus of celebrations.

"Fuck yes!"

"Hellyeah."

"Praises to Allah!"

"Woot, woot."

That last one made their leader grimace a bark of laughter and shake his head. Though there was one disgruntled, "About fucking time," grumbled from someone who all their comrades managed to spare the time to turn their attention to for a second of glaring.

"Hi. I'm Kyle Wattkins." Kyle introduced himself. Normally if someone made the connection between his last name and his famous mother it made them think that he was a super dope battle warlock. That stupid assumption that his mother's badassness had been passed onto her son. This time though he was met with dismayed cries.

"The cook?"

"No." Kyle sternly replied. "Not the cook. The warlock of the Archivist, curator for the museum." He released his identification card and resettled his high collard warlocks robe over this suit. It was a kind of classy look, Jones had to admit a bit grudgingly. "Now. Specialist Jones and I need to get through this herd to the New York Preparatory Academy. Is it possible to open this barricade to let us through? And we will draw off the herd as we go?"

Jones didn't have a thing in his mouth, but he was certain he'd just done a spit-take and choked on his own tongue at the same time. The S.W.A.T. officers gave Kyle incredulous looks too.

"You aren't here to clear out this herd?" The guy who had been the S.W.A.T. team's spokesperson questioned dubiously. "We can't open this blockade. We won't be able to control the herd if they get past us, we've got them pinned in for the next several blocks between all the teams. And you can't get through the herd, they are coming from New York Prep."

Kyle climbed up on top of one of the vehicles to see sleek metallic wolves pacing impatiently just beyond the reach of the defenders' weapons. These weren't the clumsy, nearly mindless half-formed manifestations Anna had described to Sam. No. These were fully manifested class three monsters. Fast, deadly, and partially protected by magical properties from the elements they had formed out of.

"I see." One of the more ambitious monsters crouched low as Kyle eyed them critically. It saw one of the food sources it had been watching resentfully from a safe distance and decided to risk an attack. It bunched its hind legs behind it and launched for a huge jump from over thirty feet away. "No." Kyle spoke to himself quietly and he summoned his magic.

Power flowed from his being and out his mouth, twining with his words as he spoke the spell he needed.

"Shield of Aeneas."

Chapter 27

"Kyle!" Jones rushed forward knowing that he was going to be too late to do anything. It felt like he was moving in slow motion. By sheer reflex he unholstered his wand and prepared to fire off the basic fireball spell that he'd been trained to use, because…when in doubt, burn it. But he wasn't going to be in time to protect Kyle.

The monster was moving too fast. And though Kyle was clearly trying to defend himself, his hand was raising so slowly. It was moving mere inches while the metal wolf monster the size of a large sedan was traveling feet. Blood thundered through Jones' ears and the words Kyle spoke felt distorted by time dilation even if they were quiet and soft.

"Nooooooo," followed what felt like an eternity later by, "Shield of Aeneas." Jones recoiled hard as he choked off his spell mid summon. Because he'd been pouring everything he had into in a last-ditch effort to save someone who…clearly didn't need to be saved.

Lines of fire blossomed outward from Kyle's raised hand tracing swiftly out to form an intricate and ornate shield of images. Scenes out of history and myth drew themselves into existence in the wall of magical light sprouting from the warlock's hand. The two babes suckling on a female wolf were Romulus and Remus, the twin brothers who founded Rome. There were several depictions of battles, Rome under siege, ancient peoples and events set against epic landscapes and buildings from times long past.

"Holy shit." Jones breathed out an appreciative sigh. The spell was known. It was famous. But it gobbled magic limiting those who could cast it to those with naturally high reserves of innate magic, or those who could channel and focus high levels of ambient magic. The second wasn't recommended. Taking in and channeling that amount of ambient magic had a tendency to make a human sick.

The monster impacted hard.

It yelped and howled with a sizzling hiss as the fiery shield of solid magic burned the metal shell of the monster straight down to its gooey mutant insides. It landed with a whump, twitching a few times before it struggled to stand and limp away. The shield stayed up for as long as Kyle chose to hold it, burning down the arcanes in the immediate area every second it was active. Even so, the notoriously power-hungry spell was hardly making a dent in the Prometheus purple levels of AMD. But it was having an effect on Kyle. He staggered under the weight of the massive shield.

"Okay." He grunted as he released the spell. "That's enough of that." Turning to the awed swat members he rolled his shoulders. "Right." It was casual, nonchalant even and he sighed sadly before continuing. "There's between sixty to eighty students, faculty, and security guards trapped in the New York Preparatory Academy, with active monster incursions of at least four different levels and no shielding except a fourteen-year-old cryomancer."

He stopped for a breath and before anyone could speak, he held up his hand to forestall questions. A gust of wind blew his hair dramatically and a ray of bright sunlight shone off his blonde highlights. Was that just super coincidental or had Kyle actually made the effort to make that happen, Jones wondered. Taking another breath, the young warlock continued.

"That is just confirmed in the school. I'm not even taking into account the hundreds of people trapped in the buildings surrounding the herd that has formed there. People who aren't getting any assistance because the buildings they are in are being used to contain the monster herd manifestation. I need to get there and get those people out. Preferably without any casualties."

"I'm sorry, son." The head S.W.A.T. officer interrupted apologetically. "But we can't do that. None of my men are trained for this kind of combat. We don't have the magic for it." Kyle's expression turned thunderous.

"You don't have the magic for it." His tone was furious as he hissed vitriolically back at the speaker. "There is more than enough magic to go around if you are willing to *use* it." But he visibly restrained himself and tempered his tone. "I'm not asking you to help me. Just let me through and keep quiet about it later."

"If you die, we'll need to explain to somebody what happened to you." Another S.W.A.T. officer added unhelpfully. Jones rolled his eyes at that.

"I'm not going to die."

"Right." Someone scoffed and it wasn't the same asshole who had previously protested.

"I'm not going to die." Kyle assured the police. "And I'm not asking you to come with me. I'm a warlock from the museum. I know what I'm doing." Jones had to admit that just hearing those words, *'from the museum'*, did make nerdy dorky unthreatening Kyle seem like maybe he knew what he was doing, that was how strong the belief and faith in the magical knowledge curated by the museum was to citizens.

"Annnd…" the young warlock hesitated nervously as he spoke, "I'm about to do something that is only possible because of the extremely high levels of arcanes around us right now. Any other time, I'm just an average warlock. Right now?" He shrugged self-deprecatingly and gave a quick nervous grin.

Specialist Jones felt a sinking feeling in his stomach. Yeah, there had been that rumor about Kyle's 'real' job running around the military personnel who were assigned as guards at the museum. But Jones hadn't put any credence in it. It was just a rumor…

And sure, Jones had been pretty sure that he was going to be in deep shit for the shenanigans that Kyle and Sam had gotten up to earlier. However, it was just shenanigans. Poking dragon corpses that were only safe to be around because of portable magic collectors was dangerous. Driving across town during a high magic event before monster formation started, dangerous but doable. That was quantifiable deep shit. He was aware of exactly how much trouble he would be in for that.

Letting Kyle drive through herds of actively evolving monsters with the intention of fighting said monsters? Not great for Jones' career. What Kyle was saying now?

He was going to die. The Last Line was going to hunt down one Specialist Jones if he managed to survive this. Because, he hadn't even dreamed of stopping Kyle when they found out that little Anna was trapped in her school under active monster attack.

Chapter 28

Jones clambered up onto the vehicle next to Kyle. He'd intended to try and help save Anna from the start. But the reminder that he could draw on the ambient magic to perform feats of sorcery far beyond his normal capacity had calmed his galloping heart. It was weird that it hadn't occurred to him before Kyle had mentioned it.

Kyle turned to face the milling herd. Some were keenly watching them, looking for an opportunity to attack. Others were actively gnawing their way through the walls of buildings or widening holes where glass doors had once been. The normally goofy warlock who sang along with the jingles he used as cell phone ring tones, had narrowed his hazel eyes. The light of laughter was gone from them, replaced with keen seriousness.

"You should stay here, Jones." Kyle was quiet enough that only Jones could hear him.

"I'm going to help you." The Specialist insisted. He wasn't full of bravado, just determined to do the right thing, protect the American people like he was paid to.

"Anna is my priority. If it comes down to it, I will sacrifice every single other person in that hellscape to get my baby sister out." He turned his intense gaze to Jones who met it stoically. "Are you good with that?" Jones shrugged before replying flippantly.

"It's what your mother would want." His reply brought an ironic laugh from Kyle who smiled ruefully at the soldier.

"Oh, you clearly don't know my mother very well." As Kyle spoke, he began shrugging off his warlock's robe dropping it to the hood of the car. Next, he took off the suit jacket that matched his slacks revealing the fitted holster for his magical tome that he wore over his dress shirt.

"No?" Jones was doubtful as he kept one eye on the monsters. They were getting riled up way down the street. There was something *big* moving around there. But like every other street in the city at that moment, there were abandoned vehicles lining both directions interspersed with dozens of vehicles and other things that had already transformed. Hell, there was even a little manhole cover monster sliding around on its back. Like a moving mouth facing upwards. It was sliding underneath other monsters as they walked and biting off feet as they came down.

"She's not here, is she?" Kyle was fussing with his tie and lanyard, debating whether to take the lanyard off or not. It was clear that he'd made the decision not to when he dropped it and focused on taking off the tie.

"She might not know?" Jones offered. but knew it was a bad excuse even as he'd said it. Her flight should have landed by now. She would know something was seriously wrong in her city.

"Or she's been ordered somewhere else." Dropping his tie with the rest of his extraneous clothing, Kyle changed his focus to taking off his holster, his fingers moving with practiced ease. "Either way, it's not a great look for a parent." Jones acknowledged Kyle was right with a tilt of his head and a raise of his eyebrows as everything that the Wattkins boy had discarded levitated and began floating itself back to the armored vehicle behind the barricade. "Need anything from the vehicle?"

"The biggest most effective weapons stored in there?" Kyle smirked at that response and nodded as he turned his back to monsters as he focused on what he was doing.

"Watch my back a minute." Jones obliged and turned his full attention to the city street. Devoid of people. Bright and sunny with shadows between the buildings, most of which towered over them. He focused on watching the monsters, shooting off a few fireballs that glinted off the windows when he felt a nudge on his shoulder. It was a large riffle, semiautomatic, magically hardened, that shot enchanted alchemy charges with a mount for a bayonet on the muzzle. Standard Magicorps issue. It was one of the weapons that were stocked for the museum guards.

"Nice." Then he saw a cross-shoulder double-bandolier of alchemy shots, and a bayonet to attach to the gun. "Feels like home." He smiled ruefully at his charge.

"Be careful with the sword," Kyle cautioned, "It's a lot more magically conductive than standard military issue. Have you trained with the museum standard enchantments?" Jones nodded as he geared up with the new weapons in addition to his sidearm and his wand.

"I've been familiarized with it." Jones assured Kyle. "You want me to take point?" He offered, because he didn't think the nerdy young man had ever done something like this."

"No. Stay behind me." With nothing other than a wand in one hand and a plain leather notebook in the other hand, he hopped off the vehicle he was standing on top of into the danger zone.

Immediately, all the monsters who were focused on trying to get past the underprepared police holding down the street at the barricade zeroed in on Kyle. They hesitated, confused as to why food was coming to them. The soft squishy thing didn't seem dangerous. Did it not know it was in danger? Had it not realized there were monsters about? So, they waited and watched.

And gave Kyle the time he needed to prepare.

Kyle paused for a second after he'd hit the ground. Squaring his shoulders, he took a deep steadying breath. Could he do this? Maybe. Technically. Was he ready for this? Unlikely.

Despite the danger, he closed his eyes for a second and took a second breath. It was fine. He could feel the arcanes in the atmosphere. As a warlock of the Archivist, Kyle had access to the vastest collection of documented spells and magical enchantments in existence. Anything that had been scanned by the archive, his pact item could teach him how to recreate it. And he had a lot of powers granted to him from the Archivist, were primarily used for the preservation or dissemination of knowledge. Something that was exceedingly useful for someone who was also a wizard.

True, Kyle Wattkins was an average warlock.

He wasn't super powerful; he wasn't particularly talented. But he was also a wizard with small amounts of natural magic. He was a wizard, and wizards didn't have large reserves of internal magic, so they specialized in using the magic from the environment around them. He was a wizard with access to the greatest library of spells to ever exist, a natural proclivity towards electricity he inherited from his father, and the ability to channel magic from the environment.

Opening his eyes again, Kyle began drawing on the seemingly limitless ambient magic. With nothing more than a wand and a book, he began walking into the fray.

Chapter 29

Up. Up high above the city Kyle could feel the static electricity of nature in the atmosphere. There wasn't enough infrastructure functioning in the city for him to draw from the grid. Normally he wouldn't have even bothered trying to do this. But with so much magic saturating the city, he could.

He reached to the sky with his wand and gathered the awesome power of nature stored there. He was burning arcanes like mad, channeling magic through himself at higher levels than he'd ever done before. It was terrifying, and exhilarating. Honestly, a once in a lifetime opportunity for a wizard really. After all, when else would he have unlimited access to raw magic without having to become one of those crazy loons roughing it out in high magic zones of the wild for the sake of magic.

He far preferred the comforts of a city. Plumbing, cell phone reception, the internet…doughnuts. Kyle was exceptionally fond of roads and vehicles. Sure, he walked or took public transportation most of the time, but he loved the convenience of being able to hop in a vehicle and go when he needed to. Buildings and roads were pretty important to Kyle, too.

The buildings and roads were crawling with monsters. Distant screams, intermittent crashes and wailing of sirens were interspersed with the howls and growls of newly manifested monsters. The very infrastructure of modern society that Kyle cherished and had forsaken his wizard training and became a warlock instead for, were turning on the city he loved. It wasn't just vehicles that were turning.

Yet the power in the air, it called to Kyle in the way that magic called to all those with the proclivity toward wizardry. A craving that he dared not feed. The heavy taste of the arcanes in the air was sweet and savory on his tongue. He licked his lip then bit it in pleasure as he drank in all the power he could ever want. Arcanes flooded Kyle's body, coursing through his veins and making him feel like he'd grown a hundred times larger without changing at all.

He was going to regret this later.

But he watched the monsters noticing him. The bright fall sunlight was glinting off so many metallic hides making random wild blinding reflections of light playing across the shadowed areas on the street and up the sides of buildings. More magic than most wizards ever saw in their lifetimes.

Kyle grinned. Fixing his targets in his mind.

Though no one could see it, his eyes were glowing. Static electricity arced in little crackles over his body. The scent of ozone wafted from him as flashes of miniature lightning bolts played between the rising hairs of his head.

"Jones?" Kyle felt the weird metallic taste on his tongue that he always found when he tried to speak while casting this type of magic. It mingled deliciously with the flavor of the arcanes. "Stay at least thirty feet back from me so you don't get hit by a bolt grounding on you."

"Yes, Sir!" The specialist called to Kyle's back. Then Kyle started walking forward. Maybe the class three metallic wolf-form monsters sensed the growing danger that Kyle represented because they hesitated to attack, instead growling menacing as they backed away. The class one and two incomplete manifestations of the vehicle form monsters only saw him as a source of delectable edible magic. Emboldened by the retreat of the class threes, the class ones and twos began lumping and huffling their way towards him.

His steps were slow at first, but Kyle grew more confident with every arcane he absorbed. His pace gradually increased until he was walking briskly through the chaos while less evolved forms of monster hurried toward him. Before those beasts could get within attack range, Kyle acted.

"Lightning bolt!" Though his words were spoken at normal volume, they seemed louder, echoing with the dangerous levels of arcanes reverberating in his being. A bolt of lightning split the heavens, momentarily striking down to ground on Kyle with a crash of thunder. He held the thousands of joules on his wand for a split second, before discharging the electricity in dozens of arcs simultaneously onto the monstrous targets he'd chosen.

The creatures were killed in their tracks or maimed enough that their forward movement was halted. The sound of electricity crackled and hissed as the unfortunate creatures were cooked inside their metal hides. It was quiet for a second, then Kyle, wand still raised to the heavens spoke again.

"Lightning bolt." Again, a flash of electricity cracked down from the heavens to race through Kyle's wand then out to the milling monster herd. A thunderclap deafened him then rolled off into the distance as sound does. More monsters fell, screaming and roaring their defiance, some just going silent when the electricity he'd pumped through them had dissipated. Others didn't fall. They just started charging if they hadn't already been converging on this new source of sustenance.

Jones stayed well behind what Kyle had deemed the safe radius. The soldier was glad he had because Kyle was arcing bolts of lightning and conducting electricity for dozens or even as many as a hundred feet away. The bolts of plasma heated air were directed forward and to the sides and never backwards toward the anxious specialist. That didn't make him feel any safer about it.

Absolute shock had frozen Jones after the first volley of lightning that the nerdy-history-buff-museum-employee, Kyle, had held in his hand, and then used to drop over a dozen monsters ranging in size from two-door hatchbacks to extended cab pickup trucks. It wasn't until the second spell had triggered most of the monsters in the next two blocks to charge, that he pulled himself from his temporary stupor. There wasn't time to be surprised after that. The monsters were coming, and Jones and Kyle had a three-block gauntlet to run of class one, class two, and class three manifestations with no backup coming.

Chapter 30

Jones steadied his heart with slow even breaths. He could do this. He'd done this before. Okay. Not *this*, but similar. There were places where he'd been deployed where the monsters ran in packs and overran smaller villages. Or demons had escaped and in an orgy of freedom made things unpleasant for the locals.

Heck, even plain old magical creatures could be a problem if they were big, hungry, or ornery enough.

And that's what the Magicorps trained for. Days like this when magic wasn't a helpful aid to civilization bestowing boons of knowledge and safety, and instead, was a bitch. That's right. Magic was being a sonofabitch today and someone had to kick some monsters in the mother effing teeth. It might as well be the Magicorps. Couldn't leave it up to the civies, or worse yet, the jar heads.

Yeah!

This? This was just a regular old day at the office for Jones. Not like the lazy lying around the museum shit he'd been tasked with since his transfer to New York. Jones performed another quick scan of the battlefield – this was definitely a battlefield, or it would be soon at least – and chose what he thought was the most immediate target.

Kyle seemed to have a radius on his lightning bolts of not more than about a hundred feet. And he was only aiming forward of his line of sight. Jones focused on the monsters who were parallel with them or slightly behind Kyle, the ones who had been missed in the first salvos. There were three currently under fire from the swat officers behind them, but their plain chemical projectiles weren't packing enough punch to do the kind of damage necessary to put them down.

Jones lined up the sight of his semi-automatic rifle with the first monster he'd targeted. A smooth squeeze of the trigger made the familiar crack of a chemical projectile weapon. The monster practically ignored the impact thinking at first it was one of the police's ineffectual bullets. Until it noticed the round had not only penetrated its body, but that the alchemical components within the round were reacting.

Alchemical rounds could do a lot of things. It was alchemy after all, and alchemy was a broad and diverse school of magic. Alchemy was used just as frequently to create, heal, or modify, as it was just for destruction. The ammunition that Jones was using had been mixed to do some awful things. Or maybe it was meant for *fighting* awful things because the wound in the huge metallic class three wolf monster began smoking.

Then it began flaming, jets of white-hot fire spitting out of the hole in the thing's chest. Probably some kind of magnesium concoction with that coloring. Which some might try to argue was just a chemical reaction until they saw what happened next. The monster began whining. Shaking, and pawing at itself in an attempt to remove the burning mass of alchemical reaction that was not so slowly consuming it from within.

When it began howling and running blindly, Jones turned his attention to the next target. He still caught the monster rebounding off when it hit the wall of a building and chuckled at its misfortune. The lay twitching until it popped with small explosion that sent the organic metal guts flying a short distance from the creature.

He kept up firing short burst of rounds into one monster after another, carefully sighting on the creatures and secure in the knowledge that the alchemical rounds would only react with the mutated flesh of the monsters and not with anything else if he missed. While that was a safety measure enchanted into all alchemical ammunition, it didn't change the fact that he was firing bullets in a city. If he missed, the speed of the weapon firing might just send a bullet through a wall and injure an innocent person if he wasn't careful. Bayonets, like the enchanted one on this rifle, were distracting to people who weren't familiar with them. That was probably why Kyle hadn't taken one of the weapons himself. Jones had been watching the young warlock surreptitiously, partly situational awareness, and partly just because he was so damned curious about what the kid would break out next.

But the lead creatures in the charging horde were getting too close for Kyle to continue fighting the way he had with mass area lightning bolt dispersions. When he saw Kyle calling down another bolt of lightning that was going to be far too late to do any good, Jones was afraid he might have to intervene. A class two manifestation that looked like it used to be a *really* expensive sports car was rushing forward on stumpy rubber and steel legs. It was nearly upon Kyle and nearly crushed him as he waited for another bolt of lightning to fall from the sky.

It was going to be too late. Even if lightning did travel at the astounding speed of two hundred seventy thousand miles per hour, the spell was not going to strike fast enough to save the warlock of the Archivist from being crushed from several thousand pounds of mutated metal flesh and exoskeleton. Incongruously, Kyle charged the oncoming beast, launching himself – wand, open book on palm and all – up onto the monster. Jumping and running up the hood-head to leap from its highest point over the open convertible top to catch the bolt he was summoning. It coalesced into a long shaft of buzzing light shaped somewhere between a spear and a sword.

The bolt grounded in the pulsating cream leather interior of the monster with a dramatic shower of sparks erupting around the pair. Like a pole vaulter hanging in midair from the top of a rod of lightning Kyle bore his weight down the shaft extending from his wand, piercing deep into the back of the beast. His pillar of electricity shrank as it discharged until he was left with something the size of a billy club or a nightstick.

Kyle awkwardly clambered out of the interior of the transformed vehicle, one hand holding a hot current lengthening the reach of his wand by about two feet. The depleted energy weapon glowed a dull red, fluctuating slowly. For his part, Kyle's face wore a look of complete disgust as the formerly sumptuous leather interior of the luxury vehicle was now gooey with some kind of slimy biological fluid. It coated his legs with slime that made his trousers stick to his calves and shins.

"Ohhhh…. Gross. Shi –" Another several thousand pound monster nearly collided with the warlock as he dodged backwards with a yelp. "Oh, no you don't." His makeshift cutlass swung and began hacking parts off the vehicle-form. The blade grew brighter, stronger, larger, and more refined with each swing he took. Its color gradually going up the light spectrum as Kyle fed it more of the ambient magic from around him. From the dull red of hot metal, the sword of captured lightning changed to orange, then yellow, and green, all in the neon brightness of a storm's captive might.

Sword and warlock became a swirling mass of stop-motion light trails and phantom images. He ran from one encounter to another hacking, cutting, and mutilating monsters to incapacitation. A gathering Roy-G-Biv of destructive force blazing brighter and brighter into the upper echelons of visible light, bright enough to make even the sunny day seem dim.

Chapter 31

11:30 AM September 13ᵗʰ, 2026
35,000ft Altitude between New York City and Washington DC

Poor Jim was nervous. He was handling it well, but now more of the flight's passengers were asking questions about why they were so long overdue. Some of them were getting angry. It was keeping the already stressed-out flight attendants, who didn't seem to know what was going on themselves, very busy.

For her part, Camina was fairly certain she knew what was going on. Not exactly, no. She wasn't clairvoyant. But she could put her observations together and make some educated guesses. Observation one, the ambient magic density had spiked significantly. Observation two, the plane had turned around and flown away from New York. Observation three; none of the passengers, and possibly none of the staff not in the cockpit had been informed of these changes.

Of course, Camina couldn't be positive she was making the correct deduction, but she was fairly certain that there had been some kind of major magical incident in the vicinity of New York. It hadn't been cataclysmic. At least, the levels of magic she sensed didn't feel cataclysmic. It was definitely bad though. Very bad.

Part of her, the maternal part, wanted to scream at the flight attendants and demand some answers, much like the other passengers were doing. Another part of Camina was patient. It sat and waited, legs primly crossed, partly because it knew that staying in tight control over her emotions and biding her time would bring her answers faster than throwing her weight around.

The other reason was that she was a prominent magic wielder, and her actions had very far-reaching consequences.

"Listen here, young Miss." An angry blonde with twang was shaking an admonishing finger as she harangued the flight attendant. "We've been on this here flight for hours longer than it was 'sposed to last. I think we all deserve some answers. Now aren't we going to New York or ain't we?" She'd switched to gesturing around the cabin and trying to get support from her fellow passengers.

"Ma'am." The exasperated female flight attendant tried to reinstate order one more time. "I've already told you. We are being redirected to another airport. But because of the magic arrow swarm intersection happening today we won't know if we have a path to land anywhere for a few hours." Well, that sounded like a lie if Camina had ever heard one. The magic arrow swarms weren't set to intersect for another two or three hours. And they were coming from nowhere near D.C.

"I've been watching the news on my tablet thingy that the grandkids got me for Christmas last year." An elderly gentleman chimed up from a few rows behind the obnoxious twanger. "And the news is saying there's been some kind of catastrophe with New York." He smacked his lips against his gums in irritation. "Nobody can communicate with them except by message spell. Was there some kind of blackout of something? They lose their electricity?"

"Sir. As I've said before…" Before she could finish her thought, the man that Camina had bet Jim was the U. S. Marshal on the flight stood up and indicated the woman should stop talking. He had been closely monitoring a low-magic communications scroll strapped to one wrist. When he'd stood to deal with the unruly passenger he'd pulled his sleeve down over it.

"You owe me five bucks." Camina chuckled quietly to Jim who groaned as he pulled out his wallet to pay up.

"You're lucky I even have five bucks. Any other day and I'd have to use an app to send it to you electronically." Giggling with glee, Camina settled in to watch the unfolding diversion.

"United States Marshal, Ma'am. The flight crew will keep you apprised of any information you need to know. Could you please sit d –" Before he could even fully intervene, the passenger address system came on.

"This is your captain speaking." The words crackled with the weird not-so-great echoey quality that all passenger address systems seemed to have no matter how luxurious the interior of the plane. "Would the passenger in seat forty-four A please come to the flight deck. I repeat the passenger in seat forty-four A please come to the flight deck."

For a second, just a second, Camina glanced eagerly around to see who it was that would respond to the captain's call. Who else besides herself could possibly be important enough for the captain to call upon. Then her shoulders slumped, and she glanced furtively at the seat number above her head…and sighed dejectedly.

"Forgot what your seat number was for a second there didn't you?" Jim quipped quietly beside her.

"Oh, shut it Thafesh." It was a habit really, to call a comrade by their last name. It made her just a little bit amused. "Don't let them toss my coffee while I'm gone." She whispered urgently and stood as nonchalantly as she possibly could. Most of the other passengers were still looking for the row and seat the captain had called out, but their searching gazes zeroed in on Camina like homing missiles despite her attempts to look completely casual.

Sure, the tall, gorgeous brunet with her tropical tan and dark eyes could have just been getting up to use the restroom. But did anyone really think the exotic, muscular beauty that looked like a supermodel had become a professional athlete, and walked like she was marching was just coincidentally getting up right after the pilot called someone to the cockpit. Naw. From his own seat, Jim snorted in amusement. It was funny.

Murmurs started up around the cabin. People turned around in their seats to watch her approach and slowly walk past. There were whispers talking about how familiar she looked. Damn right she should look familiar. One person who made the comment was literally holding a magazine with her picture on the cover and Jim had to stick a finger in his mouth and bite it not to laugh out loud. He had no idea how she was keeping her composure and not rolling on the floor in hysterical laughter. Like, he could just see that the effort of not rolling her eyes at that one, was giving her eye strain.

Finally, she reached the flight deck door and pushed the button for admittance. There was a brief quiet exchange over the intercom, and she disappeared into the interior. The quiet murmurs became an almost instant buzz of gossip.

"Oh, my good Lord." Someone exclaimed. "Was that Camina Wattkins? The Harbinger is on *our* flight? How much trouble are we in?"

112

Chapter 32

"Holy crap." The copilot and pilot had both turned to look at their guest when she entered the cockpit and apparently the copilot hadn't believed he was genuinely about to see who he thought he was about to see. "It really is you." Now, he was jerked back in his seat as far from Camina as he'd been able to move.

"Come on, Earl." The pilot scolded. "Try to pretend you're a professional when there are people around to see." Though his words were weary sounded, there was a twinkle of mirth in the older man's eyes. His salt and pepper hair was cut high and tight, and his profile could have been a generic former military white dude with a chiseled jaw.

"Sorry." Earl coughed apologetically and settled himself down into his seat properly and he glanced between the pilot and Camina. "It's just that, it's her. I mean. It's *you*. And you're *her*." Familiar with this phenomenon, Camina merely smiled politely while retaining her grip on her patience.

"It's alright." She assured him and turned her focus to the person who was actually focused on his job. "I assume you both had a reason for calling me up here?"

"Yes." The pilot responded and keyed up the radio. "There's a call for you."

"I see." She wasn't surprised. Honestly, Camina had been expecting something like this. The military officer on the other end of the transmission gave their credentials and confirmed hers. Then she listened as she was briefed and received her orders. Her stomach sank with every word spoken.

"Communication has been limited. But reports say that it's Prometheus Purple in Manhattan."

She'd known. Not precisely, but Camina had known something was very wrong in the city. The city where her children and husband were at this very moment. Had Lance ever gotten Anna? Or was she separated from family in the middle of what was happening there? Kyle would be fine; the museum was practically a magic proof bunker when all was said and done. Sam was…Sam. And her husband wasn't great at emergencies.

No.

Lance surely would have gotten Anna as soon as he was done with whatever patient he'd been dealing with at the time. Surely. Of course, Camina didn't expect Lance, an untrained civilian, to risk his life though…for their daughter…

"What do we…" Her voice was tight, strained. Tears weren't in her eyes yet, but they were stinging. She stomped hard on that train of thought before it could take her mind places that she couldn't afford to let it go right now. Taking a brief moment, Camina cleared her throat and lifted her gaze to the ceiling of the cockpit. Then biting her lip, she steeled herself and asked the question again with a shake of her head at herself. "What do we know about the monster manifestations?"

"Hundreds. And those are just the class three and lower ones. There's at least one class four that we know of because it can be seen across the bay." Camina froze.

"In the city?" It came out in a breathy whisper.

"On Manhattan Island." Apparently, her whisper had been loud enough for him to hear and respond. Or maybe she hadn't been as quiet as she thought.

"What are my orders?" It wasn't resignation, per se. But both the pilot and copilot glanced up at the woman as her voice changed yet again. While she wanted to go and help her children and her husband, she knew that there were others who needed her help, others who were less gifted, less capable. But she wasn't the person that got sent in to rescue people. She was the person who got sent in to deal with dangers the rescuers couldn't. Camina knew she wasn't a precision tool.

"The class four monster manifested at the airport on the North end of the island." Gasps came from both pilots at the news. For her part, Camina focused on the sleek black plastic of the instrument panel, her eyes roving over familiar gauges that she knew enough about to not accidentally crash. "It's just a standard jump into a high magic monster hot zone. Disable or contain the monster. *Do not* let it leave Manhattan."

"Understood." Her face was bleak. All those people. There would be thousands of deaths, if not from the monster, then possibly from collateral damage. "Will I have a team? Or any…" She stopped and swallowed the hard lump of dread. "Is anyone documenting what's happening?"

"No, you'll be jumping from the plane you're on now. It's just you for now." She nodded stiffly before realizing that he couldn't see her. "The pilots already have their orders. You'll be descending to twenty-five thousand feet for your drop. I've been told that's enough time for you to suit up?"

"Yes, Sir."

"I'm sorry." He offered, only halfheartedly. Because he wasn't really sorry to be ordering her to save lives. Yet he knew what she was risking, how difficult this was emotionally, and how bad things were going to be for her in the future without an embedded journalist to document what she was doing to combat the vitriol of the conspiracy anti-magic nuts. "There just aren't any other military personnel on the flight with you. The closest thing there is to an embedded journalist is the journalism student, but he –"

"He'll go." Camina gasped quickly. "He'll absolutely be willing to deploy with me." Hurrying to add before she could be cut off. "He's been sitting next to me the whole flight and I've been looking over his work. Good solid stuff. I was going to recommend scouting him. If he's all I have to choose from, I'll take back up with a Level Four magic license."

"Fine." The officer acknowledged. "We vetted him before calling the plane just in case." She pumped her fist and did a happy little dance in the cockpit without letting any sound escape her lips.

"Yes, Sir. Thank you, Sir." She was giddy with excitement now when she'd been morose only moments before.

"Right." He already sounded like he regretted it.

Chapter 33

Camina exited the cockpit not in the best of spirits, but at least relieved that she might get one thing going her way today. Sure, she was about to rain fire down on civilian airport and that was going to suck in ways she couldn't allow herself to think about right now. But the young man she thought she was going to have to nursemaid through endless bureaucratic hoops to get on her team was getting the catastrophic event short cut. So…bonus.

"Mister Thafesh," She called out loud enough for her seat mate to hear her voice. He half stood with an anxious look on his face and the rest of the first-class passengers glanced back and forth between the two with confusion and concern.

"Ma'am, what are…" a flight attendant tried to interrupt but the copilot opening the cockpit door behind Camina shook his head for the flight attendant to let it be.

"Yes, Camina? Uh, Ma'am?" Jim ran his hand through his hair and glanced at all the people focusing on the two of them. It made Camina chuckle. He might as well get used to the attention now.

"Have you ever performed a HALO jump into a Prometheus Category Purple zone with active monster formation?" The young man's eyes nearly bulged out of his skull as he drew a sharp intake of breath. Around the cabin, passengers gasped and murmured.

"Uh. No, Ma'am." He admitted shakily, "I can't say that I have."

"Well, you're about to." Camina gave just a second for him to process that information before she continued, nodding in his direction. "Gear up. I got called in to work on my time off again and you've been approved as a replacement for my regular embedded team."

"Seriously?" The young journalism student gaped then grinned. Then he hurried into the isle. "Thank you. Thank you." He was already pulling his carry-on bag out of the overhead compartment, glancing back at Camina ever few seconds as he pulled out more camera equipment. "Thank you, for this opportunity. You won't regret it." Behind Camina, the copilot was murmuring for the flight crew to go through the plane and start another trash run and make sure that everyone put any lose belongings in the overhead compartments.

"Wait a minute!" The woman with the twangy voice stood self-righteously, arms crossed. "You're going to do a HALO jump? I know that that is. It's a high altitude jump with a low opening of a parachute. Just where are you going to do that from? Passenger planes don't carry parachutes. They travel too high and too fast for it. And the doors can't open once they are in the air because of air pressure." Camina actually laughed at that.

"Oh. You're not wrong. But you are so *very* wrong." The copilot gave Camina a put-upon sigh and shook his head as he fished in a storage compartment for a harness and line to secure himself with. "You might want to secure any belongings you have out."

"Ladies and gentlemen, this is your captain speaking." The captain did not have the confident tone he'd had at the beginning of the flight. Instead, he sounded weary and not entirely pleased. "As you are probably aware by now, there has been some kind of magical event in New York City which is why we didn't land there. Our intention was to return to D.C. when reports of class three and class four monster manifestations necessitated our intervention."

"The woman standing at the front of the cabin with my copilot is Camina Wattkins. She was returning home from Washington. We find ourselves in the predicament of having on board with us the one person who actually needs to be in New York right at this moment. So, we have been ordered to let her off to go deal with this emergency. What we will be doing is not normal, but if you follow all of our instructions, it will not be unduly dangerous."

Camina let the pilot drone on about descending below cruising altitude and using oxygen masks while she strolled back to her seat to stow her purse and carry on in the overhead bin. Her adrenaline was already starting to ramp up and it felt good, relaxing muscles that stiffened during the hours on the flight. Her face carried a slight smile, and she hummed a bit. It had been a while since she'd had a really good workout. The hum faltered and her smile faded to bleakness when thoughts of her kids intruded into her pre-fight mental preparations.

"You can't make us let you open the plane of the door for her." Twangy was back at it and this time, other passengers were on her side. It was starting to look like it might get ugly. But Camina plastered her biggest I'm-probably-on-camera smile and turned to face the rest of the cabin and the shrill woman from a place that Camina was seriously going to look into the feasibility of removing it from existence for producing that particular accent.

"Yes, I can." This was one of the parts of her job she hated. "I have orders to deal with a class four monster manifestation at Manhattan North International Airport. It poses a danger to dozens of cities, not just New York or Manhattan Island. I will be leaving this plane. I do not require a parachute. I will fulfill my orders as they are entirely ethical, and I will not be endangering any civilian on this plane if I leave." Pausing, Camina cocked her head and threw a little attitude while she gestured around the cabin. "Now, I can wait for you all to stow any personal belongings, so they don't fly away when the door opens, *and* wait for you to have oxygen masks. Or I can follow my orders without making considerations for the civilians onboard this plane. What do *you* prefer?" She stared down at the obnoxious blonde, taller than the woman by several inches.

"But...but..." It seemed as if the twanger didn't have anything to argue against that with until a nursing baby started snuffling and crying. Then she sniffed triumphantly and spat out as if it was the greatest argument of all. "But there's children on board." Yet Camina was prepared for it.

"There're children in Manhattan, and Newark, and Brooklyn, the Bronx, Staten Island, and Hoboken. Do I put the comfort, not safety, just comfort, of the less than three hundred people on this plane before the immediate safety of millions? And remember, every second I remain on this plane, is another second that people are dying in New York." As she'd feared, she was being recorded by more than one person's cell phone, but also by her new journalist and she tried not to give him an annoyed twitch of her lips at that. He was just doing the job she gave him.

"It's still not right." The woman grumbled and Camina was going to leave it at that.

116

She scanned her eyes across the passenger compartment. They were scared. Scared and angry. Worried for themselves and for anyone they might know in New York. Then her gaze passed a man in, maybe, his fifties or so with a U.S.M.C. ballcap on. He looked like he was sleeping with his eyes closed and his head lowered, and it took a second for her brain to catch up with the fact that no one would be sleeping right now. Camina's eyes jerked back to the man and looked him over more carefully. *Oh, no! Sonofabitch.* Quickly taking a few steps, Camina drew level with his row. She wanted to confirm her suspicions before... He had one.

A protective prayer charm for the patron saint of warriors.

It was on a chain around his wrist, and he was rubbing the worn surface compulsively as he murmured something under his breath. The image was barely recognizable as an angel with wings spread holding a large naked blade.

The Archangel Michael.

Chapter 34

"Haaahh-ah-ah-le-lu-jaaaaaaah!" A familiar heavenly chorus sounded behind Camina. It was accompanied by the oh so very familiar sounding whoosh of air from a physical body essentially teleporting into existence, and a rustling like the flapping of very large wings. There were gasps and murmurs from the passengers who had seen him arrive.

Camina's brow furrowed and she closed her eyes with a happy wince. Happy because she loved her patron like a brother. Wincing because he was…a lot. Over the top? And there wasn't much he was allowed to do right now beside freak the heck out. Divine beings were not permitted to take direct action with their full divine powers on the mortal plane anymore.

No. Michael hadn't told her why. Just that 'there were rules' and if he didn't follow them, 'there would be problems'. Gods were extremely limited in what they could do per The Treaty. Demi Gods, angels, and other semi-immortals had more leeway. Miracles were another matter. All divine beings were permitted to influence events through miracles when granting prayers. But there had to be a lot of damned prayer energy going any one way for that to happen.

"Oh, thank goodness." His familiar voice called out, and the tall brunette turned slowly around to take a look at her patron. He was rolling his eyes with the most put upon expression on his face. "It's about damned time someone said a prayer to me."

"Hi, Michael." She smiled with genuine, but restrained, delight. There he was in his human form. A young ethnically ambiguous man. Possibly Asian-mixed, possibly Hispanic, maybe there was some middle eastern in there? No one could tell and he wasn't saying. But he clearly wasn't *only* Caucasian.

He had thick dark curls that sometimes came down to his shoulders, and sometimes were kept short around his ears, or anywhere in-between. Right now? They came down to just about around his square jaw. Below the large ridiculously lustrous curls of his bangs – which dangled over his high forehead almost to his eyes like some schleppy-in-a-cool-way skater boy or surfer dude – were wide-spaced heavy brows, also black. Enviously prolific lashes framed brown, almond-shaped eyes.

The immortal patron, who had looked a decade older than her when they'd formed their pact, now looked younger than her by several decades. It didn't bother Camina at all anymore. Nope. Just like she hadn't been jealous of the freckles on his broad cheeks when she was a teenager. Michael's age seemed to fluctuate slightly with his whim and Camina suspected that he could look older than her if he wanted to.

Her patron looked somewhere between his mid-teens to mid-twenties. Michael liked dark colors. Blues, greys, and blacks, colors and shades that went well with everything. Dressed in a pair of designer athletic joggers, tennis shoes, a T-shirt, and a zip front sweater jacket, the angel looked like an average high school or college athlete who was out for a morning run and planning to stop for latte after. Or he would have, if he hadn't also been noticeably soft around his edges. A stark contrast to Camina's own svelte physique. So, he looked athletic, but not exceptionally so.

“I’m so glad you’re okay.”

Rushing the twenty feet or so between himself and Camina, Michael took her up in a quick, desperate hug. Though taller than his chosen form, the woman felt herself lifted off the floor momentarily before she was placed ever so gently down again. Concern suffused the angel’s face and his pearly white wings, politely folded and contained by his sweater jacket, were quivering over his shoulders.

“Are you okay?” His large hands grasped her shoulders and gave her a tiny shake as if to test that she was really there. “I’ve been waiting for the kids to call me, but they haven’t. Not one phone call, not one prayer.” Though he might have been known as the unyielding general of God’s armies, Michael was incredibly passionate and caring in his relationships with mortals. And he took his job as God father and honorary ‘uncle’ of Camina’s children quite seriously.

“If they haven’t called for help, they are probably fine.” Assurances fell from Camina’s lips despite fearing that her words were false. But she was trying to project calm.

“Are you sure? I can’t see anything in New York. The arcanes are way too high. Us angels can’t even hear anything out of there but a muddled muted mess and even though we want to go down and get up close so we can hear any prayers just in case, the boss is all like ‘Naw dawg. Dems da rules.’” When excited. Her patron tended to get a little hyperfixated and somewhat motormouthed. Words were coming at her fast and she was pretty sure those sentences would have been without punctuation if they were written. Then he hurried onward.

“And I was all like ‘I don’t care about no rules, if my gurl Anna calls I’mma gonna go and get her because she’s my godbaby and I…I…’” his tirade devolved into a sob of disconsolate worry. “I can’t hear her, Camina. I was supposed to – It was so sudden.”

Giving an empathetic sigh, the warlock patted her patron on the shoulder in a there-there kind of way. Then, because the mom in her just would not sleep ever, she picked some lint off his jacket and flicked it away. It was tough being an angel. Being able to hear all the world’s woes but unable to act on most of them. Having to wait until the power of prayer was strong enough to act but that strength was not necessarily dictated by the number of people praying for something nor the passion behind their faith.

“Hey. I don’t know if it’s going to be okay. But I’m going to go down there and clear out the worst of the monsters.” Cupping his face in her hands, she smiled her bravest, most encouraging smile at her patron. “Why don’t you stay with these people and give them some faith. Answer their prayers and keep them safe until they get to a safe landing somewhere.” Gently, the warlock guided her patron to her vacated seat and Jim Thafesh, pockets bulging with gear and cameras strapped to his limbs and head, scooched out of the way around them.

Michael almost didn’t notice the young man at all until something caught his attention. Camina was trying to push the angel into her seat when he stopped and resisted. Putting a hand on the back of both Camina’s seat and the one in front of hers, he pushed back against her guiding hands. Head jerking up in sudden alarm, the dark-haired angel sniffed the air. Once.

"Wait a minute." Eyebrows lowering in consternation, the words were growled out deeply with just the slightest hint of a chorus behind them. Divine power escaped in wisps and curls from his lips. He sniffed twice in succession. "What. Is. That."

Chapter 35

Dark eyes with a hidden light behind them found Jim Thafesh as his gaze snapped to the source of whatever had caught his attention. His gaze narrowed with the unpleasant malevolence a father or uncle might give a man who was talking to his teenage daughter or niece. Realizing the jig was up and her patron had caught on to…something…about her new possibly-protégé that he didn't like, Camina's shoulders sagged like she was said teenage girl knowing her 'uncle' was about to give some young man a talking to just for being friendly.

"Stop." The softly spoken command resonated through the air and stopped Jim in his steps despite the young journalist's back being turned so he didn't know that it had been directed at him. "Come here." Now Jim became aware of the archangel's malice on his back as his feet began walking backward on their own accord then turned him around to face the angel.

"Oh. You meant me?" Gesturing at himself as he asked the obvious question, Camina realized that Jim was just digging the proverbial hole bigger. Though for the life of her, she couldn't figure out what her patron's problem could be.

"Michael –" She began before the archangel lifted and hand and made a 'shut it' gesture clamping his fingers together like a shadow puppet mouth.

"Quiet, Camina." He'd silenced her in a way that he never had before and she immediately shut her stunned mouth, straightened up, and paid attention. "Let me just check something first." Slowly, the archangel reached out one large, manicured hand and extended his index finger. Unable to move his feet, Jim began to lean away from the incoming finger. "Stop moving." Michael commanded.

Concerned, the journalist glanced at Camina worriedly, but she gave him a distracted and reassuring nod. Jim's focused eyes appeared to cross as they watched the incoming finger looming closer to his face. For his part, Michael's gaze was fixed on a spot somewhere on the trembling journalist's forehead. In a careful movement, the archangel swiped his index finger over Jim's brow as if he were stealing a taste of frosting off a cake.

Michael then switched his focus to the finger as he critically examined whatever he'd gotten off of Jim. For his part, Jim looked even more confused as he couldn't see anything at all on the finger. He kept glancing between Camina and Michael in befuddlement. After several seconds of intense scrutiny, the angel lifted the finger to his face and touched it daintily to the tip of his tongue.

Immediately he pulled the finger away. Making a tight-lipped grimace, he dropped his hands in defeat. Then sniffing disdainfully Michael turned to Camina.

"He's…" Pausing as if he couldn't even bring himself to say the words, did not reassure Jim about whatever the angel was about to reveal about him. Then exhaling with a vibrating of his lips like he was blowing raspberries, Michael shook his head in disgust. "He's been snared by fate."

"Ohhh!" A disappointed groan escaped the soldier. "No. Not again. He's mine now. They can't have him back." Her shoulders dropped and she gave them a little shake before straightening again and heading to the front of the plane to remind the copilot that he needed to let them out from a rear door. He'd need to unstrap himself and connect his harness again after relocating.

"What's happening?" Jim had been working his tongue in his mouth before finally getting up the nerve to ask.

"Nothing." Michael assured him in the most unconvincing way. "You'll be fine. Just stick with Camina and do what feels right to you." Absently, the archangel patted the young human on the shoulder before sitting down and buckling himself into Camina's vacant seat. Noticing that the speechless journalist was still standing where he'd forcibly drawn him, Michael looked up.

"Shoo, shoo." Hand gestures accompanied the instructions and Jim Thafesh, newly appointed embedded journalist of, arguably, the most famous warlock alive wandered towards the rear of the passenger compartment that he'd been shooed towards. More nervous now from pondering whatever had bothered the archangel than he'd initially been at the prospect of jumping out of a plane without a parachute. *Wait a minute! They did say that there's no parachutes on this plane?*

Red-faced with embarrassment, the copilot huffed slightly as Camina ushered him toward the back of the plane. He clipped his harness onto a seat leg across from the door and adjusted the length of the tether before locking that in place also. Almost as if on cue, the speakers for the announcement system came to life and the remarkably professional voice of the pilot was broadcast to the passengers.

"Ladies and gentlemen, this is your captain speaking." Did he sound just the slightest bit excited about the crazy shit he was about to do? Maybe. "The oxygen masks are about to be released. Please put them on as quickly as possible. Secure your mask before securing the mask of anyone you are assisting. As soon as I've been notified that everyone has their mask, I will begin depressurizing the cabin."

Short, startled shrieks sounded as oxygen masks descended suddenly. Cumulative hisses filled the compartments as air began to flow. People fumbled with their masks and put them on. It was at this point that Jim realized that he didn't have one. Neither did Camina, but she had divine powered battle armor. Or did she?

"You aren't going to suit up?" He whispered to her quietly. "Also, we don't have masks." Smirking a smile out of the corner of her full lips, Camina shrugged nonchalantly.

"Can't suit up in this confined space. I'd damage the plane. We don't need oxygen. We're honestly not that high." Her assurance had serious overtones of being superior to civilians. "Deep breaths. Exhale fully and quickly, inhale slowly and shallowly. Once you're out of the plane, even deep breaths. You first, I'll follow and catch you. But you'll be falling for a while because we need some distance for safety while I summon my armor."

"Okay." Jim nodded. And he kept nodding. More than he really needed to. Was he starting to shake? "Oh, God. What am I doing?" Camina smiled kindly at him with a brilliant flash of her celebrity-white teeth. She placed a reassuring hand on his shoulder. Jim noticed that there was an ornate white metal combat knife with gold inlay strapped to one muscular arm. Her pact item.

"You are about to help try to protect and save over eight million people from class one, class two, class three, and class four monster manifestations." Jim had looked away from the warrior before him, ashamed that he was considering backing out of his dream job because he was afraid of jumping out of a plane. Her words drew his gaze upward once more. When Jim met Camina's eyes, there wasn't any condemnation there. Just faith.

"This is the captain speaking." The hollow tones of the announcement system started again. "I've been informed by the flight crew that all passengers are ready. Depressurization is starting now. Remain in your seat with your seatbelt secured." Dull and muted roaring began. Growing in intensity until it stopped, still mostly muted.

The copilot grimaced as he held up his hand with three fingers, then two fingers, than one and opened the door and Camina helped him swing it inward. More likely, she was helping him prevent it from swinging in too quickly. Jim staggered as the wind pummeled the interior of the aircraft. Grabbing on to the seat behind him, Jim steadied himself. Which lasted a moment before he felt Camina's hand on his shoulder again.

He looked up at her as the wind howled around them. She was grinning wildly, excitement lighting up her eyes. Then she pulled Jim forward to the edge and his eyes widened with burgeoning panic. Before he could react though, Camina Wattkins pushed Jim Thafesh out the open door of the plane and down forcefully into the empty blue expanse of the sky.

Chapter 36

"Oh Shiiiit!" Jim's scream came out breathy and he tried not to lose consciousness. Sky howled past him, his journey deafening. His unprepared exit from the plane had resulted in him being in a sideways position. Off in the distance, the horizon was a vertical line from his current orientation.

He was falling and the ground was far, far away but it was also entirely too close. Because it was everywhere below him. Everywhere. Remembering that the least he could do was document what was happening, Jim pulled his splayed arms to his chest and carefully braced the camera securely strapped into his white-knuckled grip to his eye so he could focus it. After filming a few seconds of the ground, he windmilled his arms and flipped himself onto his back.

There the plane was flying away in the near distance. Already further away than he'd like even if it was entirely too late to get back inside. As he watched, Camina seemed to fall out of the opening in the rear of the fuselage. Brown hair streaming behind her, the distant woman spread her arms and maneuvered away from the retreating aircraft which began banking almost as soon as she was clear.

A golden light enveloped the woman gradually coalescing into armor. Glistening pearlescent in the bright sunlight, the summoned armor transformed her clothing around her. Or maybe it covered her clothing. Honestly, he couldn't remember if that had been covered in any of Camina's interviews before. Right now, it didn't matter what the nitty gritty was, just that he was watching, and filming, the magnificent transformation of The Harbinger of Light.

Yep. He was fanboying out hard core while trying to keep his camera steady. A full body suit of what looked like powered mechanical armor out of some kind of science fiction movie. Instead of being powered by some kind of convenient unobtainium MacGuffin, the Saint of Warriors Armor of God's General was powered by magic and divinity channeled through the warlock pact with the archangel Michael. It was based, vaguely, on the armor her patron wore in battle. Though, historical renderings made Michael's armor looked decidedly less technological.

What had been the knife strapped to her forearm enlarged and morphed into a giant rifle mounted on the pearly white metal of her gauntlet. All the segments around her joints and her waist were covered in some kind of flexible gold scale alloy. Then Camina's body spasmed, her spine arching and her appendages splaying wide as her wings erupted from her back in a spectacular display. Multi-segmented wings made up of huge shimmering armored plates shaped like feathers. The individual pieces were jointed together with golden divine magic.

Despite the edges of his vision trying to darken, the journalist fought his body's desire to faint. These were the moments he lived for. The shots no one else would get, the stories no one else would tell. Camina's eyes were covered by the sleek white helmet of her armor behind the reflective polarized visor. Her wings flexed as she slowed in the air and Jim saw the distance between them had begun to widen.

Just as quickly though, she'd tucked the wings close and dove after him. Drawing near, she swooped to match velocities with the plummeting man. Tracking her relentlessly, Jim never took his camera off the armored woman. Even as she approached and seemed to hover beside him, taking the time to de-polarize her visor and smile at him before holding out her arms to *very* carefully cradle his falling form. Ever so slowly, Jim Thafesh felt resistance against the pull of gravity pressing him into the mech armor.

Once she arrested their uncontrolled fall, Camina started flying.

It was glorious.

They were still high up and the ground was still rushing toward them but not nearly as fast as it had been before. Now they were soaring, gliding on air currents. Towering skyscrapers solidified out of the blurry landscape. Then smaller buildings, the river, tarmac and streets. Vehicles and things that had once been vehicles.

They began slowing and the scents and sounds of the city hit Jim even as he continued filming. Smoke, trash, the acrid stench of jet fuel and too much magic filled the air. Sirens were wailing both near and far. An emergency response vehicle lodged upside down in a second story window gallery overlooking the airport tarmac was making an intermittent 'whoop', 'whoop' as it tried to sound its siren. Its light flashed periodically from beneath it, reflecting eerily from the shaded walls of the terminal.

The intact windows of the terminal were polarized and reflective, so it was impossible to see if there were any injured people around the damage. Roaring and crashing came from further on beyond the weird angular construction of the airport terminal. Whatever it was, it was massive. Especially if they could see glimpses of its limbs over the roof of the building and hear it over the rushing wind and the hum of Camina's powered armor.

With what felt like not nearly enough caution, Camina set down on the closer side of the terminal roof. Thankfully, she'd chosen an area that was still structurally sound. Relieved to touch a flat surface again, Jim almost forgot that he was filming. Her face showing just the right amount of concern, Camina opened her visor.

"You alright, Mr. Thafesh?" Eyebrows raised in inquiry; Camina spoke quietly to avoid drawing attention to them before she was ready. The woman somehow managed to convey the image of friendly neighbor…clad in magical armor and toting a giant pulse rifle that could transform into a wicked lance or sword. Nodding, Jim responded haltingly.

"Yes…yes, Ma'am." He'd started straightening his clothing without thinking about it with one hand while the other was still trying to keep his camera steady.

"Excellent. Let's go take a look at what is making such a racket, shall we?" Camina's wings retracted into her suit. Crouching, she gestured for the journalist to follow her to the side of the building where the monster was actively moving around.

Archangel Michael Vs the Fates (Part 1)

Aaaannnnd…they were gone! He absently answered the prayer of that veteran with the Saint charm of him, and sent a bit of divine miracle to help the copilot close the door quickly. Michael sighed and tried not to fidget nervously.

Camina was a big girl now; she could take care of herself. Okay. To be fair, she'd been fairly damned capable of taking care of herself long before she ever met him and that's why he'd fought so hard to become her patron.

She was a warrior. Through and through. Her battle instincts were spot on. Quick, capable, and filled with determination even against insurmountable odds.

Archangel Michael had seen a girl fighting alone and unwilling to ever give up no matter the odds, and he knew that if she survived that first battle, she was going to keep taking on those fights. It had called to him. That little girl had been exactly the kind of person the patron saint of warriors was meant to protect.

Camina had been the youngest warlock Michael had ever taken. Considering the religious connotations of the pantheon he belonged to; warlocks were somewhat rare for angels. Even more so for Michael, their religion generally attracted paladins and those were generally directly affiliated with the boss. For Michael, his warlocks were precious. Sanctified magic wielders touched by the divine and 'blessed' with a mission to protect those who could not protect themselves.

Nurturing and protecting these rare individuals whose faith in right and wrong, and the power of their patron was stronger than any faith they would ever have in his deity was sacred to him. But Camina was different. She'd been ten. And she hadn't fit comfortably into the world even before she'd completed the summoning ritual for a patron. Afterward, things had been unpleasant to say the least.

Not because of Michael. Partially because of Michael. It wasn't his doing. There were laws about how young a person could be when they took a warlock pact. And while Camina had known that she would face some challenges for breaking this law, she hadn't expected to be punished for doing what she'd needed to, to survive. She wasn't the same as other kids anymore. Pacts brought knowledge with them that changed a person. But ten-year-old Camin, who now had senses and instincts from her pact with an archangel that drove her to battle evil and protect the innocent, wasn't looked upon by the adults as anything more than an impetuous young girl with talent. Someone to be manipulated and reigned-in.

It had led Michael to be a little more hands-on with this particular warlock than with any other he'd ever had. If his warlock called, Michael came. So far, she'd never called him for anything that would 'break the rules', but the archangel knew full well that he totally would if asked. Camina knew it too, so she never asked. The 'rules' of non-interference were starting to seem particularly stupid since he'd taken Camina as a warlock. Needless to say, Michael was seeing things differently nowadays.

Which brought him to his next item of business.

The Fates.

Those Greek hussies who kept trying to slyly weave the mortals with potential for greatness away from other pantheons and sneak them into the purview of their fellow *Greek* gods. Ugh. Like some creep sliding into the DM's of a mortal's life and surprising them with dick pics and thinking they should be grateful. In this case, the dick pics were actually surprise opportunities to do dangerous things and become a 'hero'.

Becoming a hero for the Greek pantheon was a surefire way to end up dead quick if the chosen wasn't able to live up to the gods' expectations. And heaven forbid the chosen actually dedicate themselves to one particular god or goddess. Favorites were often punished in unpleasant ways when there were feuds among the deities or pantheons.

The cabin had been repressurized as the archangel fumed silently and the flight attendants were now helping passengers stow the dangling oxygen masks out of their ways. He sighed and pulled out his cell phone before scrolling through his contacts and selecting the one labeled Three Cunty Biotches. Drumming his fingers, Michael listened to the phone ring as he waited for one of them to pick up.

"Well," An ancient cracked and breathy voice spoke in a trembling fashion as if the effort was overwhelming. The speaker took a long slow breath as if just that one word had exhausted them. "How kind of you to call and check up on a couple of little old ladies." Rolling his eyes, Michael tried to keep his voice level.

"Knock it off." He scolded impatiently. "I' not some ignorant mortal you can play your head games with." They really could be as young and beautiful as they wanted. All three had two functional eyes if they so choose. And a mouth full of teeth was in each of their mouths.

"Someone's a bit testy." A second, younger voice purred seductively. Either the call was on speaker on the fates side, or they were just using power to hear and make themselves heard.

"What could possibly have upset you?" Called the third. Sucking on his teeth angrily, Michael kept his wrath in check as he replied.

"I told you to stop using my warlock as a shepherd to level up you chosen heroes." Cackling laughter came from the crone intermixed with the tinkling laughter of her sisters who were projecting at least the sound of younger women at the moment.

"What are you going to do about it?" It was the crone this time. "We've got just as much right to weave the fates of mortals as you."

"First of all, I don't weave the fates of humans." Balling up his fist because he wanted to hit something, Michael reigned in the flash of temper that roiled through him in a hot wave. "Secondly, The Treaty specifically says you can't weave the fates of mortals claimed by other pantheons." Tittering laughter continued and Michael wished he was permitted to take up arms against these three menaces who genuinely pissed off every single divine being who had to deal with them, including the deities of their own pantheon.

"Oh, no." Suddenly the plane, which had been climbing steadily for the last several minutes back up to cruising altitude, dropped in a stomach clenching plummet. Screams filled the passenger compartment as the turbines outside the windows stuttered. The plane stopped falling but rocked and jerked in the air as laughter cackled over the phone louder and louder.

Pulling the phone away from his ear, Michael glowered at it as the laughter continued growing in volume. The laughter filled the cabin as if his phone was on speaker, and now terrified passengers were looking at him. Looking upward Michael made a beseeching gesture at the sky before the buffeting stopped just as suddenly as it started.

"Oops." The loud voices on the other end of the line spoke in the saccharinely sweet voice of someone who was entirely insincere. "My hand slipped, and I just almost accidentally cut a bunch of threads at one time."

"Oh? That's how you want to PLAY THIS?" Michael's voice grew louder, and the chorus of heaven crept into his voice, bells and horns trumpeting faintly. His ordinary garb was briefly overlayed with his warriors vestments. "I DEMAND ARBITRATION." He roared and a flash of light filled the plane with a golden glow as the oppressive presence of hundreds of minor and major deities before dozens of voices responded.

"ACCEPTED."

Chapter 37

Sam was…not good after the call from Anna. All this time, she'd assumed that her little sister was safe. If not at her very expensive, prestigious, and supposedly *extremely* secure private school, then at home or at work with their father. Either way, she should have been in a safe location.

Not only was Anna not secure, but she had also been unable to get ahold of their father. So, in addition to the horror of listening to the screams of terror from the people with Anna over the call and the sounds of a large monster manifestation. Sam was also imagining all kinds of crazy shitty scenarios vying for space in her brain, narrating what horrible things could have happened to their father both before and after the incident.

Had he tried to get to Anna only to be eaten by the very monsters that were now endangering her younger sister? Maybe. Possibly. Sam didn't know. She didn't know.

Why hadn't her dad gotten Anna when the school called? He never had appointments that lasted more than one hour let alone multiple hours. Had his secretary not given him the message? Had he been mugged on his way to work this morning or on his way to get Anna and was lying in a gutter dead or dying somewhere and no one had found him because of the emergency?

Ahhhh!

And why didn't Kyle have his phone on him?

What the artificers fuck, Kyle!

Sam was on the verge of hyperventilating in concerned fear and outrage at the unreal and unholy combination of negligence and general incompetence that had led to this situation. If dad or Kyle had answered their phones or checked their messages, Anna would be much safer right now. Okay. In all fairness, if that damned school had proper magic shielding this might not have been an issue at all.

Maybe. Was the school building able to withstand an attack from a class three or four monster? Or a herd of them? She didn't know.

"Fuuuck!" It came out as a long, frustrated growl and Sam ran both hands through her hair, mussing her perfectly smooth tie back. Much in the same way her brother did when he was frustrated, she grabbed her roots and gave a gentle tug of pent-up emotion. Then Samantha Wattkins swallowed down her feelings.

This was not the time. It was not the time at all. Wrenching her thoughts back to the present, Sam got to work.

"Okay." One more deep breath steadied her and a calming pat on Gleipnir where he nuzzled her waist comfortingly settled him as well. Their combined auras had been doing that thing again. When they were agitated, well, it wasn't good. It made the area around them unpleasant to be in. And if pressed hard enough, the aura alone could become a weapon that injured anyone who came within its radius.

"Okay?" Frank questioned from a distance. He'd called back the team he'd had guarding the perimeter of the primary danger zone when Anna's call notified him of much more dangerous monsters than he'd been anticipating.

"Yeah." Though Sam's voice and expression were reassuring and calm, Alex eyed her partner skeptically. And Frank's eyes darted from Sam, to Alex, and back to Sam, clearly wondering if the younger agent could tell whether or not Sam was lying. Dropping her shoulders, Sam rolled her eyes at Alex then gave her field boss a flat look. "We. Are. Fine." The magical engineer gestured between herself and Gleipnir's 'head' still cuddling his warlock consolingly along the curve of her waist.

"Yes." Gleipnir agreed, the emotion of his voice giving the impression of someone who had been crying but had now pulled themself together despite their sore throat and stuffy nose. "My Sammy is a big strong girl. She'll be able to fight even if her sister and brother are off dying under an overwhelming wave of monsters and her father might be having an affair."

"Gleipnir!" Alex was equal parts amused and aghast and she choked back a laughing gasp. "That is…that is *not* how you comfort someone." Frank was less decorous and actually snorted before covering his mouth with one hand as if he were just thinking. Then he turned back around to face outward for signs of monsters.

"Thank you for that Gleip" Dry and caustic, Sam's tone may be, it was lost on her oblivious pact item. The sentient artifact merely acknowledged what he thought was his just dues.

"You're welcome, Sam." The munificence of his reply indicated he had no idea that he'd made a grave faux pas. Even Sam snorted at that as she blinked back the wet glimmer in her eyes. Because it was clear that Gleipnir deeply cared for his warlock and was just showing that he had her back, however clumsily.

Then he sniffed.

At first, Alex thought he was being stuck-up Gleipnir again, but no, he sniffed again. Then twice more. Swiftly the artifact unwrapped his chain from around his warlock and shifted more of his bulk into his sword-shape. That made Alex take note as he lifted himself up slowly to whisper in Sam's ear.

"Do you feel that?" His voice was low but not so low that he couldn't be heard by the two agents closest to him and Sam. Gleipnir's 'face', or the part of his sword-shape that Alex had come to realize he'd designated as his face, was angled toward the warehouse they had yet to investigate.

Sam was nodding, her eyes narrowing as she too turned to face whatever he was sensing. Alex found herself nodding as well at the sick twisting churn of magic coming from the building which had, until moments before, just been a part of the oversaturated chaos in the ambient magic levels. She almost wanted to vomit. A few of the agents that happened to be closer to the building began retching uncontrollably.

"What is that?" It was unnatural. Unholy. A filthy perversion that Alex desperately feared and felt needed to be immediately cleansed from existence. Yet it was just a feeling, a sensation. Nails on the chalkboard of reality.

134

"Monster manifestation." Gleipnir whispered. "High level. Too high level. Turn your magic collector back on. Now. Now. Now. PERSONAL SHIELDS NOW!!!"

Chapter 38

Alex hadn't waited for Gleipnir to finish his scream. She'd switched her portable magic collector on the second the other agents had started vomiting. Magical engineers had to be sensitive to the currents of magic. It was a requirement for the job. Whatever was brewing in that warehouse near the second magical source, the source that hadn't been directly dampened at all, was bad news.

"Integumentum infernis." Sam whispered and a whooshing followed by the muted crackling of flames began as a circle of fire surrounded her. The circle grew up into a wall that then collapsed onto her body. Now, the warlock was covered in a second skin of enchanted fire.

"Good choice, my girl." Gleipnir approved loudly, projecting his voice so that all the agents could hear. "A very arcane hungry spell, it should help burn off a significant portion of the magic before it reaches your body and causes magic poisoning."

"You heard the men," Frank roared to his subordinates. "Cast your highest cost shield spells. We're going to drain arcanes right out of the air by brute force if we have to." From the warehouse came the sounds of something large stirring. Huffing, growling, clanking. A screech of tearing metal and then the roof of the building began sinking where a support was clearly no longer doing its job.

"Scutum fedei." A paladin that was on his knees coughed out between retches. Sam was somehow beside the man already. When had that happened? She'd just been back over to Alex's left a few seconds ago, hadn't she?

As soon as the spell summoned by the paladin was in effect, he became noticeably less sick. The magic hungry spell eating up the ambient magic around his body at a terrific rate. For a moment, Alex watched dumbly as her partner was running from one downed agent to another, standing beside them for a few moments until summoned their own spell, and then running off to the next one. It was as if Sam's presence was making the sick people better.

"She's syphoning off the magic around them with her spell, so they have a chance to activate their own defenses." Frank grabbed Alex by the shoulder and pulled-shoved her along with him. "Come on. We have to get them out of there. They're too close to the source. Shield up!" Frank's spell was just the basic shield spell that all agents learned in training. But he was clearly modulating it to feed more off the ambient magic as a glimmering aurora surrounded him with arcane symbols.

Alex…was a magical engineer. She was not a front line, first responding kind of agent. This wasn't what she had trained for. Was it? She was supposed to be in a hygienic, sealed lab somewhere dismantling and examining illegal magitech. Not running into a Prometheus purple zone that was about to turn pink really quick. Today was seriously making her rethink her career choices.

She was proficient with the standard shield. But it really wasn't sufficient for this situation. She couldn't use the one the paladin had as that was a faith-based spell. Maybe, maybe she could do the one that Sam had used?

"Rosolvere et effingo, integumentum infernis." She directed the analyze portion of her spell at Sam, and then the copying portion at herself to initiate the spell. Hot damn. Her vision flashed blank and white as the knowledge of the spell wrote itself upon her mind. "Shit." It came out breathy and she gasped a short cry of alarm as she was engulfed in flames for the first time in her life.

Taking a brief moment, she examined her hand and saw the inferno blazing around her. Satisfied that she had completed the spell correctly, Alex ran off to join the fray and rescue some of the agents who were still debilitated by the high levels of arcanes in the area. Sam had glanced up with a frown when she felt herself at the center of the rosolvere spell, but she smiled at Alex and called out as she was standing over another coworker waiting for them to regain their breath so she could help them up.

"That was great, Alex. Excellent control in the examination. Nice and steady." Did Sam just compliment her? Well, miracles came in all sorts of forms apparently. Skidding to a halt in front of a young Asian man, Alex focused her thoughts into sucking up as much magic into her shield as was possible.

She was directing external arcanes in a way similar to what she did with enchanting, but instead of directing magic into an object or intention, she was lighting it on fire and using it up. It was something her artificer instructors in college would have been appalled to see. Such waste. The young man's bowed head was bobbing as his stomach emptied its contents without his control and the sounds and smell was making Alex sick to her stomach as well.

"You're gonna be okay." She offered the suited agent unhelpfully, hoping that she was pulling enough arcanes away from him. Glancing at the Prometheus sensor on her wrist, it was clear that the magic levels were dangerously close to pink even inside her barrier.

"Tai…Tai…" He was trying to cast his spell, but he was choking on vomit between gasping attempts. Knowing that she had to do more but knowing that he wouldn't be able to control the shield if she placed one on him herself, Alex did the only thing she could. She increased the flow of arcanes into her fire skin and grabbed the man's arm.

He screamed and spewed flecks of vomit all down Alex's front as she yanked him to his feet and pulled his arm over her shoulder. Her shield burned him where it touched him but if she let it down, she'd be as debilitated as he was. "Taiyō…" He screeched, not even trying to pull away because the fire that burned him was also burning up the arcanes that were poisoning him. "Taiyō no yoroi"

Chapter 39

Once the words had been uttered in full, *then* and only then did he lunge off Alex's support and stumble forward. A brilliant flare of light engulfed him, erupting in a blaze that rivaled the bright light of the sun. Shielding her eyes, Alex tried to focus on the man. Was he okay? Had something gone wrong with his spell?

He looked like he'd combusted into a pillar of white-hot molten…something. Then, Alex saw the bright pillar-blob start moving. A blurry slightly darker triangle began to appear and disappear on the undulating lower half of the pillar, and he realized he was walking. Not fast, but he was not bent over and vomiting like he had been a few moments before.

"I'm fine." He gasped out, then bending over, waved her off. "Go help someone else. I'm as good as I'm going to be." With a shrugging shake of her head, Alex headed off to find someone else who needed help.

A glance around showed her that her earlier hesitation meant that other agents had rescued most of the people who'd been in distress. Those who had recovered quickly, had helped others. It had been fast. Now the last of the group were hobbling towards their vehicles in preparation for evacuation.

Seeing that her charge had already taken off towards the vehicles, Alex looked for Sam. Sam and Frank were escorting a pair of agents, one of whom was too injured to manage on their own. Somewhat jealously, Alex noticed that her fellow magical engineer was able to manipulate her shield so that she didn't burn the person she was helping.

Behind them the rumbling from the building became a deafening roar. Concrete and metal crumbled and fell. Chunks impacting whatever they landed on with echoes and crunches. Chancing a glance back, Alex saw what resembled an avalanche in reverse. Debris launched itself into the crystal-clear sky. Huge, medium, small as dust? It didn't matter. It was all going up in what would have been spectacular special effects in a movie.

Yeah! She could admit that. Her mind admitted numbly. Even as a remote and tiny part of her mind was urgently screaming an alarm for her to flee, flee now because her life depended on it. Alex's legs had slowed in stunned awe. What on Earth could it be?

Was it the unidentified source of arcanes? Was it a monster manifestation? What had transformed? Legs slowing further, the magic technician came nearly to a stop half turned to watch her approaching doom.

Sam, Frank and the others were nearly to the first group of vehicles by the time she realized that Alex wasn't with her anymore.

"Where's Alex?" She shouted over the man supported between her and Frank. Her words were eaten by the sound of imminent death coming from behind them.

"She was right behind us." Frank shouted back, the lines around his eyes and mouth drawn in a tight grimace. Sam's forehead furrowed and her head jerked around to look for Alex as Frank yanked open a car door.

"I'm going back for her." Before he had finished helping the person they were supporting into it, Sam had dashed back into what was now a billowing cloud shooting the occasional sizzling boulder of warehouse into the air.

"Fuck. Sam" Checking to make sure the person they'd rescued was secured, Frank looked back into the cloud that was making its way toward them as it fell toward the ground.

"Don't wait up." She screamed back to him as she loped away. Gleipnir was in her hand, and she plunged into the dust, her body nothing more than a faint glow in the growing darkness of the cloud.

"Damnit." Shaking his head, Frank almost tossed his keys to someone else, but changing his mind hurried around to the door. Several vehicles had already evacuated but some had stopped to watch Sam with horror as she ran into a churning maelstrom. "What are the rest of you waiting for. Fall back. Fall back." He circled one arm in the air for emphasis and pointed out the difficult to navigate terrain before he swung himself into his vehicle and left as quickly as the damaged infrastructure would let him.

Meanwhile, Sam didn't slow in her sprint back for Alex despite the reduced visibility. Spells rattled off her lips for additional physical shielding, for sight int the dark, for heat vision. She was flipping through spells as fast as she could trying to find where her new junior agent had gone.

Ignoring the blisters forming on her lips from her rapid-fire incantations, the magical engineer faced a living embodiment of destruction in little more than her pants suit. The coppery taste of blood in her mouth mixed with the sweet-savory heaviness of the arcanes she was pulling through her. Was that maybe slightly brighter spot in the cloud Alex. It was impossible to tell under these conditions.

"Oh." Shaking her head in disgust, Sam yanked the buttons on her wrist open and rolled up her cuffs. "The *hell* with this."

As a warlock, Sam wasn't used to taking in ambient magic. Her power was granted by her patron, the Norse goddess Frigg. Because of this, a large majority of her magic was creation related, weaving in particular. Which was why Gleipnir, a needle and or thread type sentient item, had been her granted pact item.

And while many might think that the creative and fiber arts-oriented obsession of Frigg's nature might be exceedingly limiting on the magics available to her warlocks, it gave them an advantage that many warlocks lacked. Creativity. And the ability to layer styles of magic and spells to make them more powerful than they would ever be just relying on the magic granted to them by their goddess.

"Vefa ok sauma." Weave and sew. Sam spoke it quietly, whispering it almost lovingly from her lips as her intention gathered both the power granted by her patron and readied the spell to be fed by the ambient magic. Despite her soft voice, the words of power seemed to dampen the raging noise around her, an all-encompassing command in the vortex of dim yellow light. Raising her hand, the young woman faced the obscured potential doom defiantly and spoke three precise words.

"Bregðandi. Nordr. Kaldr." For a second, all the world stopped.

Archangel Michael Vs the Fates (Part 2)

10:55 AM September 13th, 2026
Central Manhattan near the Empire State Building

"Nicholas Everstone" The slim and lanky man in his mid-thirties had stopped to place one foot up on a planter and posed with his hands on his hips like a conquering hero so he could admire himself in the mirror-like reflection of the coffee shop window. The golden light of morning caught his bright red hair and set it aflame. Not really. But it shined brightly in the sun. "Arbiter of the Gods."

Okay, sure, he got weird looks. But at least one woman walking by gave him an encouraging nod and an eyebrow lift, that he returned with a genuine smile. At which point the eyebrow lift turned into a sniggering smirk and a hand over her mouth as she hurried away.

"Eh." Nicholas shrugged it off and laughed at himself. Because he was being silly. But that was okay too.

Truth be told, women laughing at him would have sent him spiraling when he was in his twenties. Now, he knew better. Laughter was good. Usually. And if this was the bad kind of laughter, then she wasn't the right kind of woman for him.

Though, damn, he bit his lip and tried not to turn and follow that oil-rubbed-bronze goddess with his eyes. Her thick dark hair straightened, then styled a gorgeous cascade of fat gurls down her back. And what even was she wearing? Was that string? Rope?

He didn't know.

The red-headed dork did know that her collection of fiber, artfully arranged as it was over her torso, didn't leave much to the imagination. Determined not to be a creeper, Nicholas averted his eyes and checked himself. Sheepishly grinning, he shook his head at his silly self.

This was something he did every morning to start his day. Just for a couple of seconds. Not like he stood around waiting for women – or anyone for that matter – to notice him. It was just a thing he'd done one day to cheer himself up from keeping the biggest secret in the world that he couldn't share with anyone. It was like having the worst NDA contract in history.

Imagine if you did something so utterly cool that it could probably get you laid every day for life. But…you couldn't tell anyone that's what you did because everyone would think you were out of your ever-loving mind. Yeah. That was Nicholas' side gig. And it paid, oh ho, so well.

It made his attorney's salary look like chump change, and the stress? Now, lawyer is supposed to be a high- stress career. Being a lawyer for regular everyday humans? That was easy. Dealing with the scum of the divine planes? That was stressful. When the cases you presided over affected billions of people? Yeah.

Taking his hands off his hips and his dress shoe shod foot off the sidewalk planter, Nicholas straightened his suit. Then he headed into the coffee shop where he completed his morning ritual in front of for his daily It's Definitely Not Dairy latte. Which was one thousand percent better tasting than ambrosia.

It's Definitely Not Dairy was an entirely non-dairy coffee slash sorbet shop and café. All of their food and beverages used vegan substitutes for dairy. No. They weren't a vegan restaurant. Just their dairy was vegan. Which was great, because the Irish American attorney was decidedly lactose intolerant. Which had sucked, since until he found out he was lactose intolerant, he almost exclusively snacked at Thirty-Four Milks. It was a very lactose-oriented establishment that boasted an inventory of dairy from thirty-four different types of animals.

Being an adamantly unapologetic carnivore, Nicholas had been thrilled when he discovered It's Definitely Not Dairy. So many lactose free restaurants were really just vegan and that was so difficult to deal with for a carnivore that was already suffering from dairy deprivation. Somehow, Nichola had soldiered through the crisis with his vast wealth and two amazing jobs until he'd found his new haven.

"Oh, hey, Nick." Sherral the barista greeted him with a familiar smile and a wave. "You were looking good out there this morning. Almost reeled one in." She giggled and winked. Smiling, Nick hid his grimace.

"You saw that crash and burn?" Though his tone was lighthearted, Nick's old insecurities started bubbling back up. His sheepish chagrin causing him to duck his head shyly.

"It was more of a rug pulling." The pixie-like barista assured him. She'd had the hair on one the left side of her blonde head shaved to about a quarter inch then bleached and dyed to look like hot pink leopard print spots. On the right, she'd left it about three? Maybe four inches long, dyed it neon blue and spiked it in every direction. Straight out from her head.

"Rug pulling?" Nick was trying not to stare at the rosettes, which was what they were called wasn't it, of pink and black on the left side of her head. Intricate work like that must have taken hours and cost a fortune. Or was it magic?

"Yeah. She made it seem like she was interested and gave you an ego boost before laughing at you. Let you have a leg to stand on then pulled the rug out from under it." She shrugged her tan shoulders in a careless way that made the delicate skin over her collar bone move delightfully. "I mean, it's not terrible. But it wasn't nice."

"I suppose." Honestly, Nick hadn't thought about it that much. He'd just been embarrassed for thinking she might be down with his awkward shenanigans.

"It's a hot chick thing."

"You would know." It'd been meant just as an acknowledgement that Sherral was both attractive and bisexual, but she took the unexpected compliment with a heated flush to her cheeks.

'Uh. Um." She licked her lips nervously. "Thank you." It came out softly around a sudden lump in her throat and she looked down, then away, and anxiously fidgeted for a few seconds before Nicholas managed to break the moment.

"So…"

"Are you gonna order dude?" A third party called from behind him. There was a line. Oh Gods. A huge, long line of patrons all observing their interaction in various degrees of amused, or unamused, thirst.

"Oh. Right. Your regular, right?" The cute but probably way too young for him barista hurried off to go and start on the same beverage he had every morning. Was ten years too big an age gap? Was she really that much younger than him or did she just seem younger because she was short, petite, and did funky things with her hair? Or did she just use one of those really great magical cosmetic creams that kept her skin looking like she was in her twenties?

There was no way to know without asking.

And if he asked then she'd know he liked her. At the very least she'd suspect he liked her before he was ready to make a decision about whether or not he really wanted to ask her out. And should he even bother? His work was always getting in the way somehow. With all those thoughts swirling around in his head Sherral had to call his name twice before he realized his drink was ready for him.

"Oh! Oh! Thank you so much." Nervous wreck that he was, Nick clasped both his hands over and around Sherral's as he was grabbing the cup from her such that she couldn't let go without spilling hot latte all over both of them. "Oh, Gods. Sorry Sherral. I'm just not, with it today."

"It's fine." Sherral assured him as they maneuvered their hands for a safe and non-mess-causing exchange.

"Just ask her out already buddy" The heckler from before called out and this time the guy had a chorus of agreement from the other dairy-free patrons.

"Oh, my Gods," A clearly-younger-than-Sherral woman with green hair and matching eyes who appeared to be on the phone with someone, gave commentary to her conversation partner, "Did I totally just watch a meet cute. I did. I mean technically they seem like they know each other, but it was adorbs."

"Agreed." A white-haired older gentleman smiled at them then over at the mature female warlock with dark hair and lines of grey and steel threading through it who held his arm like damsel from decades past. "You only get one chance to find the right one."

"Hah. You got two chances." She grinned with gentle mirth as they took Nicholas' place at the counter.

"But that's because you are exceptional."

"Aww." Sherral cooed in delight seeing the older couple who had clearly spent years together bantering like lovesick youths. It was charming, and much as it might have seemed as if Nick was interested, he had already turned belatedly away as she got back to taking orders. He would always be back tomorrow.

The lights flickered.

Then they went off.

Everything went off. And the valley girl who had gushed about the meet cute shrieked.

"My phone. Someone stole my –" Someone grabbed her phone from her hand in the sudden dimness which flashed brilliantly as the phone erupted into flames and burst into shards that showered over the confused and milling crowd.

"There, there, dear." The older woman who had just been at the front of the line was standing beside her and the elderly husband was holding a shield…that was also his arm? Maybe?

Chapter 40

"Bregðandi. Nordr. Kaldr." Wind. North. Cold. In that second, a wave of cold billowed out from Sam. In her hand Gleipnir shivered. Sam had used the spells for weaving and sewing to combine the essence of wind, the North, and cold. Essentially creating a spell for the North Wind on the fly.

"Brrr." He gasped, as ice crystalized outward leaping from one dust or debris particle to another. "I hate that spell."

His words rang clearly as the spell worked to freeze the chaotic movement around them. The crackling of frost was the only sound for those instants. With a cracking whoosh that swiftly grew thunderous, the grit and debris hindering sight was blasted away with the magical engineer and her pact item as the epicenter. Able to see once more, Samantha Wattkins wiped some dirt from her sweat streaked face.

A quiet sob drew her attention. *Finally!* Sam thought in exasperation. *That was Alex for sure.* She'd expected her partner to be looking for everyone else. But she wasn't. She was staring at something. Something that was behind Sam and a little to the right. Something high. Transfixed.

Then Sam heard it.

The rumbling of concrete slabs grinding against one another was back. With it, the squealing screech of tearing and bending metal. Then there was a crumbling boom. It shook the ground and made all the destroyed asphalt of the parking lot she was in tremble at the impact. Followed by more rumbling and screeching, and another boom. More trembling.

"Oh, for the love of doughnuts!" Gleipnir used one of Kyle's favorite Anna-safe-Camina-approved curses. He wiggled out of Sam's grasp and turned to glare in the direction of the noise. He gave a small, strangled yelp. "Don't look, Sam." He admonished in a quiet whisper, as swiftly returned himself to her hand. "Just grab Alex and run."

"I think maybe perhaps I should look, Gleip." Sam countered with trepidation. "It can't be that bad."

"No. Just run. Right now, it's attention is on Alex, but the second you move it will notice you, and we are much closer to it that Alex." Low and tight, his voice had no levity in it. Just concern for his warlock.

"Is it about to eat Alex?" It was still a bright sunny day, and Sam was starting to wish she'd wore sunglasses. She could feel sweat that was from more than her exertion saturating the blouse under her jacket. Like, what she wouldn't give to be able to adjust her bra right now.

"Ehh." Gleipnir waffled, as another footstep slammed down more to heir right than behind them this time. "It's looking like that."

"Fuck it." Sam exclaimed, a little too loudly then hushed her voice as she continued. "I'm looking." She turned to her right, not sure what to expect, but not at all expecting what she saw. It was…

…a building?

With legs!

"Fucking, *what*!" the shout got its attention and the front? The head? Whatever it was swung towards Sam and Gleipnir. It lurched ponderously towards the pair and the warlock was already sprinting towards her partner as her pact item screamed at her.

"Run! Damnit. Run! I told you not to look, you stubborn warlock." Though he could have far surpassed her in speed, Gleipnir stayed with his warlock, letting her hold him like a weapon as she ran for her coworker.

"Now's not really the time to rub it in, Gleip!" She shouted back, regretting the last cup of coffee she had as the strenuous activity brought a burnt coffee and bile taste to the back of her throat.

"Now's the only time to rub it in." He hollered back unrepentantly. "If you die in the next few minutes, I'll never get to tell you I was right!"

"Fphft." She tried not to laugh as she continued running.

"Okay. I fear to say it again." The sentient pact item was keeping a look out for the oncoming warehouse which had somehow become an entire monster manifestation. "But don't look now, it's decided you are too fast and gone back to targeting Alex."

Redoubling her efforts to reach her partner, Sam did chance a short glance to her right that nearly sent her stumbling as she miss judged the height of an uplifted slab of asphalt. Catching her balance, Sam kept running. But though she was fast, the head of the larger monster was nearing Alex.

"I told you not to look, again." Grumbling continued, but quietly to not distract her.

"Why is she just sitting there?" Had Sam ever run this fast in her life? Maybe. She didn't know. "Get up!" She shouted at Alex. "Get up and run, Alex. RUN!"

But Alex didn't run. She stayed there on the ground in the half-stupefied trance of horror as a behemoth of corrupted magic bore down on her. It's maw gaping. Huge teeth dripping the lubricating oil that had kept the warehouse's machinery working. A body hung from a shattered hole in the carapace. Small streams of blood flowed from various cracks.

"Alex. Alex. Run." Still, she hadn't moved. Her eyes were transfixed on the body hanging out of the mouth. With a safety helmet on. A factory worker. Shit. There had been people working in there.

"It's no good, Sam." Far too calmly, Gleipnir informed her. "I suspect that monster has some kind of paralysis or trance effect on its prey. I can feel the magic emanating towards us but I'm keeping it at bay."

"Well, fuck!" Pouring on the speed, Sam ripped her wand out of its holster and pointed it at Alex.

"PRAESIDUM!" The spell tore out of her mouth at her top power level, scorching her lips as it went. A spherical invisible shield sprang to life around Alex with seconds to spare. The invisible shield flared as jagged steel girder teeth impacted on them. Two snapped.

Hearting hammering, Sam plunged through the shield and yanked Alex to her feet. Now the terrified agent shrieked. Screaming loudly in Sam's face before realizing that it was someone there to help her. Without slowing her rush, Sam dragged the hapless Alex along behind her.

"Come on." Gleipnir wrapped his tail around Alex to shield her from the mesmerizing effects of the monster as they fled.

Chapter 41

Alex wasn't doing well. Her legs were barely moving, and it was slowing Sam down. This was a problem because Gleipnir could *see* the glee come over the warehouse monster's face as it realized that and changed its ponderous trajectory to hunt them. This was not good.

"Carry her." He shouted at his warlock. For her part, Sam rolled her eyes so hard she could have sprained them.

"With what superhuman strength genius?" Always feisty, Sam's snap took Gleipnir by surprise.

"Your patrons. Duh." If he had a genuine face, it would have sneered at her incredulously. As it was, his voice dripped with disdain. "Use. A. Spell." Sam gave a single sharp bark of laughter because she couldn't afford more while she was exerting herself so strenuously.

"Which one. I don't know a strength spell." For a second, Gleipnir was stunned silent.

"Of course, you do." He argued, because how could she not?

"No." It came out as a huff between gasping inhalations. "I don't."

"Yes. You do!" The pact item insisted. "Fortification."

"That just makes… me resistant to things… that could harm me… it doesn't… make me able to… preform… feats… of… strength." Sam was coming to a gradual stop and took a second to catch her breath. Glancing over her shoulder, she saw that the monster was far enough away for a break, but not far enough to be safe.

"Well, shit." It wasn't eloquent, but it was a succinct evaluation of their situation. Her pact item paused for a moment, then wiggled the end of his ribbon tail in his version of a shrug, "Eh. Then leave her. No one will know."

"Gleip!" Eyes widening, Sam gave a chuckle. She could tell from his tone of voice that he didn't mean it. Things weren't that dire yet. But Sam also knew that he'd knock Sam unconscious and drag her to safety while leaving Alex behind in a second if he thought that's what was necessary to keep her safe.

Twisting her body to get a better look at the monster as it closed on them, she sighed, lowered her shoulders and lifted her wand again.

"Vefa ok sauma. Handleggr. Grund." Weave and sew. Arms. Earth. Two disturbingly human-looking hands of soil erupted from the fractured and uneven asphalt. The hands were attached to arms of earth. And the hands secured themselves around the monster's rubble and twisted metal legs.

A brief struggle showered the trio with rubble and dirt. But the improvised prison held, and Sam took the opportunity to hurry Alex to their car. Shoving the shivering and shuddering junior agent into her seat, Sam began fumbling with her seatbelt only for Gleipnir to interrupt her.

"Forget that." He hissed, as the monster continued struggling against the restraints on its legs. "I'll secure her." To show he meant it, Gleipnir floated into his spot behind and between the two front seats, but instead of letting the length of his flexible ribbon tail drape beneath him, he looped it over and around Alex, securing her in place. "I got you, kid." He patted her face as her frenetic breathing finally started calming.

Sam had already hurried around to the other side of the car and after securing herself, started up the vehicle. Slamming it into drive, she accelerated. Though she'd been careful on the drive in, Sam did not take the time to carefully navigate her way through the large, uplifted chunks of asphalt, cracks in the road, or the overturned vehicles that littered the sides of the street.

Instead, she took the turns as fast as she could, dodging around obstacles recklessly. The communication scroll on the dash showed the last instructions from Frank. She gave it a tap so it would reroll and display messages from where she had last checked it when she parked.

"Gleip, could you read that for me while I drive?"

"Indubiously."

"Indubitably. Gleip." Alex corrected as she started becoming a bit more coherent and her shivering subsided. Sam chuckled with relief as she rounded a sharp turn.

"If you're fighting with Gleip then you must be okay." There was grunt from Alex and a glowering growl from Gleipnir, then silence. "Could you read the messaged for me?" She gently reminded Gleipnir as the silence droned on.

"Ah. Yes." He made a throat clearing sound, the one that always annoyed most people because they assumed that he didn't have a throat and began narrating. "Frank says, 'Sam, Alex, or Gleipnir, if you're still alive, we've withdrawn to the secondary perimeter.' I think," Gleipnir added helpfully, "That he means they ran away to where the destruction of the road stops so it's easier to flee like the cowards they are if we aren't able to take care of that thing on our own."

"Ahahahaahaha!" Borderline hysterical laughter came from Alex as she listened to Gleipnir. The pact item turned the blank metal of his 'head' to 'look' at her. Which was unnerving because he had no face and no expression. Sam just raised an eyebrow and smirked. What? That was funny."

"You think I'm joking?" Voice a little higher with indignation, Gleipnir confronted the woman.

"Well, of course." She nodded amiably. "No one could possibly expect the two of you to handle something that size on your own." Now Sam chuckled, covering her mouth with her hand for a moment, then quickly putting it back on the steering wheel to correct course around another hole in the road.

"Oops. My bad." She made a show of focusing on the road and straightening in her seat. "You gonna tell her Gleip?" The befuddled Alex looked between the warlock and pact item pair with amused suspicion. They were putting her on, pulling one over on her. It was just another one of their jokes. Gleipnir turned to his warlock.

"I will tell her." He spoke with all the superiority he could muster then swiveled back to Alex. "I…" he paused for dramatic effect while drawing himself up his ribbon tail lengthening with additional coils around him, "am Gleipnir."

That was it.

That was all he said.

Glancing at her partner, Alex could see that Sam was sucking on her lips to prevent herself from laughing. Whether at her partner or at her pact item,

Alex wasn't sure. But even though she was blocking the sun with one hand and squinting through the sunlight, Sam's face was fighting a smile.

So, Alex focused on the proud and posturing Gleipnir.

"And…?" she prompted. "I knew that."

"What? But…" The haughty set of his ribbon and the jaunty angle of his body shifted down slightly. "Don't you know what that means?"

"That you are a sentient magical pact item from some famous powerful magic being." She paused thoughtfully before adding, "Oh yeah, and you're old as dirt." Sam laughed. But it was a short terse laugh. Despite the levity they were trying to bring to the situation, Alex couldn't help but notice that Sam was checking the rearview mirror regularly.

She took a look herself and regretted seeing the moving form of the thing that had almost eaten her struggling to escape the bindings that Sam had placed on it. Maybe they could handle it themselves? No. Maybe? No…?

"I'm Gleipnir." He corrected her gently. Alex refocused her attention on him. Still the words didn't mean anything to her other than his name. So what? He was Gleipnir. How was that name significant?

She searched her mind, and she could have sworn that the needle-sword thing was gazing at her expectantly, searching her face even though it had no eyes to see with. Gleipnir. Norse mythology. Fenrir. Ragnarök. That was back in 2012. Scary shit. Gleipnir was what they called the thing that they tied up Fenrir with.

"You're named after the thing that used to hold Fenrir before Ragnarök." Alex guessed. If anything, the sentient pact item seemed to become more disappointed with her.

"I *am* Gleipnir." He told her firmly but softly. "I was created specifically to hold that poor child, Fenrir, restrained and imprisoned for hundreds of years before my conscience finally won out and I released him. But the point is, *that* monster," he nodded behind them, "…it's just a manifested being. Powered by the arcanes it's leeching off the dead creature within it. It's small, compared to Fenrir."

"Oh." Finally understanding why Gleipnir had the kind of cocky swagger he did in every aspect of his personality, Alex's eyes and mouth had formed round 'ohs' of understanding long before the word had escaped on a breathy sigh.

"Yeah." Sam grimaced, getting their attention. "We've found the calvary." It wasn't said with sarcasm, but it did take on another meaning now that Alex understood that all those mages barricading the street with their vehicles and flashing lights weren't super necessary or doing anything particularly helpful. "This is your stop, new kid. Hop on out."

Archangel Michael Vs the Fates (Part 3)

Back in the bad old days, when gods had a disagreement, they fought. The most powerful won and the Earth, along with all the little mortals on it, suffered. At some point, the gods realized that this was a Bad Thing.

One might wonder why it was a Bad Thing for Gods if mortals suffered. Well, because when they suffered unduly, they stopped praying. They stopped believing. They stopped worshipping. And the Gods, started losing their powers.

Even that hadn't been enough of a reason for them to stop using the mortal plane as their personal PvP arena. But eventually, after thousands of years, they had got it through their heads. Arbitration was a relatively new thing.

It had come about after Ragnarök, in the year 2012 by human reckoning, when the recently freed Loki and his remaining living children had approached the other Gods and demanded justice against the rest of the Norse pantheon and safety from further reprisals. The whole situation had been bad, because well, everyone was culpable. Any god or goddess who was aware of what had happened over in the Norse pantheon could have stepped up and said or done something.

They knew Loki and his children had been falsely imprisoned because of a prophecy. Which literally *everyone* also knew could not be taken literally. Most of prophecies were self-fulfilling anyways. Which meant, the Norse Gods had literally deliberately created the circumstances which led to Ragnarök. And while every god, goddess, or spirit of justice was aware of the injustice Loki and his offspring had suffered, no one felt that they were impartial or free enough of guilt to come up with the appropriate solution and punishment.

The gods and goddesses who did think they were fit to judge, the rest of the gods and goddesses agreed were not at all fit to judge and just as guilty as the rest of them for letting the travesty happen. It was at this point that Loki turned to mortal law for inspiration. There were hundreds of years of history and social development for him to catch up on and surely, *surely,* there was something that could help him in his cause.

That was how he learned of lawyers.

Attorneys.

Restraining orders.

Yes.

But before a divine court could be convened to pass judgment or grant a restraining order, they first needed to agree on a system of judicial process for the pantheons. Laws needed to be written and decided upon amongst all of the pantheons and all the gods, goddesses, and demigods that took their power from the existence of mortals. A system of determining when someone had really broken a law. How severe the punishment should be. Who got to decide? A judge? A jury?

And were they really all *peers*?

Because some gods and some pantheons had a lot of power. While others were barely above the level of a very gifted magical hero on Earth. Immortality and the ability to gain strength from worship being the deciding factor of whether they were divine or not at that point.

Every pantheon had their own morality. Every divine being had their own laws they felt should be adhered to above all overs. There were exceptions, special cases, and factions began forming. Like players on an elimination reality television series, agreements to support one law in favor of supporting another were the final straw.

Schisms started. Little cracks in the unified decision that they had to *do something.* They had to have some kind of order in place to prevent what happened to Loki and his children from ever being perpetrated again. Spreading fine tendrils of discord throughout all the pantheons as like-minded divine beings rallied together to push their influence on the new laws being created.

If an accord couldn't be reached soon, something was sure to happen. A war to rival all prior wars because it would have shattered pantheons. Since they had already all sided together, the deities that embodied truth, honesty, and justice called for an outside advisor.

Because they had come to the simple realization that before the gods could do anything purposeful, the pantheons really needed a treaty that spelled out what was allowed and how they would interact.

Who better to advise them than an attorney?

Surprisingly, the other divine beings agreed to the suggestion. No one really wanted the kind of fight that had been brewing. Except for maybe the war gods, who had decided to band together, eliminate all other divine beings, then have a good old fashioned battle royal until there was only one god left standing. Oh. And the gods of destruction who really hadn't had as much fun as they'd prefer since the last big argument between the pantheons. Or any deities that might get a chance to rise up in stature of another divine being feeding off the same mortal concept and prayers were to die…

Okay. Almost every god was hopping for a tussle.

That's not the point.

The point was this entire situation had come about because the Norse pantheon had done bad by Loki and his children. And no one had stopped them nor held them accountable. As much as every stuck up, egotistical, big-headed divine being thought that they would come out on top in a battle, it was clear that if enough gods ganged up against one by themselves, they would lose.

Everyone knew that if something wasn't done to prevent it, they could be next.

Which is how they agreed that they needed guidance. Unbiased guidance. That, of course, meant it had to be a mortal because no divine being could be entirely unbiased whether for their pantheon or against it. Loki was decidedly *against* his own pantheon. A mortal was the only choice.

The mortal could not have any religious affiliation with nor worship any specific pantheon. They had to believe in justice, truth, and honor as something to live by. An incorruptible mortal who could not be swayed by intimidation or greed. A mortal who would be fair and impartial but could understand the unique demands and challenges divine beings faced.

After paring down the list of attorneys with all of their requirements, there were still, surprisingly, several thousand to choose from. How did the gods find their one chosen mortal ambassador? Not by comparing to see who was most just, or most impartial. They were all equally up to the task. Probably.

No.

They picked their attorney by what his name was. How it sounded. What it meant. And how much that person embodied the meaning of their name.

Odin, Zeus, and the gods that represented war and conflict thought it should sound tough, because... of course, they did. The intellectual deities thought the name should reflect how smart their attorney was. Sophistication and elegance were the votes of the representatives for love.

A sneaky, quiet voice from the Earth mothers reminded the pantheons that the name Nicholas was one of the names that represented 'victory'.

Because victory was what they all wanted for themselves, but disguised as just and fair, nearly everyone agreed that the first name of their attorney would be 'Nicholas'. What should his last name be though? Of all the Nicholas' who were also attorneys on Earth, which one would be best? Smith, whose name meant that someone in his family had been a smith at some point? That Ikeda person whose family is named after a rice paddy by a pond, or maybe a rice paddy pond? What about Kumari? That meant princess or royalty with riches.

Victory of riches?

Nah!

Everstone. Unchanging, unyielding strength of stone.

That seemed like a winner when paired with victory. And all the pantheons agreed, after so much debate and reviewing hundreds of names, that this was the right choice.

Nicholas Everstone.

What they never bothered to think about is that the full meaning of Nicholas wasn't just victory. Yes. It represented victory. But not just any victory. Not for just anyone. The full meaning of their chosen attorney's name?

Victory of the people. Unchanging, unyielding stone.

As a coherent sentence?

Eternal victory of mortals.

The pantheons had chosen an attorney who would always put mortal concerns and safety first.

Chapter 42

1:00 PM September 13th, 2026

Street that the New York Preparatory Academy is on.

Jones was catching his breath after he and Kyle had cut a swath through a literal horde of monsters. Big monsters, too. Made from fucking vehicles. Like cars and SUV's and shit.

And it had been easy. Really easy. Way too easy.

Why had that been so easy?

Sure, it was class one and class two monsters, but that didn't explain how easily they'd massacred monsters made of actual living metal. But behind them, all the manifestations were dead. Their carcasses already losing their false matter to arcane sublimation as it evaporated away. They stank, the organic components rotting faster with the high ambient magic of the area.

He'd never seen someone wielding magic like the apprentice warlock of the archivist just had. Not even the kid's famous mother could bend magic to her very will like that. Was it even legal for a non-enlisted mage to wield magic like that?

Nausea roiled in Jones' guts as he realized that he may now have a new phobia of the stereotypical academic librarian looking kind of guys. The reason behind that being the fact that Kyle was the least impressive looking person one might ever meet. He was just average in every aspect of his looks. From his height to his hair, to his personality, to his general attractiveness, even his intellect and normal magical ability was exceedingly average. How had this unstoppable mad man switched places with the affable, cautious, young nerd who worked in a museum?

Taking a quick sip of water from a canteen, Jones wondered, yet again, if the new rumors were true about Kyle. Because as he surreptitiously watched his charge from the corner of his eyes, Kyle looked like maybe…just maybe…he *knew* what he was doing. Cold flinty hardness had overtaken his gaze, replacing the spark of friendly humor. It drew attention to the keen intellect that must have always been hiding there.

Scanning the street for more immediate threats, Kyle stood guard as Jones rested. Finally ready to proceed again, Jones replaced the cap on his canteen and stored it on the bottom of the bandolier it had come on. An odd place for a canteen, but it was museum issue gear. Only once Jones had taken over watching for threats did Kyle take the time to relax and have a drink himself. It was fast. Efficient.

Kyle wasn't wasting time.

With a silent nod to each other, the pair left the shade and shelter of the building they'd stopped in. Returning to the center of the street, the pair began walking at a quick pace toward the school. Most of the remaining monsters were there and they were not happy. Luckily, those monsters had yet to notice Kyle the two men coming up the street behind them.

At first, Jones had been puzzled by the lack of response from the larger horde as he and Kyle were cutting, eviscerating, and alchemy shotgun shelling their way loudly, *very loudly*, through the monsters gathered near the blockade. But as the pair of men drew closer to their goal, the specialist realized that the monsters were fixated on the school and a wall of ice that they were frantically trying to dig their way through.

To the tasty morsels of people within the ice encased building.

Because it was ice encased. What seemed like a vertical wall of ice, was met at the roofline by a flattish dome that encompassed the entire building. Monsters of various sizes – most in the sedan to sport utility vehicle range – surrounded the abstract bubble of ice.

"I see Anna's been holding the line." It was the first thing Kyle had said, growled really, since they'd started fighting. Monster fluids had stuck his pants to his legs up to the knee and he kept trying to shake the clinging fabric away from his skin. Guts and shattered windshield bits splattered his chest up the side of his neck where a blood vessel throbbed angrily. This was the first time that Kyle had a bit of a facial tick when he clenched his teeth that way. "Those fucking bastards couldn't even evacuate all the kids."

"She did that on her own?" Jones was… yeah… that was impressive. A kid doing that kind of magic? That was pretty damned good.

"Yeah." Kyle wiped his sweaty face on his shoulder then spat as he got monster muck smeared across his lips. "Bah.'

"The entire building?" It was not long after midday and the sun was angling down between he taller buildings around them, so Jones was shading his eyes with one hand to see better.

"Probably." The apprentice warlock sucked his teeth a bit before spitting again as he continued forward determinedly. His head swiveled from side to side looking for threats from the damaged lower floors of the buildings. Within the buildings, the higher floors were quiet.

"How do you know it's all her?" Yes. He knew he should have kept his mouth shut. But the question had popped out unbidden. Also, if they drew a monster out of a building, it was one less monster the survivors hiding inside wouldn't have to deal with.

There were survivors. There had to be. Evidence of magical battles and residents or employees fleeing were everywhere. Bridges of vines from someone who worked plant magic were retracting slowly from a third story window. A flare of light went off two blocks ahead of them where the next concentration of monsters started.

"I recognize my sister's magic. There's –" Here Kyle paused as if he wasn't sure how to describe what he meant so the warlock's next works surprised Jones immensely, "…I'm not sure if I should tell you if you don't already know. But magic, has a… flavor. Which most people know. But there's a nuance to different sources. Not just fire or ice, but if you're familiar with a person's magic, you can tell when a spell or magic comes from them. That's Anna's ice. I can taste it in the air."

"Oh." When he put it that way, it made sense to Jones. "Like the way the weather changes before snow? Or old people with old injuries who can feel the rain coming?"

"Something like that." A rueful smile played at Kyle's lips as he chuckled darkly. But the focus of his gaze never left the dome of ice they were approaching, nor the mass of monsters spread across the no longer pristine green lawn of the school. Their lunging, lumping gaits had torn chunks out of the turf

156

and huge gashes of bare soil marred the landscape. He slowed as they neared the next corner, holding up a hand to indicate he wanted to stop.

Jones heard it too. More clumping and lumping of partially transformed monster manifestations hunting awkwardly on their rubber paws. A small herd that seemed to have made it through whatever barricade that should have been here as they sounded too far away to just be harassing the local swat. The were returning though. The crunching of pavement and the squealing of metal on metal as their organic monster parts integrated with their non-organic immovable parts.

In front and among there were dozens and dozens of smaller, extremely vicious little monsters. They were boxy, kind of like whatever they had been manifested out of had been rectangular blocks with pointed tops. Leaking a white fluid from their whitish bodies as they went, these smaller monsters were agile, leaping from the ground to ride other monsters, or darting into buildings with their nimble little legs gnashing wide mouths that almost split them vertically.

"What in the hell are those? Is that milk? Are those milk cartons? And milk jugs?" Following the little swarm, Jones realized that the building they had been going into and coming out from was a grocery store. "Milk jug monsters. Well, I never."

Kyle's shoulders slumped like a kid who'd just been told he had to do his homework before he could go out and play.

"Ugh! We don't have time for this. Jones. Can you buy me ten seconds? I need to do something stupid."

Chapter 43

"Yes, sir." Jones was already agreeing before his brain registered the 'stupid' part of that request. He thought that what they were doing, waging a two-man campaign against monsters that way outclassed them was stupid. So, he was having trouble imagining what could possibly make their already deranged lack of a plan even stupider.

But whatever.

Jones reloaded his weapon with more alchemical ammunition and started taking even, measured, unhurried shots at the fast evil little milk jug buggers that were hurrying toward them. Peripherally, he was aware of Kyle doing things. His book was still balanced on one hand and Kyle held another over it before giving a command.

"Archive query." The book glowed and its open pages seemed to lift slightly as if in anticipation of his next request. "Retrieve spell." The pages lifted higher and began thrumming. "Battle Armor – Saint of Warriors, Armor of God's General. Replicate." The pages flipped frantically through the book until opening on what Jones could only assume was the page that the spell was referenced on.

Wait a second? Wasn't that the name of a certain famous warlock's armor? That was a spell granted to another warlock by their patron. You couldn't just learn a patron granted spell, could you? Maybe that's why Kyle thought it was a stupid idea. He was clearly hesitating, unsure whether or not he should continue with the spell. Jones was about to speak up when –

"Oh. Shit!" One of the little meat jugs, that's what he was calling them because the milk jug manifestations had already turned almost completely organic having been mostly organic to begin with, had made it close enough to bite him on the knee. "Mother fucker." A swift kick had it exploding into a pink spray of…sludgy meat. He tried once again.

"Kyle, I don't –" The young warlock had steeled his nerves in that moment that Jones was distracted, and his words didn't come fast enough.

"Configure, Replicate, Activate!" They'd been said with such finality, as if Kyle had been expecting something to go horribly wrong. And for a few moments, nothing happened. With a shrug, Jones returned his full attention to the cartons of meat and the larger monsters that were shepherding them. Because those were some big MFers.

However, behind Jones and to the side, Kyle's book flared brightly, and a rising sound of trumpets began. Brilliant golden light shone from Kyle's location and Jones chanced a glace over at the young man. Sure enough, there in the center of the light, armor was forming over the grinning warlock.

Where Camina Wattkins' armor was white and gold, this armor was different. Anywhere that Camina's armor was white, this shone a gleaming midnight black with metallic blue accents where the original had gold. While it had the same general outline as the armor famously worn by Camina and her patron the Archangel Michael, this armor was decidedly in Kyle's style.

"Fuck yeah!" Kyle screamed and pumped a fist before it was jerked out by an invisible force and a gauntlet formed over it. "It worked. It worked. Ahhhh…" The triumphant shout ended with a gurgled horrified scream.

Whirling, Jones was faced with Kyle, swarmed by more meat jugs that had somehow snuck the fuck around his guard through the corner building they were beside. A stream of the little fuckers was flooding out of a door behind them and had attacked Kyle from behind as his transformation was finishing.

A gauntleted hand reached up and tore the creatures off Kyle's face and head before a helmet flashed into place. The floating segments of his wings started flexing and shaking off the mini monsters clambering on them before they became charged with electricity. Sparks traveled between the wing segments as they started floating away from the suit in a very un-wing-like fashion. Then they became an electrified blender of death.

There were squeals, popping explosions like water balloons impacting on something, and a fine pink mist with larger white chunks floated away from Kyle as the whirring sound died. His wings returned to their normal position, flexing in the way a bird's might when they were anxious. Jones stared dumbfounded.

"Well alright then." Then he grinned and chuckled a little because Kyle had forgotten to close the faceplate of his helmet first. Absolute disgust was written all over the warlock's face as he tried to spit out the pink mist of monster parts which had covered his entire head. The armor, of course, was somehow spotless. Which was even funnier.

"Note to self." Kyle called out to Jones. "Close the faceplate first. Yeah." After a quick second of thought, he added with a concerned voice, "Where'd my Codex go?" He looked over the ground near his feet, turning in a circle as he went. "Locate Codex." Faint chiming started in response to Kyle's call.

The chiming was coming from the suit and after a few befuddled seconds of patting himself down, he located the book in a pocket-slash-drawer on the exterior of the suit in the general area where his concealed carry magic book holster had been. Pressing on the location with one of his gauntleted hands caused the compartment to open.

"Noice!" He exclaimed. Breathing a visible sigh of relief, Kyle closed the compartment again with a grin. "Oh. Behind you, Jones." Jones spun on his heel at the warning just in time to dodge the surprisingly quiet larger monster that had been sneaking up on him along with several others.

'Crap!" Jumping out of the way, he stabbed a monster through the side with the bayonet on the end of his rifle. Screams came from the creature as flames erupted from the weapon plunged into it. A quick pull of the trigger blew Jones backward off the beast as the alchemical charges in the rounds sent him flying backward into a brick wall.

"Jones, I got this." Kyle called out then then took off flying at the group of larger monsters. His wand flared up with a larger electric blade than before and he began dodging and weaving among the larger manifestation, slashing and stabbing at them as he went. Shrieks and screams gurgling into silence drew the attention of observers.

Chapter 44

Kyle started moving with more force than necessary. His armored boots crunched into the pavement where he kicked off leaving twin overlapping miniature craters in the asphalt. That was the least of his worries. Jones made a decent showing of it popping little milk cartons of goo while the nerdy museum kid he was supposed to be protecting went on a haphazard manic killing spree of destruction.

That first shove off from his powered armor had sent Kyle careening past his intended target, an SUV sized class two manifestation that was quickly growing in size and organic content making it well on its way to becoming class three. Arms windmilling wildly, the warlock of the archivist caught his balance and leveled the lightning bolt he was using as a sword.

He charged at the creature on foot, each heavy boot clanging metallically. After a brief run up to speed, Kyle tried using his flight again. Unable to fully control his movements, the mech-suited figure zipped past his target again, but with more control this time. It was only his ability to control the length and force of his lightning sword that allowed him to slash the monster nearly in half as he skidded past.

"All right!" Pumping a fist in exaltation, Kyle adapted to his lack of control over flying and instead used a combination of hovering and short powerful sprints to dash from one large manifestation to another. Jones followed Kyle as they cut a swath of gore up the street. Kyle was leading in his nigh indestructible armor. Meanwhile Jones brought up the rear with a wand in one hand and his enchanted bayonet in the other, a semi-automatic rifle that shot alchemy bullets, and a bandolier full of the best damned magical charges a mage could ever hope for.

He was pretty sure that he was hearing muted cheering drifting down from the windows of the buildings above. It was difficult to be certain over the loud snarling attacks and pained roars of monsters. But in the occasional lulls where the melee was less loud, it did seem like maybe, maybe the occasional screams of pain and horror from inside the buildings lining that street were more like cries of joy. At least, that's what he was telling his conscious.

The school had to come first.

It wasn't shielded like it should have been and anything inside the building could turn at any moment. Everyone else in proper buildings could wait. They had to wait. The kids came first.

No.

Anna came first.

Kyle was only here for Anna.

And Jones was only here for Kyle.

Those were his orders.

Then he looked up, up to the sounds that he couldn't block out of his head. And there he saw them, people. Leaning over the balconies of apartments screaming encouragement, or pressed against the windows of offices, restaurants, or shops and waving wildly. One idiot decided that they'd cleared enough monsters from their part of the street and actually dropped down from a second-floor fire escape while other young men of about the same teenage shouted at him. Encouragement? Admonishments? Jones couldn't tell.

Said idiot stumbled as he landed, twisting his ankle. Jones had to fire a shot over the kid's head as one of those little milk jug bastards tried to eat said head. The boy lost the ball cap he'd been wearing revealing a head full of sandy blonde curls. He stood, favoring the twisted ankle. Yep, it was definitely hurt. Not enough to keep him from trotting around carcasses and over slippery guts to a point in the street with a good view.

That little shithead snapped selfies with Kyle and Jones killing things in the background. Then he took a couple more actions shots of the pair as Jones shook his head in disgust before the teen limped hurriedly back into the building from which he'd come. His friends were screaming kudos about how big his balls were and what a boss he was. Jones started to shake his head –

Well, shit. He thought to himself. *I wouldn't have the cajónes to come out on this street with nothing but a smart phone.* After a few seconds of continued mop-up of monsters, he went back around to his original thought on the subject, which was… *Of course, I'm not an idiot.*

Jones hadn't been watching how close they were to the school. After a particularly vicious one-on-one with a manifest that had to have once been a limousine, he found that he'd run out of adversaries and finally glanced further around. That had been sloppy. He needed to pay more attention. Especially to Kyle, who was the whole reason he was here.

Kyle was standing still. Helmet visor open, head tilted back, he gazed up at a monster that was nearly three stories tall. Three stories and focused entirely on the dome of ice it was trying to gnaw its way through. It alternated between trying to chew its way through the ice and beating on it with earth shaking brutality. After a few attacks it would get winded and as it caught its breath, the monster's bright headlight gaze focused on something directly beneath it in the ice dome.

Jones watched his charge's face harden with understanding. Jaw tight, fists clenched, teeth grinding with rage, Kyle's eyes followed where the monster was looking. The Magicorps soldier didn't have to look to know, but he did anyways, found Kyle's sister facing the beast defiantly. Though the dome of ice had seemed as if it was mostly opaque from a distance, it appeared mostly transparent up close. They could see a white-haired teen in her private school uniform. Brown eyes wide with terror and leaking tears never wavered as she fed every ounce of magic she could to reinforce the shield of ice between her and the monster.

Dozens of students huddled around her as behind them, inside the protective shield, the teachers and security fought smaller monsters encroaching on their rear. Monsters that must have gotten into the building before she put the shield up. Or more likely, they had manifested inside the building afterward.

"Look at her." Jones breathed wondrously. Because it was a wonder to see magic so pure and powerful without the taint of a patron or the confines of a spell. "That's amazing. She's holding off a class… what do you think that is?" Jones turned to Kyle briefly before looking back and forth to the power struggle between the fixated monster and the… "I want to say it's a class three but it's gotta be at least a class four manifestation." It was the kind of power that every mage longed for.

"I'm coming, Snow Cone." Kyle's words were growled low, almost breathy, and his tone of voice snapped Jones' attention back to his ward.

The click of Kyle's visor closing in preparation for battle was deafening to Jones. Kyle might as well have been bellowing a challenge to the twisted amalgamation of matter, magic, and life before them. Because that's what it meant. Play time was over. It was time to go to war.

Chapter 45

The now clearly class four monster had lost all resemblance to whatever it had manifested from. Nearly completely organic, only the tough metallic segmented hide hinted as to its possible vehicular origins. The thing resembled a giant millipede now. Four clusters of too many legs to count lined its body. The eyes were bright glowing orbs that flashed off and on in time with its attacks on the ice shield, as if it was blinking to protect its vision of the shards that it sheared off the dome.

The first two clusters of legs lifted up every time the millipede, as big around as a bus, reared up. Then the dozens of limbs came down on the cracking and weakening shield pummeling away as much of the ice as possible. Each blow was backed by the weight of its massive upper body. End to end, it could have stretched the entire three block gauntlet that Kyle and Jones had just fought their way through.

Somehow, Anna was holding off the mass of about a block and a half of a New York City Street. But she wasn't enough. And the monster could tell it was going to win that fight eventually if nothing changed. There was an evil gleam of delighted anticipation about it, as if it was already imagining the taste of those refugees.

Why it was so determined to breach the school's defenses when there were so many easier to reach people in the surrounding buildings, Jones didn't know. Before he could say anything to deter him, or even just confer about their plan of attack, Kyle took off. Once again, the force of his launch into flight cratered the ground around his boot prints.

This was no semi-controlled skimming of the street like his previous careful attempts at flight had been. No. This was a full-on flight. Like a missile, the armored warlock shot straight for a point in the center mass of the monster. Unerring and determined, he pulled his course up just barely at the last moment before impacting.

In a maneuver that he couldn't possibly have ever practiced before, Kyle flipped around and shoved the blazing arc of his lightning wand-sword into a junction of the overlapping steel plate segments on the monster's body. A high, multi-voiced scream came from the monster's head as it whipped towards the searing pain that an angry big brother was dishing out. It was fast.

Faster than Kyle had anticipated.

In a flash, and distressingly soon after the start of the battle, Kyle found himself caught between the crushing mandibles of the monster. Sizzling and popping, the monster's venom ate away at Kyle's protective shell everywhere it splattered on him as the enraged monster shook him like a dog shaking a toy it was having a particularly great time destroying.

"Ha, ha. This is not good." Kyle coughed, immediately regretting the loss of space in his deflating lungs. How to get out of this little pickle? How to get out of this? He didn't know. Being shaken was making it a bit hard to think. And Kyle was more of a reader than a fighter. An eater, really, if he was honest about it.

The monster finally stopped shaking Kyle. While the creature worried him in its jaws, Kyle had a moment to think. His eyes focused on Jones down below him. Not nearly as far down as Kyle had thought he was. The soldier hadn't cut and run like Kyle half expected him too.

Instead, he was charging. His yellow Magicorps beret a bright beacon of hope to those who saw it. Mainly Kyle. Sporadic bursts of precisely aimed alchemy ammunition were wreaking carnage on the millipede legs supporting the behemoth. But it wasn't enough. Not for as many legs as this creature had. Jones would run out of ammo long before this beast ran out of legs.

Still, he fired. Alternating between the semi-automatic and his wand, the soldier ran straight up onto a group of legs, tossed something under it, then dashed away hastily. A flash followed soon afterward and as Kyle's dazed eyes cleared, he saw that it had been one of the alchemy grenades he'd given to Jones.

If only there was a way to disable all those legs at once.

Also…

What was he doing?

Why was he just laying here limply, while Jones did all that fighting? Why was Jones fighting? He should have just left the dangerous big monster to Kyle. Jones was going to have all those other smaller monsters on him any minute now because his attacks on the class four monster that Kyle had run off halfcocked to fight without any kind of plan, had drawn a lot of attention to the soldier.

Oh. Kyle shook his head and felt it pounding angrily. His vision swam and he almost blacked out. That was not good.

"Okay. Don't do that." He admonished himself, feeling a trickle of something running down his face to dribble against his lips. Licking them, he tasted blood.

He needed to get free, but even in the armor, he wasn't strong enough to just force his way out of this predicament. When he struggled, the monster just bit down harder. Which he definitely didn't want it to do because it sent a stabbing pain into the right side of his chest and made breathing infinitely less pleasant.

"Fine," he grouched in his semi-delirious state. "We'll do it the slow way." Gradually Kyle slipped one of his arms out of the monster's tight grip. It was tricky. The thing didn't want to let him go. But it didn't seem particularly invested in trying to open up its chew toy just yet. It was just slowly letting its venom-acid-saliva burn its way through Kyle's armor as it gnawed Kyle between its mandibles.

Every time the mandibles would loosen, Kyle moved his arm a little more. He was only able to move the one arm, the other being too firmly stuck in place. That was fine. He could do this. The lightning sword he'd been using had gone out. Which was good, otherwise he might have electrocuted himself.

While he carefully wiggled his way to freedom, Kyle started calling the ambient magic to himself again. He'd been careless, shoving himself into this fight the way he had. This was the Armor of God's General… with fucking tornado razor wings that he was pretty sure the original didn't have. And he'd wasted that by letting his fear for his sister and his anger at this creature that was after her get the better of him.

So, he gathered magic. More than enough magic. So much magic it might make a person sick if they tried to hold it all for a working. But that wasn't what Kyle was doing. He was channeling every subatomic particle of it into his wand in preparation of an instant release spell. Finally, after a few more chews, the warlock was able to point his wand into the soft organic interior of the monster's gullet. Triumphantly, he gave a hoarse whisper to trigger the spell he knew would do the trick.

"Fireball." It was quite possibly the largest fireball that Kyle had ever seen. Certainly, it was the largest he'd ever cast. Added to the fact that the monster's acid-venom was flammable, it gave a most spectacular sight for those watching. An enormous gout of fire plumed out of the monster's face, and Kyle in his armor along with it.

He shot in an uncontrolled arc, wobbling in the air for several meters before he'd regained control of his attitude and altitude. Swinging himself around as fast as he dared as he was still at risk of blacking out if he moved too quickly, Kyle prepared the next stage of his assault. Because, the Warlock of the Archivist had a plan now.

The legs were the problem. The legs had always been the problem. Get rid of the legs and what could that thing do? It couldn't run; it couldn't fight. It would only be able to thrash wildly and try its damnedest to spit on its attackers. And Kyle was pretty sure that it couldn't spit very far.

"Archive Query." He commanded, knowing that his pact item was safely with him and would heed his call. "Retrieve spell. Snare of Arachne. Activate." Lines of magical light poured from Kyle as he fed the spell with more ambient magic. The lines flowed together into an intricate web, ensnaring and tangling the dozens of monster legs flailing against it.

Soon the gigantic monster was fully cocooned and immobilized by layers of magically entwined cords. Cords that Kyle held the ends to in one large mechanically armored fist. So restrained, Kyle found the creature a bit pitiful. It whimpered evil wheezing hisses at him with sad headlight eyes. Yeah. This had definitely been some kind of vehicle at some point.

He didn't want to kill it. It was a living thing. Kyle didn't even really like killing bugs. Though he might never think a millipede was cute ever again after this. However, he knew he couldn't leave it tied up for someone else to deal with. That wasn't how the spell worked.

It was now or never.

Below him, Jones was inundated with smaller, but still very large monster problems of his own. In the ice shield dome, Anna was running out of time. So, while Kyle wanted to give himself several minutes to come to terms with the reality of the fact that he was about to kill a living creature – even if it was just another monster, and even if he'd already murdered dozens of the things that day – he couldn't give himself time to think about it.

None of the other monsters had been restrained. They had a fair chance at a fight when he'd killed them even if his intelligence, magic, and equipment had made the match unfair. Could he kill a thing that was not currently a danger to him in cold blood? It looked up at him with what almost seemed like pleading in its eyes.

None of the other monsters he'd killed had anything that seemed like real sentience or life in them. They'd just been mindless things devouring life and magic. They hadn't really seemed to know what they were, or care about anything other than the moment they existed in. This one seemed to know. It knew it was about to die.

"I don't have time to feel sorry for you or think about the morality of what I'm doing. I'm sorry." He took a deep breath to steady himself. The finishing blow was not one that should be used lightly. Nor was it one that he could have used in any other circumstance. He adjusted the ties in his hands and fed more magic into them covering the face of the struggling creature.

Sensing the end was near, it struggled more, so Kyle directed the snare to tie itself to the ground and prevent too much movement. Sighing, he let his shoulders sag.

"Archive query. Retrieve spell. The Curse of those who Witnessed the Curse of Sodom and Gomorrah." The struggling stopped and the shrouded form of the millipede became less defined. Kyle dropped the magical ropes holding the Snare of Arachne, then he turned away. There was no reason to make sure, Kyle knew it was done.

Instead, he cleaned up the monsters harassing Jones, once again relying on his whirlwind bladed wings to blender up the manageable sized monsters surrounding the dome and providing Anna with a route to safety once she opened a spot in the shield.

Archangel Michael Vs the Fates (Part 4)

Nicholas ducked reflexively from the flash and bang of an exploding cell phone. That's what it had been, wasn't it? That green-haired chatter box's phone exploding as the arcanes surged like mad. Even if he hadn't been able to feel the change in the ambient magic levels like everyone else, all the electronics going out and the Prometheus Magic Detection Lights coming on were a dead giveaway.

Every building had emergency magic detection lights that came on in the case of high magic levels. Okay, not *every* building had them. And Prometheus wasn't the only brand that manufactured them. But they were on. And they were…

Purple?

They were purple.

"Sonofabitch." This *had* to be Zeus' fault. That asinine shag bag was consistently one hard on away from accidently destroying some civilization because he tried to fuck around on his wife. One of these days Hera was gonna give her husband the 'find out' instead of whatever poor nymph, dryad, or minor goddess – or god, Nicholas amended his internal monologue – that asshat was chasing. Zeus would stick it in anything pretty enough, regardless of its sex or gender…

…or species…

Eww…

Nicholas shuddered at the gross thought. All that had flashed through his mind in a matter of seconds after the room became bathed in the lurid purple glow known the world over as Prometheus Purple that any sane person dreaded. Everyone else was still coming to terms with the situation and realizing what kind of Ragnarök level shit must be going down for the AMD to be Prometheus Purple while Nicholas had already assessed their level of fuckedness. He was fairly certain it was somewhere between 'guess who's going to be a step mommy again' and 'I'm leaving Zeus and taking the mortals as my alimony'.

Which meant that any second now, there would be an insane posse of divine beings to Shanghai him to another bout of 'but is it really cheating if…insert narcissistic gaslighting abuse here…?' In other words, arbitration.

He cracked his neck in anticipation. Somehow, he was always caught off guard when they came for him. But not this time. This time, he was going to be ready and keep his composure, no matter how fucked up their attorney-napping of him was. So, the red-headed attorney looked around with eager anticipation for once.

Because, this, you know, everything going on around him, he could do something about. Getting divine intervention in whatever emergency those fuck heads had caused, that was something he could make happen with some court ordered community service and restitution for the victims. The biggest victims being the humans who had to deal with the fallout from the problems the Gods made.

"Okay everybody," Sherral called out over the murmuring voices that were quickly rising to hysterical. "The building is supposed to be magically insulated to Prometheus Blue, but as you can see," She gestured around the room which still had some bright sunlight shining through windows but was also filled with purple light. "…ambient magic is at Prometheus Purple. So, if you know someplace shielded nearby, then I recommend you go there."

"What if there's monster's outside?" The man who'd heckled Nicholas to ask Sherral out asked loudly. Loud seemed to be his default volume setting.

"I don't know if there's monsters outside yet." The barista was holding it together quite well so far, the attorney conceded to himself. Her two coworkers backing out of the kitchen behind her, mumbling fervently and wielding a pot and a long ladle respectively, weren't handling the situation nearly so well. They were so stoned their eyes were nearly drooping shut, and the mumbles that drifted towards Nicholas through the various voices were saying something about bad weed.

At that point, Nicholas stopped paying attention. A dinging from the bell on the café door drew his attention as he sipped gingerly at his still almost-too-hot Definitely Not Dairy latte. Several other customers turned as well. Some were startled by the sound and jerked around as if they feared monsters had decided to politely open the door instead of crashing through the glass windows of the building.

'Meet-cute', which was what Nicholas was dubbing the green-haired loud public phone conversationalist, jumped particularly high. Though, he supposed she was entitled to be extra upset seeing as how her cellphone had nearly exploded in her hand. It would have been a nasty wound if not for the quick actions of the elderly couple who had grabbed her phone.

They hadn't seemed concerned at all when the lights went out and a phone exploded. Just did their thing as if they were responding to a sudden Spring shower while on their afternoon walk. Nor were they concerned about the door as Sherral started talking to the newcomers.

"Hey there, new people. This building is only magically shielded to Prometheus Blue, so if you know of someplace nearby that is rated for Prometheus Purple, I recommend going there." Three people left. Five more came in through the open door and the barista repeated the process. It became a revolving refrain as those seeking shelter in the café realized that it wasn't there and decided to move on. Or decided that it was good enough and stayed.

Nicholas decided that here was good enough. Mostly because he couldn't remember where the nearest magically shielded building was. Most buildings were magically shielded. At least, residential buildings were supposed to be designed to prevent magic reaching Prometheus Purple levels indoors. Since he'd decided to stay, he moved into a corner to make room for others as they moved away from the glass window front of the restaurant.

There he stayed, sipping his latte for several minutes occasionally eyeing the high kitchen staff as they babbled about being too high while there were monsters about. The interesting elderly couple were also eyeing the incredibly not-sober duo. That old man had seriously high-grade magic tech in that prosthetic.

A terrible thought occurred to Nicholas at this point. It was taking an awful long time for the gods to come and get him. What if this wasn't some deity related incident that he could fix somehow? All this time he'd been assuming that the danger level wasn't going to actually be too bad because arbitration would happen, he'd rule that the gods fix their fuck up, and life would return to normal. What if that wasn't what was happening?

Then a loud sound from the kitchen drew everyone's attention.

"Hey, guys." Sherral glanced between the cooks out into the dining room and the closed door to the kitchen. "Who's in the kitchen? I thought it was just you two today?"

"Oh. That's just the toaster that we hallucinated coming to life." One of the men responded. "But it's fine, because we are just really high on a bad batch of weed that probably got laced with something, so it's just a hallucination." Oh, fuck. Nicholas and everyone else who'd moseyed on over towards the kitchen to be away from the storefront windows, scooted away from the kitchen door as quickly as possible.

Except for the elderly couple. They went toward the kitchen. Just as the wife was about to open the door, her husband stopped her. For one second, Nicholas thought that the old man was going to talk some sense to his wife. Instead, he did something entirely different.

"Let me get the door for you, my beautiful wife." He made a flourish with his remaining natural hand and bowed. His wife blushed and giggled. "After you."

"Thank you, darling. You're always so sweet to me." To the horror of all watching, her husband opened the door for his aged wife. No sudden attack came from the dark depths of the kitchen. A soft snick and the ring of metal sounded as the woman, who Nicholas now realized was probably a very skilled warlock, unsheathed a sword belted to her waist. Hand in hand, the couple disappeared into the kitchen.

Chapter 46

1:30 PM September 13th, 2026
Inside the New York Preparatory Academy Ice Bubble

Oh, the Gods! That wasn't Camina Wattkins. Camina's armor was white. And clearly female. Like, it left nothing to the imagination. Sara's mother always told her that it wasn't classy. Even if her own clothes were far more revealing than a mech battle suit.

It was the principle of the thing. You know? You didn't dress to kill in order to actually kill. You dressed to manipulate people and get what you wanted. So, no. Sara was one hundred percent sure that… that was most definitely a dude in that suit. He was sporting a whole different sort of curves.

"Do you know who that is, Anna?" Liam had asked. "He's wearing armor similar to your mom's." Anna squinted at her ice dome, smoothing it further with a wave of her hand to see more clearly through it.

"I… I…don't know." She finally answered. "It's not Uncle Michael." Sara gave a snooty shrug from where she stood eavesdropping and rolled her eyes. Calling an archangel 'uncle'? *Show off.* "Michael's armor is different."

Ugh. Liam Ecclestone, the guy who *claimed* she didn't even know, well he'd been hanging very close to her ever since they ran out of the darkened hallway together….

Sara clicked her tongue against the roof of her mouth making an annoyed tisking sound. Yeah right, Anna wasn't interested in Liam at all. The cheerleader's eyes rolled as she tucked a lock of hair behind one ear and smiled at her unknown hero while he mopped up the monsters outside. That white-haired frosty bitch could have Liam. Sara had just wanted him because he was the cutest and the richest guy in school.

But a guy who killed monsters in a giant mech suit? That was. Yeah. He'd taken out that monster so fast. Stupid Anna couldn't do that. Even if she did manage to create an ice shield.

Grinning, Sara giggled as she watched the mysterious hero working. Then she covered her mouth. The distracted girl didn't even notice her fellow cheerleader standing next to her giving her an astounded and disbelieving side-eye.

While Sara wasn't the only person cheering for the pair that was coming to rescue them, she was the only one who had made fan-girl giggles while still trapped between the wall of an ice dome and a group of monsters. It was fine. It was all good. Mystery hero was going to save them.

After the big monster was dead, and the smaller monsters outside had been killed or driven off, then the guy in the suit came up to the dome and opened his helmet. He was… so… cute. Not cute-cute, but normal cute. Sara did a little happy dance. He didn't look that much older than the teens huddled together either. Yeay.

This was nice. Maybe, maybe she'd get to talk to him? Thank him for saving her? Things were looking up if Anna would hurry up and let the armored guy in so he could finish off the monsters that the trapped warlocks and security guards inside were currently fighting behind the students.

Things were going well indeed. Until that freak Anna Wattkins let out a shout of delight as she got a good look at their savior on the other side of the, admittedly, easy to see through ice.

"Kyle?!" Sara's head jerked over at the pale-haired girl. Jumping for joy that Wattkins brat waved her arms to open a door in the ice. "He came. He's okay." Bouncing and beaming, the freak grabbed Liam's hands excitedly. "Yeay!"

Oh. Look at that. Poor Liam looked just as disappointed as Sara to see that Anna knew their rescuer. Which actually cheered Sara up a bit. Now he got to see how it felt. With a self-satisfied smile, the blonde smoothed her hair and straightened her uniform. Twirling a lock of smooth unfrazzled hair around one finger, she shrugged happily that everything was going to turn out okay.

And she probably wouldn't have to come to school again for a while.

Except for cheer practice. That couldn't be canceled. There were competitions to prep for.

"Who's Kyle?" Liam's question went unanswered as Anna dropped his hands and sprint-hopped happily to the armored man chanting.

"You're here. You came. You're okay. Hooray." Flinging herself into his arms, her voice almost broke on a sob, that she quickly stifled.

"Hey. When my sister calls, I'm going to show up." His brown hair glinted with sun bleached highlights in the bright sunlight coming through the opening in the glass. It matched the gold accents of his armor. Anna was still hugging him tightly and he gently pulled her arms off him.

"I gotta go help your teachers." He explained when she tried to tighten her grip. It was so… didn't she care what her classmates were going to think? She was being so emotional. Like…ugh. Nobody else knew if their families were okay and they weren't crying. Okay, well the boarding students knew. But… "I promise, I'll be right back."

He smiled, and Sara kind of sighed as she felt her heart flutter a little bit. He was such a good brother. Then he was off, a swirling whirlwind of blades and tightly controlled magical spells. While the freed-up school staff were organizing the students to follow the yellow-bereted Magicorps soldier who was covering the exit from the ice dome.

Some of the students had wanted to stay and watch the creatures that had terrorized them through the halls get demolished by the badass who was apparently Anna Wattkins' brother.

"Dude…why'd the papers claim he was a cook?" An eyebrow rose on Sara's face. *Interesting?*

"What do you mean?" She asked the no-longer-hot Liam as she fell into line, letting the teachers calling for an orderly evacuation as if they hadn't just been shitting themselves seconds ago corral her out the opening of the ice dome with her fellow student.

"That article about Anna's family this morning. It said that her brother Kyle was a cook." Gesturing at the clearly skilled spellcaster who was absolutely wrecking the remnants of the monster horde on the second-floor cafeteria. "Does that look like a cook to you?" Sara wasn't the only one who paused and turned as Kyle Wattkins bathed the shattered roofless room in a wash of magical light from one of his attacks.

"Maybe he's called The Cook because with all that firepower he's able to bring the heat," someone enthused before giving a cheering hoot. "WOOT! GO KYLE! BRING THE HEAT!" Then shaking his head with a grin, he turned and walked out into the open air and dis-a-fucking-peared.

"What the hell just happened?" Sara stopped dead when – *What was that kid's name again?* – dropped out of sight.

"It's fine." An almost bored sounding voice came from beside the door in the dome. Searching for the owner, Sara found an exhausted-looking Anna. For the first time ever, the other girl's enviously tan skin was pale enough that she almost seemed to match her hair. Not like legit pale, she was still tan. But she had a pallor to her. "I had to make a slide for us to get down so no one would get hurt. Ice, stairs, and warm sunny days don't mix well."

"Oh." Straightening and trying to hide her moment of sudden panic, Sara squared her shoulders. "That's fine then." She sat and immediately regretted the chilly wetness that soaked through her skirt as she tightened it around her knees. Taking a deep breath, she kicked off and started her slide to the grassy field below.

Chapter 47

12:30 PM September 13ᵗʰ, 2026
Manhattan North International Airport, New York, NY

Jim's legs had almost given out when Camina first set him down. It was Sheer adrenaline alone that kept him standing. The rush. His heart was jackhammering in his chest so loud he was certain that every monster on the island could probably hear it. But that woman didn't make a big deal out of it. She didn't call attention to how green he was at this.

When she realized he wasn't following her over to the edge of the rooftop because he was scared shitless, Camina had just given him a kind, mothering smile and encouraged him to follow her with a nod in the direction that sounds of destruction and horror were coming from. There were screams. So many screams under the sound of crumbling concrete and the screeching of metal tearing apart. Glass crunching.

The screams were quiet compared to the angry roars of the monster.

Camina got down on all fours and crawled to the low wall that lined the edge of the rooftop they were on. Summoning his courage, Jim followed with his camera recording. The gravel and debris bit into his elbows despite the reinforced patches on his jacket. And his armpits chaffed as he tried to keep the camera steady through his crawl. This. Was. Not. Fun.

The midday sun was beating down on his back while rivers of sweat were saturating his shirt. Scorching heat rose up from the tacky tarred roof that he stuck to, just a little bit, with each forward motion. Hot, rich, and volatilely resinous, the scent of tar filled his senses until there was no room for any other sensation during the long tedious crawl toward danger. Or at least he thought it had, until he inched his head slowly up to see over the wall and got smacked in the face by the updraft off the tarmac.

Dry air clogged his throat and left the young journalist gasping for air while trying to stifle his body's autonomic desire to cough. Smothering his mouth against an arm, Jim convulsed with his silent struggle. When his tearing vision cleared after a few blinks, he was staring at a canteen or a water bottle. Camina's outstretched hand was holding it mere inches from his face.

Yep. Now she knows you're an amateur, stupid. The disappointed thought popped into his head. Didn't think to bring anything but my camera gear.

The woman didn't say anything. She wasn't even looking at him. Those eyes of her's were focused on the thing that really mattered. Not some kid wannabe reporter catching his breath, but on the people who genuinely needed her help. Jim took the vessel and drank, quickly. Opening, sipping, and closing the lid took only moment before he placed it back in the waiting hand that closed reflexively around it.

She didn't even have to look to return it to where it belonged as it disappeared smoothly into a clip on her white and gold armor. Feeling less dizzy and back to himself, Jim Thafesh made a second attempt to do the job he was here to do. Taking slow careful breaths, Jim peeked his head up above wall he was behind…

…and wished he had stayed on the plane.

It was huge. The monster looked like it used to be a plane. A big one. It had sprouted small hindlegs, mostly walking on its wings like a wyvern, and the glass of the cockpit window was gone. The behemoth had a jaw that opened wide low on what had been the nose, filled with sharp jagged metal teeth. Eyes were located to either side of that.

The clawed wings were burrowing into one of the terminals across the way from the building they were located on top of. Short sharp retorts from the weapons of security guards rang out. Shooting was futile, but they were trying anyways. Bright flashes from wand thrown spells spilled around the contours of the metal horror.

Holding up the camera strapped to his hand so he could zoom through the lens, Jim was astounded to see what looked like a few regular civilian passengers standing side by side with the airport security. A valiant last stand while those without magic fled deeper into the maze of corridors in the terminal.

"There's civilians working alongside TSA agents and airport security trying to hold off the class four monster attacking North Manhattan airport." He began narrating quietly into the mic for the benefit of anyone who might watch later.

"None of those spells are a high enough level to do any damage to a class four monster." Camina commented beside him.

"Do you think that they waited too long to try taking it out instead of destroying it while it was a lower class?" Jim cleared his throat trying to sound more professional for the recording as he swung the camera around to focus on her, The Valkyrie still had her faceplate open, and she never bothered to look at him as she shook her head in denial.

"No. Look…" One gauntleted hand pointed down and swept across the loading and unloading area where a cluster of cargo carrying vehicles were strewn about in pieces. Red and pink smears were interspersed among the destruction. "…I think they didn't have enough time once the transformation had begun. Even if they had, the monster's skin is still that of a plane. Its mass is even greater now as it fills in with magical organics. They just don't have enough firepower."

As she was speaking a rumbling started in the distance. Growing loud quickly, Jim recognized the sound of a jet and turned his camera swiftly to catch it as it flew overhead. There was only one model of plane magically hardened enough to come that low, the ARC-17 Aegis Magically Enhanced fighter. Two more screamed past just as loudly but not faster than mach. A tickle of fear ran through Jim as he briefly wondered if the country had just written off New York and decided to 'sterilize' Manhattan from the sky.

"Oh. Look who's here." Though her voice was light and calm, the grimace of disgust Jim saw on Camina's face out of the corner of his eyes said a lot. He was very careful not to get it on camera. "I'll go take care of this. Those guys are just here for recon." She stood suddenly and the journalist startled as the woman beside him stepped away to make room for her wings.

"You sure?" God damn it. He'd tried so hard not to say it even as the words were elbowing their way out of his mouth.

"About what? It's just a class four." Then Camina's visor snapped shut and her wings sprung open. She launched herself high enough into the air and turned herself into a blazing comet fired at the monster across the way.

"Holy fucking shit!" The force of her passage knocked Jim from his knees onto his ass, but he miraculously managed to keep the camera trained on the rocketing woman as she punched through the monster with a screech of tearing metal. Bellowing the transmogrified jetliner reared up on its tiny hind legs, ichor and hydraulic fluid gushing from the Camina-sized wound in it.

Furious but unhindered, it began searching for the thing that had hurt it. Jim wanted to get a shot of the reactions from the brave mages who had been trying to hold it off, yet he also didn't want to miss a moment of the fight. He was riveted anyways. Where had Camina gone? She'd gone through the former plane and out the other side. Her passage had left a gushing hole.

She was lost to his sight. A distant cheer let him know that the famous warlock must still be fine and in view of the people she was rescuing. Hoping that Camina was okay, the journalist focused his camera on the monster which was humping its body weirdly. Twisting and hopping from its center as if it couldn't quite lay down because there was something beneath it. That something was a certain warlock as she lifted the monster over her head and flung it away from the building it had been ravaging with a mighty heave.

It arced through the air hundreds of feet high but still low compared to the size of its body. Landing stunned it momentarily as it cracked the tarmac in a spiderweb tracery that was probably a lot more damage than it looked like from so far away. However, it wasn't long before the wounded creature began wiggling on its back to right itself.

Focusing his shot back to Camina, Jim was just in time to catch the distant figure in armor spreading its wings. She launched into the air. He was expecting another inferno run but instead she drew her pact item weapon, Ascalon, the dragon-slaying lance of Saint George. A transforming, shapeshifting weapon so powerful, that it could kill dragons.

Dragons, the most magical creatures on the planet. These monsters plaguing the city were nothing compared to the magic contained in a single proper dragon. The lance in her hand thickened as it became a heavy laser rifle. Jim zoomed in, mesmerized. Thank the Gods he had splurged on the good and expensive magically hardened cameras with the best zoom ever.

Camina had never taken the time to darken her faceplate again, so he was able to catch every nuanced micro expression as the woman took aim at her target. The hate and rage she clearly felt drained away as Jim watched. Replacing it was a still kind of calm that he'd never really seen on anyone before. No animosity, just someone so engaged in what they were doing that there was no room for any other thought or feeling. Then, ever so slightly, her eyes narrowed, and that calm was replaced with a vicious teeth baring snarl in the split-second instant before her visor darkened.

"Oh shit." Flinging his free arm up, the hopeful journalist covered his eyes and face just in time before a searing light ruptured existence from the muzzle of the weapon Camina was holding.

The roaring explosion was fast. Wind buffeted him with debris. Then it was quiet, and he looked again hoping against hope that he'd managed to catch that on film. Dust and rocks were falling around the blast site and as it cleared, a hovering figure appeared out of the cloud. It turned and flew over to him, not fast but not slowly either. When she reached him, Camina opened her faceplate and smiled in a bittersweet way.

"Let's move on to the next one. We've got a city to clear."

Archangel Michael Vs. The Fates (Part 5)

After some scuffling, a couple a gurgling screeches, and squelching that made many of the refugees gathered in the café glance at each other uncomfortably, the couple returned mere minutes later. They had a few splashes of the magical false matter gore from the small monsters they had slain on their clothes. Other than that, they were fine. The wife's eyes in particular, sparkled, as if she was on the most romantic date of her life.

"Oh, sometimes I miss the occasional monster fight." She sighed expressively and flicked a bit of pink and silver flesh from her husband's cheek before giving him a kiss. Nicholas blanched a bit. Gross. Then someone shrieked behind him, followed quickly by the sound of glass shattering.

The elegant older woman's eyes jerked in the direction of the sound, then widened. At first, Nicholas thought she had been surprised. Then her smile grew brilliantly, and she jumped up and down like a schoolgirl.

"Oh, goody." Her husband sighed good-naturedly as his wife skipped away from him to meet the new threat. Turning, Nicholas fearfully looked behind him.

Yep.

It was monsters.

Lots and lots and lots of monsters.

Swallowing hard, the attorney really wished this had been a gods thing. However, maybe…nope. That sentence didn't have a finish in his mind. Instead, he watched spellbound as an elderly woman ran at the creature forcing its way through the broken coffee shop window. It looked like it might have once been a postal drop box. Like, the kind that letters were dropped in.

She dodged and wove around it, slicing it into chunks as if she were cutting… something really easy to cut. Not butter. Butter didn't peel away along graceful lines of separation like this. It was mesmerizing. And from every slash and wound, false matter ichor spilled like red oil covered in an iridescent sheen. Transfixed, the redhead was unable to look away until someone jerked him almost off his feet by the arm.

Snapping jaws whizzed by his ear. Startled and terrified, the attorney scrambled for balance and hurried away from the… was that one of the hanging lights? Not anymore. It had grown a mouth and… oh shit… *all* the lights had grown mouths and were straining at the structures they were suspended from. Angrily, the collective lightbulb creatures hissed in frustration when the coffee shop's patrons ducked below their reach.

"Could you get that honey?" The sword-wielding woman was facing down another monster lumbering off the street between two trees. "I'm a bit busy." Hopping out the window and over shards of slippery glass to meet the thing before it could cross the sidewalk. Beside Nicholas, the embattled woman's grey-haired husband sighed and smiled fondly at his wife's back as he let go of Nicholas' arm.

"Of course, Dear." He called out then gave the attorney he'd just rescued a conspiratorial shrug. "Women. Am I right? You can take the take the girl out of the Magicorps, but you can't take the Magicorps out of the girl."

His focus shifted swiftly, and a soft mumbled whisper caused the enchanted prosthetic arm which had already transformed back into an arm from the shield he'd used to protect everyone with earlier, now shifted into a sword.

"Useful that."

"It quite is." The elderly gentleman agreed before Nicholas had realized he had spoken out loud. Then he took a step forward and murmured another phrase under his breath. The leg he stood on elongated and lifted up. He rode the forward momentum of that step up towards the ceiling in a smooth swift motion like he was a pole vaulter.

Hopping and dancing around the coffee shop floor, the old man severed the light monsters from their mounts and destroyed their false matter insides before they grew the ability for independent movement. As more of the inanimate objects in the building began to show signs of transforming, those were skewered as well. While the husband didn't show the same rabid delight as his wife at the prospect of fighting for his life, he did have a certain grim satisfaction on his serious face.

"Oh, wow." Sharral commented as she shuffled out of the way and over to stand beside Nicholas. Which he did not mind at all, even if he would way rather prefer one of tiffs between the gods than to be in this place right now. "His arm and his leg? I wonder what happened?"

"You want to know what happened?" How had that old man managed to hear all the way from over there. But he was grinning at Sherral now as he hop-dashed between opponents. Aghast that the very able amputee had heard her speculation, the barista covered her mouth in shame.

"Oh. I'm so sorry. I didn't mean to be so rude."

"Pshaw. Nonsense, young lady." A slick movement with his bladed arm made quick work out of a table that was getting a little rambunctious. "I don't mind sharing." A cackle left his mouth and for the first time he seemed to really be enjoying himself.

"I used to be a medic…" Without missing a beat, the old fighter started into his story between breaths. "…Spent a lot of time in offices…" Another table was hacked to gooey bits and an espresso machine launched itself off the counter. "…anyways, you know how everyone complains about the printers in their office?" Nicholas found himself grimacing in understanding. Printers were fucking assholes when they were just regular machines. "Well…" the expresso machines sloshed into coffee ground guts mess on the floor. "…shredders? Just no. Don't mess with the shredders."

Nicholas waited for more, but there wasn't more coming. Their defender just grinned at them between actions. Like he knew they had questions but didn't dare ask him if he didn't volunteer the answers.

What?

That was it?

"A shredder? Did… I mean…both? At once?" Sharral was stunned but Nicholas could tell from the gleam in the old man's eyes that he was messing with them and smiled along with him. Despite their dire circumstances he chuckled. A smile cracked Nicholas' face. Until the booming sound that shook the building and rattled every piece of drinkware on the shelves.

Nearly everything froze.

It came again. Then again. Even. Measured. Footsteps.

"Aw heck." The old man called out. "What in the apple-picking wonders is that? I am never coming to the city again." He hurried over to the broken window to check on his wife. She was well out into the street, reveling in battle with a trail of carnage behind her.

"Amanda, get in here." It was clear that he was terrified for his beloved wife. "Whatever that is, it's too big for you to fight alone and you know it." After she'd finished dispatching the manifestation she was working on, she put a hand to her brow squinting into the distance against the bright midday sunlight.

"It's fine." She called back before going about with what she was doing.

"It's damned well not fine. You promised not to do this again." *Again?* Nicholas wondered. How many times had she risked her life against impossible odds?

"No. No. It's Heavy Step and The Fancy Prodigy." Her laughter was meant to calm and sooth her husband, which it kind of did. "We've got backup. The superheroes are here."

Chapter 48

"Yeah. About that...." Jim was staring wide-eyed at a small herd of monsters that had appeared behind Camina. Catching the look on his face, she rolled her eyes, turned around, and fired off some kind of rapid-fire spell that was bright, hot, and destroyed the monster herd in a matter of seconds.

"I told you, there's lots more to kill." She shrugged nonchalantly as if it wasn't that big a deal.

"Will you be going through the airport to clear out any manifestations and find any people who may be trapped?" Even before the sentence had finished coming out of his mouth, Camina's face froze into a polite and beautiful masking smile.

"Of course, I'll do that." Wow, there was that brilliantly gorgeous smile that the world was so familiar with. Yet as one of Camina's biggest fans, that smile seemed a lot less genuine when Jim was the one behind the camera. It seemed pained. Very, very pained.

Being the quick-witted camera man and fan of Camina that he was, Jim shifted the camera to the damaged building across the tarmac as soon as he realized the mistake he'd made. She didn't want to do that. He'd just accidentally committed The Harbinger to a search and rescue operation because if she said 'no' now that it had been recorded, it would not be a good look for her.

"Yes. Of course, we'll do a walk-through of the airport, see if anyone's trapped and put down any manifestations that might be roaming in there." As she spoke, Jim focused tightly on the mages who had been defending the terminal unsuccessfully. They were pulling people out of the rubble and trying to fortify the collapsing ceiling.

"We'll need to be particularly carful, Mr. Thafesh," Her tone of voice when she said his name felt like a cue, and Jim turned the camera back to her. At that Camina folded her wings and latched her lance into the holder on her back. "...my warlock spells and pact items aren't suited for close quarters combat, and I might accidentally damage something or hurt someone if I use some of my spells inside."

OooooOOOoooohhhhhhhh! Well shit!

Realizing his error, Jim peeked out around from behind the camera and mouthed the words 'I'm sorry' at her. Now he understood his mistake.

"Come along, now." That bright smile broadened wickedly, and over six feet of magical battle armor stalked toward the journalist. Jim yelped as Camina scooped him up in her gauntleted arms again. Heavy running steps jostled him against the cold metal armor. Until the inevitable powered leap that launched them into the stomach lurching drop to the ground below.

One... two... three... four... Jim opened his eyes, which turned into huge saucers of horror at the rapidly approaching terminal building. They were going to smash into the building. So, he braced hard. The smash never happened. But although Camina landed smoothly and the mechanisms in the suit lessened the impact, he knew that was going to bruise.

Then he was down on his own two feet again. Camina was all business as she found an open door with employees waving her into a stairwell. The survivors cheered. It was reedy and thin though and many of them were wounded. And she couldn't do anything for them.

First aid. That's as much medical knowledge as she had. Sure, her dad had been a medic back in the day so, she knew a little more terminology than the average soldier. Not a single iota of her warlock magic was based in healing. It was all destruction and shielding. That was it.

"Miss Harbinger." A young woman, teen really, ran over to her. "Can you fly someone to the hospital? My Gran's injured." A girl pointed to where a few travelers were hiding and cowering far away from the large glass front windows of the terminal. 'Gran' wasn't the only injured person there.

Her gaze was dispassionate as she surveyed the injuries. Young, old, male, female, or whatever else they identified as disaster did not discriminate on the basis of gender, age, or ethnicity. Though it probably did have a bit of a bias based on religious beliefs since that was going to be affected by whether or not a deity deigned to answer someone's prayers.

"I'm sorry, Miss. I don't really know if that would be the best thing for her." Camina responded with as much regret as she could put in her voice. "Anyone who is injured enough that they need a hospital may be so gravely injured that they could be killed by the flight." Explaining this was horrible. It always was. "I'm somewhere protected inside the suit, but it isn't very safe for the people I carry."

"You carried him." The teen pointed to Jim who wanted to melt into the floor at that point but instead spoke up.

"She did, but I'm all bruised up from being pressed against her armor during flight." He used one hand to pull the collar of his shirt out of the way and the nasty red mark that was just starting to color the arm.

"I'm sorry, Jim." The contrite look on Camina's face was, well it was endearing. Then she turned back to the girl and began looking around. "Point me to whoever's in charge and I'll see how I can help."

"You can help by clearing out monsters and helping us evacuate as many of the injured as possible to hospitals." A man in a suit called out from where he was bent over an injured security agent. His ID badge dangled from a lanyard around his neck. "I know you can't carry them, but you can push a bus, can't you?"

"Why, yes." Camina's eyes brightened knowing that she had suitable work to do that would allow her to protect these people. "I *can* do that."

"If you take care of the monsters, my people will get the injured organized and loaded." He patted the security guard who was no longer gasping for breath as a mage with healing abilities treated whatever was wrong with them.

"Then I'll provide both the motor and the escort for the busses." She rallied the security guards to her. "Alright, who's coming with me?" A ragged group of about half the uniformed security personnel formed around her. "Which way first?"

"Clear a route to the loading and unloading area where the busses are." The one who seemed to be in charge volunteered while gesturing in the appropriate direction with his wand. "Then meet up with the survivors in the other Terminals. We've confirmed injured in nearly every group of survivors."

186

"Right. Let's get going." The armored figure took the lead, and Jim fell back to film the intrepid group of heroes who were going into battle supporting her. Not *really* supporting her. That was just the way it was going to be spun by the news outlets and the military's PR people when the footage aired.

Chapter 49

Did you know that walking in powered armor is slow, and tedious? Well, it is. Whenever Camina found herself in a situation where she had to 'work' with civilians *on camera* she always found herself fantasizing about giving a truly candid interview. One where she could just tell everyone how it really was.

And no, it was not a good idea. She would never, ever, actually do that.

But God damn it. She hated walking through buildings in her armor. It really wouldn't have been that bad if not for the trail of airport security following her around like baby ducklings. Obediently, in a line, and so very, very fragile. The civilians had no understanding of the danger they were in if Camina accidentally bumped into one even with the highly controlled movements she was using to limit her suit's strength.

Familiar yet somehow inordinately annoying at this moment, the suit's hydraulics whirred rhythmically inside her helmet with each step. *Whirrrr-clunk... whirrrr-clunk... whirrrr-clunk... whiiirt?* A sound. Even her armor seemed to question what it was.

She'd heard it and sensed a disturbance in the ambient magic levels. Arcanes were swirling around her in current she understood. Around the corner ahead, something was disturbing the flow of the currents by soaking up free arcanes.

Watching it with her eyes and her magical senses, Camina could feel the eddies swirling and interfering with the natural flow of this unnatural quantity of magic. Well, that wasn't entirely true. The unnatural quantity of magic part. New York had a pretty high natural magic level before the first large scale magic collectors had been built to bring the AMD down. Certainly not Prometheus Purple *all the time*, but it had been high enough often enough that the Magicorps, a military branch dedicated to fighting monsters and magic, had been necessary for the nascent United States of America.

Pushing back the vaguely remembered history lesson that was squirreling itself to the forefront of her mind at the most inopportune of times, Camina held up her fist in the gesture telling everyone else to stop. From the muted sounds of bodily collisions behind her, followed by murmured sorries and hissed shushes, not everyone in the party was aware of what a raised fist on a bent arm meant.

Amateurs! The scoff was internal as her helmet's external speakers were on, in case she needed to shout warnings or commands. Instead, she indulged in rolling her eyes before twisting her waist to indicate to the civilians that they were to wait there. At least they had caught on that pointing at them and then at the ground by their feet meant for them to bleeping stay put. The first monster she'd come across, one of those idiots had tried to come after her to 'help' and had ruined her element of surprise.

That had been a mess. Slow learners some may be, but they were catching on. And Camina was moving quickly. Sure, it felt slow to her because her tall, powered armor gave her longer legs than those not in powered armor. It was slow to her even if everyone else was creeping along in a slow jog.

Stepping around the corner, Camina swiftly located the hostile targets in her heads-up display. The hallway had opened onto a long airy corridor with high ceilings lined with baggage check and ticketing counter, with sporadic self-serve kiosks along the way. It was a decently sized area for an engagement. She'd be able to maneuver her bulky armor around without doing excessive damage.

There were six manifestations. Launching herself at them, she fired up her propulsion and spread her wings for stabilization. Pulling her lance from her back it morphed into a sword suitable for use in her gauntlets and backed by augmented strength. One, sliced in half and spilling ichor from its steal and rubber body. It had been small, possibly a former luggage cart.

Crunching her body to flip into a new trajectory, she focused on number two and three. A self-service kiosk and what had to have been the very last coin-operated pay phone in existence were snarling and snapping at each other as they fought to free themselves from the bolts and electrical infrastructure that tethered them to the floor. Two and three went as she landed in a hard skid between the two. Tiles and grout sprayed up before her as her weight shattered it in a moving wave.

As she slid between the two her body twirled in a swift double pirouette, her weapon flashing out and severing both in half then freeing their remains from the floor. The movement ended is a graceful bow, like in the dance practices she'd go to as a child before her pact with Michael. A girl had to have fun somehow, and this had not been a fun mission. No. It had not been. That level four had been… nothing. It had been nothing.

Ever since the battle of Ragnarök – which had been disappointing in and of itself with the way it ended – work had been so boring. There were no challenges. Camina never got to really let loose and go all out. It didn't help that monster classifications weren't just based on how powerful they might be magically but on their size. So, that airplane manifestation had been a class four based on size alone… even if it had been dumb and not even remotely close to what its final form.

Pushing down with a foot, Camina went for the next manifestation. Her mind wandered to the old children's rhyme a bit as she did a quick flash sprint up to the beast and ran it through as it lumbered along.

Prometheus Purple do beware,
Monsters, monsters, everywhere.
Rock or metal…,

Humming the tune to herself, she jumped up onto number five's back. It was a suitcase. Or it had been before the manifestation had begun growing out of control. Stabbing the rollicking creature that was now the size of a horse big enough to ride in her powered armor, Camina rolled expertly with the bucking monster. She was tempted, really tempted, to raise one hand and pretend like she was in a rodeo, but experience had taught her that this would be the one thing those who disliked her would focus on out of everything else she would do that day if it were caught on camera.

Too bad that wasn't quite true.

It took far more effort than she'd expected to kill the thing. Stuff that didn't have a clear solid form when it manifested could be weird to get rid of. With a more flexible framework to build upon the manifestation sort of distributed whatever it was that kept it alive to disparate parts and sometimes, she had to completely disassemble it to get it to die like she wanted.

Six now.

Six was across the skywalk to the parking garage. She didn't strictly need to deal with it. However, Camina grimaced, it was going to be an issue if she ignored it, and they drew its attention while trying to get people out of the building and onto the line of hotel shuttles and tour busses that seemed abandoned in the bus loading and unloading zone.

Snorting and growling, the monster was moving in a very organic way. It was mottled brown and green, and an odd sort of squarish shape. A pelt of flopping green and brown circles hung from cracked gray-brown-green skin. If Camina didn't know better, she would almost think that it had evolved from...

... a shrub.

One of the kinds that were trimmed into cubic box shapes. A box bush... or whatever the heck they were called. Gardening wasn't really her thing.

"Oh, hell." That wasn't good. While living organic material rarely mutated in Prometheus Purple levels, it was possible. Really high purple might as well be really low pink. *And once you're in the pink, everything stinks.* A lewd rhyme most Magicorps soldiers learned in basic to remind them that Prometheus Pink basically equals death if you weren't protected. Camina had picked it up from her parents, and their friends, and all the soldiers she was around in military school, and her older brother... Okay, fine, Magicorps was steeped into every moment of her life.

With a sigh, Camina checked the seals on her suit and trudged after the last obstacle in her path to leaving the claustrophobic confines of the airport. Once she was out on the street things would be better. A fully organic manifestation was slightly harder to kill even if it wasn't made of reinforced materials. They were *too* alive. Too full of muscles and sinews even if their blood and bone weren't like normal animals. They felt like real animals. Dispatching them felt like killing and butchering real creatures sometimes.

Like now. But she did it quickly.

Then, turning in place, she returned across the skybridge leaving a trail of sappy blood footprints. There was Jim. Filming her like he'd promised to do, he'd left the corridor that the others had been instructed to wait in. Behind his camera the youth was beaming that silly excited grin that had first made her afraid that he was a gore groupie. It reminded her of her kids, and she tried not to let that flash of emotion show on her face.

Never be sad in front of the camera. Someone had told her that once. Never show emotions that can be used to make you seem unstable or unsuited for the job. Determination, satisfaction at a job efficiently done, but never sadness or worse yet, any indication that she might actually enjoy her work. Hell, the only spell she'd even used today was the spell to summon her suit.

"We're all clear." She spoke loudly through her external speakers- as her helmet was still closed- to let the people who were driving know it was safe to prep the buses. She intended to keep her helmet closed now that she'd seen how high the AMD really was. The magic levels in parts of the city weren't just Prometheus Purple. They were high Purple. Closer to Pink really and that… that wasn't good. Jim hurried forward and was about to pass her to get a closeup of the monster remains. "Don't."

"But it's dead right?" Too damned focused on the shot for his own good. Maybe it had been a bad idea to bring him in to this. Camina would never forgive herself if something happened to him.

"The AMD is too high. It's almost pink over there. That was living plant mutation." Jim blanched, his face paling terribly at the realization of the danger he'd almost put himself into. "Stay close to me. Not out of my sight. Unless I tell you to run. If I do, then run and don't look back or stop until you are off Manhattan Island." She kept her volume low so that the airport security who were closer now couldn't hear what she was saying. "We're higher up on the Prometheus Scale than I thought we were. Let's not panic anyone though, okay?"

Other security staff went back to notify the various pockets of survivors that they had liberated and unified know that it was safe to start bringing injured people forward for loading. Things moved quickly and she watched dispassionately as he first bus was loaded. She gave the warnings to everyone about the parking structure being too dangerous with higher magic levels than the airport building itself.

Camina knew the warnings didn't matter. There was bound to be someone who didn't listen to her and would choose to risk getting to their vehicle to leave. They'd found four buses that were parked, intact, fueled, and in drivable condition while being magically hardened enough to function. There was almost a dozen more which hadn't been hardened but could be put in neutral and she could push them one at a time.

Good. Five was a lucky number, wasn't it? Once loaded, she waited for the driver in her dead bus to give her a thumbs up out the window. Positioning herself behind the bus she braced her hands, planted her heels firmly into the asphalt of the street, and leaned into the bus with hard even pressure.

Wheels rolled, and a weak cheer came up from inside the vehicle. Those watching, the remaining injured and the uninjured who had helped them to reach this point, also cheered from the loading and unloading curb before the terminal they were leaving from. This was it. They were on their way. Through a city full of monsters which could now be made from anyone or anything living or dead.

Her heart thudded in her chest in a tremulous and unpleasant way. She hated city combat. The damaged vehicles, the desperate wounded people hoping for survival. How many times was she going to be the one saving people from monsters in high magic zones? And would they still be people by the time she reached the hospital?

Luckily, Camina was distracted from her morose descent into depressive memories by a bright moving light moving across the sky. At first, she tensed in her steady trudge behind the bus, thinking that it might be another monster. But no. It… was a chariot? A magical chariot? The chariot of heaven? Michael? Had that silly Archangel broken the rules to come and help her?

No. That was *not* Michael. Michael did not cackle maniacally like that.

Archangel Michael Vs. The Fates (Part 6)

"Oh, thank God." Someone exclaimed. Nicholas wasn't ever sure who. But regardless, they all settled in to watch the arrival of powerful mages who used their powers to protect and serve. Licensed superheroes whose anonymity was protected by law behind their colorful costumes if they fought and patrolled when they were scheduled to and came to the city's aid during disasters.

Hours they watched the battle. Sharral stood beside Nicholas, and they squeezed together a little while with the others crowded at the windows. They couldn't always see what was happening as the heroes moved around the city and beyond their line of sight. Amanda had traded quips with the various heroes that joined her occasionally. There were four more who came down streets they could see along but when the manifestations thinned and the heroes moved on, a guilty glance back at her anxious husband kept the woman who was clearly reliving the glories of her youth from following.

Amanda had just started a casual stroll back towards her audience when the building shook again. This time it was far stronger than any of the shaking that Heavy Step had caused. The tremor knocked Sherral off balance, and she fell against Nicholas who caught her with all the regular mortal strength he had. Which wasn't much. But still.

Her eyes were round saucers as she stared up at him. Maybe it was his overwhelming masculinity, but he was pretty sure it was sheer terror. Wrapping an arm around her they hurried further into the building, away from the large windows and behind the counter where they could hide. The next tremor didn't just shake the building, it made it lurch so hard things fell over.

Tables – the few that remained – chairs, a ventilation duct broke loose from the ceiling with a creak. That creak just barely gave Nicholas enough warning to lift his hands overhead with the full knowledge that the impact of trying to catch this falling object was going to break both of his arms. He'd never felt a force so hard and painful as that heavy duct hitting his hands. It stung. A lot. But it held.

At least, the half he'd caught was holding. The other half was almost pinning Sherral to the counter. Had pinned her between the duct and the counter. His muscles shook with the effort. He wasn't weak. But he was no mage and certainly no superhero. If he let go, would she be…?

"Can you move? I can't hold this long?" Sherral didn't answer at first. Her breath was coming in quick little gasps, and she was trying to wiggle free.

"Yeah. Just give me a sec. Can you lift it a little higher?" It was quiet and breathy. Nicholas really couldn't tell if she was just in pain from being squished or if she was seriously injured from being *squished.*

"Someone. I need help." The refugees had almost all been shaken by the last tremor. Several had fallen and were being helped off the floor by those who hadn't. But when he called they started towards him. This was bad. This was awful. He was staring into Sherral's gorgeous eyes while she struggled to worm her way free.

Was he getting lightheaded? Had he gotten hit in the head by something? His vision was getting brighter. As if it was being suffused by a glow. White light formed around him casting a shadow on the staring barista.

"Nicholas? What's happening?" She was asking him a question, but he didn't know. He didn't have magic. What was this? A monster manifestation? He couldn't see over his shoulder while supporting the weight of the metal tube. But he wouldn't be doing it alone for long.

The sensation of lightness grew. Suddenly the duct seemed to rise and Sharral was moving more freely. But she felt lower. And lower. And lower.

This…

…felt familiar…

He was moving. Nicholas Everstone, Heaven's favorite attorney, was being lifted into the air.

"Someone, quick. Grab this from me." If he kept moving he wasn't going to be able to support the piece of building in his hands. It would end up falling on Sherral again. "No… No. Not now you bastards!" The end of the tube slipped from his white-knuckled grip as his fury grew. The metal fell, it almost looked like slow motion to him but the light around him grew and he couldn't see if anyone had been there to support the duct when he lost his grip.

Like an alien abduction, Nicholas was levitated out of It's Totally Not Milk. He fought it every inch of the way, grabbing corners of walls, the counter, a duct that hadn't fallen off the ceiling. At last, the beam of light completely ignoring the thrashing man inside, stopped abruptly.

The light was coming through the wall and like a magnet pulling something it shuffled him around, higher, side to side. Nicholas took the opportunity to try escaping by pushing off the wall where it met the ceiling with both feet. This only succeeded in making him spin wildly before he was yanked hard against the wall again.

This time his head smacked the concrete with a dull wet thud and a not-quite fuchsia light flashed behind his eyes before turning a throbbing teal. After a few more shifts sliding his much more pliable body around, the light beam finally lowered him enough to slide out the edge of the shattered window. However, Nicholas couldn't see any of this.

The light was too bright, and he was in too much pain. He did hear quite well over the rushing pulse of his own blood filling him with agony every time his heart beat. So, he recognized the voice which spoke to him even if he couldn't remember why.

"Hello, Nicholas. It's been *far* too long."

Chapter 50

1:15 PM September 13ᵗʰ, 2026
Industrial Park District Near the Port of New York

Sam gripped the steering wheel tightly. Palms slippery with sweat, she made sure to keep her grasp secure by occasionally rubbing them dry on the leg of her slacks one at a time. She waited until she had the wheel firmly clasped in her hand before taking the other off. Gleipnir had taken the front passenger seat and was humming *In the Hall of the Mountain King* to himself softly.

Despite his relative bravado when he spoke to Alex a few moments earlier, once it was just the two of them, his attitude changed somewhat.

"I couldn't help but notice that you seem to be a little nervous, Gleip?" Though she'd tried to keep her voice neutral, her own apprehension came out as she spoke.

"What?" The pact item exclaimed with the high-pitched screech of someone who is totally lying. "Me? Nervous." He laughed haughtily. "You must be mistaken?!" His voice ran haltingly through the octaves like the terrible actor he'd always been.

"You are shaking like a chihuahua that's been approached by a great Dane." Her dry voice was matched by a wry smile, which quickly faded with worry. "Are you not sure that you can contain this thing?"

"Oh, Sam." Gleipnir patted her on the knee with the end of his ribbon in a way that she knew he meant to be reassuring but which would have been utterly condescending if anyone else had ever done it. "I'm not worried that I can't do it." He sighed, or at least, simulated the sound of a sigh. "I'm worried that you might get hurt in the process. We've never fought something this big together. But we got this."

Her pact item, who was really more friend than anything else, moved his long sword portion as if he were nodding in affirmation. It reassured Sam because she could hear the solemn smile in his voice, and she glanced down at him just in time to see him turn toward her. He patted her knee again and she grabbed the tail of his ribbon and gave it a comforting squeeze.

"Yeah." She scoffed with false bravado. "We gots this." Then she yanked the steering wheel hard over to the right and skidded to a drifted stop with her door facing the oncoming behemoth. Taking in the towering figure, Sam suddenly found that her mouth was very dry. She pulled out some lip gloss and smacked her lips with a pop to spread it. "Though this is one time I really wouldn't mind having mom bail me out."

"Oh, pashaw! Sam. This will take us no time at all." Gleipnir opened the door and hopped out on the side of the vehicle opposite the monster. Yeah, it really did look like he'd hopped out and his 'body' bobbed along around the front of the car as he moved to join her. He opened the door for Samantha bowed with a flourish, "Mi'Lady. Would you care to join me in a dance?"

It made his warlock smile, and that was why Gleipnir had done it.

"Sure, Gleip." She giggled at his silliness as she clambered out of the vehicle with her wand at the ready and reactivated her most arcane hungry spell to assist her personal magic collector with reducing the dangerous levels of magic around her. "Integumentum infernis. Do we have a plan?" Brilliant flames erupted around Sam.

"Yes." Gleipnir replied assuredly…. Then he was silent. The monster was not, however, as it realized the prey that had so recently escaped was now returning. It trumpeted angrily, a blast of sound and force that revealed its jagged teeth of twisted broken steel beams.

The crushed and mangled body was still there lodged inside its maw. Even more blood oozed and dripped from the cracked and crumpling concrete walls which were now the beast's hide.

"Are you going to tell me," She asked as the lumbering giant broke into its version of a run.

"I don't want to" He admitted with a shout to be heard over the growing thunderous noise.

"What? *Why?*" Despite being in the middle of facing down a charging monster, Samantha Wattkins took the time to slowly turn her head to her pact item and give him an incredulous wide-eyed stare.

"You aren't going to like it." He admitted as the monster's jaws came for them. "DODGE!" Samantha had been waiting for the order and she grabbed him and rolled out of the way just in time to avoid being bitten in half by the head the size of a school bus. She was up and running with Gleipnir in hand before the monster even realized it had missed them.

"Tell me what the heck the plan is, Gleipnir." Sam commanded as she pointed her wand at the ground and conjured a blast of wind to propel her up onto the monster's back. "Bregðandi." Her feet hit the sloping fractured wall of hide and she ran up the side of what was once a building.

"I need to get to the magic source and cut it off so that you can kill the monster." It was a good thing that Sam had just about reached the former roof of the building because she sort of choked and stumbled as she understood what Gleipnir meant.

"We have to go inside?"

"We have to go inside" He confirmed gravely.

"This is so far beyond my pay grade." Muttering between gritted teeth, Sam fought the revulsion she felt against deliberately placing herself inside a living body even if that body used to be a building. "Especially because inside that monster is either a lot of dead people or one really big dead dragon." She pointed to the trail of blood that was leaking from the monster.

"It could be both." The lumbering creature was turning and twisting as it searched the ground for them trying to figure out where the tasty little mortal morsels had gone.

"Why would you do that?" Shaking her head in exasperation, the warlock blinked at her pact item again. "I was trying to psych myself up to do this. Now I'm even more grossed out." Gleipnir laughed. Sam laughed. Then they sobered.

"Cut a hole." Gleipnir instructed. "I'll go in and secure the probably-a-dragon corpse to suppress the arcanes it is emitting. Then you come in afterward and kill the monster before it finishes manifesting to a fully organic state."

"Okay." Gleipnir transformed in Sam's hand to a sharper blade, making himself look more like a fencing saber than an oversized sewing needle. She slashed downward through what seemed to be a particularly vulnerable portion of the back. This roof had been covered in gravel and tar prior to its transformation and the portion she'd picked had partially caved in. It just needed a bigger opening; one she could climb through on her own.

Together they hacked apart the concrete and steel beneath them. Every few strokes they'd hit a newly formed blood vessel or a pocket of false matter flesh that would spurt and splatter on the pair. This was gross, dirty, and difficult work. And it was made more difficult by the heaving of the monster upon which they stood even if the creature's back had its own safety wall around the edges. The enraged thing was trying to remove them with short hops and flexes now that it realized where they were and that it couldn't reach them with any of its limbs.

"I think that's good, Sam." When Gleipnir finally spoke, Sam was more than ready to stop. Her arms were tired and sore. Her feet hurt. And she was pretty sure that she'd pulled a muscle in her abdomen in the constant flexing and standing as she brought Gleipnir's blade down over and over again.

Alex had been watching through a pair of binoculars shed snatched from Frank the second Sam sped back off again. When they'd stopped in front of the manifestation and Sam had just stood there? She'd never been so terrified for someone else in her life. Had Sam fallen prey to the same fear or terror field that Alex herself had?

There was no way to know. Because Alex wasn't there. Because she should have stayed with her partner. Like her partner had come back for her. All the probationary agent had been able to do was watch as that bloody mouth of horrific metal teeth came closer and closer to eating her partner.

Oh, God. Run. Why won't she run? Oh, God. Oh, God. OhGod! OHGOD! I can't watch!" At the end, she hadn't even been able to watch and had tried to fling the binoculars away.

"Give me those." Frank, of course, had taken them back so that *he* could watch. "Ah, hell!" He cursed as he focused the magnifying device to his own eyes. "Did they just get eaten? I can't see anything through that dust cloud." Alex hadn't actually stopped watching. Instead, after a brief eyes-squeezed-shut moment, she raised a hand to block the bright sun from her eyes and tried to survey the fight unaided.

"I can't see anything either, boss." Someone commented. Alex didn't care who. Nothing mattered right now except for whether or not Sam was okay. Sam was what mattered. Not just because she was Alex's partner, but because that monster was being fueled by something inside it. It wasn't going to just 'go down' without a big, damned fight.

"I see her." Another voice commented.

"Where?"

"Where?"

"Where, where, where?"

Even among the chorus of 'where's' Alex knew hers was a little more intense than the others. She was just concerned for her partner. That was all.

Sam had just saved her life. It wouldn't be fair if something happened to her before Alex could properly thank her.

"She's climbing up the side of the thing."

"Holy shit."

"I see her too."

Sure, there were a lot of people talking and running commentary. Yeah, there was a lot at stake. Beside her Frank was scribbling frantically on his message scroll requesting backup yet again, conveying every bit of data about the thing they were going to have to fight any minute now if Gleipnir wasn't as all-that as he thought he was.

"What's she doing? Is she…?" But Alex could see it too. The distant warlock was wielding Gleipnir like a regular old cutting implement and slicking chunks out of the roof-back she was standing on. Her hips and knees flexing like she was surfing a wild wave on the most effed up board ever.

"She's cutting her way into the monster." It came to Alex as she realized what the pair had to do.

"Why wouldn't she just try to kill it?" Who was that? Not Frank, so Alex didn't look.

"Because there's something in that monster fueling it and it will just keep regenerating until it's removed." *That* was Frank. And he sounded sadder than Alex had ever heard him. Okay. To be fair, she'd only just met him. But still, it was a kind of awed sadness that meant he got what was happening.

"But whatever that thing is, it's Prometheus Pink outside of it. Inside will…does she even had a spell that can protect her from that?" Again, it was another mage, not Frank, not the previous not-Frank. Alex didn't care.

A disgusting numbness was welling up in her stomach. Nausea was rising with it, and she couldn't be horrified at what was happening. She just felt a terrible sadness as she felt the stinging prick of tears welling in her eyes.

"It doesn't matter." Her voice broke on the soft words, and she sniffed at the snot that was suddenly trying to run out of her nose. Stupid nose.

"Why not?" Alex didn't bother responding and one glance at her told Frank that he might as well field that question for her.

"It doesn't matter because it has to be done, and somebody has to do it." Frank glanced at the other agents then back to Alex before returning his focus to the outline of a warlock on the back of a giant monster manifestation. "Either Sam and Gleipnir do it, or they fail, and we do it, or we fail and the people who come after us do it."

Sam dropped from sight.

The monster gave up on trying to remove her from its back a few moments later. Alex guessed that was because it couldn't feel her hacking at it anymore. Alex gripped her wand tightly and took a deep steadying breath. Now that it wasn't distracted by Sam and Gleipnir's attack, the monster began its heavy stomping way towards them again. Sam's words echoed in her mind.

"It doesn't matter who does it as long as it gets done." It was something Sam and Gleipnir always said. Probably quoting Sam's world-famous hero of a mom. The sentiment had always annoyed Alex who felt that there should be clear lines of responsibility. Not having agreed upon delegation meant that some people slacked off while others were taken advantage of. But Sam had insisted that there was always a time when those words applied.

"Get ready, people." Frank hollered as he readied his wand and sidearm. "I don't think backup is going to get here in time." The monster started moving faster and faster, though it was still slow due to its size, it was doing its equivalent of a full-on sprint.

All of a sudden, it tripped and faltered.

Falling hard, the manifestation began crumbling as it skidded to a halt mere meters away. Many of the other agents had already begun fleeing out of the way to attack it from the side and behind. Now they were sheepishly avoiding eye contact with the agents who had stayed to face the monster head on.

Alex hadn't fled.

And she didn't quite believe the danger was over, so she stood there, wand at the ready, as she watched the carcass warily. The remnants of the building were still holding together but also, they were coming apart from structural damage. When the sound of moving rubble drew her attention to the sinking roof, she pointed her wand to the location she estimated whatever it was would enter her line of sight.

The gathered agents waited tensely as the noise became louder and louder. Then a mop of frazzled light-brown hair surrounded by a halo of fire poked over the edge of the building. Alex's heart clenched tightly, as if it was squeezed in a vice. While her shirt was torn and soaked with blood and false matter flesh, Sam was alright. She was more than alright. She was blazing, brilliantly beautiful beneath the dirt and bruises.

This was…

This was amazing. This was something that was going to live in the memories of the world centuries. When one warlock and their pact item saved a city from a monster invasion by going *inside* a manifestation. Someone pulled out a magically hardened camera they'd been using to document the crime scene earlier and snapped off a few quick shots of Sam as she clambered down with pained awkward movements.

Sam had *never* been arrogant. But that was how Alex had interpreted it. Because Alex had never bothered trying to understand what her partner was capable of. In her overabundance of self-confidence, the younger agent had always assumed that Sam had an inflated ego because of who she was related to. Alex had thought that all of Sam's achievements had been easy due to favoritism and her mother's fame paving the way. And she had been wrong.

Alex was just realizing that Sam really was amazing.

For her part, Sam was shielding her eyes, squinting out over the heads of the assembled agents. She had a quizzical look on her face, as if she couldn't quite believe what she was seeing. She pointed out a spot in the sky and called out to her fellow agents down below.

"Hey… Is that a chariot, or did I hit my head at some point?"

Chapter 51

2:00 PM September 13th, 2026
Outside the New York Preparatory Academy Ice Bubble

It was done. Or at least as close to done as it could possibly be until the corpse contaminating the city was removed. He'd killed all the monsters which had been besieging the survivors of the school attack. The ones inside Anna's ice bubble were gone. Most of the ones outside had either been killed or driven away.

So, why was Kyle more on edge now than he had been at any other point through this entire ordeal?

The warlock took a minute and surveyed the interior of the ice bubble to ensure the monsters really were all dead. They were. That was good. Then he steeled himself for the uncomfortable part, squaring his shoulders as he did so.

People had noticed him. Not just noticed him but noticed that he wasn't really known for being an overpowered warlock. There would be questions. So many questions. Ugh! His shoulders, which he'd just straightened, slumped dejectedly.

Kyle hated those questions. Whenever he did something exceptional like this everyone was like: 'OMG how did you do that?' 'You claimed you were just an average warlock, why would you lie about your abilities?' 'You do know that deliberately hiding your magic level from the Department of Magical Licensing is a felony that comes with fines up to one million dollars and up to twenty years in prison?'

Yeah.

It was a pain. But the problem was, Kyle really was just an average warlock. It was his talent for wizardry that let him do incredible things. And wizards didn't have a reliable internal source of magic, they took their magic from the surrounding environment. That was why most wizards lived in high magic zones. Kyle liked living in low magic zones. He liked civilization. And he honestly loved studying magical artifacts and history.

All those reasons were why he had chosen to become a warlock. As a warlock of the archivist, his almost non-existent internal magic stores were seriously augmented by the archivist. He got a cadre of spells from the archivist, and access to the greatest collection of magical knowledge the world over. Being a warlock meant he didn't have to risk his life every single day in the back of beyond just to quench that tiny thirst for power that gnawed at him.

Because he was man enough to admit he thirsted for power. Magical power, not you know, power over others. But it was a thing with him. A tiny thing, yet still a thing. So warlocking it had to be.

His mom hadn't been pleased at his choice of patron. She hadn't been happy with yet another one of her children choosing to go another route with their magic. Not a one of the three older siblings had followed her family's tradition of making a pact with a powerful military minded patron. Yes, they'd continued the tradition of service to others, but in their own way.

Davelor, the eldest had become a healer. Samantha was an engineer working with the Magic Crimes Division of the FBI. Kyle worked at the most prestigious educational facility for the investigation and containment of magical artifacts. None of them fought like Camina did. Davelor, had the build for battle. He was huge and ripped with muscles everywhere. Sam, had the pact item for close combat with magical creatures. Gleipnir, was flexible and had that nifty magic containment ability. And Kyle, if the ambient magic was high enough, Kyle could copy pretty much any spell that had ever existed.

So, Camina was most disappointed with Kyle's choice to become the studious academic that he had become. Even with the magical boost from his patron, Kyle's abilities under normal circumstances were extremely limited. The warlock of the Archivist's magic was so limited that under normal magic collector protected location circumstances Kyle was just barely able to meet the Magicorops requirements for recruitment. One might argue that it didn't matter, since fighting would be done in high magic zones where he'd have free reign with all the magic his wizarding ways could ask for. One would be wrong.

Train how you fight.

Kyle couldn't put up a good fight in low magic. This meant he could not protect a populated area from a monster incursion. He could only go to high magic areas and fight there. What was the point in killing monsters in their home territory and releasing their magic into the environment to raise the AMD? What was the point in killing monsters in an area that would just spawn more monsters? As a warlock, Kyle Wattkins was worthless to the Magicorps.

Sighing again, Kyle launched himself off the ice ramp that everyone else had slid down. He didn't use his suit's thrusters but had spread his wings to slow his descent. Even doing that made him morose as it reminded him that the very suit he wore, was a spell he could only use due to the high AMD flooding the city at the moment. The group of waiting teens cheered as Kyle landed with a thud. Wings spread, he let the joint mechanisms in the suit absorb the force of his fall and he landed down on one knee like a superhero.

Okay. That had been fun. They began a rush toward him until Jones called out.

"Keep the kids back. That suit is mighty powerful and one of you all could get hurt if he bumps into you." That had the teachers and staff urgently joining in to get the group back and ordered.

"Where are we evacuating to?" Kyle asked as he opened up the faceplate in his helmet. A tall serious and rather severe looking woman stepped forward and spoke up.

"The rest of the students were evacuated to the   about eight blocks away." She informed Kyle while looking him up and down in a way that both confused him and made him uncomfortable. It was that way educators had of assessing a student to see if they could maybe, possibly, under the best, most optimum circumstances pass muster. And this woman's look said she seriously doubted Kyle could handle the task.

Well, excuse her.

"Alright, Ma'am." The young warlock decided that *not* showing how much she intimidated him was the right course. "Let's get everyone there." The woman's eyes narrowed.

"Do you know where it is?" She genuinely seemed to think Kyle didn't know she was talking about the oldest most famous Vampire run luxury hotel in the United States.

"Yes, Ma'am." Clenching his jaw so that he didn't say something flippant that made the staff mistrust him, Kyle kept his tone neutral and steady. "I know how to get there on foot." The principal – this could only be the principal that his mom hated for letting that brat Sara bully people for years – harumphed and placed her fists on her hips.

"You don't think it would be better for us to seek shelter in one of these buildings?" She gestured to the relatively intact buildings around them. Most of them had shattered windows on the first floor where monsters had penetrated the buildings. Her eyebrows and chin lifted, and her head tilted ever so slightly to one side. It almost was as if she was hoping he'd say what she wanted him to say, and he frowned at the woman.

"No, Ma'am." Now Kyle thought he understood what she was doing though his brow still furrowed with confusion. Anyone could see that those buildings were not particularly safe from external monster attack. "Those residential buildings might be magically hardened to protect against monsters forming inside. But even if they are up to the mandatory basic code for New York City, you can clearly see they've already been breached by monsters." Then Kyle's frown deepened as he recalled the desperate chaotic drive to get there. "Or possibly looters. We ran into some earlier."

That caused the woman to draw back in alarm. Her eyes widened and her sharp exhale was echoed by several of the other survivors.

Alright." It was quite possibly the weirdest, most passive aggressive standoff Kyle had ever participated in. "Lead the way Mister Wattkins. I'll have my head of security coordinate with you to keep everyone safe." She waved her head of security forward as she retreated to relay the news to the rest of the staff and students.

"Holy shit." Kyle exclaimed as he took in the appearance of the man before him. "I didn't know the school hired mercenaries for their security." He chuckled a little and kind of internally gloated that he got to meet a mercenary while Sam was stuck babysitting dead dragons.

"Private security contractor. Mister Wattkins." The man who was dressed all in black corrected him. He was in black pants with lots of pockets. And wearing a black long-sleeved shirt with lots of pockets.

His name was on a patch on one pocket like it was a military uniform and his company's logo was on the arms like military service patches. A protective vest full of huge pockets with ammo and gear covered his chest, a magic message scroll was on one arm, a wand holder on the other. The look was finished up with a loaded handgun in a holster strapped down on one thigh.

Kyle laughed thinking it was a joke.

"I am not a mercenary Mister Wattkins. I'm a private security contractor. And for legal purposes I will require you to say that to anyone who may inquire in the future." The definitely-not-a-mercenary made a big obvious wink at Kyle.

"Oh. Oooh." Kyle's lips pursed in an 'o' shape for a bit as the words sunk in. "Gotcha." With a shrug, Kyle accepted the statement. There wasn't time to ponder over the implications now.

"Call me Kyle." The warlock offered. And that was that.

Chapter 52

After a brief consultation with the head of school security who was definitely not a mercenary – which Kyle now knew because he had stated it several times – they headed off. The 'security contractors' formed a perimeter around the herd of students and teachers while Kyle took the lead and Jones pulled up the rear.

Things were going really well. And that was scaring the heck out of Kyle because he could see and feel the currents of magic twisting, in preparation for another manifestation. The longer it took, the bigger the monsters were going to be.

However, there weren't any new monsters coming out to attack them. The people who had cheered Kyle and Jones on their gauntlet to the school were relatively quiet. By relatively, they were cheering like mad. Some screaming for the group to take shelter inside their building. Others asked to join them.

"Please stay inside your buildings." Kyle shouted to those who wanted to come with them. "We are relocating because the school's magic shielding has been compromised. If you are safe, don't leave safety." It became monotonous as he repeated it whenever someone requested to join.

Only one small group of a few bank tellers joined them. Two were bloodied and bedraggled and they were supporting a third between them.

"We don't have access to the apartments upstairs and the manager," the breathless blonde speaking gestured to a gray-haired elderly man draped between her and a dark-skinned man in his twenties wearing the slickest purple suit with all the accoutrements, "is unconscious and can't get us into the vault." It took only a quick survey of the ruined row of ground to ceiling windows for Kyle to realize that there was no safety there. "The only reason we aren't all dead is because the monsters trying to eat us went after you two on your way through here earlier."

"Fall in with everyone else." The definitely not a mercenary cocked an eyebrow when Kyle said it loud enough for the whole group to hear. They shared a look which said neither of them liked the idea. But Kyle wasn't about to abandon someone he'd already accidentally saved.

They continued on without incident. When they reached the barricade with the S.W.A.T team they'd passed earlier, the officers helped pull the civilians over the barricade. Despite congratulating Kyle and Jones on a job well done, they weren't effusive in their praise. They were quiet and speculative. The captain nudged Jones as he passed and murmured low so that his voice wouldn't carry.

"Can everyone at the museum do that?" The captain gestured towards Kyle with a nod in the warlock's direction and Jones smirked, shaking his head negatively.

"You should help us get the kids out of here." The officer in charge jumped at the unexpected closeness of the voice as Kyle came up behind him.

"We were supposed to…" He tried to argue that they had orders, but Kyle stopped him.

"Another big one is coming. The other barricades were overrun before we got through there. There's no one to back you up if you stay. But if you help us your vehicles will get this group to safety at the Plaza de Saint Germain hotel." Something about the look on Kyle's face must have made his point and the officers started loading up the refugees into their vehicles.

Not everyone could fit inside but a few of the older boys volunteered to ride on the running boards holding on to the vehicles' exteriors. An excited hope that was quickly squashed by every adult present. The children were safely ensconced within the vehicles. When necessary for someone to ride outside, it was an adult, usually one of the S.W.A.T. officers.

Jones, Anna, and the principal were all bundled into the museum vehicle that Kyle and Jones had driven there with a couple more kids. Kyle was standing on the running boards next to Anna's window. She was behind Jones in the driver's seat so Kyle could talk to her and Jones through Anna's window without blocking the driver's line of sight. There were two security personnel standing on the running boards on the side opposite Kyle. Jones had one of the communication scrolls from the school's security personnel, which the principal was holding for him in the front passenger's seat.

There was a girl on the far side of the back seat that kept giving him the oddest wide-eyed look which was making Kyle wonder if she was suffering from magic sickness. And between that girl and Anna was a boy *sitting next to his sister*. Kyle narrowed his eyes at the young man suspiciously through a murder-red haze of hate. The boy looked slightly older than Anna which automatically made him an 'older boy' and therefore not allowed to be that close to Anna.

Now was not the time for that. He'd get 'Uncle Michael' to deal with it later. Or maybe he'd just let slip to one of the pantheons that a boy might like Anna, then stand back and watch. It would be like the Little League debacle all over again. Word would spread. Boys wouldn't risk sitting next to Anna Wattkins ever again. A tight determined smile ghosted across his overly-protective big brother face.

Back in the direction of the school the previous monster had dissipated its false matter back into the ambient magic. The arcanes had begun twisting darkly. Whatever it was, it was coming fast. There was no time to waste on nonsense.

"Let's go people." Kyle called, slapping the roof of the vehicle for emphasis before throwing his arm forward so that the other drivers could see his command. He pointed repeatedly in the forward direction and the principal repeated the command on the scroll in her lap, relaying it to dozen or so vehicles around them. "Go now!"

Every person with even a little bit of magic sensitivity had to have felt that. The vehicles moved out, lurching forward in a line. But it wasn't fast enough. Kyle twisted his body so that he was facing backward. He watched as a part of the street began heaving behind them.

A creature erupted out of the ground, asphalt rupturing around it. It snarled, snapping its teeth as the rat grew and mutated faster and faster. Organic mutations were fast. Kyle knew their impromptu convoy wasn't going to make it. There was only one thing to do. Around him, the S.W.A.T. members and security personnel riding outside the vehicles were firing their wands and munitions at the monster scrabbling after them. Its huge beady eyes jerking from

208

target to target as if it was dazed. Or it just couldn't make up its mind. Bending down he took a moment to speak to Anna.

"Hey, Snow Cone." Anna, the boy beside her, and the girl on the other side of the vehicle were all turned around facing the direction they were fleeing. Fear was plain on the children's faces. The principal hadn't turned but her gaze was riveted on her view in the sideview mirror, and her hands were unconsciously clawing at the magical scroll in them. Anna turned to Kyle, and he could see in her eyes that she knew what he was going to say.

"I'll come help you." Before he could even say anything, she was reaching for the door to open it when the child safety lock clicked on all the doors as Jones activated it from the front seat. His sister hadn't had any time to recover from her standoff with her last monster and she swayed in her seat as the vehicle went over a bump. "Let me out." Her head turned to glare at Jones, but Kyle drew her attention back to him.

"Hey. It's going to be okay, Snow Cone." His lips drew back over his teeth in a snarled grin as he tried to pretend that everything was going to be okay. Because it would be. It was just going to be, well, there wasn't going to be an easy way. "I've got awesome armor and I'm going to use that spell I've always wanted to try but there was never enough magic around for it. So, I need you to make sure everyone gets away."

"Kyle..." Anna nodded, tears filling her eyes because she hated that he was going into danger without her.

"Good enough. Get my sister to safety, Jones." He shouted then leaped off the back of the vehicle where he'd been standing guard.

"What? Kyle, no!" Anna shouted as she turned to look behind them. She saw her brother facing off against a monster far faster and meaner than the thing he'd previously fought. She immediately tried to get out of the vehicle and Jones enabled the child safety locks. "Let me out. I have to go and help him." She started crying harder.

"No. Anna." Jones told her as stoically as he could. "You really don't." She turned in her seat as Liam tried to comfort her and keep her calm. The sky was still blue and clear. The bright sun illuminated everything clearly. Kyle looked so small compared to the thing rising up behind them.

"Anna. Anna." The principal had turned around when she'd heard Kyle and wanted clarification. "Anna, I need you to focus for a minute. What spell is Kyle talking about?" Anna's face drained of what little color it had regained since her epic display of magic use. "What tier is it? How much distance do we need?"

"Oh, shit." The teen breathed as her mind registered what her brother had meant. "More. We need more distance. As far as we can get. Then turn so there's a few city blocks cutting off a direct line of sight." Tense silence filled the vehicle as it sped away from the following monster. Anna watched her brother grow smaller and smaller until her view of him was cut off as Jones took a sharp right. She angled her head to look up at the sky knowing what to expect.

Clouds began rolling in. Dark. Heavy. Ominous. Within moments the bright sunny day had transitioned to an unnatural twilight. Her fellow passengers became concerned. From the driver's seat, Jones looked up at the sky and murmured "Oh shit…" before refocusing his eyes on the road to keep driving. A few seconds later a booming voice rang out.

It sounded like Kyle, but also not. Tinged with an unnatural power of the divine. The sky flashed brilliantly, painting the thick cloud cover with stark shadows of skyscrapers.

"WRATH OF ZEUS!"

Chapter 53

The heavy clouds overhead tensed up, then seemed to flinch away slightly as the shockwave hit. Anyone indoors or safely enclosed within a vehicle was momentarily deafened, while those unlucky enough to be outside suffered slightly worse and were buffeted with wind for a few long seconds. Their ears popped as if equalizing to a change in pressure, and the heavy scent of ozone was only barely dampened by the rain that had just begun to fall.

If anyone had bothered to check, they would have noticed that the sides of buildings exposed to the blinding flash were now noticeably warm to the touch. If someone had been watching the spell unfold without eye protection, they likely wouldn't be seeing for a few hours, though there would be no permanent damage from the light.

From her position in a fleeing vehicle with several city blocks worth of buildings between her and the spell, Anna was spared temporary blindness. She also wasn't sure if she was okay. Sure, if everything worked the way it was supposed to, then Kyle had just obliterated the very dangerous monster. Which was good. But Anna didn't know how Kyle had fared channeling that kind of magic through him.

'Wrath of Zeus' was the kind of spell that could kill the caster.

Most magic users relied on external sources of magic whether it was ambient magic, divine magic, or warlock patrons. Those were wizards, clerics or paladins, and warlocks. Most of the magic Kyle normally used was from his warlock patron, but he also had a wizard's ability to control, manipulate, and use external sources of magic. Clerics and paladins got all of their magic from the divine beings they served and their faith. Warlocks got magic from their patrons and their pact items.

But the fourth type of magic user was sorcerers. Sorcerers had an internal source of magic. It was a part of their very being. They lived and breathed magic in their sinew and bones. Now, anyone with natural magical abilities like wizards or sorcerers could augment their powers by becoming a warlock or serving a divine being as a cleric or paladin. But the spells available from a patron or a faith were limited. To use the full range of magic out there, a sorcerer or a wizard was needed.

However, wizards were limited to only the ambient magic around them. Whereas sorcerers were limited to their internal stores for spells. Or their affinity. Like Anna's practical limitation to ice magic. Ice was just easy for her. Other spells took so much more effort and used so much more of her power than ice. The point was that neither she nor Kyle could perform Wrath of Zeus under normal conditions.

Anna couldn't because though her magic was enough, using it for a spell that wasn't ice magic would multiply the magic requirement significantly. It would take her magic and then her life. Kyle couldn't normally use the spell because there wasn't enough ambient magic in any of the livable areas of the world and he had pretty much no internal stores to use whatsoever. So, he couldn't even cast the spell. Today though, today he could cast it. And if he managed the magical flow correctly, he might have survived.

He probably survived.

Still, Anna couldn't help worrying as she watched the rippling clouds above. They hadn't cleared away yet. How long were they supposed to stay after the spell had been executed? Minutes? Hours? She searched her mind for the answer and couldn't find it.

"Huh. What's going on? Where are they taking my students?" The principal's sharp question broke Anna out of her examination of the sky. Her gaze focused on the street in front of them. There was a large group of military vehicles in front of the Plaza de Saint Germain hotel. Yeah, there were a ton of vehicles, all-terrain vehicles, jeeps with turrets attached, hummers, and even several tanks. But there was also a convoy of vehicles loading up students. The ones she recognized loading up all looked like international students.

"About time the Magicorps showed up." Liam huffed from beside Anna and Jones made a non-committal grunt of displeasure at the implied criticism before he spoke up as well.

"They should have been here hours ago. But it's not just the Magicorps. Look." The soldier was right. Sure, there were squads of soldiers in yellow berets with wands and magical munition coming and going from the command tent as they left for assignments and returned for new orders. The ones standing around as guards and driving the vehicles looked like regular army though. As she watched, a group of soldiers with gods damned useless standard issue weapons approached their line of fleeing vehicles.

"Fucking army?" Jones muttered angrily. "Might as well be feeding the monsters. They're practically civilians. Everyone keep quiet, they'll be twitchy." Jones gritted his teeth in frustration and tightened his grip on the steering wheel while they waited for the soldiers to reach them. The vehicles ahead of them were already being directed out of the way to park.

But the principal couldn't wait any longer as she saw more of her precious students being loaded into vehicles. The last straw was when the student that had come with her started getting out of the vehicles and the school security personnel resisted the kids under their charge being led away by a military officer.

"No more. That's it. I need to see what's happening." She was unbuckled and out the door before Jones could stop her. Her headlong sprint towards the students and the school security who now had weapons pointed at them was halted when the approaching soldiers raised weapons to point at her as well.

"Well, that's happening," Jones growled in frustration. "If I'd known we'd been dealing with these idiots I'd have brought some crayons as bribes." But he quieted, kept his hands non-threateningly on the wheel, and forced himself to have a neutral semi-smile on his face. After a few tense, shouted exchanges where the soldiers verified who the principal was, they lowered their weapons, and one peeled off from the group to escort her somewhere while the rest continued on towards the vehicle that Anna was in.

Archangel Michael Vs. The Fates (Part 7)

Michael was ticked off. The pantheons had all agreed not to interfere with each other's followers. That had worked out wonderfully for a really long time. But for some reason, Camina Wattkins seemed to be the gosh-darned exception in everyone's mind.

Was it because of how she'd come to be a warlock? The competition had been quite fierce amongst certain echelons for the honor of being her patron. Because they had all known it would be an honor to have a mortal like Camina as their warlock. And honestly, Michael had only ever so slightly just nabbed her from Thor because the Norse already had Camina's mother.

It didn't used to be that way. When the divinities had used their power directly upon the mortal plane rather than only acting indirectly through their mortal servants and worshippers, they hadn't treasured the great ones as they did now. Mortals had been toys to entertain them back then. Even his father had been like that, killing off all the mortals willy-nilly every time he decided that things hadn't gone the way he wanted and trying to start over with his chosen few.

Most of the angels did not like when they saw that disregard for life or free will from the god who had created them. It made them wonder what would happen if they displeased Him. And the scenarios that played out in their minds had not been reassuring. Once the gods had all agreed to take a step back and only act indirectly, the mortals were no longer toys to them to be used and discarded. Their agents had become a precious resource.

Here was the thing. The divinities needed mortals to believe in them. They needed faith like a human needed air. Okay, not really. But the belief from faith was an integral part of their makeup. It was part of why the gods had all been so loose with their actions over the Millenia. They had been making sure mortals knew what was up, whom to pray to, and generally being the shittiest self-promotion team ever.

The world had suffered for it.

And the gods had all almost ceased to be because of it.

Now that they only really acted through proxy and prayer, life was both more enjoyable and they actually had more shit to do so they weren't making trouble out of boredom. *Earning* the faith of their followers was an intricate dance of answering prayers and acting by the proxy of their servants. A good strong servant had a much greater ability to generate faith and accumulate new followers.

While paladins, clerics, monks, nuns, and priests were great vessels for carrying faith, the miracles they performed also cost it. Warlocks on the other hand ran entirely on magic, even if it was divine magic, and generated faith at no real expense to a divine being. But it was hard to find a good warlock. There was a certain mentality necessary for it. They had to mesh with the morality of the patron and work to forward their agendas on the mortal world.

This had resulted in the various patrons cultivating lineages of warlock families. Hereditary servants one generation after another. But there was another kind of warlock bloodline. The kind who followed a particular concept or goal. Camina's family were warriors. They made pacts with patrons who either represented fighting or protection. Or patrons known to have powerful weapon pact items.

That was just one bloodline. And the warrior patron tradition was not nearly as common as Michael had expected it to be. Fisher, artisan, or farming bloodlines were far more common. Heck, there was even a few flying families. These families usually had a prescribed time or age when a child would become a warlock and take their place as a full participant in the family tradition.

Camina was from a warrior tradition. But she'd made her pact early and unscheduled, fighting for her life against impossible odds. It had caught the eye of every deity who was interested in that sort of thing. She'd been a desirable warlock because of her spirit, ingenuity, and determination. Someone who lived purely by spunk and grit.

There had been a fight over who was going to be her patron because so many had wanted to respond to her summons. And ever since then, the ones who'd lost out had been trying to mooch some of Camina's greatness off her onto their own chosen. *That* was the problem Michael had with what the fates were doing. They weren't just trying to build their own Camina by shoving someone into his warlock's sphere of influence. They were trying to justify influencing *his warlock* because their chosen hero was linked to Camina by fate.

Back in the bad old days before arbitration, Michael would have rounded up a posse of his fellow angels and any other divinities who were willing to side with him – though that was iffy because you never knew when someone was going to stab you in the back and switch sides – and just gone and hashed things out with a good old-fashioned rumble. It would have been messy and bloody, but once it was done… It would have been done. That is, until the next time, after the losing side had regrouped and decided to try again.

Arbitration, however, was forever.

The decision was backed by all the pantheons and enforced by all the pantheons. They didn't just take it upon themselves to act against arbitration because it would be acting against all the pantheons and all the divinities. That was one of the greatest reasons why arbitration was necessary now. There had been a lot of competition when it came to deciding who was going to be patrons for the Wattkins children.

Some of those who'd wanted to partner with the children hadn't been doing it entirely for the right reasons. A few had been bitter that they lost the bid to be Camina's patron. As Anna's godfather, he didn't want anyone negatively affecting Camina's life through her affiliations just to use Camina to help level up their hero faster. He was pretty sure it was already happening. Or was it entirely coincidence that the first major magical catastrophe in centuries just happened to occur the same day Jim Thafesh's thread of fate was twined with Camina's?

The odds were against it.

Chapter 54

"I'm so happy to see you guys." Jones' big smile and the tone of absolute welcoming in his voice as if it was the best thing in the world for the army to show up, shocked the children inside the vehicle. Anna found herself blinking in surprise at who well the Magicorps soldier was lying through his teeth. "We've had a rough time of it. So glad the calvary has arrived."

A couple of sniggers came from the two guys who were still standing on the running boards outside the vehicle. Jones had been selling it so well until the last sentence took it a little too far. Still, the soldiers were almost immediately more friendly toward Jones despite them glaring at the other two individuals who weren't nearly as impressed by them.

For her part, Anna wasn't particularly impressed either. They were of low rank. None of them were magic users, otherwise, they would have had the insignia for it, which was universal across military branches in the United States. These weren't rescuers. They'd be almost useless in a fight, and they knew it was the reason they were directing traffic.

Jones knew it too. He hadn't rubbed it in and had lumped this small group in with the overall efforts thereby not offending them. Which was smart. It kept people who weren't super significant from using the little power they did have to be jackasses. It was one of the things that her mom gripped about all the time. Small-minded people being petty because they could be was a common complaint in the Wattkins house.

After a brief friendly exchange, they were directed to park out of the way of ongoing efforts. Then the kids were escorted into the building to be sorted and sent home if their homes were safe. Boarding students were being sent back to whatever city or country they were from. It seemed a bit wrong for a military operation to be involved with a private school. Like, that was definitely unfair favoritism towards the wealthy and influential. It made sense of a sort though because so many of the students were the children of diplomats, politicians, and various other foreign dignitaries. For example, cough, a couple of members of royalty that everyone pretended were normal students, cough.

There were students of way more important people than Camina Wattkins there, so both Anna and Jones were surprised when Jones was stopped and told he had to report to the command on the scene.

"You need to be debriefed and assigned to a temporary team." Jones was informed coldly.

"I'm under assignment from the Museum." He pointed at the patch that showed he was assigned to the National Museum of Unnatural Science and History. "I'm under orders to escort Miss Wattkins until she's transferred over to Museum personnel, or she is returned to her parents' custody." One of the soldiers drew back as if Anna was a venomous spider and she was about to bite him.

"Wa – Wattkins?" He stuttered. "As in...*the Wattkins*?" Anna snorted and rolled her eyes.

"Was that you?" One of the soldiers turned to Anna with admiration. "Doing the 'Wrath of Zeus' spell and that giant ice shield?" Before any of the teens around him could speak, Jones answered for Anna.

"She did the ice shield. We did not witness who cast that Magekiller spell." He turned to the three students with him and gave them meaningful looks disguised as seeking confirmation. "Did we kids? We were several blocks away at least and our view was cut off from wherever the epicenter of the spell was by buildings." They had given quizzical looks at first and then they realized that no, they hadn't really *seen* who cast the spell even if they had assumed that it was Kyle.

"Oh." Clearly disappointed, the soldier's excited look turned downcast. Anna and Liam were both put out that he didn't seem impressed at all with her ice shield. To everyone's surprise, it was Sara who spoke up.

"But her ice shield was amazing." She placed her hands defiantly on her hips, tossed her long blonde hair in the epitome of spoiled rich mean-girl fashion and stomped a foot for emphasis. "She held off a gigantic monster for hours with it until the museum guys showed up."

And that's what did it. If Sara had stopped at 'but her ice shield was amazing', they could have been overlooked a little bit. But it was the big monster being stopped by the 'museum guys' that got them singled out and truly noticed.

"Yeah." The squad leader looked lazily back to a nervously grinning Jones and then at Anna with a raised eyebrow. "You definitely need to come with us and talk to command."

"Damnit Sara." Anna glared at her bully. "Even when you're nice..." She wanted to kick the girl. But they didn't get the chance to as Sara and Liam were led off to join the rest of the students and Anna somehow got lumped in with the S.W.A.T team, the school security personnel, and Jones for debriefing.

It wasn't bad. In fact, it seemed like things were going to go very well. They asked her about the ice shield. She admitted to it. They were like 'cool, we already knew you could do that you're a registered sorcerer with an elemental affinity for ice'. Then they asked about the Magekiller spell, and she told the truth, she hadn't *seen* who had used it. And they believed her.

Everything was hunky dory. Her and Jones were loaded up into a jeep in the convoy and driven out of town. Over the bridges, into New Jersey, and then to some kind of military base or office building. Honestly, she'd fallen asleep at one point, so she didn't know exactly where they were. Just that when they stopped, the sun was out again. When she got out of the vehicle she looked around and could see the dark clouds gathered over Manhattan and it was not as far away as she feared.

Chapter 55

"I thought I was being taken home?" Her question was ignored, and Jones shook his head while drawing close to her. "Jones…" she hesitated speaking his name because it was the first time she'd ever said it and was worried that she'd misremembered it. "What's going on?"

"I don't know Snow Cone." He'd used her brother's nickname for her without thinking. Kyle had referred to her as Snow Cone so many times that he'd just started thinking of the kid as Snow Cone instead of as Anna.

The soldiers escorting them, who were not the same as the ones who had originally approached them in the city, exchanged glances. They entered the building and after passing a few security checkpoints were led to rooms. They opened one door and gestured for Jones to enter.

"No." He insisted adamantly. "I'm under orders from museum personnel to protect Miss Wattkins. Until she is reunited with her parents or museum personnel, she is not to leave my sight." Again, the soldiers exchanged glances with each other as if Jones' words had confirmed some kind of suspicion they had.

"She won't be leaving your sight." One assured him. Then the other walked a few feet down the hall and opened the door there. When he flipped the light switch, the far wall of the first room lit up. It was glass. From an observation room. Jones rolled his head back and looked up at the sky with a sigh.

"You have *got* to be kidding me." Because now he knew or at least suspected what was going on. When she saw the interrogation room Anna's heart leapt into a gallop.

"Am I in trouble?" Her soft voice was incredulous as she stared at the room.

"No. We just got on the radar of someone who thinks they have clearance, but doesn't, so they don't realize how much trouble they are going to be in. Go on in, kid. It's fine. They're just going to waste a bunch of time and piss off your mom." Anna hesitantly entered the clean eggshell-toned room and immediately knocked on the mirror there.

The door was still open, but a soldier was standing at it between her and freedom. She heard a knock in return, but it didn't reassure her.

"How do I know that's Jones?" Ana called out just as she heard Jones shout coming from the open door.

"It's me, kid. Sit down and rest. I'll see if they can rustle you up a mana potion. I know you're exhausted." It was true. Anna was exhausted. She'd been running and fighting for hours, without breakfast or lunch.

"And some food? I haven't eaten today. And since Mom's been out of town Dad cooked last night. It wasn't good." After she'd said it, she wondered if maybe she'd crossed a line. But Jones just laughed.

"I feel ya. My dad's a shitty cook too. I'll see what I can do." Then Anna heard some quieter muttering as Jones conferred with the others. She sat down to wait and found herself resting her head on her forearms on the table.

In all honesty, Camina Wattkins was a terrible cook. Really, really, awful. But she was smart enough to acknowledge that she sucked at cooking and made sure that the house *had* food. Those pre-prepped meal boxes were lifesavers. And sometimes one of her grandparents would come over and cook. It was best when Kyle came over though. He was a great cook.

Her dad did food like a bachelor who thought cooking was women's work. Take-out and microwave dinners were his staple. Unless he forgot to go grocery shopping and was too cheap and lazy to buy delivery. They'd had fried jelly and pickle wraps for dinner. Which honestly wouldn't have been that bad if they'd had peanut butter or strawberry jelly. Nooo… all they had was grape jelly and pickles.

And the wraps hadn't been deep fried. They were pan-fried. So, they were burnt in spots, undercooked in others, and filled with scalding melted jelly and hot pickles. Sweet, grape, salty, dill in a whole wheat flour tortilla. Who does that? Why? Grape jelly in fried pickle wraps? Whole wheat tortillas?

Everyone knew it was supposed to be *fresh* strawberries, dill, salt, and cucumbers with sour cream in a corn tortilla that was deep-fried. The outside was supposed to be crispy. like a taco shell and have malt vinegar sprinkled on it. The flavors were supposed to be sweet-salty, and umami. The inside was supposed to still be cool while the outside crunched.

It was only a few minutes before someone showed up with a juice box, a bottle of cold water, a bag of nuts and a vending machine sized bag of corn chips.

"We weren't sure if you have any allergies? The sailor who brought them in stated in a questioning tone. Do you want the nuts?" Navy now? Interesting. Anna felt her eyebrow raise at the new development.

"No allergies." She responded and took both bags and the juice box. "Thank you." Tucking into her food, Anna settled in to wait while she glared intermittently at the mirror on the far wall. This was not how she had expected to spend the rest of her day.

It was not until she had clearly finished snacking and tossed her trash in the little bathroom-sized bin in the corner, that someone finally showed up to talk to her. She knew they were coming when she heard footsteps, a lot of them, coming down the hall. Which was easy to hear because the door was still open to both rooms. Anna heard the familiar sound of soldiers standing to attention and saluting as the newcomers shuffled in.

In the other room, Jones felt his heartbeat quicken as he watched a familiar face enter the room. It was the Vice President of Daedalus Engineering, the foremost military contractor in the country. Jones had never met the billionaire, but he'd seen him on TV enough times to recognize him. He was accompanied by a group of rather serious men in black suits, and some higher-ranking military officials. Not super high, not people who would have met Anna through interactions with her mother. None of them were Magicorps, however, and that was concerning.

Jones had stood and saluted like a good soldier should. And he'd gone along with things so as to not get Anna or Kyle in too much trouble while there was a crisis going on. But these chuckleheads taking advantage of that crisis to corner Anna for some reason was going too far.

"At ease, soldier." The highest ranked officer told Jones and his escorts. So, Jones relaxed and took the proper stance before addressing them. And no, he wasn't particularly polite about it.

Chapter 56

"Sirs," He addressed them through gritted teeth and an unfriendly smile. "Why is Anna Wattkins being detained and questioned? She has had a very draining day holding off a *class four manifestation* for several *hours* alone before a combined task force of Magicorps and museum personnel were able to relieve her. I respectfully request that my charge be released and allowed to go home to her mother."

"Ha!" the Army Brigadier General who happened to be the highest-ranked individual in the room, gave a bark of laughter. "Respectfully my left butt cheek. Nice try, but no." He turned to the others. "Take a seat gentlemen. You too, Specialist. I can't question you because you aren't in my chain of command and are assigned to the museum. But Miss Wattkins has answers we want."

"Your funeral, Sir." He muttered darkly to himself. Jones returned to his seat in the corner and sat down while the others took seats of their own. The lights went off, which made the view through the mirror much easier to see. A few moments later, a man in a black suit and an Army Colonel entered the room with Anna and sat down facing her but away from the observers.

"Hello, Miss Wattkins." The man in the suit greeted her. "Are you feeling better?" He was friendly in the way people who weren't used to dealing with kids were friendly. Warily. Awkwardly.

"Hello...Sir...ers?" She glanced between the suit and the Colonel. "I'm still tired, but okay."

"That's good." He shuffled some papers in front of him, aligning their edges on the table with a few taps. "We have a few questions for you."

"Uh...huh..." Anna might have been a kid still, but she knew that this wasn't a smart thing to do. This was all kinds of bad-idea on this guy's part. "Do my parents know where I am?" This jackass had the affrontery to look surprised that she would ask. That didn't seem to stop him though and he continued on.

"Are you aware that it is illegal to lie about magical ability to the government?" His question seemed nonsensical to her, and the teen frowned at it.

"Does General Wickers know what's going on here?" General Wickers was the man that her mother reported to. He was the Magicorps person who would normally interact with the Wattkins children for things like PR opportunities or bribery for Anna's cooperation in making Camina look more human to quiet the people who were afraid of one woman having the kind of power she did.

"Eyewitnesses at the New York Preparatory Academy incident state that an individual in a cutting edge magitech suit came specifically to rescue you. Who is he?" What the artificers fuck was this? They were worried about Kyle? There was a real genuine threat to American soil and these jackasses had kidnapped her because someone was doing their job for them?

"Does the Secretary of the Magicorps know this is happening?" Because this was bullshit. It was getting clearer by the second that there was no one of an appropriately high rank who was aware that she was being held and questioned.

"Where did the man who rescued you get his magitech suit?" Anna stared at her interrogator and snorted in amusement.

"Do any of the Joint Chiefs know what you are doing here?" *Because you are going to lose your job when they find out.* She thought maliciously at the jerk.

"Do you know which Daedalus Engineering employee leaked the plans for the Valkyrie flight suits?" That's what they thought was going on? Were these people fucking morons? Her head turned sideways as she looked closely at the man before her. Then she turned her incredulous look towards the blank mirror behind them.

"Wouldn't a magitech suit like that be the purview of the Magicorps or the museum? I don't see any Magicorps or museum personnel here. Except Jones." She was done being nice. No. This was some kind of idiocy and she checked out of the experience and stopped taking anyone seriously. "But you aren't questioning Jones, are you? Probably because you know you aren't allowed to know whatever he would have to say."

"Eyewitnesses claim that your brother, Kyle, was the individual flying the magitech suit. But Kyle's abilities are well documented. And he does not possess the magical capacity nor compatible warlock powers to use that type of tech. Especially not in his profession as a… cook." That made Anna laugh. Kyle? Weak magically? And cook? Was this guy who might have been from one of the three-letter agencies actually using a magazine article as a reference for what her brother did for work?

The Colonel had been silent until now. He'd been just watching impassively until Anna's tinkling laughter had been the straw that broke the camel's back of his patience. His eyes narrowed angrily.

"The narrative survivors provided does not mesh with the known facts. How were you able to contact the mage in the magitech suit if you were trapped in a school without power or a means of communication?" In the observation room Jones rubbed a finger nervously against his forehead as he recognized the look that had come over Anna's face. Yeah, he'd seen that look on her two older siblings' faces that very same day.

"Well, I called his cell phone, but he didn't pick up. So, maybe a fairy took a message to him for me?" Anna's flippant remark was meant to be humorous and break the tension a bit. More for her to relax than anything else. But it had the opposite effect on the man questioning her, his eyes widened, and he jerked his eyes to laser focus on the young woman attentively.

Watching through the one-way mirror, Jones covered his eyes with a hand as he felt the beginnings of a headache starting.

"Oh, kid. No. Now is not the time for jokes." He groaned as he realized that Anna had just made things go from inconvenient to probably bad. Beside him, his own guards and the higher-ranking officers had perked up at the idea that another species of sentient lifeform might exist on their world then relaxed and chuckled as they realized what was happening.

"Are you saying that the fae are real?"

Chapter 57

"Are you saying that the fae are real?" The suit and the Colonel were deadly serious, and Anna rolled her eyes in frustration. But it was on now. She was done with these fools.

"Clearly you weren't issued a sense of humor. Maybe you should see the quartermaster about that. Jerry, are you back there? We need a sense of humor up here." From behind the one-way glass, Jones suppressed his laughter with a snort. Jerry was the God of bureaucracy and just about every person in the military had prayed to that fuck head at least once.

"That's what you've been stuck babysitting?" One of Jones' guards asked quietly as they watched the exchange unseen.

"Not that she's wrong, that guy is a dick." The General added under his breath.

"Ha!" Jones gave a soft bark of amusement. "You should see her older siblings. This one's a veritable kitten." Then they quieted for a few seconds. Jones had gathered from the facial expressions on the other's faces and the way they grimaced at the interrogator they were watching that they did not like that man one little bit. He added thoughtfully before settling in to enjoy the show, "I should have told you guys to prepare popcorn for watching this. Snow Cone's gonna teach him what's up." In the room, the questioning continued.

"This is a serious matter, Miss Wattkins. It is a crime to lie to the government about or hide magical capabilities. The individual in the suit has gotten a hold of classified technology. You need to cooperate with us." No. She didn't need to cooperate with them. They were doing something illegal themselves and she wasn't going to give an inch now that she knew what was up. Not only were these guys dumb, but they were not the people who should have been doing this if it had been justified.

"Tells us about project Snow Cone!"

The young Elementalist leaned back in her chair, holding it suspended and rocking on the two rear legs with her feet braced against the table. Then she very deliberately and slowly, while looking the interrogator dead in the eyes, brought both her hands together. Her fingers laced together, and her palms rested against one another. Lastly, she bowed her head and closed her eyes gently.

Anna's face smoothed with serenity.

"What are you doing?" It was the suit asking. Anna could tell the two interrogators' voices apart and she opened one eye with a slight smirk. The Colonel looked slightly concerned, as he should have.

"Praying to my godfather." Her innocent reply was sweetly saccharine and confident. Despite her apparent confidence, the suit chuckled cockily.

"The AMD is too high for the Angels to see into the city." He looked around and gestured to the empty air. The lack of an immediate response from her prayers and the suit's words emboldened the Colonel.

"No one's coming. Please cooperate and answer the questions." No sooner had he spoken than the ceiling dissolved into light and an angelic voice echoed down from above.

"Anna, I'm kind of busy. Is this important? I thought you were safe already." There was a cacophony in the background. A multitude of voices arguing querulously. A sharp shrill female voice pierced the sound.

"Don't you run off. The boy is going to be *our* hero. The Greeks haven't had a hero in centuries." The protest was followed by a gusty sigh from Michael.

"You got one of the kids already. You can't just keep poaching heroes off of my warlock. She's not a crutch for you to limp your heroes through trials with." Well shit. There was stuff going on with her mom among the divine pantheons. As interesting as it sounded, Anna had to interrupt and get Michael's intervention.

"I'm in an interrogation room without a legal guardian, and I don't think the people who took me have told anyone important that they did it." Michael suddenly descended out of the glowing light in his heavenly armor. It was a white and gold version of the armor that Kyle had been wearing earlier, though Michael's was less technological-looking and more ancient. He positioned himself next to his goddaughter and glared menacingly at the men interrogating Anna.

"Normally when I appear before mortals, I tell them to 'be not afraid'. Your answer to my first question is going to determine whether I say that to you also, or if something else happens instead." The suit had jumped back from the table, his chair clattering on the floor. The Colonel was stunned into the stillness of a statue.

"But, but, but you aren't allowed to interfere in the affairs of mortals." The jerk in the suit protested ineffectually.

"I'm allowed to answer prayers," Michael replied with a toothy grin. "Now," Michael pulled out a chair to sit down. "Please get me whoever's in charge. Who's the big boss? I want to talk to…" he nudged Anna to prompt him for the right name.

"General Wickers." The teen whispered out of the corner of her mouth.

"Ah, yes, General Wickers." The angel was just settling in for a proper session of intimidating the mortals when another angel looked down through the glowing hole in the ceiling.

"Michael, you can't just leave in the middle of Arbitration, especially not one that you called for." The Colonel squeaked as Lucifer peered down at them with one of his demons next to him. The demon's nightmarish features contorted in a perpetual snarl beneath dark horns contrasted with Lucifer's angelic beauty.

"Oh, hey Anna, how's my favorite god-niece? Are…" The beautiful angelic features frowned like his brother's as he took in the scene below. "Are you in jail?" He turned to speak to someone beyond the sight of the people in the room below. The shrill voice was still speaking, and Anna was catching bits and pieces of the conversation.

"See, we should be able to turn Jim Thafesh into a Greek Hero because Michael doesn't even care enough to stay through the arbitration he –"

"Hey!" Lucifer interrupted the argument. "Did you three bitches do this to Anna to distract Michael during the arbitration?" Lucifer's accusation finally prompted the Colonel to speak.

"Mister Morningstar?" The Colonel squeaked in confused terror. Finally, another entity poked its head over the edge of the portal to the divine plane. It looked like a woman, but her age shifted from young to old and all the ages in between. She held a golden thread in her hand and was staring at it quizzically.

"What are you talking about? We did nothing. Anna's fine. She's supposed to be waiting for her brother to retrieve her from the…Anna dear. What are you doing here?" The Greek Fate looked between the thread in her hand and the girl below in surprise. "Mortal." Addressing the Colonel her voice took on more authority than the shrill whine she'd used when arguing with Michael. "What are you doing? You are interfering with the natural affairs of Fate." Turning to speak with someone behind her, the Fate called for backup. "Sisters, some mortal took advantage of the Fates' absence during arbitration to bully Anna."

"Who's bullying Anna?"

"Who's bullying Anna?"

"Who's bullying Anna?"

A chorus of divine voices rang out. They echoed and shook the room as the shimmering faces of divine beings filled the hole above and looked down upon the mortals menacingly. Both interrogators shrank back against the one-way mirror in terror. Then a louder voice called out deep and powerful above all the others. It reverberated throughout the building and the suit sank to his knees.

"Who's bullying my god-granddaughter?" A booming thud sounded, shaking the building. Then another. And another. Heavy footsteps coming towards the portal.

"It's okay, Dad," Lucifer shouted over his shoulder to the giant deity that was still some distance out of sight. "I've already got him on the list." The footsteps paused, then boomed a retreat.

"Not unless he makes it to my realm first." Another voice called out and the darkly handsome Hades poked his head over the portal and peered down as well. His long lashes framed eyes simmering with anger to see who needed torturing.

"Oh, yeah. Totes. I'm putting him into the pool with the standard shared custody agreement that all of us punishment afterlife deities worked out for people who bully Anna." Lucifer grinned and held up a hand.

"Sweet." Hades high-fived Lucifer's waiting hand and gave the suit and Colonel a nasty smile from behind his glasses. The acrid stench of urine filled the room as Anna realized that one of the dumbasses had pissed himself. Lucifer and Hades' malicious grins widened.

"Okay." A new voice came from above and out of sight beyond the edges of the portal. The sound of someone struggling through a press of bodies was punctuated by a couple of grunts of effort.

"Why has arbitration been interrupted? Michael, you can't just leave in the middle of a court proceeding. What are you all looking at?" A red-headed man in a suit poked his head over the portal, blinking his eyes as they adjusted to the difference in light. When his eyes finally focused on Anna, they opened wide in surprise. "Is that a minor being interrogated without a legal guardian or representative present? Do you need legal representation, Miss?"

Michael's smile broadened as he glanced up at Nicholas then back down to the interrogators.

"This is Nicholas Everstone, Heaven's attorney and legal representative of the divine pantheons." Michaael introduced the recently abducted attorney. In the observation room chaos reigned. The Brigadier General had immediately sent his subordinates running for ways to cover his ass and justify his actions when Michael first arrived. From their position in the observation room, the observers hadn't been able to see the portal to the divine realm. However, they'd heard everything.

Now, the general's stare was transfixed by the muscular divine warrior of Archangel Michael, because after the angel had introduced Heaven's attorney, he had changed his focus to the general. He could see through the mirror and knew exactly who was there and who was responsible.

Archangel Michael Vs. The Fates (Part 8)

The divine courtroom was stuffed to capacity as Nicholas Everstone gingerly pressed a magical un-melting handful of snow to his head wrapped in a piece of somebody's robes… toga… whatever. He didn't care what it was as long as it did the job and wasn't off someone's godly genitals. The last thing he needed was some kind of venereal disease from a God.

Thronging masses of deities from dozens maybe hundreds of religions – honestly he'd never bothered to research them and also didn't know the exact number – were talking animatedly. Off to the side, the big guy sat on his throne, head so high up into the ether that Nicholas had never seen his face. Though occasionally there were flashes of light from what had to be his eyes hidden in the murky multicolored celestial twilight.

Nicholas liked looking at it. Not God's face. No. Nooo. He wasn't trying to see it and suspected that bad things might happen to him if he did. Out of courtesy, the other divinities took forms that were safe for Nicholas to be around as a mortal during Arbitration. But the one, *the one*, he kept an immense form, seated on a throne off in the distance, shrouded from all as he watched impassively from afar.

That was fine with Nicholas. There was yet to be an arbitration that directly involved that one. Oh, his angels, sure. Yeah. All the time. Those kids got in spats with the other divine beings like preschoolers fighting over toys.

The attorney didn't think that one god's aloofness was because he was better than the others or more mature. In fact, he was one of the younger gods. No. Nicholas was fairly certain it was just because there wasn't something yet that one cared about enough to make a stand on it against the others. It made the mortal wonder if that god was capable of feeling love, or desires, or anything, really.

And when that thought occurred to the attorney it was very unsettling because there were literally billions of people around the world who thought *that* god *loved* them. Nick winced as he frowned, the movement pulling his sore flesh painfully. There was more than one lump on his skull throbbing in time to the ebb and flow of conversation around him. It was possible that he had a concussion from that jerk angel's abduction of him, but Nick hadn't been thinking about it much. Mostly because he'd been unconscious until a few minutes ago.

He probed gently at the tender lumps on his skull and hoped that nothing was broken. Normally, if Nicolas had been injured during the 'retrieval process' an angel, probably Michael, would heal him. Or one of the Greek divinities that represented healing. This time the angels and the Greeks were at odds and neither wanted to be seen as trying to curry favor. As usual, it was the mortal that suffered because of the strife between the pantheons.

Nick's eyes were blurring, and his vision swam when he touched his head in the wrong way. Yeah. Definitely a concussion. He was going to have to refuse to hear the case until someone, anyone – aahhh, maybe not everyone, he quavered as a dealmaking demon strolled by behind Lucifer – healed him. There were worse fates than dealing with an angel-induced concussion.

Out of the foggy brilliance of the heavenly court, a pale-skinned goddess drifted toward Nicholas. She wore some kind of ancient traditional garb. The kind of thing one saw in anime depictions of goddesses, but more. So much more.

She had long dark hair and luminous dark eyes. Her shimmering locks were done up in an elaborate style with decorative golden combs encrusted with flowers made of jewels and sticks that dangled beads and tassels. The dress? Kimono? Not specifically a kimono but robe-ish with a sash. What were those called in Chinese, or any other language? Surely the Japanese didn't invent that style of dress? It was silky and sparkly.

The garment was embroidered with scenes of great import to the goddess's worshipers. Probably? Nicholas didn't actually know. He just knew that it was ornate, lovely, and flowed around her ankles in such a way that she appeared to be floating over the ground. Maybe she was? Maybe he was hallucinating. The pulsating pain in his head was making it difficult to think.

As the goddess neared, Nicholas found himself mesmerized by her ruby lips. They parted as she spoke, and Nicholas had no idea what she said. He'd only realized she was speaking when she frowned kindly at him and raised one graceful arm, her shimmering sleeves trailing low beneath it. Her hands rustled around her sides as if searching for something and when she found it, she held it out to him.

Nicholas stared at the delicate pale hand with long crimson nails. On the palm was a round…thing. It was white and pink and lovely. Soft and fuzzy. Pretty. He smiled at it dreamily and the goddess sighed with frustration before gripping the fruit in her fingers again and shoving it into Nicholas' mouth.

He froze dumbfounded for a few moments. What had looked like soft fuzz on the object was not a pleasant feeling in his mouth. Before he could spit it out or push the hand holding the object away, the goddess used her other hand to push up on his jaw. His teeth pierced the fruit and juice flooded his mouth. Peach!

Not just a peach, the peachiest peach that had ever peached. The essence of peach burst on his tastebuds and filled him with contented clarity. That was nice. Finally, the thrumming din of the massed arguing assembly seemed to come into focus. Words registered in his mind for the first time since arriving.

"Bite it." The goddess was instructing him with a kind but urgent voice. "You need to bite it, chew and swallow." Who was Nicholas to refuse such a pretty goddess? Yet as he chewed, and critical thinking returned to his mind; the attorney began wondering if it was safe to be eating magic fruit from a goddess.

"You should feel better now. One bite to heal you. That's all it is." His concern must have shown on his face because the goddess put the fruit back into wherever it had come from with another smile.

"Thank you." Nicholas grinned at the goddess sheepishly. Here she was doing a good deed, and he was thinking negative thoughts about her trying to sneak him a divine… something. Honestly, what was he worried about? There weren't any bad myths about food from the gods were there? "I wasn't doing well, was I?"

"No. Not at all." She giggled and blushed as he bowed to her with a smile.

"Thank you for saving me, fair lady." It wasn't the way the attorney dealt with the divinities. He wasn't all that big on flattering them and was more about equitable treatment for all divine beings and mortals. But it had felt right.

"I couldn't let our noble arbiter perish due to our mishandling of him." And that made Nicholas like her. She was pretty and kind. She didn't think it was right to hurt mortals just because you could. Yeah. Nicholas was about to try his hand at flirting with a goddess who was still blushing prettily from his calling her a fair lady when a growing disturbance caught his attention.

"Oh, no. What's going on over there?" He'd finally noticed the crowd gathering around something. All the other divinities were heading their way over to the gathering and Nicholas realized that he might have to go break up a fight soon.

"Michael's goddaughter prayed to him for help, and he's run off in the middle of arbitration." The goddess informed him, and he slapped his forehead and groaned. "He's left the portal open. I think it won't take much time at all to straighten out."

"I better go see if I can help things along." He bowed to the goddess again. "Thank you for healing me. I greatly appreciate it." He missed the goddess' calculating smile behind his back as he strode into the press of bodies observing Michael.

Chapter 58

4:22 AM September 14ᵗʰ, 2026
Outside the New York Preparatory Academy Ice Bubble

Twelve hours. That's how long he'd spent looking for Anna and Jones. After nearly frying his brain performing a mage killer spell that he never should have attempted, Kyle had collapsed on the destroyed and crumpled asphalt of a New York City street. There he'd lain until someone had worked up the courage to run out from shelter and see if he was still alive.

Surprise, surprise, yes, he was still alive and kind of wishing he wasn't. Sure, everyone told you that performing mage killer spells was a bad idea because if you didn't have enough stored magic it was going to kill you. But nobody told you that performing them even when there was enough ambient magic to use them without fearing death was still going to hurt like you'd just mainlined a sack of bricks.

The kid who had run out to help him had been none other than the crazy selfie guy. And he had saved Kyle hours of agony with a pretty decent quality healing potion. Not museum or Magicorps field kit quality, but better than he'd been expecting someone to have on hand for general first aid. It had done the trick and got him up and moving again with a groan of regret.

"Oh, God." He'd wondered while working the cotton sensation out of his mouth and waiting for his head to clear. "Is this what a hangover feels like? Because gross!" After thanking the kid and declining a second photo op because he was too burnt out to conjure the armor again, Kyle started hobbling back in the direction of the Plaza de Saint Germaine hotel.

It was time to get his sister and head home. When Kyle arrived at the hotel he was stopped by the regular soldiers and then was hustled over to the remaining students and faculty who had been evacuated from the New York Preparatory Academy. He could recognize a few of the students there and knew that they were all individuals who resided within the city. The kids he knew didn't live in the city were all gone.

His sister was gone too and when he inquired as to her location, he'd been told that she had been evacuated to her home…in the suburbs.

Which was a lie.

"Anna Wattkins doesn't live in the suburbs." He'd snarled at the lieutenant who was referring to the list in front of him. "My sister and parents live in New York. It's close enough to this hotel that Anna could have walked there in under twenty minutes on a normal day. Why –" his hands slammed down on the folding desk and it sank three inches on the front side as the metal legs bent beneath the weight of Kyle's anger " – was she taken out of the city?"

"It's possible that she wasn't sir." The Lieutenant offered helpfully. "If her home is as close as you say it is, she may have been taken home if it was deemed safe enough." This mollified Kyle a bit even though he was still pissed off.

"Okay. Then I'll go see if she's there. Could you point me in the direction of the museum vehicle that Anna's security was driving? It's got all my gear in it." A pained expression passed over the lieutenant's face as he wet his lips uncomfortably.

"Ah. Your… ah… vehicle and the gear it contains has been… commandeered for rescue and evacuation efforts."

"Sonofanecromancer!" Kyle's tossed his hands up in frustration. "Do you have any idea how much one of thos – never mind." He'd cut himself off midsentence and thought furiously. How safe would it be to hoof it alone to his parent's apartment? Maybe.

His own place was in the opposite direction in the museum employee housing complex, and it was possible that Anna had herself taken there. Of anywhere in the city, the museum complex and the museum itself inside Central Park were the safest places to be. So, she could have gone home or there. Snow Cone had a spare key.

However, there was a third option. As unlikely as it was, Anna could have had herself evacuated to their grandparents' house. Which set, he was unsure of. But his mom's parents, who were actual fighters, were the logical choice. Though… the Wattkins did live further from the city and would therefore be safer.

Frustrated and pissed off that Jones had allowed himself to be separated from the museum's vehicle, Kyle waved goodbye to the officer who'd been helping him and then headed out toward his parent's townhouse. In less than half an hour he'd know if Anna had made it home. When the jeep full of soldiers decked out in alchemy munitions, wands, and the yellow berets of the Magicorps pulled up next to him to warn him that it was dangerous and that he should get indoors, Kyle almost lost his shit.

It was a good thing that he was too tired to channel more magic because the young warlock was one stupid question away from committing murder. Today had been rough and it wasn't ending anytime soon. So, he gritted his teeth, put on a wary but reassuring smile, and let the concerned soldiers know that he was fine, he was with the museum but that his vehicle had been commandeered.

A few exchanges later, Kyle was crawling into the back of the jeep. He was crawling because every overworked muscle screamed with agony. The smiling soldiers reached down, and he was pulled into the vehicle by multiple hands.

"Wizards." One scoffed as he took his seat and gave a friendly nudge to let Kyle know that he wasn't making fun of the class of mage. "All the wizards in our unit have been casting every major spell they use for high magic zone engagements, and they look like they're on death's door until they have a chance to recover.

"I just need a better-quality healing potion." Kyle waved dismissively. "There was a bunch in my gear but the entire vehicle and all the weapons and gear inside it had been commandeered before I was able to reunite with the evacuation group, I was buying… time… for."

The soldiers glanced at one another as Kyle's sentence devolved into a dry hacking coughing fit. His voice had been thin, hoarse, and reedy as he spoke and the blisters on his lips betrayed the nature of the spells he'd been casting.

"Buying time, eh?" Tears had filled Kyle's eyes as he coughed, and he blinked them tightly to clear his vision as he nodded. When his eyes cleared, Kyle realized it was the team medic who was speaking to him. He had that speculative analytic look in his eyes that all medical professionals give you when they realized you were downplaying what was wrong, but they weren't quite sure why. "Don't worry. We've got the good stuff."

Chapter 59

The medic made a gesture and one of the others opened up a locked and insulated impact-resistant chest. Kyle could see from the glow that reflected off the soldier's face that it must have contained very high-quality potions. He rustled around and pulled out a mana potion, a stamina potion, and a healing potion.

Kyle began shaking his head. There were so many reasons wrong with that, not the least of which was that it was too much potion for a person to take at once on an empty stomach. Not at that high a magic concentration in this level of AMD. But he chose to focus on the most important aspect.

"No mana potion." He insisted and the medic nodded in approval. "I've channeled too much magic today."

"He's right." The medic must have been using some kind of passive appraisal or examination spell on Kyle. "Grab him another healing potion, put the mana potion back." The medic smiled kindly as he took the bottles. When he handed them to Kyle, he took the warlock's hands and cast a diagnostic spell on him.

"It's rude to cast spells on people without their permission." Cocking his head to the side, Kyle sighed in resignation even as the medic's eyes widened into big round orbs. "Are you more surprised by what you read or by the fact that I could tell you were doing it?"

"Ahem. Sorry." He blushed in a way that probably got him a lot of attention from girls and pulled back with a wince. "Just wanted to make sure I was giving you the right things and could recommend a dose."

"What's my prescription doc?" Kyle croaked while uncorking the healing potion without waiting.

"A bottle and a half of healing potion now, the rest in six hours or after your next major injury. Two cc's of stamina potion every hour as long as you need to stay up and functioning." He paused, seemed to consider adding something else to it, then changed his mind.

Within minutes Kyle was feeling more like himself. He was still tired, but the blisters on his lips were healing quickly while the raw flesh of his seared throat smoothed. He hadn't even been aware that his breathing was being interfered with from all the damage he'd done casting powerful spells.

"That's my stop," Kyle called out as he realized they'd almost passed the intersection he needed to head for his parents' place. The jeep stopped and Kyle hopped out easily. The aches and pains in his body were almost entirely gone. Almost being the keyword there. He was still in pain, but it was far more manageable.

"You sure you're okay?" One asked.

"I'm fine." He replied at the same time as the medic answered for him.

"He'll be fine." Kyle waved and started off towards his parents then thought of something.

"Hey," He shouted to the jeep before it took off again. "When you see Camina tell her that Anna was 'evacuated to her home out of the city' by some Army officials. But I'm looking for her." He'd made air quotes so that the soldiers understood he was quoting someone. "Say it just like that with the air quotes. That had been all he'd intended to say but one of the soldiers shouted back at him.

"Camina? You mean, The Morning Star?" Kyle nodded.

"Yeah. You'll run into her if you keep going straight and then make a right turn when you hit the monsters."

"Right. Yeah." There was some muttering among the Magicorps soldiers as they took off again. They were discussing publicly known information about Camina Wattkins' family and they knew that Camina's family lived in New York City. From the sound of it, they'd figured out the message he was trying to send his mother and it was good enough.

He trudged on until he hit his parents' building, one home in a row of many. It was an expensive home. Not because it was particularly nice, just because Manhattan was a pricy place to live. Luckily, Camina and Lance Wattkins had decent salaries. More importantly, they were both from long warlock lineages and generational wealth had accumulated through centuries of service.

Kyle had nothing with him but his wand and his book. His keys were with the rest of his belongings wandering around the city in the museum vehicle he and Jones had lost the first time they went out on a call unsupervised. That was fine. He whispered a spell to unlock the door and the tumblers turned with soft snicking sounds.

Within three minutes of entering the house, Kyle had ascertained that not only was Anna not there, no one had been in the home since she and their dad had left for work and school that morning. Fine. Back the way he came to check his place.

He worked his way around the city hitching rides with various squads of soldiers working monster suppression. First to his home, then to the museum proper where he was unable to enter while the building was in lockdown because his museum ID was in the vehicle with everything else, he'd put in there for safe keeping while he was playing with too much magic.

Then he headed to his dad's office, hoping to at least find Lance Wattkins there. But no. Not only was Kyle's father nowhere to be found, the spell he whispered from the glowing pages before him told him that no one had been there since hours before the shit hit the fan. His dad hadn't been at work when the school called him that morning about Anna.

Dejected and trying not to assume the worst about his dad, Kyle returned to the street with a sigh. All the magical creatures in the city were starting to come out of hiding to take advantage of the high ambient magic density now that they realized that the humans were staying inside. A herd of prisms were basking in moonlight. Something that was rarely seen in New York City.

It was late and dark already. He'd been participating in search and rescue efforts as well as suppression efforts for hours. So many hours. It was only by virtue of the stamina potion he'd been given that he was still able to function. Yet he still hadn't been able to find Anna nor anyone who could give him a hint of where she was. Taking a deep calming breath while he watched the prisms, Kyle made the rational decision to go home and start the search again after a few hours of rest.

236

Archangel Michael Vs. The Fates (Part 9)

That had been the most satisfying bit of intimidation that Nicholas had ever engaged in. The way that officer freaked out from the Archangel Michael glowering across the table from him while hundreds of deities and demons observed menacingly through a portal to the heavenly courts? Priceless.

Normally, the attorney didn't really like that part of his job. Intimidating people on behalf of his clients wasn't something he enjoyed. He loved helping people though and that kid, Anna? Was it Anna? Well, she had needed help.

It wasn't like an Archangel couldn't handle some basic intimidation on his own, but Nicholas was pretty sure that if he hadn't stepped in, he would have ended up having to mediate the divinities arguing over who got to destroy those assholes and their families for the next…ever. Those idiots would have been fighting over who got to destroy them forever. It was easy to see why, Michael's goddaughter was a good kid, and she didn't deserve to be interrogated like she had been. So, Nick had done some pro bono work because no one should be bullying kids.

What surprised him had been the way all the divinities had stood behind Michael. Nicholas had heard of Michael's goddaughter. It was impossible not to have, since she was in the media regularly as the child of a famous mage. But she was a regular topic in the conversations of the divinities. As heaven's favorite attorney Nick heard Anna' name in passing conversation at least once every time he'd been summoned since her birth. The human had thought the frequency she was mentioned was because it was weird that Michael was so abnormally involved in his warlock's life.

Michael got a lot of flak for it, but he didn't care. The cynical part of the attorney had always assumed that the Archangel's involvement in his warlock's family was just a bit of entertainment. Yet, as he watched the absolute burning fury on the archangel's face, Nicholas realized that his affection for his goddaughter, his warlock, and her family was very real. The feelings every divinity felt towards the girl were very real. There was a depth of emotion for this one particular mortal shared among all the pantheons.

What had caused it? What had made her special? Was it just because they saw her as a person? Did it come from watching her grow? Her first steps? Her first words? The fact that she believed in and respected all the gods and goddesses as people? As family?

Heck, even the Big Guy moved when Anna was in distress. On the other hand, was that really a surprise? With the blessing at her birth?

It had taken a while to get things sorted out, waiting for a general and a politician with high enough rank to negotiate on behalf of the country.

"You want to negotiate a national policy regarding Anna Wattkins?" the stunned soldier had inquired in a trembling voice.

"Don't you think that's a bit excessive?" The voice had come over a speaker from the observation room and Michael passed a note to Nicholas letting him know that the person speaking wasn't even military but was a representative from Daedalus Technologies. His green eyes had narrowed in fury because he was starting to understand what this was really about.

Profits.

Those mother fuckers had essentially kidnapped a kid because they wanted access to technology or magic from someone affiliated with her. A fire of rage built in his chest from the kindling of that injustice and his voice became very precise… and *very frosty*. The archangel beside him arched an eyebrow and scooted his chair away from the attorney realizing that the lanky redhead was pissed off.

"I represent the *entirety* of every single pantheon. I want to stress this; I represent every single pantheon and all the divine beings in all of those pantheons. Do you get that?" Nick spoke slowly and deliberately hoping to impress the seriousness of the matter on everyone present.

Yes. The lords of the afterlife and underworlds were audibly debating the best way to torment those who upset Anna for all eternity right above their heads, but it was the tacit agreement of every other divine being observing that really drove home the point. Messing with Anna Wattkins was bad on a whole different level. These mother fuckers hadn't just pissed off one archangel whose powers of retaliation were limited.

"My clients want to speak with –"

"General Wickers."

"General Wickers."

"General Wicker." Michael spoke and all the deities who had been observing through the portal in the ceiling chimed in also. Nick grinned and felt a trill of excitement as he tried to hide the excited flutter in his fingers.

"– Yes," he continued. "General Wickers. We'd also like to speak with Wicker's superior –"

"The Secretary of the Magicorps. the Chief of Magicorps Operations, the Chief of Staff for the Army, the Commandant of the Marine Corps, and my congressional representatives." Anna chimed in.

"Really?" Nick turned to Anna to ask if she was sure that was something she could make happen. She was glaring with cold confidence at the man in the suit and the colonel who smelled like he had peed himself. Wisps of condensed air billowed out of her nostrils with each angry breath. The girl nodded.

"They owe me." He shrugged and accepted it because even if whatever favors she thought she had coming were denied, those people would come when they heard that every pantheon wanted to talk to them. Heck, there might even be a few extra individuals trying to worm their way into that kind of meeting.

"You heard my clients. Get us those people, whoever is authorized to engage in negotiations for the country, and someone in your chain of command with enough authorization to have you fired." Nick pointed at the suit who never did identify what organization he represented. Then the attorney leaned back in his seat and folded his hands in his lap. "We'll wait."

Chapter 60

Trudging along his way back home, Kyle came across a site that was uncommon in the busier parts of the city. A herd of tiny crystalline creatures, no bigger than a toddler's hand, leaping and playing on the sidewalk. Usually, they stayed out of sight, hiding from the dangers of a modern city like cars, people, dogs, cats and all the other things that could harm something so small.

One might not realize what the small creatures were doing if one could not see the currents of magic flowing through the city. But if one could, as Kyle could, then they would understand that the cute little crystal creatures with no head or tail that were basically four legs with a torso, were splashing in a riverine flow of concentrated arcanes. They drank it in and sucked up as much as they could.

A rustling caught his attention, and he noticed a raccoon stalking the group just in time to see it snatch up one of the little magic creatures.

"Oh, no you don't. Static zap." It was a small spell. One meant to hurt instead of maiming. The raccoon dropped the prism with a screech and a hiss before bounding away. Kyle stared after it, resisting the urge to take out his frustration on the creature. It was just an animal. It wasn't its fault someone had abducted his sister or lost her.

Piteous meeping drew his attention back to the herd of prisms. They had gathered around the one which Kyle had saved as it twitched piteously on the sidewalk. It also buzzed a bit with residual charge from betting hit by some of the static spell. The amount of charge was not enough to really harm it, but just in case, Kyle picked it up to examine it.

The prism's crystal body was somewhere on the scale between opaque and translucent and looked like a collection of quartz crystals joined together into a quadruped body. It also had a tiny current of electricity running through it which meant it had absorbed enough of Kyle's magic to change its magic type to electricity. That was one of the coolest things about prisms, they ate magic. Pure magic, elemental magic, it was all the same to them as long as they got those sweet, sweet, oh so tasty arcanes. But whatever kind of magic they absorbed, that was the kind of magic they became able to use.

This little guy or girl, was now an electric type. Kyle smiled as it rubbed one of its ends against him like a cat. Anna would like this as a pet. Kyle gently fed it a tiny bit more magic and set it down. The prism promptly ran to his feet and tried to climb one leg. Laughing, Kyle picked it up, gave it a bit more static electricity magic to eat and then tried setting it down again.

The little sucker clung to his hand as Kyle carefully tried to shake it off onto the ground. It would not let go. Now all the little prisms could see what was happening and were watching avidly.

"Fine, you can come home with me." The warlock grumped and placed the tiny creature small enough to it in his palm, into his shirt pocket and headed off. It meeped happily and hungrily and with another sigh Kyle brought a hand up to his chest to pet the prism. Immediately it grabbed his hand and began rubbing what may or may not have been its face on the finger Kyle had used to feed it previously. Piteously buzzing and mewling for more sustenance, Kyle relented and fed it lightning magic as he walked until it was vibrating contently in his pocket.

Maybe his bone deep weariness was the reason Kyle did not notice the other prisms take notice of him generously feeding their fellow. Nor did the warlock notice that the herd had started gathering around him hopefully. Because yes, there was plenty of magic around, but a nice mage that would feed them even once this windfall of magic had gone away was even better. Though the city was abnormally quiet with few vehicles on the street and the regular nightlife absent because of the emergency, it was still loud.

Monsters roared, sirens wailed from one hotspot to another, and screams and shouts punctuated the night. The noise and not the fact that Kyle was practically asleep on his feet meant that it was almost a mile before Kyle noticed the clicking. It was faint, just barely there under the sound of the wind which had picked up after night had fallen.

Yet, as he slowed and tilted his head to one side, Kyle focused on the sound which almost seemed to be getting closer. Click, click, clickclickclick. Clickity-click-click-click. Click. He stopped walking and the clicking stopped. Listening for a moment, Kyle shrugged and began walking again. Click, click, click, clickclickclick. He stopped again and to listen but again the sound had paused.

He took one slow step.

Clickity-click-click.

He took another step.

Clickity-click.

Then another step.

Click.

He began walking slowly down the street and the clicking surged and slowed with each of his steps as if something was trying to keep up with him. With a sigh, Kyle lowered his shoulders and turned around with his wand at the ready. If it was a monster, he was going to be so annoyed. It… was… not… Instead of the monster Kyle had been dreading in his depleted state, Kyle saw the herd of prisms.

With his mind churning out worry over his sisters – and the rest of his family – but mostly his sisters, Kyle had almost forgotten about the little prism in his breast pocket let alone the herd it had come from. They were following him. Did they want their friend back? Okay. Fine.

He carefully reached a hand into his breast pocket and fished the little prism out. It snuggled against his palm while vibrating its contentment. The little prism was warm despite being made of hard crystal and buzzed from the static electricity he had imbued it with. In its crystalline body Kyle could see a tiny little current flickering giving the prism an internal light.

"Looks like your friends want you back little buddy." Kyle tried to set him down on the sidewalk gently, but the prism clung to him again as it had done previously. For something that had such a smooth surface and no fingers, it had a remarkably tenacious grip. The other prisms reached their little stubby crystal arms up towards their fellow who just waved at them with one arm before latching tightly to Kyle's fingers again.

"Okay. If you want to stay with me, you can, but you have to tell your friends that they can't come inside with you." Gazing expectantly at the prism in the palm of his hand, Kyle waited to see what it would do.

It waved a limb at the herd. Then they exchanged a buzzing humming conversation in vibrations. Finally, his prism seemed to point in the direction Kyle had been walking in, nodded one end of its body, and then scurried up Kyle's arm, over his shoulder, and down his chest to disappear into his shirt pocket. After a few moments of rustling the prism poked what must have been its head, though Kyle couldn't really tell, up over the edge of the pocket to watch where they were going and waved in the direction Kyle had been walking.

"Oh." He laughed. "I see. You're ready to go?" The others were still watching, waiting expectantly. "I hope you told them that they can't come home with me." He shook his head as he continued on his way home with a herd of prisms following behind him. Those poor things were going to be so disappointed.

Chapter 61

It was the clicking that woke Jones. But it was coming closer like a stampede of tiny little feet in high heels. It had been growing steadily closer and louder on the street outside then stopped suddenly. So, when the slumbering mage had finally forced himself awake enough to focus after an exhausting day, he wasn't sure why he'd woken since it was now so quiet. Ugh. That was a nightmare. He stirred briefly before settling down into deeper sleep.

Kyle had left the herd of prisms on the street when he entered the locked building his apartment was located in. There weren't a lot of buildings inside the grounds of Central Park, but the employee housing for the museum was one of them. His apartment was nice, and he dreaded ever leaving his job and needing to move. As he was currently an intern and not a regular employee, moving was probably more likely than not in the next few years.

Not only was the apartment close to the museum, but it was also surrounded by natural beauty and central to everything good about Manhattan. His best friend lived down the hall so late night hang out sessions didn't require sleeping over somewhere or getting a cab home. The best part was that he was close to school, and his parents, and could help out with Anna still when they needed him to.

What was he going to do about Anna?

Mulling the question over, Kyle closed his apartment door behind him and headed to the kitchen. As the employee housing had been built by the museum it had magically powered emergency lighting crystals that cast a soft bluish-purple glow about the room. The blue was reassuring since the color of the emergency lights were Prometheus scale indicators and reflected the magic level outside.

Blue was the next level down from purple. If the ambient magic level was going down it meant that Sam and the F.B.I. had managed to secure the two magic emitting corpses. That was good. Dragon remains stuck around for centuries emitting high levels of magic the entire time. That property had made dragon parts a critical component in so many schools of magic. Enchanting, potions, technomancy, one dragon corpse was worth millions – no, billions – of dollars.

The same features that made dragons such coveted ingredients also made them dangerous to have around. Living dragons, not a problem. Heck, their bodies acted almost like natural magic collectors when they were alive, absorbing arcanes out of their environment. But once they died? All that magic started to release.

And that was the problem.

Their magic *started* to release upon death. Yeah, their corpses would up the local ambient magic levels, a lot. But it shouldn't have been enough to overload a major city's magic collectors. Strained the system, sure. Increased the local ambient levels. Absolutely.

The way it happened, though? No. That didn't track with how dragons worked. It was almost as if magic had been sucked out of the dragon instantaneously. Enough magic to overload the magic collectors. Dragons needed a certain level of ambient magic to survive. The amount each dragon needed varied depending on different factors like age, variety, size, and whether they were in their natural form or shifted to a lower maintenance shape.

Old dragons, the ones with enough magic saturating their bodies to overload a city-sized magic collector wouldn't be able to just wander around New York in their true form. Not without some kind of external magic source to feed on. Kyle mused as he puttered around the kitchen finding things to fix himself something to eat.

The power was still out but the backup runes in the refrigerator were functioning perfectly, and cool air greeted him as he opened the door. The glowing rune didn't cast quite enough light for him to see everything he wanted, so he held up the glowing tip of his wand as he pulled out some leftover pasta, butter, eggs, and sliced mixed vegetables.

Kyle was afraid to try lighting the stove. It was gas and he didn't know if there were any problems with the lines anywhere. At the moment he felt it was safer to avoid that because the last thing he needed was for his kitchen to blow up in his face. Instead, he went into his laboratory and grabbed the hot-cold stone he used in potions and enchanting work.

A soft glow came from the Daedalus Industries logo on the side as he activated the stone's heating enchantment. He set it on top of his kitchen counter and adjusted the heat before placing a sauté pan on it to heat. Once it was up to temperature, Kyle began tossing ingredients into the pan and pondered the question of the dragon corpse.

It had been in its natural dragon form. That form had been too big to fit in the truck without damaging it. Which meant that the dragon had died in the back of the Mountain King Movers truck while in a smaller form and reverted back to its full size after death. Something in that truck had killed a dragon.

Or someone?

He was making a carbonara, stirring the pasta with a silicone spoon and drinking milk out of the carton like a heathen. He smiled as he caught himself doing it. There wasn't much milk left, and he was planning on adding most of it to the carbonara anyways. No, that wasn't the way it was supposed to be done, but desperate times, eh.

Something killed the dragon in the truck. Something sucked so much magic out of a dragon while it was in a truck that it wiped out the city's magic collectors. Something triggered the dragon corpse to discharge magic at a much faster rate than normal. Whatever it was, Kyle was certain it would be found in the truck.

Was it a device? Or was it an artifact? If it was an artifact, it might be in the archive. Kyle glanced at his pact item on the counter. Just seeing it there was reassuring and helped calm some of the stirring anxiety he felt at the implications of his thoughts.

Not tonight. He'd look it up first thing in the morning. Still, a dead dragon was bad. The dragons might be fractious, but they didn't respond well to the death of one of their own. Despite the contention between the various dragon nations, they always came together for something this serious. No one was allowed to kill dragons but other dragons.

244

"Well...?" Kyle paused in his stirring, "that could be exactly what happened..." But no. The facts just didn't line up. That second magic source had been thrown into a building by extreme force. Could a dragon in a small form, presumably human to fit in, throw something that large through an industrial wall?

Probably not. Something drained that dragon in the truck which killed it and then discharged the magic it had accumulated so forcefully it threw the second magical source hundreds of feet through the air into a building. That had to be it. Kyle would stake his reputation on it.

With the food ready he activated the cooling feature on the hot-cold stone and cooled the bottom of the pan. Fatalistically, he touched a finger to the bottom of the pan to see if he was cool enough to not burn himself. Sam would shout at him for doing that every time she saw it, but he rarely burned himself. Which amused Sam anyways when it happened, and Kyle could heal himself so...

Sleepily, Kyle searched around for a fork and his wand. The fork was easy. It was where clean forks were always kept. Though, there were an oddly large number of dirty dishes in the sink that Kyle didn't remember making that morning. He frowned at the sink and then shrugged; he was too tired to think about it right now but couldn't remember why he wouldn't have washed the dishes the night before.

After at least a minute of searching, he realized that his wand, with the glowing tip that was illuminating his search, was in his gosh darned hand. Well, that was... Sheepishly, Kyle ran a hand through his hair and chuckled at himself.

"Glad no one else was around to see that." Sticking his clean fork in his pan of carbonara, Kyle headed into his living room and sat down on his couch groggily.

"Ow!" Kyle jumped up and froze, afraid to turn around. There were lumps on the couch, and they talked. "Kyle?" Why did the lumps on the couch sound familiar and just as tired as he was?"

"Who is that?" He turned slowly and pointed his wand's glowing tip at the lumps on the couch, which were under a blanket. A hand rose out of the blankets and blocked the dim glow of the wand from as face beyond.

"It's Jones. Could you lower your wand, Kyle? I know what you can do with it and I'm a little uncomfortable being on the business end of that thing." Yep. That was definitely Specialist Jones' voice. Kyle lowered his wand warily because while he knew Jones, the Magicorps soldier shouldn't have been able to get into Kyle's home.

"Hey, Jones." Kyle yawned then perked up as his tired brain realized that his missing sister had been with Jones. "Is Anna okay?"

"Yeah." The soldier yawned as well as pushing himself into a sitting position. "She's fine. Sleeping in your guest room. We had a bit of an adventure, but her godfather came and bailed us out with...yeah..."

"Oh, yeah." Kyle didn't know, but he knew. There was a reason that Anna didn't play sports or do anything competitive. And that reason was a very proud and protective Archangel and his friends in the pantheons. "Say no more. You can tell me in the morning. I'm going to go check on Anna and head to bed. Go back to sleep, Jones."

"Yes, Sir." He acknowledged with a habitual salute and collapsed into unconsciousness almost immediately. His snores began once again before his head even hit the pillow.

Kyle snorted his amusement and strolled into the spare bedroom in his apartment. There was Anna, like Jones had promised, a few tiny little snowflakes swirling out of her nose with each breath. It was cold in there. Not cold enough to prevent the snowflakes from evaporating into the air. But still cold, nonetheless.

Elemental magic seeped from Anna's very pores as she slept, saturating the air. She probably raised the arcanes in the room just with her very presence. Movement in his breast pocket notified Kyle that the prism had sensed the magical currents in the room as it popped its head out. It was cute, but it was just with him for food.

"Okay, little guy or gal." The warlock scooped the prism out of his pocket, and it eagerly climbed onto his hand. "This is my sister, and I think she is going to like you a lot." Kyle held his hand down to the bedside table and unlike when he'd tried to return the creature to its herd earlier, the prism hopped right off his hand. "I see how it is. No loyalty." Shaking his head, he watched as the prism clicked its way across the table and hopped across the gap between the bed and the table. It clambered onto the pillow and made itself comfortable in a nest of Anna's long white hair.

Relived that his younger sister, at least, was safe, Kyle headed to his bedroom, eating his carbonara on his bed. He'd meant to change out of his sweaty and monster guts-stained clothing before getting into bed. It was fine. He could wash things. To mitigate the spread of grossness Kyle decided to just sleep on top of the covers. Seconds after closing his eyes, he was asleep.

Archangel Michael Vs. The Fates (Part 10)

They were waiting for less than an hour before the high-ranking officials Nicholas had requested on behalf of his clients showed up. Which meant that they must have used teleportation to get them there A.S.A.P. That was nice. Heck, were there any other divine godchildren who needed representation? Because Nicholas could get used to having this kind of authority.

"Get this sonofabitch out of my sight and have his DD-two-fourteen processed by midrats." The woman giving the order as she entered the room followed by a trail of military police in Magicorps, Army, and Marine uniforms. She looked familiar and Nick eventually placed her face as belonging to the Chief of Staff for the Army. After the two jerks were escorted out, more individuals trailed in.

It was clear that no one had been prepared for this meeting. Some were already in their uniforms having been on duty advising politicians about the emergency in New York, others were in suits. But there was one guy in a pair of sweats, tennis shoes, and a zip-front sweater jacket. He was red in the face and sweaty like he'd just finished a run. His over-the-ear around the back of the head headphones were still draped around his neck haphazardly while one side clung to an ear.

Introductions began and those who knew Anna greeted her respectfully and with genuine kindness and affection. They eyed Michael's feral predatory grin with his ever so slightly elongated canines flashing whitely. Then a few shuddered as they looked up to the portal to the divine court and saw the rest of the gods, goddesses, and etcetera, watching angrily from above them. It was really a very good start to negotiations.

"Hello." Nick greeted the assembled military officers and politicians. "I'm Nicholas Everstone. I am the on call legal representative of the divinities when they deal with official legal matters in the mortal realm as well as the Arbiter of the Divine Courts." As he spoke, the attorney passed out his business cards to the assemblage. "When someone like Anna Wattkins who is divine adjacent, has legal problems, I am the agreed legal representative to be contacted on behalf of the pantheons."

"Which pantheons?" Someone questioned staring at the card dumbly.

"All the pantheons." Michael snarled and his statement was backed up by a rumble of agreement from the divinities watching from above. The questioner made an 'ah' sound and quickly placed that business card into his wallet with utmost care.

"As I have stated, my clients," Nicholas continued, "are *all* the divine beings. This includes representatives of the underworld and the demon hierarchy." That made someone gasp while most of his audience also showed signs of surprise. Nick noted the ones who weren't surprised. They were people he would have to watch out for and checked out of the corner of his eyes that Michael was watching those same individuals closely.

"And my clients *all* have a problem with what has happened here today. My clients want to know what you are going to do to prevent them from venting their wrath?" That brought more surprised looks from the officials and Nicholas looked over to Michael.

"The pantheons… are upset about one child?" One of the guys in suits, who had to have been the congressional representatives because Nick really couldn't imagine a general squeaking like that.

"Yes. They are upset about one child. There needs to be a policy in place that prevents government or military, or private industry interests from abducting a child or person that every single god, goddess, demon, deity, and astral being in existence has affection for. Your country," He smiled politely at the military officers, and career politicians sweating with concern as he paused for effect, "has angered every pantheon and you can either provide restitution and settle this my way by ensuring that you create a policy to deal with those who are affiliated with divine beings, or they…" Gesturing upwards Nick let his face turn grim. "…will settle it their way by seeking vengeance. And I won't try to stop them."

"What do your clients want?" When it was done, Nicholas wouldn't remember which general it was who asked that pivotal question. It was enough that someone had the good sense to speak up first to get the ball rolling. There were legal aids taking notes, advisors whispering for information. But by the end, they had a legally binding document and the outlines of a national policy which granted protections from harassment for divine beings, demigods, halflings, demon born, and those who were divine-adjacent like Anna. People who were mortals of this world but who had the favor of those who were not.

The document didn't interfere with warlock pacts, or existing religions, nor did it grant immunity for crime committed by the individuals it protected. It was just for people living their life, not causing issues, to protect them from imprisonment, interrogation, coercion, or exploitation by the United States of America or any of their officials or industries. And it was a masterpiece because there were literally thousands of deities looking over his shoulder to make sure there were no loopholes or means of exclusion.

When it was done, they took Anna and Jones first to the home the kid shared with her parents. There was no one there. So, she said she wanted to stay at her brother's place near the museum since it had better magic insulation and he would return there eventually. That was fine with Nicholas, he was tired and still worried about the people who'd been left behind when he was nabbed by the retrieval angel this time. As long as her godfather was sure she was safe, then Nick couldn't care less where they left the kid and her guard.

Which yes, seemed callous, but come on. The kid was fine and safe. She was literally being watched over by *all* the pantheons. At least, she was when they weren't fighting amongst themselves. Which brought him around to what needed to happen now. And it wasn't the hot shower, meal, and a good night's rest that he wanted right then.

Michael opened the portal back to the heavenly court and the other divine beings gathered around. While Anna unlocked the door to the building Kyle lived in. Before the attorney and Arbiter to the Divine Court could step through the portal though, a crowd of gods, goddesses, astral beings, and demons gathered around to wave goodbye to the teen.

"I'm glad you're safe now, Anna." Artimis called out. "If you ever want to join me on a hunt just let me know."

"I will." Anna grinned and nodded.

"Dreadful stuff today, Anna." Aphrodite purred with her very intentional sensuality. "Let me know if you need any help with that Liam fellow." The teen's eyes widened, and her face flushed with a furious blush. "What? Eww! Boys?! NO!" Jones chuckled and Michael turned to Anna with one eyebrow raised.

"Who?" The angel's head tilted to the side as he gave a very not happy stare in the direction of first Anna then Aphrodite, before swiveling back to Anna. "Do I need to go talk to someone else today?"

"No. No. Michael. He's just a boy I go to school with. It's not like that." Shaking her hands, Anna reassured her godfather that he did not, in fact, need to *talk* to Liam. "Boys are gross." The girl emphasized adamantly her brown eyes oozing sincerity. Aphrodite giggled at Anna's denial and shook her head in amusement.

"Okay, Anna. If you say so." Knowing that the Greek pantheon was already in the shit because of the crap the fates had pulled, she smiled knowingly and left it as it was.

"It might not be like that for her, but I've received three prayers from him in the last hour alone." Venus muttered to her fellow love goddesses. A chorus of quiet 'same' came from Hathor, Rati, Freyja, Oshun, Parvati, Juno, and at least a dozen others that Nicholas recognized were associated with love or marriage or relationships in some way.

They had spoken too quietly for Anna, who was standing in the doorway to her brother's building to hear them. Nicholas and Jones, who were right next to the portal, heard it all. Michael's face twitched violently.

"I'll look into the kid." Nick offered quickly to mollify Michael. Then Michael grinned a death's rictus as he waved goodbye to his goddaughter.

"Love you, Anna. Call me *immediately* if you need anything." Smiling sweetly and completely oblivious to the fury boiling inside the angel, Anna called back.

"I love you too, Uncle Michael. Come on Jones, I know where Kyle hides all the good snacks." Nick's stomach rumbled at the reminder of how long it had been since he'd eaten.

"Thanks for your help everyone." Jones bowed to the portal before quipping to the goddesses who were already gossiping about Anna's love life and debating whether or not the young Liam *deserved* to have any of his prayers for Anna answered.

"Well, we can't do anything that would influence the way Anna feels about him." Venus was adamant and Aphrodite gave her agreement, nodding emphatically.

"Absolutely not. I was thinking we'd make him like her more if she were interested. But that's no good. Not with how she feels about boys."

"He already likes her quite a lot, I think." Was Eros opinion. "She doesn't like him."

“I suppose someone could give him a few hints about what he could do to get to know her better and the two could decide for themselves how to go forward.” Rati suggested. “But I don’t know how I feel about a young man with so much pent up…” she frowned in distaste as she searched for the right word, “…affection… pursuing our precious innocent, Anna.”

“I give it four weeks before she stops saying he’s gross,” Jones piped up. “Anyone want to place a wager?”

Nick stole a look at Michael who turned around to Anna again, his face thunderous.

“No dating until you are one hundred years old, remember.”

“I remember. Bye everyone. Thanks so much for your help.” Anna waved and Jones followed her over to the apartment building then disappeared behind her. The archangel huffed a disgruntled sigh.

“I’m willing to negotiate on the Greek hero being partnered with Camina in exchange for keeping the love goddesses from interfering with Anna’s life.” It was growled from a place of loathing deep within Michael. Nick shook his head before following the angel back to the divine court. It was going to be a long and boring night of placating jumped up egos with too much power.

Chapter 62

2:15 PM September 14th, 2026
Museum of Unnatural Science and History Employee Housing

A beam of sunlight stabbed through Kyle's eyelids, searing his weary eyeballs. Groaning in protest, the young man rolled over and grumbled. Or more accurately, he tried to roll over and gasped in pain. Why was his body screaming at him?

"What in the artificer's heck was that? Why do I hurt so much?" He moaned under his breath.

It almost made him cry because the longer he lay there catching his breath, the more Kyle felt like the sunlight was burning his eyeballs inside his skull. It seemed like an hour of him gradually feeling the pain in his body fluctuate from sharp stabs to roaring aches to dull throbbing but was probably closer to five minutes. The lowering sun in the sky was also beaming more and more of its traitorous cancer particles through his window and onto his face.

As the minutes passed and consciousness returned, the warlock remembered what exactly he had done to make his body hate him so much. Monsters. Metal and false matter, flesh and bone flashed through his mind. One monster after another, sliced and diced, squished squashed, and squelched. In his hands. Under his boots. Bigger and bigger until the last thing screamed its unholy rage at him while the Wrath of Zeus spell rained down death around them.

Hazel eyes popped open in an effort to banish that horror from his mind. Then those eyelids immediately closed in reflex as the bright afternoon sunlight shone straight through his retina. Reflexively the young man closed his eyes and succeeded in rolling over, yelping through the agony as his abused muscles and joints protested. But at least he wasn't seeing the nightmare memories of the prior day anymore. He fervently hoped that wasn't going to be a recurring problem going forward.

Yesterday there hadn't been time to feel what he'd been doing at the time. Sure, there was fear under the determination to rescue his sister. He'd even had a not so healthy dose of self-loathing that he was killing living creatures even if they were monsters. Killing had never come easy for him and was one of the reasons he'd avoided the military career his mother had so desperately wanted for him to follow in her footsteps. Kyle had felt so much guilt beneath the disgust for the evil manifestations trying to consume the life in his city.

Guilt for killing. Guilt for being good at it. Guilt for disappointing his mother when he was fully capable of doing the job she'd wanted him to do, just because he didn't want to do it. Then more guilt for having to do it anyways after all the time the two of them had spent fighting over it. *I'll never be like you mom. I'll never enjoy killing living things even if they are monsters.* But he had.

Kyle loved magic. He loved it. He loved using it. Yesterday was horrible and he'd been terrified and angry, and disgusted, but what made him feel absolutely filthy inside his own mind was that he had been good at it. Casting spells of such magnitude and power requirements that they were colloquially known as mage killing spells? Kyle had murdered and danced his way through a city full of monsters, covering himself in splatters of flesh, and splashes of blood and despite the gnawing terror from the constant threat of death… he'd been good at it.

Shuddering painfully, he blinked tears out of his eyes. It was going to take a while to unpack all of that. And he wasn't going to enjoy doing it.

"I made you breakfast." A young, familiar, feminine voice spoke softly from over near the door. He turned his head gingerly in that direction. "And I rummaged through your cabinets for a healing potion since I wasn't sure how you were going to feel this morning."

She was wearing the spare pair of pajamas that Kyle kept in the guest room for her. It was pink with images of little cartoon cloud hopper rabbits and zigzagging lines of electricity printed on the fleece material. One of the buttons on the top was miss buttoned, illustrating how tired she must have been when she got to bed, and the hem hung unevenly exposing the drawstring on the loose-fitting pants. Kyle smiled and chuckled tiredly. That was so on brand for his baby sister.

"Thanks Snow Cone." He tried to get up, he really did, but in the end sighed in frustration and looked at his siter pleadingly. "Could you help me up? I over did it yesterday." Anna's face scrunched up in a giggle and for a second, Kyle was reminded of the happy chubby little cherubic baby she was so many years ago. Okay, so, maybe… just maybe, Kyle sometimes still thought of Anna as a little baby that needed to be coddled and protected.

"Sure." She padded into the room in fuzzy slippers and set a plate of food and a cup of orange juice on the bedside table. Turning to face him, she leaned down and wiggled a hand under his shoulder. "On three, okay. One, two three." She counted down in a voice that made it clear she was very amused that her big strong brother needed her help for once. "Heave ho."

On 'heave' Kyle tensed his muscles to rise and pushed himself up with one hand while grabbing onto Anna's shoulder for support with the other. Once he was sitting, Kyle gave his sister a flat look.

"Heave ho?" The warlock suspected that she was making fun of him somehow but hadn't been able to quite put his finger on it.

"Yeah," came her innocent admission. "It's what people say when they are working together to move big inanimate objects like boulders, stones, logs…" Kyle was certain that she would have gone on for a while if he had let her, but it only took a minute for him to get where she was going with her list.

"So, you're comparing me to rocks and wood?" Taking the plate his sister picked up and then handed to him, Kyle waited for her answer while trying to not drop the food he desperately needed.

"Hey if the object-without-a-brain shoe fits…" She shrugged impishly and easily ducked his pained clumsy attempt to swat at her playfully. "See?" Anna giggled as she turned and grabbed the orange juice which miraculously had a straw in it. Where had she gotten a straw? Did he even have straws in his apartment? "You can't even feed yourself after yesterday."

"Point taken. Is the healing potion in there?" His sister held the cup for him and steadied the straw. As soon as he put his lips on it, he realized the straw was made from ice. Taking a few sips and swallowing carefully, Kyle savored the sensation of liquid in his parched throat. Then sighed as the pain in his body first burned with accelerated healing then receded to a dull ache.

"How did you know I was going to need a healing potion?" Finally, able to support his own weight and hold the cup for himself, he took it and stirred the remaining liquid with the chilly straw. Melting liquid flowed over his fingers as he did, and he looked up at his little sister sheepishly when she didn't answer. Her arms were folded over her chest and one eyebrow was raised inquiringly.

"Really?" A snort of disbelief left her lips. "You *never* use as much as you should because you have a neurotic paranoia about rationing potions. I bet if I go through the pockets on whatever coat you were wearing when you got home last night right now, I will find a half a bottle of unused accelerated healing potion." She stood back and watched him imperiously as if daring him to prove her wrong.

"You're not wrong." Shaking his head ruefully, Kyle picked up his fork and dug into the eggs and pasta with a side of fruit salad.

"Eat up." She turned and headed out of his room. "The water's out, so you can't shower, but I made enough clean water that you can do a washcloth bath. The bowl is on the counter in the bathroom when you're ready."

"Thanks, Snow Cone." Smiling gratefully, Kyle started eating. He was still a little sore, but not so sore that moving felt like punishment. After he'd finished eating, the warlock headed to the bathroom to clean up. His clothes were stained with monster guts though thankfully the worst of it had evaporated as it had been from the false matter portion of the manifestations. Cleaning some of the muck and grime from yesterday off would be nice.

Stripping, he dipped the cloth into the bowl then yelped as the ice-cold water touched his skin. From his living room Kyle heard his sister's tinkling laughter, Jones standing up in concern and then Anna explaining between sniggers that it was just the cold water. Peering at the water more closely, Kyle saw the little ring of ice around the edge and grimaced.

"Very funny, Anna." Cold, and a little annoyed, Kyle summoned a heating spell. Whispering "Infernis," he cupped his hands in the frigid water, shivering as he did so. Though the water chilled his fingers to the bone, they warmed swiftly as his spell took effect. Then Kyle swayed as his magic levels dropped swiftly. Belated the warlock he remembered that he wasn't drawing on the magic from his pact and that magic levels inside his home weren't sufficient for him to just *do* spells all willy-nilly. His shoulders slumped dejectedly.

"Getting used to being a regular warlock again is gonna *suck*!"

Chapter 63

Mostly clean and changed into a fresh pair of clothes Kyle finally felt restored enough to walk into his living room. Yesterday's snazzy suit and dress shoes, worn purely for the benefit of looking professional while giving tours to museum visitors, had been replaced by a comfortable ensemble. Consisting of tennis shoes, a polo shirt with the buttons left unfastened, and a pair of khakis, it was what he usually wore when working in the secured rooms for restoring, evaluating, and storing artifacts.

Of course, an ensorcelled and protective warlocks robe was usually worn over anything an employee that worked with artifacts wore. It was a requirement of the job to wear the appropriate protective clothing. Kyle went to grab his lanyard and his favorite warlocks robe from the hook by his bedroom door and stopped when they weren't there. Dang it. His stuff had been in the vehicle. Oh, forget about the lost vehicle, his museum key card was missing, he was going to be screwed.

Giving a groaned sigh of exasperation, Kyle's shoulders slumped dejectedly. It was so unfair. Saving countless lives, battling monsters for hours on end, and he was still going to be canned because he'd lost a key to the most secure facility on the bunny fluffy planet. His mind was automatically editing his thoughts with his sister nearby. Even though he wasn't speaking them out loud, it was a force of habit with Kyle not to let his thoughts or words get too bad when he was with his sister, so that he never swore around her. It was their mom's rule that the older siblings were not to speak swear words around Anna.

"Jones," Kyle called out as he entered the living room, "I hope you have your key card because mine is in the vehicle I left with you yesterday. The one that the Army apparently commandeered?" Leaving the statement open, he lifted his voice to indicate inquiry and bit his lip nervously as he waited for an answer.

"No worries," The Magicorps soldier assured him as he pointed to Kyle's worn but sturdy second-hand coffee table, "The Archangel Michael hooked us up. We retrieved the vehicle, all of our gear – minus some used ammunition – and our personal belongings. It's all good." There on the table were Kyle's lanyard with his museum keycard, his not-too-awful identification photo smiling out at him, and his favorite warlock's robe.

He hadn't worn it to fight in because…? Well, he really didn't know why. Warlocks robes came in a lot of different styles and had multiple uses. The most basic was for protection from the elements and against blowback from spells or enchantments gone wrong. They were stylish, comfortable, but usually not designed for the kind of quick and indiscriminate movements required in the fast-paced combat environment.

Then there were dueling robes. Ornate and stiffly stylized, they deliberately restricted the movement of the warlock as the whole premise of a duel was to stand in one place while firing spells at one another. Combat robes went in the opposite direction and facilitated free movement with a highly flexible body that flared out at the waist, so the hem was wide enough to not restrict running while the robe was fastened down the entire length. Most were even enchanted to prevent the robe from becoming entangled with limbs as they moved. So why the heck hadn't Kyle worn his robes while fighting yesterday? That would have been useful.

Oh, yeah!

The suit.

"Thanks guys. I was freaking out that I might get canned for losing my key card." Jones, who was drinking something hot and caffeinated smelling, snorted said beverage through his nose and coughed in surprise.

"You saved like half the city yesterday. They couldn't fire you for the Army confiscating your key card." His disbelief was palpable. But Kyle knew that nothing he did would have made a difference if the museum was compromised.

"Yes. They could and should." He grabbed his robe and lanyard, donning them quickly. "We need to get to the museum and have my security enchantments changed immediately just in case someone got a hold of my card while it was out of our possession and gallivanting around town with the Army."

Jones was already dressed in his uniform from the day before. Anna had given him a pair of Kyle's pajamas the night before so that he wouldn't be sleeping in monster goo-stained clothing. So, he'd washed his uniform out the best he could with the ice water the elementalist had conjured in the bathroom sink by candlelight. He'd been too exhausted to use his wand as a light source. Then bathed himself in more ice water and passed out on the couch.

Though his clothes were still damp when he'd put them on, a quickly whispered spell had the dampness evaporating off him and steaming up the bathroom as he changed that morning. Anna had been waiting for him and Kyle to wake up as she'd made breakfast so many hours ago that it was cooled already.

"Alright, sir. Jones answered without hesitation. "Let's go then." His boots had been on and tied since he'd dressed hours ago. Part of him had wondered if he should have gone back to the museum to report in last night. But at the same time, he also had been under orders from the museum director to follow Kyle's orders, and Kyle's orders were to protect Anna until Kyle came for her. Since Kyle couldn't get into the museum, Jones knew the fastest way for him to be released back to the instruction of the museum director was to get Anna back together with Kyle as soon as possible.

Donning his robe and lanyard, Kyle rummaged through his pockets. He uttered a triumphant "Ah ha!" as he pulled out an object that seemed far too large for such average-looking pockets. It was a message scroll. The one he'd been issued by the director before heading out on his first assignment.

He read the messages waiting for him, his eyes scanning the page quickly. A little frown started on his face and the furrow between his brow grew deeper the longer he read. Kyle wasn't sharing so Anna sidled next to him to read over his shoulder. She began frowning also, which concerned Jones. After a few seconds, Jones shrugged and did the same, reading over Kyle's shoulder also.

Chapter 64

Kyle: I've reached the incident. FBI and their magitech division are on scene. Will notify you of findings after evaluation.

Director: Good. Keep me informed. I have faith in your ability.

Director: Could I get an update? It's been an hour. You should have a preliminary evaluation by now.

Director: The protective enchantments on the museum register that someone's using some high-level spells out there. Is it you? Are you under attack? Let me know if you and Jones are still alive, it's been two hours, and I can sense level two and three manifestations.

Director: There is a level four manifestation in the city. Get back here right now. Let the Magicorps and the superheroes handle the monsters.

Director: Kyle? Jones? Anyone who finds this message scroll? Please respond. There are three level four manifestations in the city. We've lost contact with anyone on the island of Manhattan.

Director: I'm getting impatient. If you don't respond in the next hour, I'm going to assume you are dead and wait until morning to send someone to retrieve your body.

Director: Gods damn it, Kyle! Someone just cast Wrath of Zeus inside the city and I'm pretty sure it was you! If casting a mage-killer spell didn't kill you, you're going to wish you were dead when I get through with you.

*Director: Kyle? *sigh* Please respond.*

Director: Jones? Anyone?

Director: It's ten P.M. If either of you is still alive, please let me know. I've been in contact with the military command that are directing suppression actions. You were both confirmed alive but that you've been taken for questioning. I'm trying to get answers, but none of my contacts with the Magicorps or any other branch know anything about it.

After this last message there were a series of scribbles on the scroll. Like a very young child had taken a pen to the page to make their own nonsensical version of writing. Nothing more than scratches really. Below this was a response.

Director: Who is this? I'm not a big meanie head. How did you get this scroll? Where is Kyle and Jones?

More scratches followed and another response. It continued this way for a while.

Director: What do you mean you 'found it under a pile of soft in tasty buzzy food man's warm place'? Who is tasty buzzy food man? Did you eat him?

More hasty scribbles that were almost indignant looking because of the hard slashes and the way the scroll was indented so deeply it almost tore through.

Director: Well, you called him 'tasty buzzy food man', how was I supposed to know you didn't eat him? We're in the middle of a magical emergency with monster manifestations. Why shouldn't I assume you ate him? He's sleeping? And Jones too? What is 'cold tasty frost sleep one'?

Another several lines of the bizarre scritches were on the scroll followed by yet another response.

Director: Of course, the word you are looking for is 'ice elementalist'. That must be Kyle's sister Anna. She does put off a lot of magic. You should probably ask if it's okay to feed off her first.

The next line of script – because it was clearly some kind of script if the director was able to read it even if no one on Kyle's end could – almost seemed to covey a sulky sadness and impatience.

Director: No. Definitely DO NOT let the rest of your tribe in. Keep those windows closed, they are the only thing keeping the monsters out. You don't want to let all the magic in so monsters can manifest and eat your new friends do you?

One last line of script was sent, and the director's response finished the conversation.

Director: I know. Your tribe is afraid of the monsters. But if they go up to the front door of the building, there's a package delivery slot next to the mailboxes. They can come in through there and then shut it behind them. Have them hang out in the mail bin and Kyle can get you all situated when he wakes up.

"I'm not the only one who can't read one side of this conversation? Am I?" Kyle finally spoke up in the deeply concerned silence that had sprung up around the three mages.

"I'm more concerned about who the fu –" Jones caught Kyle glaring at him and changed his intended word mid-syllable, "– uuudge. Fudge. Who the fudge was in here writing on your scroll while I was sleeping right next to it?"

"Then there's the fact that someone put it back in the pocket." The warlock of the archivist added looking around with alarm. "Were they being polite, or did they not want us to know that they were here? Also, who were they?"

"Where are they now?" Jones drew his wand, the end charging as he prepared a rapid cast spell in case combat was necessary.

"I'm more worried about the fact that there's a tribe of little hungry things waiting for us downstairs at the mail drop." Anna added. "And also wondering if I should be offended that I was referred to as a 'cold tasty frost sleep one'?"

A small chiming sound came from Anna. Not like a sound that a human being could make, but a ringing like crystal being struck and reverberating musically. Her eyes flew wide as she looked down at her chest where the sound was coming from.

258

"What is that?" She was clearly horrified as a lump moved on her breast. "Is it eating me? It was clearly told to ask permission!" Her indignant screech was followed almost immediately by her trying to take off her pajama shirt. But something about the moving lump stirred something in Kyle's foggy memories of the night before.

"It's okay. Calm down Anna."

"It's not okay!" She hissed back at him. Jones was now hesitantly pointing his wand at Anna appalled at the fact that there was something possibly crawling out of her body that she hadn't noticed munching on her all morning long. "You're not the one being eaten!"

Chapter 65

Kyle laughed and covered his mouth to try stifle it. Because as every brother knows, laughing at your sister when she was upset and telling her to calm down usually had the opposite effect.

"No. It really is okay." Her brother promised between bouts of laughter. "It's your new pet. I picked it up as a present for you last night on the way home. I just didn't know they had a language and could write."

"What? A present?" If there was anything that could redirect Anna's attention in fractions of a second, it was presents. She went from dancing agitatedly while trying to get whatever the thing on her was off, to calm and eagerly hopeful nearly instantly. "What kind of pet? Is it cute?"

"It's a prism. They feed off magical currents. I rescued the one on you from a raccoon trying to eat it last night." Anna stared down at her pajama breast pocket with wonder and excitement instead of the dread of only moments ago. Sheepishly, Jones put his wand away and went to run a hand through his hair. His hand paused, expecting a cap, then remembered he was indoors and wasn't wearing his cover.

"So, not dangerous, and not eating us?" He made sure to get clarification from Kyle.

"No. Not eating us. Just want to feed off our magical output. This one got a taste of my electric magic when I zapped the raccoon that was trying to make off with him. And after I healed him – or erm – it up, it refused to let go until I let it come home with me."

"It's so tiny." The trio had been watching the lump gradually worm its way up Anna's pocket and when it finally poked its head over the edge, Anna let out a breathy squeal of delight. "Hiiii cutie." Cooing at the prism in high pitched tones like she was addressing a baby, Anna held out her finger for the little crystal creature. "Are you hungry? Why were you hiding in my pocket?"

"That's probably my fault too." Her older brother admitted with a wry grin. "I let it ride home in my pocket last night, so it may think that's where it's supposed to be when it's close to a person."

"OoooOOOoohhh!" The ice elementalist continued her conversation in baby tones, cooing cajolingly to her new pet. "Did Kyle teach you to ride in pockets? That is such a good little prism. Yes, you are. Did the director and his message scroll scare you last night, so you went and talked to him? What a good brave wittle prism. You deserve some tasty magic. Yes, you do!" Jones snorted at the teen's antics as she wandered away, pointing a finger at her new pet which grabbed onto it and suckled like a baby.

"Well, that did a quick one-eighty." His dry remark was not lost on Kyle.

"Mom refused to let any of us kids have a pet because she didn't want to clean up after it or deal with all the animal regulations during PCS-ing." He shrugged in a self-deprecating way as if it wasn't a big deal. "Even if she just keeps her prism here with me, she's got herself a pet like she's always wanted now." Smiling fondly at his sister, Kyle pulled the stylus out of the message scroll and wrote a quick response to Director Arcas before rolling up the scroll, tucking the stylus back into it, and tucking the bundle into one of his pockets.

"Let's head out." Taking a breath, Kyle braced himself for the day to come. Following obediently behind, Jones spared one final glance at the teen and her new pet. He was pretty sure Kyle didn't know what he'd gotten himself into. "Hey Anna," Kyle called out to her from his front door. "Stay inside the building until we've got confirmation that the monsters have all been eliminated. Okay?"

"Okay." Her response was immediate and distracted... and utterly sincere. Kyle narrowed his eyes in suspicion.

"That felt too easy." The Magicorps soldier beside him murmured after the door had closed behind them.

"Yes." Kyle agreed.

They walked in silence toward the front door of the building, pausing to hear the little tinkling chiming sounds of the tribe of prisms that had made themselves at home in the incoming mail drop box. A few poked their heads over the side of the box and Kyle tilted his head skyward a groan.

"Easy." Jones grinned and shook his head. They exited the building and locked the doors behind them. Now in the walled courtyard that separated the employee housing from Central Park, Jones held up a hand for them to stop. There was a rhythmic pounding in the distance. Like the sound of many feet marching in step. But bigger, heavier. "What's that?"

Cocking his head, Kyle listened for a moment. Closing his eyes, the mage took the opportunity to enjoy the warm afternoon sunlight on his face. Now that it wasn't waking him up, it felt quite nice when paired with the crisp breeze blowing through the city. He was pretty sure he knew what the sound was, but he opened himself to the flow of magic around him to confirm his guess.

"The security golems." Verifying the source of the noise, Kyle opened his eyes and pointed in a direction tangent to where they needed to be. "They've been active since the initial event and have been patrolling all day. It sounds like they are actively engaged in monster suppression in the vicinity." Nodding his understanding, Jones placed a hand on his wand. "Don't," Kyle warned the Magicorps soldier, "They can handle anything tier three and under. But if you so much as flare your aura they could perceive you as a threat. Didn't you get the new employee orientation?"

"I did." The specialist agreed. "I just... force of habit."

"Have your museum ID handy. The enchantments on it let the security golems know that you are authorized to be in the area and use magic. But they're... twitchy... with me." He raised his eyebrows in a what-can-you-do gesture, and Jones raised his eyebrows back in a that-fucking-sucks response.

Chapter 66

Though the trip was a little terrifying, Kyle and Jones made the journey through the park in relative safety. Relative safety because arcanes were still saturating the area, and the high ambient magic density meant that while monsters were no longer forming the ones that had formed the previous day and hadn't been dealt with, were still active. The patrolling security golems had done their jobs in every way.

Their design was ingenious and especially suited for a disaster like this in multiple ways. First, the security golems were usually in a low-magic-use standby mode. In this mode, their enchantments absorbed, accumulated and stored the normally low ambient magic of the area for use during times when they had to be active. This process enabled them to remain active all the time. Even when there was very little ambient magic.

However, they also worked similarly when active during times of high ambient magic. This meant that in addition to killing monsters that did manifest in the area, the security golems' very presence was lowering the ambient magic of Central Park and preventing the formation of new monsters. Using their magically enchanted weapons features drained the ambient magic further still. They had been quite elegantly designed in Kyle's opinion.

Magically, that is. Not visually. Visually they were golems. Some with blocky and clunky looking. Surprisingly, those weren't the oldest golems, but newer ones designed to look like abstract sculptures. Some were elegant works of art that expressed some sentiment of myth or history. A pack of bronze wolves was snarling over the remnants of what looked like some kind of large spider beast and a trio of past presidents in marble were cartwheeling after the Enchantress Doughnuts food bike stand as it wheeled away from them frantically, its partially manifested monster form pedaling itself with arms that used to make up the poles of the shade canopy.

"Aww, man!" The warlock cried out in anguish. "Not my Enchantress doughnuts!" He grabbed at his hair theatrically and fell to his knees. Partly to have fun being over the top, and partly because it had been a while since he'd had his doughnut fix and now it was going to be even longer. His knees had actually gotten weak and if he hadn't voluntarily fallen to the ground in mourning he might have legitimately fallen a few seconds later.

"What?" Jone was startled and immediately went for his wand, unsure what Kyle was reacting to. So, Kyle pointed.

"There." After peeking with one eye to make sure he got the right angle, Kyle flung a hand and finger in the direction of the fleeing bicycle food cart then turned his head dramatically away. Closing his eyes, Kyle put the back of one hand to his forehead like a fainting Victorian maiden.

"Seriously?" His companion grunted in dismay. "A food cart? I thought we were in danger." Side-eying the civilian who – after the events of the day before Jones had started wondering if some of the gossip about the warlock of the Archivist might be true – he put his wand back in its holster.

"It's Enchantress Doughnuts." The words were said with such emphatic emphasis as if that explained everything. When the Magicorps soldier just stared at Kyle as if the words meant nothing to him, the warlock tried explaining again. "*Enchantress. Dough-nuts!!!!*" This time a shake of the head came from the soldier. "Literally the most delicious doughnuts on Earth. That was the closest shop to my home, running away on wheels."

"I still don't see what the big deal is." The soldier reached down to help Kyle to his feet.

"I haven't had my doughnut fix in days. And now it will be days longer, maybe weeks before a new doughnut bike is brought out to replace the old one. I'm not entirely certain if I can live like this!" Panic was setting in as he thought of a life without Enchantress Doughnuts whenever he wanted and decided that it was not a happy one.

"It's just doughnuts. You can eat other doughnuts." Aghast, Kyle gasped. A look of affrontery and betrayal so deep on his face that Jones was a little surprised.

"You take that back." Now standing, the young warlock crossed his arms like a petulant child and turned away from the soldier. Smothering a laugh and covering his smile with a hand, Jones agreed.

"Okay." And they began their walk toward the museum again. It was weird, walking through the park as the golems wandered about patrolling as they went or actively pursuing threats. No monsters came towards them, but the thumping of the golems feet as they moved, rhythmic as they patrolled in groups yet also out of sync as individuals broke off from their groups to engage.

It was as they neared the museum that Kyle became nervous and slowed though they had made good time so far.

"Hey." He motioned with one hand for Jones to hold back and keep pace with him while fumbling for his lanyard and employee identification card with the other. "You've got an ID card, don't you?"

"Yes, Sir." Jones nodded warily; uncertain what Kyle was so concerned about. He watched the nervous way the museum employee glanced side to side, his head on a swivel and scanning for… Jones didn't know what. But something.

"Get it out. And whatever you do, don't lose it." Something about Kyle's wariness bothered Jones. This guy had faced down class four monster manifestations without this level of concern. Heck, who was Jones fooling? Kyle had laughed in the face of danger and had fun doing it. So, for him to be concerned now, so close to the literal safest place in the city…

"What's wrong?" Jones felt his heart suddenly leap into a gallop. It thudded thunderously in his chest as adrenaline dumped into his system making him a jittery mess. Because Kyle was afraid and that was terrifying.

Was there some kind of special security precaution which went into effect during emergencies that the Magicorps soldiers weren't briefed on? Did Kyle, as the clearly more talented mage, sense a dangerous monster lurking someone in disguise that Jones didn't? The horrific possibilities were endless.

"It's going to sound stupid." Keeping his voice low and walking slowly and cautiously, Kyle explained. "But the sentry golems that are usually stationed here at the entrance to the museum, well… they don't like me."

"What?" It was such a letdown from the horrors that had been racing through Jones' mind. He'd been playing out various danger scenarios and how to get them both to safety despite potentially overwhelming odds and no cover besides some trees to hide behind. The question had come out flatly. In disbelief.

"The sentry golems don't like me. I get stopped almost every day on my way to work." Scuffing a toe shyly as he spoke, Kyle glanced up at Jones from beneath an unruly mop of hair. It had been wet when they left his apartment and had mostly dried into jagged chunky locks that looked like they might have wanted to curl.

"What?" Incredulous that something like this would make Kyle, the badass who took down at least two class four monsters the day before, nervous…well, it was just a little bit ludicrous. "That's… that's a silly reason to be worried."

"Is it?" He'd gone back to scanning for signs of the usual sentry golems, but they were off in another location as of yet, but looked back at Jones with a hard dark glint in his eyes. "Every day, every *normal* day I am stopped on my way into work and nearly dealt with as a possible danger. Golems in standby mode come awake every day just for me. What are they going to do now that they are actively seeking and destroying things they consider to be a danger?"

"Well, shit!" It was all the soldier had to say on that matter. But he did take a few side steps and sidle away from Kyle. They were still walking abreast but with a good eight feet between them now.

"That's not far enough away to not get caught in a greater fireball blast." Kyle chuckled and Jones surreptitiously moved himself just a little bit further away as they continued walking.

Chapter 67

Much to Kyle's relief, he and Jones reached the museum without incident. The normal sentry golems that provided security immediately around the Museum were all patrolling other areas of the park or further out around the perimeter. Whatever the case, the warlock was immensely grateful that he didn't have to test how well the enchantments on his museum employee identification badge worked during times when the golems were one hundred percent active.

Jones seemed to breathe a sigh of relief also as Kyle keyed open one of the unobtrusive rear service doors that opened into the loading dock. They were unable to enter through the main doors as those were covered with a security barrier at the time because the front of the building had huge glass windows. The kind of glass that was a near-perfect barrier against magical seepage, but still just glass.

Director Arcas was waiting for them as they stepped into the cooler interior and dimmed emergency lighting of the museum. The unique scent of the museum greeted him with its familiar blend of musty antiquities and clinical sterility. He took a deep breath, savoring the subtle hints of old parchment, corroded metal, and preserved inks, arts, and dust that hovered just below the air-conditioned climate-controlled breeze that was tainted with the slight chemical smell of cleaning solution and preservatives.

In the distance, his friend was cooking up a storm in the museum's café, adding his own blend of cooking magic to the arcanes that buzzed around and among the artifacts housed here. Food, magic, and old books.

It was better than home.

Kyle was relieved to see that some of the excitement of the day before had worn off Director Arcas. The bright hungry glint in his burnt umber eyes had dimmed to its normal level of bemused bewitchment. His black hair was brushed back with a few loose locks framing his forehead and highlighted the vampire's porcelain skin and perfectly proportioned face.

The director had the stereotypical too perfect features of vampires. He was fawned over by women for his god looks and unfairly muscular physique. Every time he looked at his boss Kyle was reminded that the vampire, with his perpetually sardonic half-smile and the careless ease he styled himself with, was just Sam's type. As a responsible brother, he should definitely continue avoiding the pair ever meeting. Because if the parade of dates the vampire brought to museum galas and functions were any indication, Sam was totally his type too.

That was a disturbing train of thought, and he quickly shoved it away before the recurring nightmare where his boss was his brother-in-law found any more fuel in the darkened corners of his mind. *Happy thoughts.* Kyle gave his boss a pained smile and desperately thought of anything else. *Happy, happy, thoughts.*

"So, you truly are alive. Congratulations on a successful first artifact retrieval assignment." Arcas fanged smile spread elegantly across his face with genuine delight. Though it gave Jones the heebie-jeebies so much he barely suppressed a shudder, that smile actually relaxed Kyle and put him at ease. It meant he wasn't in trouble for… everything he'd done the day before. "I was fearful that you were dead, and I'd been conversing with someone who had looted your corpse."

"Nope. Not dead." Smiling back, Kyle closed the distance between them and clasped the vampire's proffered hand.

"I bet you almost wished you were this morning. Eh?" Kyle groaned as Adrian Arcas, the vampire of an unknown number of centuries but who looked like he was perpetually in his mid-twenties, joked at Kyle's expense. They both chuckled and Adrian clapped his employee on the shoulder and then turned to walk further into the building. "You had quite the exciting day you two. While I just sat here in safety like an old hermit shepherding grumpy tourists. Could you secure the door Mister Jones?" Arcas called over his shoulder with the vaguely European accent that no one could place as he escorted Kyle along with him.

"Also, congratulations on surviving as well, Mister Jones. I didn't mean to neglect you; I was just overwhelmed with relief that I hadn't lost my Warlock of the Archivist. Please, come, join us. I can brief the two of you as we walk." He'd removed his suit jacket at some point and now had it draped across his shoulder like some debonaire trust fund playboy. However, it was also swishing behind him like a short cape and Kyle sent a silent prayer to the universe that Sam never, ever, ever met his boss.

Because…

…. eww.

But enough of that. Kyle had been worried sick about what happened at the incident site after he had irresponsibly left his sister and the Magic Crimes Division to deal with it. Though, when anyone asked in the future, he was going to frame it as heroically running to the rescue of a school full of children under monster attack even if he hadn't really intended to save anyone but Anna.

"So, the retrieval *was* successful?" If Arcas noticed that his question was hesitant, he didn't point it out. Instead, the probably older vampire nodded happily.

"Quite. Both corpses have been airlifted to an appropriate holding facility, and they have left the vehicle intact pending further advisement by a museum representative." Arcas was very satisfied with the outcome. "Though your sister and Gleipnir oversaw the transport, credit and first examination rights are coming to the museum. So, I'd count this as successful." His slight smile twisted a little higher as he chuckled and gave Kyle a side-eye. "I doubt your sister will be pleased with that."

"No," Jones guffawed from Arcas' other side and Kyle gave a small chuckle also. "She will not be pleased with that at all," he agreed as Arcas' devilish grin grew mischievous.

"She might just slap you again, Kyle." Jones and Kyle went awkwardly silent as they realized that Kyle and Sam's shenanigans had gotten back to their boss. "You're not in trouble; I understand that you can't control how your sister behaves. You are only responsible for your own actions." They continued along the broad corridor that led from the loading bays to the offices and public display rooms on the second and third floors. "I can't wat to meet the woman who isn't afraid to slap a man who can cast mage-killer spells."

Kyle gulped. Suddenly the hallway was a yawning chasm as his mind spun with his worst sibling dating fears. Then, a thought occurred to him, and he had the perfect response.

"Should I arrange for her and her partner, *ahem*," the warlock of the Archivist cleared his throat significantly as he said the name, "Alex, to come to confer with the museum in person for this retrieval?" At first, Jones furrowed his brow then understanding dawned on him as he cleared the confusion off his face just as Arcas glanced his way.

"No." If there was the ever so slightest hint of suspicion in his tone, the vampire hid it well. "It's quite alright. Your sister just seems like an interesting person, from the stories I've heard. You do have a very remarkable family."

"It's just Sam." Because while he thought his sister was remarkable for being herself, she was, after all, just being herself. She was smart and funny, and a bit of a brat. But she worked in a lab most of the time like him. They were average people. So, Kyle wasn't sure what was so remarkable about a girl slapping her wizard brother who would barely be able to cast basic spells once the arcanes went back to normal. "But she's alright."

Adrian Arcas continued smiling at Kyle and Jones as he closed the door to his office behind them. It was clear that neither of them had heard about Kyle's sister's exploits. He wasn't going to be the one to tell them.

Chapter 68

The meeting had been brief but exciting for Kyle.

"Like I said previously, the Magic Crimes Division handed the transfer of the artifact and the dragons." Arcas nodded towards Kyle. "It was definitely two dragons, which will be its whole own can of worms I'm afraid." His slight and vaguely European accent made the vowels sound rounder to Kyle. But whether that was the correct term, he really didn't know. His 'w's though, had just the tiniest hint of a 'v' sound to them. Sometimes Kyle suspected that the vampire was playing it up a bit to fit the stereotype that was expected of him by the museum's rich and powerful patrons.

"There's a registry of all the dragons in North America." Jones volunteered. "It shouldn't be too hard to identify them." Arcas narrowed his eyes just a tad before smiling again.

"If they are on the registry, yes." The Director agreed. "However," He continued, "considering the circumstances, one has to wonder…" The sentence trailed off and he left it hanging.

"Anyways, Kyle, you will be continuing the examination of the device at the facility Magic Crimes have set up." Glancing down at a very expensive pocket watch chained to his waistcoat, the dapper vampire verified the time. "Your flight will be here in about ten minutes."

Kyle's heart soared. He was so excited. Another shot at his first acquisition. But he as his eyes focused on the multitude of diplomas, certificates, and artifacts from the directors personal collection – presumably belongings from his long life – on the wall behind the director's head, Kyle couldn't help but to forcibly tamp down his eagerness. He had to ask.

"Is it really okay that I left the artifact acquisition incomplete? I know there's extenuating circumstances…" Arcas threw back his head and bellowed a hearty laugh.

"Kyle. Kyle. Kyle. It's not only alright, but it was also the best possible course of action." Nodding reassuringly Adrian Arcas began gathering up the paperwork Kyle would need for transferring whatever artifact they would find beneath the dragon in the truck from the Magic Crimes Division to the Museum's possession.

"Sir?" Kyle's quizzical and doubtful look drew another laugh from his boss.

"You rescued so many rich children with rich parents. Imagine the potential for gratitude or even guilt donations." His Burnt umber eyes gleamed with avarice. "So, many parents so happy that their children are still alive. Wracked with guilt that they were safe and sound and so far away while they experienced such trauma." Licking his slightly parted lips between his fangs, Adrian continued excitedly as his fingers steepled together. "Your actions have certainly generated so much new revenue, not to mention the potential for ancestral artifact donations."

It brought a grin to Kyle's face and a whimsical roll of the eyes. Of course that was what Arcas cared about. Money. And artifacts. As long as Kyle's actions benefited the museum.

"I'm glad to be of service, Director." Blushing a bit as the director smiled his way too handsome smile at him, Kyle bowed his head with not entirely mock humility.

"Now, stop that. Take compliments with your head high. Some might think it arrogant, but everyone has the right to be proud of themselves and their accomplishments." Upon finishing his sentence, he paused to watch Kyle and Jones, glancing between the two of them until they nodded acknowledgement of his admonition. Then he handed over the folder of documents he'd been gathering, signing and filling with stamps, embossing's, and official government enchantments as he'd spoken.

"These are all the documents you two will need. Get a full lab kit and your personal tools. I don't trust that the FBI will have the kind of equipment necessary for truly arcane magic." It wasn't said with malice, just a fact. And Kyle agreed.

"I do believe they work more with modern threats as a counterpoint to the more ancient magics and techniques that we deal with here at the museum." Kyle agreed.

"Excellent. You two, get ready. A helicopter will be on the roof in about fifteen minutes." Giving a delicate sniff, he turned his attention fully to Jones. "I suggest you take the opportunity to get a fresh uniform and a second shower, Mister Jones before you gear up."

Fifteen frantic minutes later, Kyle and an impressively decked out Jones were standing in the door onto the museum's rooftop helipad as a helicopter descended towards them. Its blades whipped the air up into a frenzy while beating gravity into submission. It was something Kyle admired about the physical sciences.

Sure, magic would have been smoother, more elegant. But there was something just as magical about the way human ingenuity could conquer the physical world in a purely physical way. It almost made him think that society would be okay if magic suddenly disappeared. Then he shook that crazy thought out of his head.

When the pilot waved them over, Kyle tightened his grip on the handles of the shock-proof cases in each hand. He moved them as a means of indirectly adjusting the messenger style magic bag whose strap crossed his body. This was it. This was his first solo acquisition. Again.

His codex rested snugly in its holster, quiet. Which meant the environment was safe and his path was clear since it had no warnings for him. Jones and Kyle ran low under the idling blades of the helicopter. Kyle hurled himself inside, grateful to be away from the heartrate raising spin of the blades. Being a trained Magicorps mage, Jones was more collected in his entry, easily taking his place and strapping himself in. The young warlock of the archivist found himself fumbling with the safety straps which Jones helped him chuckling all the time.

"Laugh it up, wise guy." Kyle grinned back and shook his head.

"You don't think it's funny that you can do the things you do, but safety belts stymie you?"

"When you put it that way…" Rolling his eyes, Kyle had to kind of agree with the fact that he had a lack-of-coolness problem.

272

"I'm really just smiling because we're going on our first solo acquisition." It felt good to hear it. It felt… Right. Kyle's smile broadened. Then the words echoed in his mind. *We're going on our first solo acquisition.* And his codex stirred. It wasn't negative, or a warning. It agreed.

Chapter 69

12:30 PM September 14th, 2026
Industrial Park District Near the Port of New York

Alex was taking a break from the long grueling hours keeping the site secure until the two corpses were taken away. It had been confirmed by Sam when she climbed out of the ruins of the collapsing structure monster, the second arcane source had been another dragon. Gleipnir was still inside the rubble wrapped around it and keeping everyone safe from it.

The sentient pact item had needed his warlock's help to get him into the mess so he could essentially – and Alex hated to admit this – save everyone. Or maybe the obnoxious ribbon-needle-thing of myth hadn't really needed Sam to go in there. Maybe Sam just refused to let him go in there alone?

Whatever the case, the magi-technician was now one of the few people known to have entered a class four monster and lived. Though from the mumbling Alex was hearing from the higher ups, the monster that had formed around the dragon corpse might have been an even higher level than that. However, Alex was finding it hard to trust anything the bosses were saying.

She eyed the pop-up Emergency Response Joint Task Force magically insulated command structure that was located a good half mile back from the ruined building. It had been there since about fifteen minutes after Sam and Gleipnir had neutralized the monster. Yeah. That whole chain of command that had been out of contact during the most dangerous part of this emergency had waited until it was safe to swoop in and look like heroes.

"*Ass*holes." Muttering under her breath, she drew her gaze back to the buzz of activity surrounding the second of the two corpses. The first, the one in the moving van had been easy to move. It had just been levitated into an enchanted net connected to magic collector and a couple of heavy-duty choppers aided by levitation specialist mages and helped move it hours ago. Frank had sent most of his people with it. As for the second…?

Industrial demolition experts in bright yellow magically shielded containment suits were swarming all over with equipment to remove the debris. One walked past her, sweat pouring down his face behind the clear mask. Meanwhile, bulldozers, cranes, and backhoes were loading the false matter remains of the monster into shielded trailers and dump trucks and carting it away to be 'safely disposed of'. Alex was fairly certain that it was code for, 'sold to military contractors and big corporations for experimentation'.

Frank had argued against that. He'd pointed out that the Eastern Dragon Empire might want the entire monster corpse because it was now part of the dragon's remains. But no one had given that a second thought. The false matter of the monster had taken on magical properties of the organic host body. Greed was fueling this whole project. All the people in charge saw were money signs. Billions of dollars of dragon false matter flesh and bones for experimentation with. Not to mention the actual matter of the building, the concrete, steel and… Alex tried not to think about it because every time the words flashed across her mind she vomited.

Organic. Matter.

Too late!

She turned and vomited onto a little strip of grass behind the vehicle she was leaning against. Frank patted her back and gave it a kindly run like he did with his daughters when they had the flu. *Such dad energy. Oh, thank God. I stopped thinking about the…* before she could stop herself the words '*Organic Matter*' popped into her inner dialog along with the images of he twisted broken bodies of the factory workers who'd been incorporated into the monster.

She hadn't known. Not until they removed the first layer of rubble armor from the beast. Like, she'd known, of course. She'd seen the corpses dangling from the monster as it came for her to eat her. But she hadn't *known* the true horror of it. That some of them had been alive when they were absorbed. That they hadn't been fully absorbed. That they'd been conscious and cognitive as the creature formed around them.

Those bodies weren't going to be buried. Those bodies were… *Some aren't technically bodies yet, are they?* A fresh wave of nausea overwhelmed Alex. Yeah, the waste removal specialist and the senior staff had tried to hide it from the FBI and military personnel – none of which were Magicorps – that were standing guard. But some of the agents had seen it despite their efforts.

Alex and Frank had already been briefed, four times, on how they needed to keep their mouths shut about what was happening with the…remains. *Remains don't fucking talk and beg for help.* An insidious little voice in her head whispered and another vicious abdominal thrust heaved nothing out of her body. She'd done this too many times already.

In the car, an unconscious Sam stirred and whimpered. Frank looked through the back window.

"She's fine. Just another nightmare." He watched her thrash feebly in her sleep. When she'd come out of the monster corpse, she'd seemed fine. 'Seemed' being the operative word. The exhausted and overspent warlock had not given the slightest hint that there was anything particularly traumatizing inside the monster. Just a regular slaying. Or so everyone thought until about seven hours ago.

After an interminable period of time, Alex felt her stomach settle. She'd started counting. Not counting anything. Just counting. Because if she put objects in her mind it would merge with the visions of the inside of the monster and prolong her agony. The first time she vomited, she was counting sheep. Because that's what she always did. Count sheep until she felt better and could control her stomach again. Alex loved sheep. They were adorable. They were her favorite. Her entire desk at work was personalized with sheep paraphernalia.

But no. This time, the images of sheep in her head, instead of jumping over a little fence on a green lawn, they had been sucked into the monster and were bleating horribly. Their little fluffy heads struggling to escape while their eyes rolled back in terror. So, now Alex just counted. Seconds.

Because seconds fed her hate. It felt like seconds after Sam had defeated the monster that the director of the New York Magic Crimes Division had miraculously appeared with suspicious swiftness as soon as it was safe. Backed up by the combat mages that hadn't been available to help out the investigative team. And the Army. Where had they been when they were needed? Huh? Why were the Magicorps monster suppression teams being sent *away* from the fucking monsters? Why wasn't there anyone who was normally in charge of dealing with monster incursions on site?

Huh?

Why?

Why had so many of her colleagues suffered near fatal or even possibly fatal exposure to magic while fighting that Gods damned zombie monster. And the nausea was gone, replaced by the calm icy burn of rage.

"You good?" Frank patted her back again which just made her annoyed this time now that she was filled with her new favorite emotion of righteous anger. The magic technician straightened and wiped her mouth on the back of her hand. A bottle of water was placed before her face, and she took it gratefully. She didn't gulp it down despite her growing thirst or the fact that today was even warmer than the previous one. That would be stupid and just give her stomach more projectile ammunition. She did, swish some around and then spat it out into the grass behind the car.

"I'm fine." Frank snorted and raised a disbelieving eyebrow.

"Really?" Rather than get defensive like she wanted to, Alex had to own the fact that he had reason to doubt her words.

"For now." Then she crossed her arms and went back to glaring between the monster-dragon corpse removal and the command center.

"You're goin' to get someone's attention if you keep glaring at command like that." How Frank had managed to keep his cool, the young warlock didn't know. If it had been her giving the briefing, she would have run her mouth something fierce.

"How are you not enraged that they sent us out here with the intention of letting us die. If I hadn't insisted that Sam and I take this call to keep her out of trouble…" Her voice broke because that coincidence was the only thing that had saved anyone.

What if Sam hadn't been here? What if she hadn't been teased in the office to the point of planning her retaliation? What if Alex had said, 'Fuck it. I don't care if my partner gets suspended for having a temper tantrum?'

Why hadn't everyone been sent out to the scene? Why had this happened the way it did? It wasn't normal. It was not the way that things were done. No one had followed protocol for an event of this size. Especially by not sending out any combat mages to back them up.

"You can't find out what's really happening if you let on to everyone else how upset you are."

Chapter 70

It had been a simple sentence that Frank had shared with the younger agent, but it was oh so important. Mostly because he was right, and she'd needed to hear someone say it to her. While she and San hadn't been partners long, Alex had learned that Sam feared no mortal… Because she was teamed up with Gleipnir and they both knew what Gleipnir was capable of. Neither had ever faced true evil though.

Until now.

Now, though neither new it. Well… maybe Gleipnir had been able to glean the situation but had kept silent for the sake of Alex? If something happened right now, the sentient artifact would have to choose between releasing the deadly magic of the dragon corpse he was suppressing to save his warlock or staying there to protect a city. On the other hand – Alex critically eyed the distance between the hill of rubble that was mostly excavated by now – they were parked awfully close to it.

"Hey, Frank?" She was quiet about it. Nonchalant even. And she focused really hard on the distance between the vehicle and the monster being torn apart. Looking at the superior agent and then significantly nodding her head and drawing her eyes in the direction of the thing. "If Gleipnir had to release his hold on that source of magic for some reason, like say to protect Sam from another monster or something, would we be in the pink over here? As close as we are, I mean?"

Shading his eyes against the sun, he made a show of squinting at the distance. Yes, it was another beautiful day. The sky was a gorgeous azure with the occasional fluffy puff of white dancing across it. So, yeah, it could be a little bit difficult to see against the glare.

She tried to hide her annoyed flat look, but Alex really wanted to elbow Frank in the gut about now. Here she was trying to be all inconspicuous about it, and he was making it obvious that they were worried about how close they were. People were going to get suspicious.

"You're right." He grumbled loudly in agreement. "If Gleipnir needs to release the dragon to fight in the case of another large monster attack, we *will* be in the pink zone. You move the car while I go and confer with the bosses about withdrawing non-essential personnel to a safer distance."

Though inside Alex was freaking out… on the outside, she was casual. Frank was casual about it too. Maybe they were too casual. Sam's keys were still in the ignition, where Sam had left them when she and Gleipnir had gone to do battle. There was a beautiful silk knotted design hanging from the ring with some tassel threads on the end of it.

A gift from Sam's pact item, Gleipnir.

Starting the engine, Alex began driving the vehicle further from the mound of rubble, flesh, and false matter. In the rear-view mirror, she watched as Frank's stroll towards the join command passed him close enough by the massive mound or Gleipnir to hear his shout that all non-essential personnel should retreat to a safer radius. Maybe it was an excess of caution. Maybe not.

Sam stirred in her exhausted sleep again. It was clear that she was sensing the increasing distance between herself and her pact item. The wrongness of it pulled at the unnatural slumber she'd fallen into after exhausting herself. Plus, the distinct possibility of magic toxicity. But she'd refused to let herself be evacuated for medical treatment without Gleipnir. The medics had declared her not in eminent danger of death, so the agent had been permitted to stay.

Then she'd fallen asleep.

A message printed itself on the rolling message scroll attached to the dash.

'Head to the containment facility. I'll stay with Gleipnir. Frank.'

Alex thought that was a good idea. Sure, there were still monsters that hadn't been caught by the squads around town yet. Sure, there was still work to be done to get Gleipnir and the corpse out of town. However, Alex didn't want to risk Sam realizing what had happened. She didn't want the warlock known for her temper and her absolute lack of tolerance for those who hurt the weak or neglected their duty as protectors, to figure out that they'd been let to die.

Okay, yeah. One could argue that their superiors knew that Gleipnir had the ability to suppress a Prometheus Pink category magic source, or even the types of monsters that would generate. But multiple sources? Like they'd reported? Multiple monsters?

Come on.

No one could ever argue that *one* sentient pact item and his young warlock who, by the way, was not a combat mage, could have taken care of that on their own. There we hundreds of people all over the city fighting. Just not the people who mattered. Not the F.B.I. And not a single high-ranking Magicorps officer to lead the groups that had been placed under the command of Army personnel.

No. Sam would make the connections eventually. And when she did, she'd be furious. But she had never fought evil. Monsters? Of course. But evil? Real evil? The kind of evil that delayed reinforcements and containment to deliberately give monsters enough time to manifest?

Sam had never met the kind of evil that would sacrifice the largest city in a country for whatever political scheming they planned. They needed to be nowhere near anyone who could observe her when she figured out what was happening. Because Sam would blow her lid. She would rage and Gleipnir would join her fight. They would take out some low-level player in whatever was going on and think they had won. Then one day, while she and Gleipnir were happily living their lives, something would happen to Sam.

Oh, it would look like an accident. They'd be separated conveniently. Then an elevator would fail, or a vehicle would run a red light. Or the containment on one of the devices she was working on would malfunction. And she would be gone. And Gleipnir's reason for interfering would be gone. Because he'd go to a new warlock. Because in the end, he wasn't really a person. Not to the gods who had created him. He was a tool to be used and bestowed for power and favor.

Chapter 71

12:30 PM September 14th, 2026
Manhattan Subways

    "All full up, Camina. We're good to go." Jim called out to her as he peeked his head around the end of the last subway car and headed toward her.

    "All right. Hop on." Her voice seemed light. Maybe tinged with exhaustion that was being held at bay with too many stamina potions. Underneath it though, the journalist could hear the seething rage that the soldier was feeling. Rage that had been boiling off her aura since she'd run into the group of Magicorps soldiers who had delivered the message about Anna being evacuated to her 'home' out of the city by Army personnel.

    Oh, yeah. The Harbinger was *pissed off*. She sure as shit had immediately worked her way to the central command and tried to get answers. Their response? *No one knew where Anna had been taken.* And that smarmy punk in charge tried to pretend that he didn't know where Kyle was and hadn't seen him at all either. It had taken Jim all of five minutes to locate at least ten different monster suppression teams that had worked with Kyle over the course of the afternoon and evening. So, yeah!

    Jim was pissed off too.

    Camina was The Last Line. And this, *this* was how their government treated her and her family?

    She'd been taken off monster suppression duty and reassigned to evacuation duty. Evacuation duty. Not guarding evacuees or clearing the way for them. No! Actual. *Evacuation. Duty.*

    There were thousands of people from out of state and surrounding cities who'd been trapped on Manhattan Island when the ambient magic levels exploded into the purple – and in some places pink. Now those people were being sent home. Not on busses because a few of the bridges had been damaged in the fighting. But via subway tunnel under the river.

    Which was fucking stupid because the alchemical waterproofing material that kept the subways from taking in water were also magical insulators. Normally, that'd be a good thing. It protected the electronics from small spikes and passing currents of slightly higher than normal arcanes. However, since the entire island of Manhattan had been flooded with arcanes, the subways had also been flooded with arcanes from the subway entrances.

    The emergency systems had worked like they were supposed to so no one had gotten hurt. That was good. It was great. The third rail had shut down when the power in New York had gone out. Backup batteries had been disengaged, and the trains' emergency brakes had locked into place, so they didn't roll on the tracks.

    But being in a low place, the magical insulation around the tunnels was holding arcanes in them. Arcanes that had nowhere to go. So, the emergency backup batteries could not be connected to the train engines. If they were… BOOOM! Because the batteries weren't magically insulated. Not against Prometheus Purple or Blue.

    And that was another dumb thing about this whole evacuation through the subway plan. Okay, *some* people were being evacuated via bus. But a majority of them were being put on subway cars and sent through the still Prometheus Purple arcane levels of the subway. Why? Why do that when there were perfectly safe Blue levels above ground right now?

Jim glared out the window of the subway car. The tunnel was fairly well-lit. Not dark. Not dim either. Ambient-magic-powered emergency lights both outside the cars on the tunnel walls and inside the cars. Standard just about anywhere in the world. Normally they were just barely enough to see by, but the high level of ambient magic had these quite bright. Nowhere near the same brightness as the regular electric lights inside subway cars. But bright enough.

This was dumb. So dumb. Camina had been assigned to *push* subway cars full of people through a high magic tunnel.

Pushing train cars wasn't the best idea to begin with. And they'd tried to argue against it. But in the end, orders were orders. Weren't they?

Jim caught himself as a sudden shift moved the vehicle he stood inside. He filmed through the rear window as Camina braced her hands on the train and pushed. Slowly at first. One step at a time he felt the cars colliding into each other, adding to the immense weight the warlock had to move with her powered armor. Each step came a little bit faster. Within a few minutes, she was jogging behind the train, her arms flexing with each footfall as she strained.

Then there came a point where she could hop onto the stand on the end of the car. After a moment of catching her breath, she positioned her back to make sure it was facing down the tunnel away from the train and turned on her thrusters. A mobile-armored-rocket-suit-powered train. Trip fourteen was off to a smashing good start. Only God knew how many more to go.

While they were moving at a good clip, that was just for now. The first part of their trip went downhill, under the river and the billions of gallons of water above. That whole crossing was fairly quick. It was the uphill slog to leave the river bed that was a slog. Jim had expected Camina's armor to lose power eventually. It or she hadn't. There was a well of divine magic fueling her right now.

The warlock herself wasn't even severely strained. Tired? Yes. Pissed off? Hell yes. But no matter how many times she had to push an entire train loaded with angry frightened passengers up out of the depths, the warlock kept going. A glowing white and blue beacon of hope that never seemed to fade.

Jim suspected that hope wasn't what was fueling her. It was rage. She'd taken a break a few trips ago to 'use the little warlocks' room' and had disappeared for a few minutes. The rictus of worry that had shadowed her eyes since she'd found out Anna was missing had faded. Jim suspected that she had gotten through to her patron and found out where her daughter was. Why did he think that? Because she was now just furious without the haunted look of a worried mother to balance it out.

Chapter 72

2:47 PM September 14th, 2026
Some Government facility somewhere relatively close to New York City.

Kyle had never seen a dragon up close before.

No.

That wasn't strictly true.

He'd seen living dragons in human form. At military or religious ceremonies, across the room at galas that'd he'd attended with his parents or while maintaining delicate displays for the museum during fundraising events. What he'd never seen up close before was a dragon in dragon form. Certainly, never a dead one – that was, baring the few minutes of examination of this dead dragon in dragon form the day prior.

It was different this time. Yesterday, the dragon had just been a source of danger. A puzzle that had to quickly be solved to make the city safe as swiftly as possible. And when that puzzle was solved, it was a moment of triumph and excitement for a young warlock apprenticing in his career field. Yesterday was something to be proud of.

Today it was a corpse.

A dead person.

The dragon had been brought to a facility outfitted with refrigeration and magical insulation that both had features of containment and collection. The magic collectors were removable, so once they were full, they could be replaced with empty ones. They were harvesting the arcanes the dragon gave off through the natural decomposition process. True, being chilled slowed organic decomposition, but arcanes came off a dragon corpse whether it was rotting or not. Those arcanes needed to be contained.

In Kyle's opinion, the arcanes didn't also need to be… harvested. Because that's what they – whoever had set up this facility, that is – were doing with the magic this poor dead dragon was giving off as the moving truck around it was dismantled. Or maybe they did. Insulating the corpse to prevent magical contamination from it getting out into civilization was all well and good. But how safe would that make working around it in a forensic capacity?

Those were questions of morality that a certain young warlock struggled with as he watched with as much detachment as he could muster. Now, Kyle wasn't necessarily cynical, but this facility was entirely too convenient. He was standing in an observation room on a second floor with reinforced glass windows looking down at the dragon from above… Ish. It was above-ish.

"It's a bit on the small side, isn't it?" That was Jones, stoically standing beside Kyle trying to make small talk while his groggy sister snickered at him from a chair. Before the Warlock of the Archivist could answer, another voice spoke up.

"It's probably young then, right?" Kyle turned from the macabre scene before him to glance at the speaker. His sister's partner, Alex, he thought her name was had finally looked up from worriedly watching Sam to participate in the discussion.

"That's…," Kyle hesitated because, "Eeh…*maaaybee*." It came out a little higher and more unsure sounding than he'd intended. He felt himself flush with embarrassment as Sam chuckled over her second cup of coffee. He'd considered offering her one of the stamina potions that were a standard part of a museum field kit, *buuuuttt…*

"You don't even have an idea?" She shook her head. "This is not looking good for you baby brother." He'd been trying. Really Kyle *had* been trying to keep their sibling issues separate, but Sam – was *SAM!* His face and voice turned cold.

"Youth is just one of the *many* reasons this particular Eastern Dragon could be so small, Sam." He shot back with as little hostility as he could manage. *Couldn't she just be, not… this… for one freaking day?* "But sure, I could be an irresponsible jerk and make the assumption that it's small because the elders let a teenage dragon, the equivalent of a human fucking baby loose in America. You know what dragons are like with their young. How protective they are. Why would anyone assume that a dragon child would be dead in an American city? Or that a dragon child could have enough magic to kill a city's magic collector?"

There were more reasons not to assume this dragon's small size was due to youth. Yet Kyle didn't have the heart to fight Sam like normal because her face, that was already paler than normal, blanched a sickly ashen shade. Her eyes lost some of their spark and a haunted expression stole across her countenance settling there like a shadow.

"The other dragon was an adult." It was quiet. Voice hoarse and thready with barely the strength to sustain itself. Those whispered words flowed through the room and stole some of the light out of it and a little bit of the joy that might ever be in the world.

Her words were significant not because she'd put any emphasis on any of them. Because she didn't. They were important in and of themselves.

"Adult dragons don't just die like that." She was haunted by whatever she'd seen while Kyle had been of saving their younger sister. "Not with so much magic sublimation that living bodies are subsumed into a monster manifestation." Setting his jaw in a tight clench, Kyle tried not to snap at his sister. He knew. He knew these things. And yet…

"You're right." Sighing, he turned back to the bloody efforts below to separate the corpse from the truck without damaging it too much. "And while dragon corpses give off significant levels of arcanes, the amount of magic that flooded the city should have taken hours, days, weeks, months, maybe even years to build up depending on circumstances. Even now, this corpse is losing arcanes faster than it should be."

"It doesn't seem that small." Alex offered hesitantly. "Maybe it's not a young dragon? It's almost as tall as this floor." That amused Kyle a little bit. Either this woman actually had no idea. Or she was deliberately trying to distract everyone by getting Kyle into an informative lecture on the dragon.

"Eastern Dragons can get quite tall in the diameter of their bodies as well as very long." The warlock's voice took on the lecture tone he used when giving tours at the museum. "Fully grown adult bodies can be two to three times the diameter of this one on average. Elder dragons will have a body diameter as tall as this floor. This one," he gestured down at the busy scene below them, "has been squished up into a cube that was over a story tall. So, while that volume makes this dragon seem like it is quite large, it's really just an optical illusion. Once it's unfurled and laid out, we'll get a better sense of its real dimensions."

"Or you could just cast one of those handy Archivist spells you have for examining things and be done with that already." Damn it Sam. Kyle could not work with her snarkiness. Regardless, he put his foot down and played a hand that was little more than an educated guess.

"No one is casting magic on that corpse until we see what is in that truck that killed it."

Chapter 73

Someone gasped quietly in the sudden silence. Kyle had been too preoccupied with his internal musings to realize that conversation around him had stopped. Not just his sister, Jones, and that other chick that worked with his sister. Oh, yeah, Alex. No. Not just them. Everyone in the observation room.

"Ahem." Someone cleared their voice behind him as the Warlock of the Archivist focused intently on the activity below them. It took a second pointed "Ahem." Followed by his sister calling out to him impatiently.

"Kyle." A shoe hit him in the back, and he turned around, put upon.

"Well, that's hardly professional." His confused scowl was entirely genuine. Sam looked up to the ceiling making an exasperated gesture and mouthing 'really God'.

"You just kind of dropped a bomb on us." The blank look on his face spoke volumes about his thought process. Or more accurately the fact that he didn't think he was the only one who'd come to that particular conclusion.

"What?" Alex and Jones narrowed their eyes at Kyle then glanced at one another as if to telepathically say 'is this guy for real'. Of course, neither had telepathic powers, they just felt that maybe, Kyle was pulling one over on them.

"Do you care to elaborate, Mister Wattkins." One of the guys in lab coats observing questioned him politely before Sam could tear into her brother. "Perhaps share your insight as a representative of the museum?" Kyle sighed. It had been said so politely but it was clear that a few of the other observers thought that he was being over cautious in recommending no magic use on or around the corpse now that the arcanes had been contained.

"Something killed that dragon while it was inside the moving truck. Right? That's why it's all squished up like it is and bursting out of the vehicle." Like he normally did when explaining things, he'd taken on his lecturer voice and started gesturing with his hands for emphasis.

"Yes, but that doesn't mean that whatever killed it is in the van with it." Someone protested disdainfully. Not the guy who had politely but sort of condescendingly asked for clarification.

"While that could be true," Kyle asserted confidently, "it's not. Think about what we know." He began pacing as he spoke, too energized by the theory and his need to see if he was right to keep still while discussing it. "The little dragon in the van died, most of its magic was sucked out of it. Enough to kill it almost instantly so it wasn't able to flee. We know it transformed upon death and reverted back to its natural form because New York city doesn't have a high enough AMD normally to support a dragon in its natural form. It's kept that way on purpose with the magic collectors."

Here, he paused, as a new thought occurred to him. Had the overwhelming of the magic collectors been deliberate? Had the goal been to make New York safe for a dragon to rampage? No. No. He shook his head in denial. That wasn't it. The pause had been only momentary, and he continued quickly.

"Something sucked the magic out of the first dragon, killing it instantly. Then that accumulated magic was released almost instantly also from whatever holding container or artifact had stolen it. The explosive wave sent the second dragon flying through a building while still in human form." His sister had been listening avidly and pitched in here.

"You're right about that. It had to have still been in a smaller form because the hole in the building wasn't large enough for the corpse that was inside." She shuddered as the memory of – everything – tried to assert itself into her conscious mind.

"Exactly!" Spinning, Kyle pointed to his sister excitedly, now that he had others thinking along the same lines as him. "The wave of energy crippled the larger dragon and sent it flying. It died in the building. Its magical structure weakened and its arcanes leeching off faster than they should have. Because even for two dragon corpses, the city being instantly flooded in Prometheus Purple and Pink levels? That's not natural."

"It should have taken hours or even days." One of the lab coats stated as he thought it out. And Kyle wondered why he was the only one in the room who had come to this conclusion. "This wasn't an attack."

"Not on New York." Kyle clarified. "Not intentionally. But I think that whatever happened was intended to kill those dragons. And they were after whatever it was that did it."

"Someone intentionally killed two dragons on U.S. soil." Alex finally pipped up. "So, we've got dragon hunters? Great."

"No." Jones corrected her before Kyle could. "No. The dragons were after whatever was in the van. They weren't fleeing. Because why would one be outside and the other inside? Why would the one inside die first and the one outside not only die second but retain more of its destabilized magic?"

It was always gratifying to Kyle when someone understood a lesson without him having to spoon feed the explanation to them. Jones was a smart guy, and Kyle was happy to have been partnered with him for this task.

"There's something in that truck that can kill dragons. And the dragons were after it." Suddenly the other observers were keener on the goings on of the refrigerated and magically insulated warehouse beyond the observation window. Alex was quick too, but Sam was the one who hit the nail on the head as she spoke up next.

"Unregistered, undocumented dragons." She thought for a few moments about that. "No one's been able to identify either of them."

"So, where did they come from? How did they get into New York? How did they find out about whatever it was that they were after?" A grim and unfriendly smile curved up the corners of Kyle's mouth. It was a puzzle. A mystery. Possibly even a conspiracy. Something that would make or break a young warlock's career.

Why did *this* have to be his first artifact?

Chapter 74

A storm of emotions roiled through Kyle as one piece of metal after another was carefully cut away from the dragon body by workers in magically sealed hazmat suits. His hands itched to go down there and help. It would be so simple. With the abundance of magic flooding that room he'd be able to lift and manipulate all the mass so easily. But he wouldn't be able to protect himself from the harmful levels of arcanes in there. So, he bided his time tapping his foot impatiently.

And occasionally pacing with glances out the window to check progress.

They were close now. A final sheet of metal had been lifted away by a winch set up in the rafters of the building. Now to unfurl the corpse from its compacted state. The coils of the body were too heavy to pass a strap under for attaching to the winch, so a forklift enchanted to protect the objects it lifted from damage was oh so very carefully levering an arm under the body to lift a portion of it.

It was a slow and delicate process. No one wanted to damage the body any more than it already was. Because being accused of abuse of a dragon corpse was not something anyone present wanted to be accused of. However, this examination needed to be done. They had to know what had caused all the chaos and destruction of the day before. A city was reeling and there were hundreds, if not thousands, dead because of this poor dead being.

"They're too close." Kyle warned the scientists whose facility they were using.

"The workers need to guide the –" The head scientist whose name Kyle had yet to bother remembering tried to protest.

"Someone is going to die if they don't back away from that corpse. If the body is moving, no one not in a protective machine should be near it." He turned away from the man he'd been addressing and glowered at the busy workers swarming over the body like ants. They obviously weren't all just there to move the body and remove the vehicle pieces. Clearly some were from various agencies trying to get at whatever was hidden in there first. Maybe make a snatch and grab before anyone would notice.

"Back it up. Anyone not operating equipment move back while the body is in motion." A voice announced to the group in the warehouse. Kyle watched them stop and look up at the speakers in the ceiling to listen. Some of the workers surrounding the creature backed away. Others edged closer. The warlock of the archivist eyed them.

With a half turn toward his sister, Jones, and Alex, he gave a little jerk of his head. Nothing overt. Just enough for Sam to notice. She in turn nudged her partner Alex before standing and brushed past Jones in such a way as to get his attention. In short order they were standing together joining Kyle at the window.

One of the great things about Sam was that Kyle didn't have to say much of anything to get her on the same page as him. They'd been two peas in a pod, the best of friends when they'd been younger. Their minds might not work the same way, but they knew each other almost well enough that sometimes it seemed like they could read each other's minds.

"Some of them not only didn't listen to that announcement," Kyle murmured "they got closer when others pulled out of their way." Sam gritted her teeth at his words.

"Who the fuck would interfere with a joint F.B.I. and museum operation?" She hissed quietly. "That's insane." As a reply, Kyle pointed.

"It doesn't matter. They are going to die in five…four…three…"

The worker's actions needed to be slow and respectful, and Kyle needed to maintain his patience which was wearing thin. He'd tried to warn them. Tried to tell them that they needed to back up… But did anyone listen to him?

As the forklift raised the coil of dragon flesh Kyle had indicated as the best place to start lifting, other coils of the dragon's long body began to shift and fall. Workers who noticed this fled further away. Some fled swiftly. Others didn't notice in time. The person manning the PA was shouting a warning. It was too late.

Part of the dragon corpse drifted sideways in an almost slow-motion looking fall. Two fleeing workers were knocked down. One had just been clipped, the other had been crushed beneath tons of weight. Chaos. Shouting. Hazmat-suited workers converging on the pair trying to help the trapped man who Kyle already knew was dead.

"At least one of them survived." Alex commented as the one who'd been clipped accepted a hand up.

"No, he didn't." It was Jones who had spoken, and Kyle was relieved that he hadn't had to be the one to say it. He just nodded and closed his eyes as the first scream started. Alex had looked to Jones quizzically at first, and then back to the scene below them when she heard the first scream. "His suit was compromised." Jones added.

The screams were short. Oh, it felt like they'd lasted hours to Kyle. Building and building up inside his head in a most unpleasant way. The sounds chasing themselves around the inside of his skull rising in pitch and terror until they ended on a gurgle.

"At least the mutation resulted in death and not…" Sam hadn't been able to continue her sentence. "Oh, Gods." She blanched, face ashen under the caramel tan. "Too soon." Her stomach heaved and she bent over to catch her breath, placing her head between her knees to reduce the nausea rising in her.

"I tried to warn them." Kyle watched the workers swarming and moving quickly, rushing to save people who could not be saved. Hours and hours later, the dragon corpse was fully unraveled, and the human corpses had been removed in their own protective containers. Then and only then was Kyle able to get his first glimpse at the device he was here for.

"Time to suit up and take a closer look at it."

Chapter 75

Forty-seven minutes. That's how long it took Kyle to suit up with a tech running a third check on his magically insulated hazmat suit. He knew he'd gotten it on correctly, but now it just felt like they were stalling for time. After seeing how careless bad actors could be in their attempts to pilfer the artifact right out from underneath their noses, Sam had insisted that one of the Magic Crimes division agents be watching the device at all times.

Kyle, for once, wholeheartedly agreed with his sister's prudence. Whatever it was, it was dangerous, and it belonged in the museum's vaults. It did not belong in some C.I.A., or N.S.A. black site. Or worse, with some DARPA military contractor trying to weaponize it in the name of Democracy. Behind his faceplate, Kyle scowled as he thought about what had happened with Anna the day before and sent a silent prayer of thanks to his mom's patron.

"Enough, all ready." Kyle groused at the technician fussing over his seals and swearing conspicuously in front of the security cameras that everything was good. "We're ready." He and Jones were joined by Alex and Sam in the first airlock before entering the warehouse floor.

"That took forever." Sam chimed in a brightly friendly tone. "Someone double check my seals." She requested quietly. "The tech helping me was suspiciously thorough."

"Mine too. Please." Jones requested in his ever-polite drawl.

"Same here." Alex added and Kyle's suspicions cemented in place.

"Since all of us had the same experience, let's double check each other's suit seals." Kyle performed a simple spell to check the integrity of the suits and the seals. Not all of them had badly sealed connections. But Alex and Jones would have had a bad time of it if they'd gone in without the last-minute double check with trusted colleagues to fix the issue.

"Why us? Wouldn't Kyle or Sam be a more critical target?" The bleak look of dismay on Alex's face had Sam patting her arm in a conciliatory manner.

"It's because we're the only ones who would be believable." The Magicorps soldier answered before Kyle could. He found Alex a bit obnoxious and therefore was kind of annoyed that he had to explain so many things to her.

"How's that?" Sam's partner moped as Kyle opened the door to the second air lock. Walking through, he detached his suit from one airline and attached it to another as he moved out of the way for everyone else to join him.

"Kyle works in these suits all the time in the lab at the museum. Sam's likely been using them for years herself. Though I've trained in similar suits, I've never worked in this kind before, and you are new enough to your position that you've probably only ever worn one in training."

Alex colored suddenly, her face blooming pinkly and she lowered her eyes. Looking at the ground she wiggled a toe nervously before looking up at Sam and blushing more.

"Oh. Yeah. That makes sense." The young woman's response stopped Kyle up short, and he gave her a keen look before glancing at his sister. His sister had frozen, turned her head slowly, and was staring at her partner with wide incredulous eyes. This was not the impudent, obnoxious, know-it-all smart ass that Sam and Gleipnir always complained about.

This was...

You know what?

Kyle had no idea what this was.

Jones seemed to actually think it was nice. He flashed Alex a charming smile for a moment until he saw the way Alex was looking at Sam. Then his smile froze on his face and his shoulders slumped ever so slightly. Kyle almost didn't notice it. Yet he had. So, it probably hadn't been subtle. Whatever that was would have to wait.

"Okay, people." He interrupted the strange interplay going on around him. "Let's get to work." The second door of the first air lock closed behind them. Kyle waited for a complete seal and double checked everyone's air hoses before opening which would be the third air lock door they were walking through.

A third set of airlines was waiting for them in the sterile environment. It felt weird to Kyle being the one in charge with his older sister around. But she didn't make a fuss as he insisted on making sure everyone's airlines were connected correctly, and their suits were properly pressurized and sealed.

"Intercoms on, everyone." They switched their intercoms on so that they could communicate with those who had remained behind in the observation room. Then he finally turned to face the gore oozing from the dragon corpse and retrieve the artifact he'd been sent here for.

In one hand, he held a large, magically insulated retrieval case with the museum's logo on it. Jones was carrying another in one of his hands. This was it. Their first artifact was mere feet away. Okay, more like several hundred feet away. But it was there.

The floor was a solid sheet of white. It had the feel of tile without the interrupted gaps between tiles that would have interfered with the building's magical insulation. Around the edges of the room and up the large white painted support beams, magical runes of preservation and protection glowed softly. Off to one side, all the metal pieces of the vehicle that had been removed from around the dragon corpse were stacked in what seemed like a very small pile. Probably for later examination or if they'd been saturated with enough magic, for use in creating future magical items.

But in the center of the room – uncoiled as gently as it was possible to do with something that much larger than a human being – sat the dragon. Long and gangly, the body was laid out along the floor. Though it was no longer looped over itself, it was sort of squiggled up to save room. There *was* another one coming after all. And that one would require even more space than this one.

There wasn't room for his magic book holster inside his suit. Which was fine. The magical insulation of the suit would have prevented the codex from functioning properly on the objects outside of the suit. But the hazmat suit was too large to wear his book holster over. Kyle's codex instead dangled from one shoulder where the holster had been carefully hooked so it would be close at hand for use. Slightly intimidated by the sight of the dragon waiting for him, Kyle patted his codex with one hand to reassure himself of its presence. Satisfied, the apprentice warlock squared his shoulders and trudged off to the body in the distance.

Cool air whispered into his helmet and each breath exhaled echoed loudly in his ears. It was just nerves. What if he was wrong? What if he'd miscalculated what he thought was going on? But no. It was there. He'd seen it.

Chapter 76

Kyle was careful in his approach. The ground was slippery with gore and though the larger pieces of the truck had been separated out from the dragon's flesh, the smaller bits had been left in place. It wouldn't do, to have come so close only to fall and puncture his hazmat suit. No, that wouldn't be good at all.

The overhead lights were bright and a cool white in color. Magically hardened electric lights to avoid interaction with any enchantments or magi-tech in the wreckage. Once again Kyle marveled at how perfect this location was for their examination. Almost like the U.S. government or one of its agencies or contractors had anticipated the need for examining a dragon corpse.

Okay. The warlock was able to admit he was being unfair even in his own mind. It was only prudent to have this kind of facility when things like dragons and monsters roamed the world. It was really, highly unlikely that some shadow agency had offed a couple of dragons and had this site prepped just for that incident. Probably. He was being paranoid.

The dragon's scales gleamed in the bright light. At least, those scales not covered in dirt and bloody flesh, or ichor gleamed pearlescent metallic colors over the deep-blue green of the base. A teeny part of his brain whispered at him to snag a few to take back to the museum for scientific and official museum business only.

Sam snorted behind him.

"I saw that." She murmured through their comms. And Kyle pretended to ignore her as he approached a crushed box on the twisted remains of the former truck bed.

"What did you see?" Alex pipped up like the obnoxious tagalong that Kyle found her to be.

"Kyle, briefly fantasizing about how useful it would be to have a couple of dragon scales in the museum's private collection." Alex's eyes widened and her lips formed an 'O' of surprise. Jones chuckled; he'd been smart enough to keep his mouth shut as he'd been wondering how technically – on a scale of one-my-momma's-disappointed-in-me to ten-there's-a-special-place-in-hell-for-corpse-looters – evil it would be to pocket a few himself.

"Nobody's taking pieces of the corpse. It's going to be repatriated back to their kin." Kyle interrupted before anyone could start one of the bicker fests that he realized started up when he and his sister were together. Then he added with less surety, "Probably."

"If it hadn't been crushed, it wouldn't look like much of anything would it?"

"Under statement of the century, Sis." The warlock turned his body so he could grin at her as they now stood in a line before the device or artifact. "But that's how it usually is with these magi-tech things."

"Right!" Sam groused, clearly aggrieved. "Not quite an artifact, but not just technology. I know it's my specialty, but the way some people cobble them together as if they are two separate fields of knowledge? Look at this piece of crap!" She gestured angrily. "No elegance, no grace, no cooperative synergy. Just two completely disparate parts forced into a semi-functional whole."

The rant had Kyle grinning. It was a common rant from his sister, something the young man had heard over and over again through the years. And she was right. A plain metal box that had been crushed so the insides had spilled out from tears in it. There were the remains of a metal crate lined with magically insulating glass lying, also crushed, a few feet away. Styrofoam insulation had been mashed into powdery bits, tinged pink in some places when it mingled with flesh and blood.

"It is an ugly piece of work." Jones agreed. "Watch your step, there's broken glass around." Murmurs of acknowledgement came through the comms.

"Let's get it packed up." The Warlock of the Archivist opened his case and placed a clean, magically insulated sheet several feet away to lay the open case upon. He wanted to make sure that he wasn't covering any piece of the device-slash-artifact that he needed to collect.

They worked quickly and efficiently after collection tools were disbursed among the four of them. Extra magically insulating gloves were placed over their gloves to protect their suits from damage and contamination. Tongs with magically insulated handles also.

"Where to start?" Alex asked with doe-eyed eagerness.

"I was thinking we secure the main box first then the smaller pieces that had burst out in the crush." It seemed like the obvious choice to Kyle who was most used to archaeological excavations.

"No, you need to secure the small pieces first, you dolt." His sister smacked the back of his head then her eyes bugged, and her mouth gapped as she realized the faux-pas she made with her reflexive big sister action.

"That's insane. No one does that." Kyle's response caused Sam's eyes to widen again, but this time in surprise and a little bit of confusion.

"So that you know where they were in relation to the box to make reassembly easier." Her explanation heavily implied 'duh stupid' as well as a clear superiority of her knowledge over his.

"Oh." Kyle laughed at his sister. "You've never worked with a Warlock of the Archivist and think we have to do everything by hand." He flicked a hand dismissively on one shoulder as if getting rid of the thought. "We don't use these kinds of plebeian methods."

"I…uh…" Jones hesitant voice came over the comms and Sam, Alex, and Kyle looked up from their sibling bickering. "I've never used these before." The soldier admitted hesitantly. "What do I do?"

"Oh, here." Alex offered. "I'll show you." Alex and Sam were familiar with crime scene investigation and retrieval of magi-tech devices. It was their profession and what they'd trained for. Sam had been doing it for years now. Kyle also had training in artifact retrieval. But Jones… his specialization was more in neutralization than preservation and retrieval.

"Oh, Jones." Kyle commented. "I totally forgot that you were… weren't… a nerd like us." He gestured between himself and his sister, conspicuously leaving out Alex with a dubious glance in her direction. Then he shrugged as Alex showed Jones how to pull the special gloves over Jones' protective suit and secure them in place.

"Now you look like a proper museum representative," Kyle smirked, and Jones made a rude gesture while grinning back at him. "Let's do this." He gestured for them to stand back, and he held out a hand with his codex hovering over it. Its tether swung slowly between the book and his shoulder where it was secured. "Archive Query. Archive Input Sequence."

The codex, a rather plain and old-looking leather-bound book, opened slowly. Pages, yellowed with age, flipped by. Mysteries and secrets of the ages flashed brief glimpses teasingly at observers before the codex settled on fresh, newer-looking blank pages singed the slight browning of almost scorched around the edges. Then, those pages flickered to life with a faint golden glow that gradually intensified. Jones wondered if the pages had always been like that, or if he hadn't noticed during the desperate fighting the day before. Kyle was frowning slightly in concentration and the soldier chose not to interrupt and ask.

"Identify and Locate, Parts of the Whole. Three-dimensional Construct with Manipulative Reconstruction. Save to Archive."

Kyle pointed at the artifact.

As he spoke the spell command sequence, the pale golden glow from the pages intensified. When he pointed, the glowing magic of the archive gently and in a distinctly non-threatening manner then *reached* out of the book. It landed on the major components of the device they had come to collect. Then other places among the bloody floor and ruined flesh of the dragon began to glow. Smaller bits and pieces that none of the group had yet identified as belonging to the artifact.

"Now, that's useful," Jones murmured in appreciation. In another area of the enormous warehouse one of the workers began shouting in panic as a glow emanated from one of the pockets on his hazmat suit.

"Yes. Sam agreed. Very useful indeed." Her wand was out and pointed threateningly at the thief. Jones joined her in pulling his wand and they both hurried over to corner the thief. More security personnel were closing in on the suspicious individual who had already put his hands up in surrender.

"I've always thought so." Kyle didn't smile. He hadn't been surprised.

Chapter 77

Kyle ignored the standoff between Sam, Jones, and the jackass trying to sneak off with just part of the device. Like, come on, did that jerk not get that he was dealing with someone from the museum? He, like every mage trained to work at the museum, had spells specifically to prevent theft from their retrieval sites and ensure the recovery of entire artifacts no matter how many pieces they were in.

Which got… interesting… sometimes.

There were stories that got shared with all the new trainees at the museum. One heard things around the water cooler so to speak. Now he'd have his own story to share about how someone tried to make off with a piece of artifact and his spell had revealed it. If only it were something to smile about and not people being disappointingly greedy.

Oh, well.

He got to work collecting pieces of the artifact as he activated his levitation ability. As a Warlock of the Archivist, that particular ability was intrinsic to his nature. One might wonder how super dope telekinesis powers were related to what was in practice being a glorified record keeper. Kyle wouldn't, but one might if they didn't know what all being an archivist entailed. Warlocks of the Archivist were keepers and retrievers of knowledge.

That was a simplistic way of putting it, but there it was. Sure, with new knowledge an archivist might find everything they wanted to know on a convenient database or printed out neatly in a book somewhere. But some records were destroyed, mangled, or damaged. Telekinesis allowed a warlock to lift an item in its totality without applying pressure to any one part to avoid damaging it further. Or applying in just specific locations to hold it together as a whole while examining it. Virtual reconstruction without getting contaminants that could destroy old papyrus rubbing off from fingers? Sure thing. How about avoiding contact with dangerous unknown substances or unknown enchantments that might be on an artifact or a spell scroll?

Telekinesis was part and parcel with the position. Kyle had magic before he'd made his warlock pact with his patron. Not great magic, not even in high magic areas because he hadn't known enough big spells to use that magic. Except for the divine fire spell that Michael accidentally taught them that one time, but that didn't count.

The shouting had settled down over by Sam and Jones and not long afterward, Kyle heard their footsteps coming back, presumably with the missing piece of the artifact. He assumed that it was Sam and Jones because Alex glanced up and didn't seem concerned. The hazmat suits they were all wearing contained each person's aura so Kyle couldn't recognize his siter that way. Which was weird, it was weird not being able to sense her aura when it was something he was so familiar with. His telekinesis would have also been blocked by the suit if not for the fact that it was augmented by his warlock power and his intentions could be commanded through his book.

"Kyle," Sam's voice came over the speaker in his suit and he felt that dopamine hit of being right about something that he had inferred. "Catch." Instinctively Kyle's body jerked around to be ready for the small object. He barely managed to refocus his magic, catching the small flesh-stained object and placing the piece gently within the growing collection of other debris.

"While I appreciate your faith in my skills dear sister, I would really prefer you not test them with something so important next time," Kyle responded dryly. Despite the near fumble, he did smile at Sam's Sam-ness.

"Well, I didn't want to keep holding it. The thing killed a dragon, Kyle. Besides, I really doubt my toss would've done more damage to it than getting blasted across the street by an expanding dragon corpse." Sam reasoned while gesturing at a piece of shrapnel lodged deep enough into the road that Kyle's telekinesis had yet to recover it.

"Road?" Kyle's face took on a look of confused concern at the word. "What road… oh." His gaze had followed three sets of fingerings pointing on the arms of three different people to another glowing spot he hadn't gotten around to yet. A large chunk of asphalt was propped vertically against a waist-sized pile of other chunks of asphalt. "Huh?!" He cocked his head at what was clearly some of the wrecked road from the incident site. There were reflectors, lane separation lines, and the magic collector grid were visible on it. "I did not see that."

"How did you miss that?" Sam scoffed incredulously with furrowed brows.

"It was organized before I got here and wasn't worked on while I was watching?" He suggested with a shrug. "But now that I see it, I concede your point about the… throwing of things."

It was a fair point. Besides that, even if the random component had fallen and broken further, Kyle and the museum were likely the people most qualified in the world to piece it back together again. Way better than the king's horses, the museum was. He worked quickly after that, his sister, Jones, and that – that Alex person pointing glows out *helpfully* as he went.

"Over here, Kyle."

"Another piece there."

"I think this is something, oh, never mind."

That last bit made Kyle grit his teeth and seethe with irritation. The freaking noob his sister had brought with her instead of a functional agent. But alas, there was nothing to be done for it. They'd just finished wrapping up the gathering when a rhythmic alarm sounded and lights near the tall doors of the sealed room began strobing in time with it.

"What's that?" Kyle questioned the observation room through his suit comms. There was a quick crackle of magical interference as someone keyed on their mic to respond. That was concerning, there shouldn't have been magical interference with them inside their suits in a sealed room.

"The second dragon has arrived; they're bringing it through the big airlock." Oh. That's what was wrong with the comms.

"Acknowledged." He picked up his case and made sure to set the location spell in his book before gesturing for his companions to follow him to the smaller air lock.

"Can't we wait for Gleipnir?" Sam inquired wistfully. Which Kyle understood, it had probably been years since they'd been apart for this long.

"Gleipnir wouldn't want you in here when he releases that thing," Kyle assured her. "It's suppressed by him and it's still glitching out the electronics through two layers of magical insulation. Which is either a sign of how powerful it is or is a sign that this facility's insulation sucks. Either way, we should get out of here."

As he spoke, the massive door on the far side of the giant room began to rise.

Chapter 78

"Puppies and kittens are fluFFY AND SWEET. WHY DON'T WE COOK THEM UP AS A SWEeet treat. Mmmm mmm mm mmmmmm." Gleipnir's singing voice had started out faint, suddenly boomed in volume as the large door between them opened wider and then became muffled again as the small airlock leading to the changing room closed after the group had shuffled through as they vacated the chamber holding the dragon remains.

Jones' eyes had widened, and his head turned slowly to glare with perplexity in Gleipnir's general direction. His face was a general mask of what-the-actual-fuck and Kyle spared a moment to smirk ruefully at the poor soldier who didn't know, that was how most people felt around Gleipnir. With the door closed behind them Kyle made for the small laboratory that was prepared for them, weaving amongst his companions to avoid tangling their air lines.

Now that they had the parts, they would need to clean them of the dangerous dragon bits. Ooorrr… the thought flashed through his mind. It would be useful for the museum to have dragon parts for enchanting in the fut– No. He shook his head. What was he thinking? That would be wrong.

"Wattkins!" A sharp bark came over their comms. Both Kyle and Sam's heads jerked up at the angry male voice. The siblings questioningly pantomimed to each other in silent inquiry as to which one of them was in trouble this time. Alex was gesturing a general 'what-the-heck' at her partner as *she* tried to figure out what kind of trouble she hadn't succeeded in keeping them out of. "What are you doing interfering in my operation? I thought I had you on suppression and cleanup."

Ah. Kyle knew who that was now. Malice suffused his countenance as Sam and Alex ceased their unspoken back and forth conversation of facial expressions, angry mouthed words, and short violent gestures.

"Son of a bitch." Jones murmured and the other three turned to him, surprised that the stoic Magicorps soldier had been the first to break the silence.

"Excuse you? Who is this?" The military officer who must have somehow blustered his way into the observation room demanded over the comm thinking he had any kind of say in the matter.

"You're that soon to be court martialed idiot who sent Anna to be interrogated by those Daedalus Engineering jackasses." Sam's nostrils flared with rage and Alex felt the adrenalin rush that was always triggered when her partner's eyebrow began to twitch with anger.

"What? Did? You? Say?" Each word was cold and precise, suffused with the simmering temper that the older Wattkins daughter was so well known for. Before anyone could respond, a roar came through the communications systems followed by an angry bellow.

"HE DID WHAT, TO MY BABY SISTER?" Gleipnir's howling anger vibrated through the walls and floor of the building. The vibration quickly became a tremor as Gleipnir released the massive weight and magic of the monster corpse he was containing. "FACE ME MORTAL FOR YOUR JUDGEMENT IS NEIGH!"

Muffled screams reached the ears of the four in the secured laboratory as the remaining workers in the warehouse fled Gleipnir's wrath. Sam smothered a harsh bark of laughter and put a hand to her head smearing a little crimson smudge across her faceplate. It would have been funnier if she wasn't so upset herself.

"Who…? What…?" The sheer panic in the fellow would have been funny if not for the fact that Kyle was infuriated with this blowhard. "What is that thing? Why is the suppression equipment reanimating?" At that, Sam rolled her eyes.

"Oh, Jesus Christ. He really is a moron." She murmured to her brother. "I bet whatever branch he belongs to would give us medals for violently removing him from the chain of command." Both Kyle and Jones snorted as he officer rambled on.

"Wattkins. Is this your doing? Cease and desist. That's an order." The building was now shaking hard as Gleipnir's wrath ratcheted up the arcanes that were filling the warehouse morgue. This time Sam rolled her eyes so hard that she might have actually sprained something because she stopped mid eyeroll with a wince and put a hand to her face again.

"None of us are in your chain of command you imbecile. This is an FBI case, we were on scene first, take it up with my superiors when communication is restored. That's not magic suppression equipment manifesting a monster, it's a sentient warlock pact item. Gleipnir. And lastly –"

"Lastly," Kyle chimed in as he activated the authority spell in his museum identification badge, a spell created by some intelligent soul with foresight a plenty specifically for dealing with asshats like this jerk, "*The Museum* has been called for consultation, and this is not the purview of our experts under the aegis of the Magicorps. You will *not* interfere."

"And he's about to lose his job and Lucifer's got a special place waiting for him in *all* the hells because he messed with an Archangel's Goddaughter." Jones murmured with a self-satisfied smirk on his face. Those words brightened up Sam's dark scowl.

"Really?" She inquired happily.

"REALLY?" Gleipnir chimed from the beyond their sight.

"Watched the main man lay the smackdown myself." He reassured them. "Should have seen the look on the interrogators' faces when the literal G-O-D started walking towards the portal to intervene. I think at least two guys fucking pissed themselves."

"Noice!" Sam offered the Magicorps soldier a bloody high five that splattered a little onto Kyle. Alex managed to smoothly sidestep out of the way.

"Noice!" Gleipnir's more reasonable tone came over the comms. "Hey, I'm coming in through the airlock to get cleaned off." The sounds of distant airlock mechanisms came through their comms as Kyle started speaking to his sister.

"On a side note," Kyle interjected. "Did you know that heaven has an attorney?"

"What? Really? No way!" They had all turned towards the airlock to the decontamination chamber to go meet up with Gleipnir.

"For real. I didn't see it myself, but Jones told me all about it." Sam spared Jones a skeptical glance.

"On my wand." He placed a fist over his heart in the formal warlocks pledge of truth and Sam gave a respectful nod.

"Holy shit!" She paused at the door as they cycled through.

"Yeah. I'm surprised mom never told us about this. Because an attorney sure would have come in handy to deal with –" Kyle's words halted abruptly and he zipped his mouth shut as his sister broke in with a threat.

"You will stop that sentence right there or I will make you suffer in ways even demons cannot imagine." Jones looked at the pair of siblings in alarm but didn't say anything.

"That's the smart move." Alex assured Kyle with a pat on the shoulder as she moved past him into the cycling airlock door.

"That's my Sammy." Gleipnir chimed in happily as he wrapped his tail around her waist and nuzzled his head against her shoulder.

"What is going on?" The officer who had finally gotten his voice back after Kyle's spell had silenced him growled over the comms. "What are you doing? You can't just come into my…"

"You are a stubborn one. Not sure how you slipped through the mental health screenings to get to your rank." Grimacing, Kyle reactivated the authority spell. Sometimes the spell didn't work as well on people who were really stupid or who had inflated egos to the point of it being a personality disorder. "I'm with The National Museum of Unnatural Science and History. This device is under our purview, and we will be taking it with us for examination in the appropriate facilities guarded by the Magicorps."

Silence.

Okay. Not complete silence.

A muffled sound of anger, as if someone were trying to speak but there was something covering their mouth or preventing it from opening. Lots of grunts and some shrieks too.

"That should hold for a bit." He let himself into the decontamination chamber as they had all been walking that way. "I hope it holds until we leave."

Showers started, water infused with magic nullifying and absorbing particles washed off their suits. They were a mess. A big one. Awful and gross and probably in danger of magical overexposure if the decontamination facilities didn't work like they were supposed to.

Should I really be that concerned about magic exposure? After what I did yesterday, what are the odds that I'm really okay? He shook his head and banished the thought. It would be fine. The codex would have warned him if he'd – wouldn't it have? It would be fine. He checked his codex making sure that it was still attached to his suit. The pact item was very well constructed and protected so it shouldn't suffer any damage from the decontamination shower.

A faintly visible field repelled most of the water raining down around the book. But did the surface seem as if it was ever so slightly damp? No. He was being paranoid.

Everything will be fine.

Chapter 79

They'd left the facility with no resistance. In fact, someone had called the asshole's commanding officers and let them know where he was, and Kyle was gratified to see him being escorted out of the building in cuffs by some very angry looking military police. Jones found that probably as gratifying as Kyle, Sam, and Alex. The siblings parted ways at the helicopter that was waiting to take Kyle and Jones back to the museum with their precious cargo with vague promises to get in touch.

Of course they were going to be in touch, they would be working the case together probably. And Sam had to let the museum take the device because while her forensic lab was good, it wasn't as great as what Kyle had access to. So, she grudgingly conceded custody of the device to her brother's lab. Gleipnir was patting her hair consolingly as they watched her younger sibling fly away.

"Okay. I guess we better report back to the office and write up our reports." Sam stuck her hands in her pockets. It was dark. Very dark. Lights from whatever city they were in glowed beautifully along the horizon. Probably near midnight now that she thought about it, and she looked at her watch to see that it was in fact still fried from being exposed to Prometheus Purple levels of AMD.

"We're a bit far from the office, Sam." There was a tone to Alex's voice that warned Sam that maybe she'd not focused entirely on things she should have.

"Where are we?"

"About halfway between Baltimore and New Jersey." Sam felt her shoulders slump at her partner's words. She'd been about to suggest that they just head home if it was too late.

"Damn, that's a bit of a drive. I was really looking forward to sleeping in my own bed for a bit."

"Our beds might not still be there when we get back to New York." Alex had turned toward their agency vehicle and waved Sam and Gleipnir after her.

"Whyever not, pray tell?" The sentient pact item had slipped into ye-olde-timey speak as part of his, 'I'm so wise and ancient act'. Normally, it annoyed Alex, but right now she was just going to ignore it.

"I don't know about you two, but my apartment's in a really shitty building and the magic shielding probably isn't rated for Prometheus Purple, if it ever was. Heck, I heard some places, not just over by the source like we were, got up into the pink where arcane currents managed to combine."

"I didn't even think of that." Sam's groaned with frustration. "I guess we'll just hope for the best. Right Gleip?" She patted Gleipnir's tail where it wound around her waist, and he chimed up in agreement.

"Right. And we'll go crash at Kyle's place if the worst comes to worst." He chortled with merriment.

"He will hate that, even if he does have that spare room." They giggled together at their malicious sibling planning. Alex grimaced. She felt for Kyle, she really did. Gleipnir and Sam were like having a pair of evil twins against the world.

"I know. But his place is museum employee housing, and it fully magically insulated and reinforced against monster attack." That sounded pretty freaking sweet, if Alex did say so herself.

"I should apply to work there." She grumbled imagining returning to a home trashed by monsters of furniture that had manifested.

"I tried, they said my craft, patron, and education was too specialized." Sam's griping surprised Alex. "But that was way back when I first got out of school, before the current director took over. Don't tell Kyle. He'd never let it go if he found out he'd succeeded to get a job there and I'd failed."

"Yeah, no." the other warlock agreed. "I'm not cruel. No way I'm telling Kyle that. Also, hotel, or two-hour-plus drive to our homes?"

"I'm not looking forward to having to deal with whatever's going on inside my apartment at this time of day. How about we go back to the office, sleep at our desks, and deal with crap when someone wakes us up in the morning." It was a decent suggestion and Alex quickly agreed.

"Sure, I second that motion."

"I," Gleipnir paused for a large annoying theatrical yawn which he didn't need to make because he had no mouth and didn't breath. "Second, second that notion."

"They aye's have it." Sam crowed triumphantly, also yawning hugely. "To the desks." They reached their vehicle and Sam took the keys. "I got a long nap earlier. You sleep and I'll pull over if I need to nap." Though the other F.B.I. magic tech specialist wanted to argue, she didn't because she knew that her partner was right. She needed more sleep.

By the time Sam pulled their vehicle onto the nearest freeway onramp, Alex was passed out, her head resting against her doorframe and little snores interrupting her deep even breathing. Behind her Gleipnir was similarly propped against the doorframe, his long tail sprawled across the back seat. Unfurled in long loping coils of lustrous shining ribbon that he didn't often show others.

He too was snoring, and it made Sam smile. Most people thought that Gleipnir faked his mortal traits. But that wasn't so. It was just… He was real. He was alive. And living things slept. They felt pain, and sorrow, and guilt. Gleipnir was alive, he knew he was alive, and believed he was alive, and so he had the traits of living things.

That was one of the wonderous inexplicable things about magic.

She decided not to pull over and would just let them sleep until they got where they were going. Was there really a rush to it? No. And Gleipnir needed rest just like every other living thing. Monsters, chaos, and reports could wait for now.

Hours passed. Lights flashing by, both vehicles and the cities flanking either side of the freeway. Then the light became fewer. Sure, vehicles were still coming from the opposite direction. But there were less lights from cities. She'd entered the boundary of where the power grid had been affected by the disaster two days earlier. Further ahead, darkness.

Or more correctly dimness with scattered patches of darkness. Only magically powered emergency lights were still functional. Even some of them had their enchantments blown out by the event. How long would it take for the lights to come back on in the city that never slept?

308

Chapter 80

Kyle and Jones parted ways at the museum after securing the artifact in one of the reconstruction labs for working on in the morning. Jones went to the onsite rooms for the Magicorps security guards after saying goodnight. Because the military security weren't actually museum employees, they didn't generally live in employee housing unless they chose to. Jones hadn't chosen to.

Instead, he'd taken advantage of the onsite dormitory housing for the Magicorps soldiers inside the upper floors of the museum itself. He still got to collect his housing allowance, which was high because, New York. But he didn't have to actually pay rent or deal with commuting in New York, which was awesome. And he had access to all kinds of amenities.

Kyle, for his part, went to his apartment to sleep and possibly to find his little sister waiting for someone to come and let her know how things were going out in the world. Poor Anna. She was probably terrified. Or… maybe not.

"The girl did face down a big scary fucking monster on her own." Kyle muttered under his breath as he let himself into the building. He probably should have checked on the prisms that were making themselves comfy in the mail drop box, but since no one was going to be delivering mail anytime soon, or checking it anytime soon, he decided to leave that problem for another day.

Trudging up the stairs, Kyle noted that the emergency lights still glowed in a rich blue. That was fine. Most people didn't realize that magic levels on the East Coast were naturally up in the high Green low Blue range without the magic collectors that protected urban areas and kept magic levels down in the more familiar Yellow zone. Just as he was about to open his door a sound made Kyle pause. There was some clicking, some buzzing, tinkling, chiming, and Anna's muffled voice coming from the other side of the door.

Anna… was… *not* asleep, apparently. Curiosity bubbling inside him, Kyle finished unlocking his door and casually entered. One look at what was happening, and he walked back out and shut the door behind him. *I did not just see what I thought I saw. I did not just see what I thought I saw. I did* not *just see what I thought I saw.* After repeating it a few times, Kyle almost believed it and was therefore far more disappointed when he walked into his apartment for the second time to see the exact same thing.

Shoulders slumping as he accepted defeat, Kyle closed and locked the door behind him then just stood and watched for a few minutes. Those prisms he'd been leaving to deal with as some other day's problem. They were a right now problem. And possibly a long-term problem because his sister was definitely invested in *all* of them. Already Kyle was trying to articulate the argument in his mind for explaining to his mother why Anna should be allowed to keep an entire herd of *prisms*.

Picture this scene.

Anna, in her pink flannel cloud hopper rabbit pajamas with the zigzag lightning bolts, buttons properly buttoned this time, was on the couch. No big deal. Right? Wrong. Because she was surrounded, completely surrounded by prisms. The herd had to have doubled in size since he'd left that morning, and Kyle narrowed his eyes suspiciously. Not doubled as in the individual prisms were bigger. No, they were all conveniently cute pocket-riding-sized. But there were definitely more of them than he originally thought there were.

He wasn't certain, but he didn't think those things reproduced that quickly. There were some smaller baby looking ones though. The babies were sitting on Anna's lap next to Kyle's personal laptop as Anna directed the prisms, the majority of which had joined together to make a scaffolding that was wielding an antenna made from a wire clothes hanger. The makeshift antenna was connected to the laptop's router port. Or whatever that port was called there the hardline to the internet would connect when Wi-Fi wasn't an option. Static played through the laptops speakers which was occasionally broken up with bits of what almost sounded like speech.

"Okay, a little bit more to the left. Left. Other left. And up, up, up. Stop. Back down. Just a smidge. Hold. Hold." The prisms were remarkably well coordinated. Even if Kyle wasn't Anna's older brother, he'd have been impressed with her magical creature wrangling. Seriously. They were an unstable tower of softly glowing, humming, chiming crystal creatures.

At her direction, the tower moved. Prisms lifting and leaning or lowering and straightening as she needed. As Anna shrieked 'hold', the sounds from the laptop grew more distinct. How was she doing that? There shouldn't be any internet. Unless…

Kyle wracked his memory. Was the employee housing on some kind of magical internet? The museum would have internet communications working instead of just scrolls if that was the case. Well, maybe they did have working communications with the outside world that Kyle didn't know about?

No. That's not right. Didn't Director Arcas say something about limited contact? He shook the whirling thoughts out of his head as a familiar theme song fuzzed its way out of the speakers.

"Yes!" Anna gave a little sitting hop in place, raising her hands together in triumph. Which was adorable, of course, while also jostling the laptop and the little prisms sitting on her lap gazing expectantly at the screen. The static surged for a second and Anna cried out with disappointment "Oh, no!" before the music came back steadier than before. "Woot! We did it guys. Let me see if I can get it to record."

What the heck was going on?

Then, a tinkling crash alerted Kyle to the tower of prisms near the window toppling over. A sound like windchimes falling in slow motion was what came to Kyle's mind. Then there was a heap of crystals with a cord running into it and a makeshift antenna sticking out the top.

"Shit. Are you guys okay?" Quickly she scooched the baby prisms onto the keyboard of the laptop and placed it aside as she rushed over to the fallen prism tower. Dejected meeps of possibly pain called out, but Kyle suspected that those little stinkers might be milking it for attention. "Did anyone chip? Are you hurt? Here, I've got some tasty ice magic for you."

Her fingers were dripping cold vapors as the mewling chiming prisms untangled themselves and scurried over to her with little clicking steps.

Chapter 81

1:25 AM September 15th, 2026
Museum of Unnatural Science and History Employee Housing

"Hey there, Snow Cone." Kyle felt like now was a good time to interrupt and grill his sister on her activities in the most casually big-brother way possible. You know, while she was distracted with her new abundance of pets. He felt an eyebrow twitch and wasn't sure whether he was upset or concerned. "What are you up to?"

"Ohhh." Though she seemed unconcerned, was that syllable just a little longer than it should be? "Hi, big brother." Anna smiled brightly and pushed some of her long loose white locks over one deeply tanned shoulder. The prisms who she had deprived of that sweet, tasty ice elemental magic meeped and chimed piteously until her fingers returned down to them again and cooed encouragement at them. "Who's my good little helpers. Yes, you are. You were such helpful little prisms. Yes. You were. Are you all feeling better now? Yeah."

I see. Oh, yes. Kyle did see. It was out with the cool big brother and all about the adorable little prisms now. When he got his sister the *best* present ever – regardless of how spur of the moment or coincidental it was – he did not anticipate being entirely supplanted in her affections by the little things. Of course, it was *supposed to be only ONE* little thing.

"Your eyebrow's doing that thing it does when you're irritated." Anna interrupted her cooing at her new minions long enough to tell him before she cut them off from the magic they were leaching off of her to crawl back up to the couch. "Okay guys, that's enough. Now you're just being gluttons." The herd had followed Anna in a way that was a little more than low-key concerning Kyle. But then one of them trotted out in front and cut the others off. It tinkled importantly and then gestured with one of its crystalline appendages for the others to back off.

"Well, at least that one's not so bad," he managed a dry comment as he laughed at the sight of his sister surrounded by magical animals as if she were some kind of princess from a storybook.

"That's the one you brought me. He's a sweetheart." From her place on the couch, his sister was stretching out her shoulders. "All right, everyone. Our attempt failed. It's way past the little one's bedtime so you need to find someplace to hunker down for the night." She was yawning her words from between fingers covering her open mouth, clearly tired herself. Her entire strain of comments opened so many questions for Kyle. Deep burning questions like; what was the baby prisms' normal bedtime and how did Anna know what it was? But he decided to leave it for now and instead go back to his first question for his sister.

"Uh. So, what were you doing?" All this time, Kyle had been standing by the door he'd just entered and realized that he wanted to come in and sit down after a fairly long day. His mage's robes, codex holster, bag, and wand never made it to their proper storage places and instead ended up off the end of the couch where he sat over from Anna. He found himself yawning having caught them from his sister when she yawned her response.

"I promised to record 'Professor What' for Sam. It's the season premier tonight." Kyle's eyes popped open when his sister mentioned the popular fiction television series about a time traveling married chronomancer couple.

"Oh, shit. I totally forgot that we were finally getting new episodes." He looked over to the bookshelf and almost got up in excitement before remembering that the whole point of the conversation was that they two, he and Anna, would not get to watch the show tonight. "Almost got up for my timeline journal." He chuckled dejectedly. "Silly me."

"At least you have yours." His sister groused and crossed her arms petulantly over her chest. "Mine is at home which I haven't been for the last two days." She sighed, only half theatrically and half wistfully for the comforts of her own room things. "I was really looking forward to seeing if Professor What was going to successfully resync his timeline with Dr. When and that T.A. Where."

Kyle was silent for a moment as he watched his sister. He knew more about the story and as he had many times before he decided to make an offer.

"You can borrow my books any –d" Before he could get the words out of his mouth Anna cut him off.

"Don't you dare tempt me into reading the books before the TV series ends," she scolded him with mock furry. "You know that the books are always better, and I want to enjoy this show as much as possible." She pretend-frowned at her big brother with a wrinkled nose and her hands on her hips until another yawn broke her concentration as he laughed at Anna's antics.

"How were you planning on recording the show anyways?" The warlock was looking at the tangle of cords and converters which were attached to his spare laptop which had apparently been charged enough for Anna to make the attempt. "The powers out and there's no internet."

"Oh, I pulled an analog to digital cable TV converter out of your storage closet for the antennae and then used an RGB to pin converter, then a –" Some of her words were lost on a yawn before she continued her explanation. "– and then I just needed a USB-C gen one for your dinosaur of a laptop and we were golden. Would have easier if it was even older and could have just skipped the other steps after the pin input but whatever."

"Yeeeeah." Kyle paused for a few moments thinking over everything he'd heard. Because he was a pretty tech-savvy guy but... "Where did you get all of this?"

"Your storage closet." She stood up and wiggled her toes in a pair of fuzzy socks Kyle had forgotten he kept in his sister's spare room for her. "I'm heading to bed. Good night. I made you dinner. There's leftovers in the fridge." Then she was off, padding away in her pink cloud hopper rabbit pajamas and leaving Kyle with even more questions.

"Okay." His stomach grumbled loudly, and the warlock looked at it with annoyance. "First food. Then I'll figure out where this mystery storage closet is that she's talking about."

Chapter 82

7:13 AM September 15th, 2026
Museum of Unnatural Science and History Employee Housing

"Nnnnooooo!" Kyle groaned as someone tapped his face insistently. "It's not time to get up Anna, my alarm didn't go off." Shaking his head, he frowned at the surprisingly sharp feeling of the tap-tap-tapping on his chin surrounded by a chilling cold. "Please let me sleep in. And maybe trim your nails."

At that he painfully rolled over with another groan, still sore and not feeling great from his magical exertions of previous days. The tapping sped up and slid along his face from his chin to his cheek beside his ear. On the one hand, as a big brother, he could admire the annoying tenacity of his sister. On the other hand, as an adult who'd had an exhausting couple of days and not nearly enough sleep. He wanted to pull his blankets over his head and snuggle down in a comforter nest.

Which was exactly what he did.

Only…

What he'd originally thought was his sister's sharp little nails were still sitting on his cheek near his ear, pressing harder into his skin from the weight of the blanket. It gave him a little jolt of adrenaline that pulled him from his groggy state and kicked his heart into a higher gear. Now more wakeful, he could hear a slight electric buzzing.

"That's not my sister being obnoxious, is it?" the warlock sighed wearily. Then he sighed again when his words were greeted with a tinkling chiming response from one of the prisms. No. Not one of the prisms. The prism. The one he'd rescued with a static zap spell.

Anna's new pet and the leader of the pack… herd… whatever.

"Why are you waking me up?" Kyle hadn't been expecting a response, but he got one. Yes, it was just more tinkling and chiming but it definitely had a cadence and *attitude*. "Riiight." Slowly, and with infinite reluctance, the grouchy warlock dragged his comforter down. Opening his eyelids, he looked out the corners without moving his head.

Sure enough, there was a certain little crystalline body there sitting on his cheek. Yes. Sitting. And Kyle wasn't exactly sure how that was working because it was positioned kind of like a cat or a dog would be, but without changing the shape of its rear legs, and also without them sticking out in front of it. Were the rear legs always so short? No. Because the prisms' bodies were mostly horizontal when he watched them walking previously.

Yet, there was no doubt that the prism was absolutely sitting with its apparent rear end on his cheek. Its crystalline abdomen was both semi-opaque and highly reflective so Kyle could see his sleepy hazel eyes staring back at him. Despite not having a face, the little prism gave the impression of gazing at him with sweet puppy-eyes and bent down to nuzzle his cheek.

That made Kyle smile. How was a walking chunk of crystal the size of a large mouse so freaking cute? Clearly the little prism understood what smiles meant because it then gave a happy little hop followed by a series of tumbling ecstatic chiming meeps.

"Okay. I'll get up. But you'll need to get off me, so I don't knock you down or squish you in the processes." Kyle didn't even have time to fear the creature wouldn't understand him as it immediately jumped to his pillow then onto the nightstand beside his bed.

"About time." Anna groused from the door to his room where she leaned against the frame with her arms crossed petulantly. "Little traitor insisted on waking you up instead of spending time hanging out with me."

"Aww." Kyle stretched as he sat up then held a hand out for the prism. It quickly ran up his arm, across his shoulder, then down his chest into the breast pocket of his pajama shirt. He giggled a little because the swiftly moving and small profile feet of the lightweight prism tickled as they ran. "Don't be jealous, sis. He's just saying 'hi' to me." After a moment of watching the cloth of his pocket puff and move as the prism got settled, it poked its upper half over the edge of the pocket and pointed towards Kyle's bedroom door with a chime of purpose. As if it was saying 'charge'. So, Kyle obliged with amusement, running a hand through his light brown hair as he stood.

"Well, he woke me up too. It's time for you to get ready for work. You're going to be late." That… caused Kyle to pause in his first step toward accepting morning.

"How do you know? All the power is still out and none of the clocks are working. What?" He asked defensively when Anna gave him a flat look before rolling her eyes and padding off toward the kitchen.

"Well, for one, you have a magical timepiece in your personal lab. So, there is that." She groused as he followed her toward the smell of hot food. "Also, do you really not think I am capable of casting a basic time of day spell to tell what time of day it is based on…" She trailed off her angry retort and gestured around her.

For a second, Kyle was a little impressed as he accepted a bowl of hot – was that bacon? Where did his sister get bacon? *And I'm absolutely certain that I didn't have hashbrowns anywhere in this apartment.* Then he got distracted and narrowed his eyes at his sister as the way her words trailed off triggered a thought.

"Wait a minute. You don't actually know how the time-of-day spell works do you?" He snatched the plate from Anna's hands before she could take it back. Instead, she folded her arms defensively, gave a sniff of distain, and lifted her chin haughtily. It was a classic Camina Wattkins move that both his siters had adopted from their mother. Kyle had seen it in movies, television interviews, state functions, and even in conversations between his parents. Anna even finished it off with tossing her hair over her shoulder which their mom often did when she was wearing her hair down. Then she folded her arms again.

"I don't have to understand how it works to perform it properly." She was cool, calm, collected – super adorable. To avoid being a jerk of a big brother, he resisted patting her on the head condescendingly like Sam would do. Instead, he smiled and took a bite of the breakfast she'd made before her pet came to wake him up.

"You're absolutely correct." He gobbled up the meal as Anna reached over the kitchen counter they stood beside and grabbed a steaming mug of something. "That better not be coffee, young Miss." He scolded only half seriously while she was taking a sip. Anna swallowed, made a face, and stuck a slightly browned tongue at her brother. "Cocoa, if you have to know. Not sure it's much better than coffee since it's only got one-third the caffeine. But parents...."

"Right. Parents." Kyle agreed with her before looking wistfully over to the other mug that had been sitting beside Anna's. "I... don't suppose that would be..." Anna gave a less snarky eye-roll and gestured towards the cup.

"Yeah. *That's* coffee for you. Figured you'd need it."

Chapter 83

After a rather delicious breakfast, Kyle headed out for an absolutely average day at work. Before leaving he gave his sister a very stern warning to stay inside once again. Which she agreed to with suspicious ease.

"This is weird." He muttered giving her the side-eye as he donned his warlock's robe.

"What's weird? I run away to your place on the weekend all the time." She responded, petting her new favorite prism in the palm of one hand as it buzzed with electricity and gave off little streams of cold vapor that pooled around its feet.

"Not that. That's fine." Kyle corrected, blowing it off as nothing. "I mean you being all compliant."

"Hey," Anna paused in petting her prism in outrage to mock punch Kyle gently on the arm. "I'm a good girl." Her high-pitched defense was both amusing and didn't do much to settle Kyle's own nerves. "Who do you think I am, Sam?" A lightbulb went off with Kyle's mind with the force of an atomic bomb and his mouth dropped open.

"You did." Anna shrieked and this time her punch was actually a little forceful.

"Oww." Kyle reached up and rubbed his bicep where she'd landed a solid but not damaging hit.

"You were anticipating Sam and Gleipnir behavior instead of treating me like me, a person who has never actively –" Here she paused and corrected herself, "d – erm, that is, until recently, and only that *one time* because I was being *bullied*, broken any rules. Ever." She finished her tirade and crossed her arms in a classic Anna glower while she waited for his response. A pained expression passed over Kyle's face and he rubbed that spot from the bridge of his nose to just between the eyebrows where he and their mom both got migraines.

"You're right." He sighed, feeling like absolute garbage for doing that to Anna. He'd hated it when his parents treated him like he was one of their older siblings. Their parents were either always expecting great things from him – like the overachieving Davelor – or expecting *so much* trouble. Like Sam... "You are a great kid. You always behave, you are more patient and amenable than anyone should ever have to be. And I shouldn't have let my negative experiences with The Prodigy of Pain influence what I think about you. Will you forgive me, Snow Cone?" He gave her a hopeful smile and held out a hand for a shake.

"Hmmm." Anna's brown eyes narrowed at her brother with suspicion. "Maybe. Pinky swear that you won't treat me with distrust because Sam and Gleipnir were hellions." Kyle agreed and closed the fingers of the hand he'd been holding out to immediately have just the pinky extended. They shook. He hugged his sister. Then he said proper goodbyes and left, whistling his way through the park to the museum.

It was a good day. The nice weather was holding despite him bringing down the Wrath of Zeus days before. Though it was weird to see the park so deserted. With the ambient magic levels still abnormally high, the golems were still active. No more monsters were visible, so he supposed the doughnut bike was in squishy pieces somewhere.

But there were no people about and Kyle wondered where they all were. Had a force come to evacuate those who had taken refuge in the museum? It had to have been yesterday while he was working because any point before that might have been too dangerous with monster manifestations happening all over.

"On the other hand," the warlock muttered darkly to himself, "that officer in command was such a moronic idiot he might have actively been trying to evacuate people prior to getting the monsters and AMD under control. Fucking idiot."

A corona of magic burst into a rainbow of activated energy around him at his frustration. Much like what had happened the last time the golems stopped him, only far, far more powerful due to the higher ambient magic levels he'd been inadvertently used.

"Oh, shit." He cried out with horror. "No, no, no, no, no. Not right now." Frantically, Kyle tried to put out the magic he'd unintentionally channeled with his emotions. There was no way that the security golems were not going to notice *this*. Sure enough, in the distance came the characteristic *whumff* of a largescale fireball spell igniting.

He turned toward the sound, scanning the green landscape and between the trees so he'd know which direction he needed to shield. Then he heard another *whumff*. Then another. And three more in close succession. All from different directions.

"Oh. Shit." He spun slowly spotting some of the car sized flaming orbs before they were thrown and some as they were already in transit through the air. They were all coming towards him. Without thought of the consequences, Kyle drew power through himself from the ambient magic and cast the strongest protective spell he could think of at the moment. "Shield of Aeneas – no fuck! That only works on forged items, not magic projectiles."

It was too late. He'd cast the spell and couldn't stop it. The agonizing and wonderful rush of so many arcanes raced into him and out into the spell. This time, it was without the buffering assistance of his codex which was uncharacteristically inert while its warlock was in danger.

Kyle doubled over, falling to his knees. That wasn't supposed to happen. Even without his codex he *should* have been able to channel this much magic on his own as a wizard. What had he done wrong? Over his head the fantastical images of the history of Rome's founding danced in choreographed light. They weren't protecting the suffering warlock from the defensive assault he was under, and the fireballs passed right through.

He couldn't appreciate it. Kyle could barely see it. He could also barely see Jones running toward him across the lawn pointing frantically with his wand. Kyle could see Jones' mouth moving, but he couldn't hear Jones' shouts over the explosions impacting the shield Jones had erected over Kyle's head in the moments before it failed.

Chapter 84

7:38 AM September 15th, 2026

Central Park between the National Museum of Unnatural Science and History and the museum's Employee Housing

Camina hated escort duty.

With a passion.

A burning unending deep and visceral loathing is what she felt for any officer who ordered her to 'escort' civilians. Almost as much loathing as she felt for the actual duty of escorting anyone to safety. And yes, she'd been to therapy for it. So much therapy for it.

Camina, and every officer on the gods damned planet knew that her dislike of escort duty came from the incident that made her a warlock and the fact that she – a sob caught in her throat, and she shoved it far down. This was not the time for that. It was never the time for that memory. But the fact that the jackass fobbit officer in charge of this shit-show, who had obviously never commanded anything more complicated than a fucking desk, had Camina-fucking-Wattkins the Goddamned Last Line of Defense running escort duty instead of cleaning up the monsters while sending *her* child somewhere without informing her *at all*…

The rage was real and well deserved.

There was going to be a reckoning.

She was already over forty-eight hours without sleep by the time Camina was assigned to cover the evacuation of civilians from the museum. Jim was basically unconscious on his feet. There were rules about how long you would work a soldier, even in emergencies. Even in combat, there were rules. But those rules were different for warlocks – who could handle higher magical loads and therefore more stamina potions – from the rules for non-magic users in the military. Even so, these orders… were not… they weren't appropriate for the circumstances.

Probably.

She was mad. Okay? And her ability to articulate her emotions, even in her own mind, was starting to flag a bit after so many hours without sleep. Or stamina potions. Which she'd been entitled to but had been denied when she requested them. Mother fuckers.

"Well, that's the last of them." Jim clicked off his camera and put it away. He had recorded video and taken photos non-stop from the moment he was tossed out of an airplane two days ago. Camina smiled at her new protégé as he put away his camera and dusted off his hands. "Good riddance." The Warlock of the Archangel Michael's smile didn't reach her eyes because she only knew that two members of her family were alive, and one of them was her eldest child Davelor, because he'd been out of the country when the magic collectors blew.

"That is the last of them." Her agreement was almost depressed and more than a little angry if her gritted teeth were any indication of her mood.

"What now boss?" The journalist swayed on his feet from exhaustion even as he rallied to her side. The older woman turned away with a weary sigh and glanced toward the employee housing.

"Now I'm going to go looking for my kids and husband. You should probably get some rest. I'm sure the museum will let you take a place with some of the off duty Magicorps soldiers in there." The thought that she now had hours of searching to do in order to find out what had happened to her kids, made her weariness weigh upon her heavily. Since she was at the museum, she might as well start with Kyle and work her way out from there. When Camina had turned her head back towards Jim, he had out another of his small handheld cameras. "Did you just record me saying that?"

"Of course, I did." He grinned at her as he paused the recording so it wouldn't catch his voice. "How could I give up on the opportunity to show the world the off-duty Camina?" When he noticed the irritated flare of Camina's nostrils, he added in notes of hopeful nervousness, "With the utmost respect and only share what you specifically give permission to share? Please?" He gave her one of those universal looks of someone pleading with their eyes and since it reminded her too much of her own kids, she relented with a sigh.

"Fine, you can tag along. Let's go talk to Kyle's boss."

"Yesss!" Despite what must have been extreme fatigue, Jim gave a fist pump and a little hop of joy. There may have even been a heel-click in there, but Camina was too busy rolling her eyes at his antics to know for sure.

"You ever meet a pureblood vampire before, Mister Thafesh?" Camina questioned as she gestured for Jim to follow her up the grand front stairs of the temple-esque National Museum of Unnatural Science and History.

"Uh… no." He provided hesitantly as he shuffled through his pockets to find the cameras that still had memory space and juice in their batteries. "I've met multiple human-hybrids, multiple generations removed. Kyle's the cook, right? His boss is a pureblood vampire." Camina laughed, her throaty tinkling laugh and it gave James Thafesh goosebumps.

"No. Mister Thafesh. Kyle *likes* to cook," Camina clarified the misunderstanding about her son. "He's the best cook in the family besides my youngest Anna – don't tell her I said that – but cooking is not Kyle's job."

Jim followed Camina's gaze toward a tall, slim, very fit gentleman standing in the shadows just inside the open doors to the museum. Red eyes glowed against pale flesh topped with dark hair. The journalist was transfixed by the glowing red eyes. Mesmerized really. Before he realized it, they were already halfway up the stairs.

"Don't look into his eyes if you aren't used to it." Camina cautioned him with a gentle touch on his arm to break the trance. "He's not even using any of his powers."

"Oh. Thank you." Came the embarrassed mumbled response from her erstwhile sidekick. He returned to filming but no longer looking directly at the vampire's eyes, which were far less crimson looking than they had been from further away.

"Missus Wattkins." The vampire greeted in his slightly accented perfect English with a broad fanged smile and his arms opened wide in welcoming. "Always a pleasure and an honor when you grace my humble domain with your presence." Camina's returned smile was far more restrained than that of the man greeting her.

"Hello, Director Arcas." The warlock declined the vampire's implied request for a hug from the open arms and instead held out a hand to shake. Of course, the vampire refused to shake and bent over Camina's hand to give it a kiss. Jim's eyes nearly popped out of his head at the sheer audacity of the vampire.

"I don't suppose you're here to finally let the museum's experts take a look at your armor or Ascalon, are you?" The raised eyebrowed frown Camina gave the hopeful director was a combination of amused and exasperated with an overtone of exhaustion because she was too tired for this shit.

Chapter 85

"Really? Adrian?" Camina's frown became a glower, and the vampire dropped her hand like a hot coal. Adrian cleared his throat and loosened the neck of his suit nervously.

"I apologize. You're looking for your son, of course." Stepping back further into the museum foyer, the vampire gestured for them to follow him. "Kyle hasn't come into work this morning, yet. He's been running late since all the excitement started, what with all the magic he's been using and fighting multiple class four monsters and helping out the F.B.I. investigation into the cause of the magic collectors failing. Camina? Are you quite alright?"

Kyle's mother had stopped short as she heard what the director said. Jim had choked on his own tongue at the words. Director Arcas had not noticed her freezing in place as her mind processed the information and had continued walking for several steps before he turned to look at the warlock he'd been speaking to. Her face was pale – stricken, and green beneath her caramel skin.

"What did you say?" It was a breathy, terrified sounding sentence. And the director seemed to have realized what he'd done wrong as understanding dawned on his face.

"Ah." He gave the worried mother a sympathetic look. "Forgive me. You didn't know. Let me rectify my mistake." He took a deep preparatory breath during which Camina interjected with dry irritation.

"Let's rectify your mistake." The Harbinger of Dawn growled and Director Adrian Arcas, a vampire of indeterminate age and origin stepped back nervously as he realized that she was still fully armored. "My son is a non-combatant. He was supposed to be here at work, and safe during this event. Or guarded by Magicorps soldiers if he was in the field."

"Yes." The dark-haired vampire agreed amenably with an audible gulp, his burnt umber eyes no longer shining crimson. "Kyle is safe. Over extended, but safe. The Magic Crimes Division called for a Warlock of the Archivist to assist in the investigation when the magic collectors blew. Kyle went with a Magicorps escort. Sam was also working the case. And while they were there, Sam got a call from Anna who was trapped in her school. Sam couldn't leave the crime scene, so Kyle went to go and help Anna. He took out the class four monster that Anna was holding off – almost entirely on her own from what I hear. Then a second at… at least class four monster that he used Wrath of Zeus on."

"Holy shit!" Jim dropped his camera ruining the shot he was recording and fumbled for it as it clattered on the ground. Camina's head snapped to her journalist shadow.

"You will delete that immediately." Gapping dumbly, Jim nodded his acquiescence to her demand.

"Camina." Director Arcas began cajolingly then amended himself when he saw how shaken and furious the mother before him was. "Missus Wattkins, I know that employees at the museum are generally looked upon as strictly academic. Most people assume our Curators are purely artifact collectors who don't fight and are primarily protected by the Magicorps officers who usually accompany them. Perhaps that's even an impression that we deliberately encourage to the casual observer, but make no mistake," here he paused, and his voice was kindly but hard as steel at the same time, "they are absolutely top-notch combatants when need be. You know, perhaps even better than I, what Kyle is capable of."

"I see." Something went out of Camina at that point. Her shoulders sagged from their normal perfect posture. Every argument she'd ever had with Kyle about his choice of patron flashed through her mind. The argument they'd had the last time they had spoken was particularly fresh. "I see."

"You're welcome to wait here for your son. We've got the golems on patrol, and they would not take kindly to a threat like yourself roaming around the grounds. Kyle should be here within the half hour. Perhaps a bite to eat from the museum restaurant?" The tall, slim, handsome vampire gestured gracefully towards the door of the museum café where tables were pushed into awkward locations and chairs haphazardly dotted the dining room recently vacated by evacuees.

"Fine." Camina gave the smarmy vampire a not quite disbelieving eyebrow raise as she allowed herself to be guided over.

"We're still a in a bit of disarray, but the food is delicious and we have a buffet set up from serving all the refugees that just left." Director Arcas pointed to a serving line that had been abandoned which employes were helping themselves from as they began to clean up. Then he waved discretely to get their attention and made a cutting across his throat motion and a crossing of his hands while mouthing 'leave it, leave it'. Which they happily did, instead filling plates and sitting down to rest themselves.

"Okay." Camina chuckled. "I can be persuaded to eat. If for no other reason than to give these employees a break." There was a weary cheer from the bedraggled group who raised glasses, mugs, the occasional eating utensil in her direction.

"Why did Kyle go home if there are employees here who appear to have not left?" Jim cut in suddenly, his camera ever at the ready.

"Oh, these are employees who don't reside in the employee housing and or who do not have magic. Those who are not combat mages have chosen to stay in the museum for the duration of the emergency or until our security golems report that it is safe for them to travel back to employee housing unescorted. If you'll excuse me I have a great deal of work to get done…" He bowed politely to first Camina and then Jim and then turned about smartly and walked quickly away. He was already pulling a communication's device out of his pocket as he walked.

Jim and Camina watched him go. Camina warily and Jim with suspicion.

"That's the walk of a desperate man." He commented drily as he turned his camera off for a moment before heading over to the buffet. "What do you think he's hiding?"

"You mean besides the fact that he genuinely has no idea where my child is or if he's even still alive but just assumed he was…because…?" She let the sentence hang there for a bit with a shrug and a withering glance over her shoulder as she turned toward the buffet. Her stomach growled loudly as her mouth began salivating. "I don't suppose you could not film me until I've gotten some food and quieted the black hole in my stomach?" She flushed with embarrassment as her hungry body betrayed her again.

"No promises." Jones said around a mouthful of bacon he had already snagged from the buffet. "If I thinks it's good, it woes in tha eel." He coughed and then swallowed the food he'd been chewing as he spoke while Camina suppressed a smile of annoyed amusement. "Ahem. I mean, if I think it's good it goes in the reel." He held his breath waiting for the beatdown that he half feared would come for being so bold. But, The Last Line merely huffed and threw up her hands.

"Fine." Then she grabbed a plate, and Jim turned his camera back on to both document the buffet and get some little seen 'humanizing' footage of Camina Wattkins being a normal person for once.

They were comfortably seated, and Camina was halfway through her first plate while Jim was contemplating going for seconds when he and everyone who was *not* Camina Wattkins was startled by a terrifying sound. First one, then another, then another. Camina stood, ready to act but uncertain.

"What is that?" Jim shouted at her as she clearly knew what the noise was.

"Fireball spells. Big ones. Artillery spells."

Chapter 86

8:06 AM September 15th, 2026

Central Park outside the National Museum of Unnatural Science and History

Jones was running across the manicured lawn of central park between the museum and employee housing as fast as his exhausted legs would carry him. They burned. And moved in a leaden clunky fashion that *felt* slow even if it was eating up ground. He didn't dare cast a haste or speed spell just in case it drew the attention of the golems still patrolling the park for monsters and unregistered magic.

Jones had not slept well the previous night or, more accurately… that morning. Between getting back to his room so late that it became early, and the shocking revelations of the past few days, he decided that there was a better use for his sleeplessness than worrying about the unchangeable facts. While there were many of those unchangeable facts – like the fact that someone had tried to kill him yesterday and he still *had not* processed it – there were also a lot of other problems. Actionable problems. Problems he could solve with some good old-fashioned Magicorps discipline.

Maybe not the most important problem, but certainly the easiest to research and most confusing problem on the list was, 'Why *did* the museum security golems seem to have it out for Kyle?'. Luckily enough, that was one mystery that a military security guard assigned to the museum in general, and now Kyle in particular, was well equipped to solve. Having scanned through a long, *looong* list of golem security protocols at Zero Dark Stupid, he had finally come upon the most likely answer.

A stupid answer for a stupid time of day to have to be awake.

Kyle Wattkins was well known in the museum as a Warlock of the Archivist. It was his most compelling qualification even among his decently impressive academic prowess and showed up right at the top of his museum ID badge. The problem stemmed from the fact that the badge *only* listed him as a Warlock of the Archivist, not also as a *wizard*. The reason for museum golems' security spells being constantly suspicious of the warlock was because his wizard skills were never registered with them. Of course, they would not like an unlisted and potentially dangerous mage coming onto museum grounds, the whole point of their existence was to stop that from happening. Essentially, Kyle appeared to have forged security clearances that the golems couldn't disregard but could not fully trust.

It was such a forehead-slappingly obvious problem now that Jones had reread the regulations manual, that Jones had to wonder if it had really been an accident. Had Kyle deliberately not mentioned the fact that he was also a wizard when he was hired on? That would have been a grave violation of protocol. A fireable offense really. *Would* Kyle have taken that chance with his dream job?

Because of course it was Kyle's dream job. Nobody had to tell Jones that. You could see the joy on the kid's face every time he came into work. Which meant that said warlock probably hadn't deliberately left out the fact that he was a wizard when he applied. And didn't that creepy serial killer-looking chef friend of his tease Kyle about being a wizard sometimes? Kyle's wizardry was common knowledge. Certainly not a secret.

Which meant that the omission had either been a bureaucratic faux pas. Unless…

Director Arcas was a shifty vamp. Could it have been a test for the youngest member of the curation team? A way to gauge his problem-solving skills or how well he was able to ferret out the solution to the problem? Maayyybe?

Whatever the case, Jones didn't know. It didn't matter because now he had an answer to the problem and a solution for Kyle. What he didn't have, was Kyle. Who would probably be sleeping right about – Jones had frozen when he'd glanced at the clock and saw that it was after seven AM and closing in on eight. Frozen in terror because it meant that Kyle was likely already on his way to work through the park which for the silly Warlock of the Archivist was now a gauntlet of death.

Because Kyle didn't know that the golems thought he was secretly a pile of wizards in a warlock suit.

Jones pumped his arms faster in the hope that his legs would follow in kind. It… didn't work. Or did it. An additional shot of adrenaline surged through him as he thought that maybe, possibly his idea would be able to fix Kyle's problem. But even if it did, it didn't mitigate the current danger to Kyle. Jones he needed to run faster. So, he tried.

He was almost ready to let himself think that things would be okay, that he was overreacting. Then he heard it. *WHOOOSHUFFM!* Big! And close. Behind him. Jones almost didn't recognize the sound of an artillery sized fireball spell. He'd never been so close to one igniting.

Out of reflex the soldier hit the ground rolling onto his back as he watched the first fireball roaring overhead in what seemed like slow motion. That was the thing about artillery magic, sometimes it was slow to start, depending on how the enchantment had been woven. Or maybe he was just panicking, and it wasn't really moving as slowly as he thought it was. *Whumpfwhumfp whumfp.*

Even though he *knew* that those spells weren't aimed at himself, Jones winced as he heard three more sounding off in quick succession. *Oh, no!* Jones army crawled a few paces as he untangled his feet, orienting himself after the direction the fireballs were going in. Then he transitioned to a proper leopard crawl, his knees moving with the opposite elbow before leaping to his feet and flat out running as fast as he could again, his eyes tracking the burning orbs in the sky.

From the angles of the fireball's convergence, their target was near. Really near. Scanning the ground below where he estimated the target was, Jones was… his view was blocked by some trees. *Really? Now? Trees? For Fu… freaks Sake!!! Did I really just Anna-sensor my own thoughts. Crap. Dodge the tree. Dodge it. Dodge… God damnit legs! HA! There!*

Jones' snaped out of his internal monologue as he spotted Kyle. The warlock was casting a spell. An awesome spell. The spell that he'd cast two days ago with such perfection. But something was wrong. Even Jones could see it.

328

Kyle was sinking to his knees. The spell? It was not going to work. Jones was going to have to try and save Kyle.

"This is going to suck." He muttered to himself then laughed, because what had he been planning on doing this whole time anyways if he had thought that Kyle could save himself? "SHIELD OF LIBERTY!" The Magicorps sorcerer flung the words out along with his wand. Pointing to a spot mere feet over Kyle's head before tucking and rolling himself under the protection also. Wouldn't do for him to be outside the barrier when the fireballs spent themselves and rained hellfire down around it.

Explosion after explosion rocked the world. Red, white, and yellow flashing across Jones' vision despite his eyes being closed with an arm over them for protection. Heat seared at his sides as molten flames dripped down around the edges of the shield he had erected, licking eagerly toward the prone duo. Then it stopped. No sound but the ringing in his ears.

A breeze blew away the heat, but his seared flesh still hurt. Burnt-grass smell met his nostrils.

"We're alive." He laughed and flopped onto his back. "Okay. I'm alive. I should really check and see if you are alive." He patted around with one hand, the other arm still over his eyes. "Are you alive? Where are you, buddy? There you are. Yep. You're alive. I'll get us out of here in a minute. But that really took a lot out of me. Phew. Being a sorcerer can *suck* sometimes." Jones relaxed with his hands behind his head until he heard a wheezing coming from Kyle.

"You aren't dying on me now, are you, Kyle?" Concerned, he removed the arm from covering his eyes and blinked until he could focus on the warlock crumpled beside him. Kyle's lips were moving, sound just barely coming out of them. "What's that? I couldn't -"

"Golems," Kyle whispered with desperation. "Golems." As if hearing the words reminded him of their existence, a jolt of fear gripped Jones' core. Then Jones felt it. The arhythmic sound of many heavy steps from many heavy feet. Dozens of golems still heading their way because their target survived.

Chapter 87

It was over. Two powerful and unauthorized shielding spells had been used on Museum grounds. The golems were closing in after determining their initial barrage had not, in fact, finished the job. Jones realized he had just tagged himself as a threat by protecting Kyle. Which meant that golems were gunning for him now too. This sucked.

Jones was frozen in terror for a moment. Wide eyes staring at the shield spell mere feet over his face. He was going to die and was taking a few seconds to wrap his head around that fact. *Was it too late to abandon Kyle and run for it?* Almost before he'd finished that thought, Jones had dismissed it. Leave someone behind? He couldn't. Regardless of the fact that The Last Line would end him if he actually did leave her kid behind.

Maybe the noise had drawn the attention of someone in the museum who could do something about this? Because Jones was tapped out. He patted Kyle. Not on the shoulder, but some part of him that just happened to be close enough to his hand for convenient reach. Kyle groaned back at him.

"Give me a second, I'll think of something…. Maybe." Jones had tried to reassure his partner but ended up doing the opposite as a thready chuckle came from the direction of Kyle's head followed by another groan. Then, as Jones made a conscious effort to continue staring at the sky and not look toward any of the coming golems because he did *not* want to see his death approaching, he felt a feeble nudging on his side. Kyle was patting him back to console Jones.

The sound of massive fireball spells had managed to gain the attention of several people. Anna, on the couch of Kyle's apartment, looked up as yet another antenna tower of prisms collapsed in a tinkling crash. Then the herd rushed her to hide inside her pockets and long hair while they cowered.

Jim Thafesh was running at full tilt as he tried to keep up with a furious and terrified Camina in full mamma-bear mode as she chased a smoking dark blur across the rolling grass lawn of central park. While Jim didn't know *why* he and Camina were heading towards the danger, again – okay, that's not entirely accurate. Camina would always run toward the danger. Which by default meant that Jim would be running toward danger if he was with her.

It was fine.

No.

Really.

It was.

Probably.

Though the journalist desperately wished he had the ability to see what the blur was they were chasing. Instead, what he did manage to see was dozens of the intimidating, blocky, scary-as-fuck security golems converging on some poor hapless monster. Or…maybe it was something else? Whatever was happening, the blur they were after was heading toward it also.

It wasn't until he was almost zapped by a bolt of lightning that Jim realized they were running through a grove of magic trees.

"Ahhhh." He screamed and stumbled away from the little explosion that had nearly knocked him off his feet. It was then that he took a moment to glance around the sun-dappled landscape to see that the trees were dozens of different colors. Not just the leaves, which would be expected considering it was getting into Fall, but also the trunks. And the leaves of the trees in this grove weren't standard 'leaf' colors either. For example, one particular tree that drew Jim's attention had Cherenkov blue leaves.

Now, it wasn't necessarily a good thing for *anything* to be Cherenkov blue, the color of light produced by a nuclear reactor in water. However, when a tree with Cherenkov blue leaves also had glassy bark and bright silver fruit hanging from it, electric currents sparking occasionally between them, it was clearly an indication that the tree was dangerous. Incongruously, cloud hopper rabbits were perched throughout the charged tree eating the silver fruit. Jim backed away from said tree and frantically searched for a safer route through what his memory told him must be the Central Park Magical Tree Orchard.

Unsure which way to go as he'd lost sight of Camina and the blur; Jim picked a direction he thought might be correct and navigated clear of the tree dodging a few more electric bolts as his pace became a run once more. Tree trunks flashed by his face now, kind of interspersed with the light artifacts dancing across his vision from the bright lightning bolts. Up and to the right, the trees seemed to be thinner as Jim could see more light between the trunks there.

He veered in that direction checking his camera once more just to ensure it was still recording properly as he navigated his way among the trees. A rhythmic thumping from all around kept distracting him as he looked feverishly for its source while trying not to faceplant on a trunk. Worse yet, the sound was getting louder as he approached the direction he believed Camina and the blur to have disappeared in.

He broke out of the orchard into the full light of day. Sure, he'd been expecting it, but he hadn't at the same time. Before Jim, laid the rolling manicured lawn of New York's Central Park. Or more of it, since the park was quite large, and he'd already seen vast swatches of it over by the museum proper. But it was out in that vast expanse that something drew Jim's eyes.

A magical shield was hovering mere feet above the ground. Below which was huddled a Magicorps soldier, his yellow beret and uniform and cape a dead giveaway of his service branch. Beside the soldier was a mage, dark robe splayed around him. What had drawn Jim's eyes though, was the circle of burned and charred ground around the shield.

"Holy shit!" Jim breathed as he continued recording and checked his camera's focus. He didn't dare add any commentary. Like speculating why, a Magicorps soldier and the unidentified mage might have been attacked by the army of golems who were emerging around the clearing. The blur that Camina had run after was nowhere to be found. Of course, if it had stopped moving…

It wouldn't be a blur anymore.

So, the question was, where was Camina, again?

There. There she was standing back from the scene around the two bodies. No. Not standing. Arguing. She was gesturing angrily as a tall and slim but muscular man with burnt umber eyes who physically restrained her with one arm as he gesticulated at the duo beneath the fading shield with the other. Jim tensed as he considered how best to help Camina with this interloper. While the pair's words were heated, Jim was unable to make them out over the ominous thumping of golem footsteps. The sound was almost thunderous, really.

"FOR THE LOVE OF GOD, WILL YOU JUST LET ME DO MY JOB, CAMINA!" Okay, that was the director. The revelation filled Jim with both relief and anxiety at once. Relief, because it was the Director of the Museum, he was the representative on Earth of the power the institution wielded. The Anxiety, of course, came from the fact that he was also a vampire, and vampires *ate* people.

Chapter 88

Across the grass from Jim, also shaded by the same grove of trees as the journalist, Camina was fussing with a vampire. No, not *fussing*. She was trying to pull out Ascalon, her incredibly powerful pact item. A holy item with the power of the Big G.

Adrian Arcas, Director of The Museum of Unnatural Science and History, was struggling with her to stop her. *WHY?* People were in danger, and he was just going to *let* them *die*? At the hands of security golems? One was a soldier. A member of the United States Armed Forces. A patriot. How could the director be so cruel?

The soldier was shouting too. Pointing to Camina and the Director as he hollered at them pleadingly. Jim couldn't make out exactly what was being said over the rumbling thrum of the approaching golems, but clearly, he was pleading with Camina and the director to save his life. And the Director wasn't letting Camina help the pair trapped under the fading shield spell.

The journalist narrowed his eye as he filmed the confrontation. This was not a good look for the Museum. Hell, it wasn't a good look for Jim. Was a licensed mage like himself really going to stand by and just let someone die because a vampire was being a prick? No? Unsure exactly what his intentions were, Jim made his way toward the struggling pair. Still filming of course. One must never stop filming.

His blood was pounding in his ears, and he was at that moment more scared than he'd probably been during the entire previous two? Or was it three days? Jim had been up and awake a long time now and even as the thought crossed his mind, Jim felt himself sway on his feet. That was not good. But bad things were happening.

While questioning whether or not he was even in a state to make good judgement calls or safely use magic, Jim Thafesh, embedded journalist extraordinaire, continued stumbling toward his boss and her opponent. His approach brought their words to him more clearly, while the increasing volume of the golems' footsteps warred with drowning their voices out. Still, he was able to catch more and more of the argument.

"Just let me draw their attention." The furious Camina protested.

"You will only increase their threat level, Camina." Adrian tried to counter as he pulled on Ascalon. "Look you idiot. You've already drawn their attention, and it's not slowed them down one bit."

"That's my son, you overgrown mosquito." She jerked back hard on Ascalon as it was growing in her hands.

"Mosquito?" Adrian growled and his eyes began to clow crimson. "See if you think the same thing after a..." The complaint died into a hurt mumble before his voice came back stronger. "I can turn them off, just stop trying to transform. You'll only further activate their threat assessments."

"I'm supposed to trust the vamp who got my kid into this situation in the first place?" Camin jerked her pact item, and by extension the very well-dressed vampire, in the direction of the bright morning sunlight.

"Oh. Woah." Adrian jerked himself back away from the sunny grass he'd almost fallen into. "You almost put me back in the light madam. I could have been seriously harmed." As if he wasn't already blistered red and slightly smoking after his run across the lawn.

"Then let go or I'll show you some serious harm." Camina wasn't relenting and a cold sweat beaded the vampire's forehead.

"Just stand down and let me –"

"Stand down? My kid is in danger you flamboyant – whufpms" Whatever the Last Line had intended to say as she gathered power around her and prepared to cast some pretty unpleasant spells was interrupted by a wordless battle cry from Jim as he barreled into her. The two fell in a tangle of limbs while the Warlock of Archangel Michael shrieked her fury and dismay.

"Jim?!" Having never actually fought a vampire before, Jim had doubts as to whether or not he could even move the man, or if the expensively suited, tall, lithe, figure would just stand there like a mountain while Jim's rushing charge bounced off of him with bone breaking force.

He just didn't know. What he did know was that he was in no state to be calling on magic. Like, at all. And Camina needed a helping hand to get her opponent off balance. So, a charge to knock the guy down seemed like the best option.

If he hadn't been awake for so many hours and hopped up on stamina potions, maybe the journalist might have reconsidered his position. Perhaps if he'd been able to hear better he would have realized that Adrian was trying to turn off the attacking golems, but Camina's mama bear reaction was creating further danger. For others, not for her. But Jim didn't know and couldn't process that right now because the last few days had caught up with him and his brain wasn't in the most rational state at the moment.

Camina was also not in the greatest frame of mind. Which is why she didn't notice when Jim started his charge yelling as he came. Adrian had noticed, with a raised eyebrow and a simple response. He just stepped back out of the way and let the young man fall into the angry mother Adrian was wrestling with.

"Thank you, Mister, I forget your name. But thank you." He stepped away from the flailing pair wiping his hands as he began whispering an incantation. A hissing sibilance of words that weren't quite understood. Were they Latin? Were they Aramaic? Greek? It was impossible to tell as they built and grew, overlapping over and over again, circling out from the vampire who now raised his arms to the heavens.

His spell had become an incoherent roaring chant in the air. Visible lines of magic with the symbols and runes that enchanted the golems of Central Park and the museum security, now linked between each and every golem. They had stopped advancing but their feet stomped and rumbled as the air hummed with magic. Then… silence.

No feet stomping. No golems moving. No echoing after the thunderous crescendo of the whispered spell.

Nothing.

A breeze blew through the meadow and Jones felt like his breath and his heartbeat were the loudest sounds that had ever existed in that moment.

"Ah… Mister Jones," the director called over to him. "Could you please bring Kyle over to us. I have a slight bit of trouble with the light."

336

"Yes, Sir?" Jones had to take a moment to let the words filter through his brain. He was still coming to terms with the fact that the golem forty feet away had been intending to smash them with its feet. He could tell from the way its foot was raise that it had entirely intended to step on the prone pair. The Magicorps soldier might have still been stunned but he complied immediately. Rolling the groaning Kyle into a more maneuverable position Jones then lifted the warlock over his shoulder. Kyle and Jones had made it most of the way to the shade of the trees when a muttering Camina finally extricated herself from the delirious young man who had crashed into her.

"Oh my God. My Baby." She staggered to her feet and rushed at Jones who kind of dropped Kyle in his terrified desire to be as far away as possible from the riled-up Camina Wattkins in mother mode.

The director shot Jones a significant raised-eyebrow look over his shoulder as he picked up the young man at his feet. Something about that look told Jones that this was going to be an exceptionally long day.

Chapter 89

9:54 AM September 15th, 2026
New York F.B.I. Magic Crimes Division

There was snoring in the Magic Technology Lab office. Frank was moseying on into the lab hoping he'd get a chance to talk to Sam and Alex, or at least warn them about the fact that *everyone* was now aware of what Sam had done with Gleipnir and she was going to be mobbed, *mobbed* by people congratulating her if she ever made it down to the rest of the building. But the snoring made him pause.

Not that snoring was unusual this time of day. Gleipnir was not a morning person, and he didn't actually work, so he slept if he felt like it. But there were three different distinct pairs… sets… what did you even call multiples of snoring? Snorts? Whatever. There were definitely more than just Gleipnir sleeping and that was not normal.

He slowed as he approached the door to Sam's domain, unsure of what to expect. Then he stifled a chuckle as someone murmured in their sleep in a classic 'mememememememe' kind of snore. That had to be Gleipnir. Taking a quick, deep, fortifying breath, the senior agent rounded the corner and peered through the door to the lab office.

A smile spread across his face.

Alex, Sam, and Gleipnir must have slept in the office after getting back from out of town. Gleipnir had made himself a hammock up out of the way in a corner on a set of hooks that, if Frank remembered correctly, had been placed there specifically for that purpose. Alex was curled up on her cleared desk head pillowed on her arms, and Sam… Sam was…

Frank had to cover his mouth as he began shaking silently with mirth. Sam was sitting in her chair with her face on her desk. No pillow. No arms. Just face turned to the side and her cheek on the cold faux wood surface, mouth open with a puddle of drool forming on the table beneath her lips. Frank rubbed his hand over his face, sucked his lips, and shook his head. This was above his pay grade. He did not want to wake these kids up.

Shaking his head, Frank did the smart thing and did not approach any further. Instead, he pulled out his wand, whispered a spell and watched as it began to lengthen. A set of footsteps drew his attention, and he peeked back down the hallway the way he'd come. It was their boss, the director of the Magic Crimes Division.

Odd. He didn't come down and interact with the Magitech people often. And Frank was worried that things might not be great for the girls and Gleipnir if he didn't wake the kids up fast.

"Come on. Come on." He muttered to his wand, willing it to lengthen up faster so that he could poke the girls with a stick from a safe distance rather than risk getting swatted by one of them if they were startled. Now it was too late to try a loud noise as that would clue the approaching director in on the fact that the main techs were sleeping on the job.

As he walked, the director stuck a hand inside his suit coat and fished something out of an inner pocket that fit perfectly in one of his hands. Was the man using some kind of movement spell because he was fast. Really fast. It was as if every time Frank glanced away or blinked, the man moved twice the distance he should have been able to in that time. The director smiled wickedly at Frank.

"Good morning agent. You can stop with that. And you might want to get behind cover." In one smooth movement, the director pulled apart the thing he'd taken out of his pocket and chucked half of it into the center of the room before ducking down behind and against the other side of the doorframe.

"What the hell?" Was that what Frank thought it was? He tried to go after it to help the girls but felt himself pulled backward by his jacket.

"No. Idiot. I said cover." Sighing as he grabbed Frank and yanked him to safety with him. "It's just a low-yield sound grenade. I use them to wake Sam up so she or Gleipnir don't accidentally maim me when she works all-nighters." Then the director covered his ears with the palms of both hands. Wide-eyed, Frank followed suite.

True to his word, a few seconds later a blast of noise came from the room beyond. As the sound died down, two feminine shouts of startlement could be heard along with the beginnings of a protective spell. Then cussing as an irate Sam realized she wasn't under attack and canceled her summoning. Alex was silent until a very, deliberately loud snore broke through the low ringing in Frank's ears as he took his hands off them.

"Really Gleipnir?" Then she laughed. So did the director who had been shaking with mirth the whole time but let it out now.

"Yeah, laugh while you can because I'm gonna skin whoever did that…" Sam was stomping her way towards the door and Frank quickly sidled his way away from the director to try and give himself some distance from the target of Sam Wattkins' ire.

"What are you planning to do to me?" Not the least bit afraid, the director stepped around the door just in time for Sam to walk into him.

"Oh. Director. Guess it's time to wake up, hey?" Like flipping a switch, Sam's building wrath petered out. Puff. It wisped away into nothing, and he smiled at her with a mischievous and knowing grin.

"It is." He agreed. "But shouldn't you be at home? Resting?" He gave her a raised eyebrow that made the magic technician duck her head, blush, and look away. Observing from a safe distance, Frank's mouth dropped open. What was that? Sam… Sam didn't… She wasn't pliant like this for anyone.

"I had work to do and someone needed to look after Alex." She mumbled grouchily before glancing up defiantly. "Plus, it was dark and neither of us wanted to see what state our shittily shielded apartments were going to be in at o'dark-stupid in the morning." The mirth faded from the director's face at that mention, and he became more serious on that note.

"Okay. Well, I need my magitechs to head home, get some rest, and take a week of leave."

"What?" Sam's eyes bulged and she glanced up, looking the director in the face again. Alex's 'what' was followed by her head popping out from behind Sam's shoulder.

"Yesss." Now it was the director's turn to look a little nervous. "Word's gotten out about what you did…" here he paused as if looking for the right words, "and about what you saw and might have experienced… and

someone's making a hullabaloo about hiding your real magical ability level…
psych evals for trauma… and maybe, *maybe*
aninquiryintomagicallicensingfraud."

The last bit had been said so quickly that it took a few seconds for the
listeners to catch up with the sentence. Especially as the director had lowered
his voice just a bit to try and make it difficult to hear.

"What?"

"What?"

"What?"

"WHAT?"

Sam, Alex, and Frank all stared at the director once the words kicked
in. But Gleipnir, who had been sawing hugely loud, obnoxious, and obviously
fake snores, shouted his question in outrage. Magical licensing fraud was a big
fucking deal and could result in serious repercussions.

"Sam, you took down a dragon. Yeah, it was a corpse. Yeah, it was
manifesting as a monster. Yeah, you had Gleipnir's help. But it was a Gods
damned real adult dragon. Doesn't matter what the extenuating circumstances
are, you aren't rated as a Dragonslayer, and neither is Gleipnir."

"Oh, fuck!" Gleipnir commented as that sunk in. He floated up behind
Sam, pointed end up, on the opposite side from Alex with a pair of googly eyes
stuck on his length near the top. Frank wasn't sure, but he could have sworn the
googly eyes blinked at him before focusing on the director. Frank rubbed his
own eyes in disbelief. "Well, it's not like I hid the fact that I am fully capable
of restraining a deity. I mean, the whole Ragnarök thing is not even ancient
history at this point. A dragon was significantly less difficult."

"Regardless," the director continued with little more than a slight pause
as Gleipnir's googly eyes had their double-take effect on him, "I need you both
out of the office and on recuperative leave or something, I don't know, I'll figure
out the paperwork," he promised as he waved a hand dismissively, "until I've
got this mess straightened out. Okay?" He shooed at the direction of the exit.
"Hurry along now before *my* bosses get here."

The two women and Gleipnir glanced at one other significantly as if
they were communicating silently with their eyes. Which was made even more
bizarre by the fact that one of those pairs of eyes wasn't even actually real, but
they were definitely blinking and moving. Yeah. They *were* blinking and
moving. Then the three shrugged. Sam and Alex, as humans, shrugged their
shoulders but Gleipnir as a, whatever he was, manipulated his ribbon tail into
some kind of approximation of shoulders several inches below his 'eyes' and
shrugged that instead.

"Okay."

"Okay."

"Why not?"

Then they turned in unison to retrieve their belongings, straighten up,
and head home.

"Really?" the director questioned in disbelief. "I was expecting a bit
more pushback on this."

"No. It's fine." Sam replied cheerily over her shoulder. "If it's
mandated, we don't have to use my accrued leave."

"That makes so much sense, actually." The director acknowledged. "Relax. Recover. And we'll see you in a week." He turned and started down the hallway, he walked jauntily as he went.

"Okay. Bye. Just don't forget to explain to your superiors why you didn't send us backup when we asked for it." He froze for a second almost out of earshot but then continued on as if he hadn't heard. Frank shook his head.

"Gods damnit, Wattkins. You just couldn't keep your mouth shut."

Chapter 90

"So, what do you want to do with our vacation time?" Gleipnir asked in the most non-nonchalant way possible. Then he gave Sam a quick worried glance before sticking his 'head' out the window again. They were on their way back to Sam's apartment in a not seedy per se, but definitely cheaper part of town. Hint, it was not on Manhattan like her parents and her lucky jerk of a younger brother.

Being on the cheaper side of the river, she hoped that it hadn't fared as badly as many of the buildings on the island. But if the damage to the buildings she was driving past was any indication, well, her hopes were sliding lower and lower by the mile. It just wasn't fair. Her sentient pact item – and best friend – had said he would keep a nose out for the scent of any monsters. To facilitate this, he had turned point side down and stuck his new 'head' out the window, letting the wind blow through the red ribbon of his 'hair' as he 'sniffed' for corrupted magic.

Sam covered her eyes briefly and winced as Gleip took a deep theatrical sniff of the light breeze their slow pace through damaged neighborhoods generated. Because *how* was he sniffing? Then, she seemed to abruptly remember that she was, in fact, currently driving and needed to keep her eyes on the road. Just in time both hands returned to the correct places on the steering wheel, and she corrected the slight course deviation that had occurred while she was indulging in self-pity that sometimes Gleipnir was over-the-top weird.

"Do you have to stick your head out the window to keep an eye out for monsters? Not that I'm expecting any." She added drily as they passed another group of soldiers providing relief assistance, passing out water bottles and canned goods.

"It works best if the old sniffer has direct access to the air, my good Sam." He responded with the Gleipnir equivalent of a deadpan straight face. Sam glanced at him again and he turned his wide jumbo googly eyes – which he had adjusted to now be near the ribbon end of his giant needle-like body – and blinked at her innocently. Then he grabbed the pair of googly eyes – which were connected together somehow - with his ribbon, and adjusted how they sat on his 'face' as the wind from the window was fluttering them and they weren't staying put well.

"Okay." Once again, Sam rubbed a hand over her face, taking care not to cover her eyes this time. "Okay." Where this sniffer was or how it worked, Sam didn't know. What she did know was that it was there. It was part of him, and it definitely existed.

Gleipnir smiled at Sam's acceptance and went back to contentedly taking deep 'sniffs' of the air out the window with his shortened red ribbon trailing along the side of her car. Not that he really smiled. It was an aura of smiling. An essence to his being that gave Sam the impression that Gleipnir was smiling.

Maybe it was a warlock and sentient pact item thing, but she could read Gleipnir's expressions as if he had a human face. So, it was a little off-putting and weird when he wore fake facial features. But also, kind of cool because they worked without being enchanted. Point in fact, the googly eyes he was currently wearing shouldn't have been able to blink and move. They just did when he wore then and there was no explanation for it. Speaking of which…

"Hey, Gleip?"

"Yes, Sammy?" He paused in his monster sniffing to once again turn to her to blink and she compressed her lips in a tight amused smile.

"Where did those googly eyes come from? I thought you'd lost all your face pieces." Because she threw them out whenever he left them lying around the apartment. There had been fights. She was sick of stumbling over fake noses, rubber lips, and… It was a thing between them. He needed to learn to clean up.

"Oh, these?" The needle-ribbon whatever-he-was pulled his ribbon back into the window to gesture at the almost fist-sized set of eyes balancing tenaciously on his inch thick body. "I remembered that I had them stashed in the back of your desk from months ago in case the pair I had been wearing at the time was damaged in the line of duty. I snagged these while you were sleeping."

"That explains… wait a minute? How did you get into my desk drawn while I was sleeping against it?"

"Oh, Sam." He waved a curly end of his ribbon at her and swirled it around in tight complicated whorls and spirals. "I'm extremely flexible." He paused and went back to looking out the window before commenting, "And strong."

"Right." She pulled into the underground parking facility for their complex and Gleipnir stiffened, his relaxed and cheery aura turning to one of concern and attention.

"We've got monsters. Maybe magical creatures. Not exactly sure. Not particularly dangerous, but definitely somewhere in the building." That sunk Sam's mood even lower as she slammed the gears into park and added her parking break for good measure.

"Great. Let's get this over with. Maybe we can go back to sleep if it's fast enough."

"Ha, haah." The characteristic laugh of Gleipnir's amusement was dry and irritated. "Are we *ever* that lucky?" The pair exited the car in the dimly lit parking structure. Someone had placed additional magical emergency lights – powered by the higher-than-average ambient magic density – and shadows from them crisscrossed one another in the pale yellow glow. Gleipnir fumbled with his googly eyes tucking them away somewhere that Sam couldn't see as she tucked her purse over her shoulder and locked her car with a beep.

"Maybe we'll get lucky this time and it's somebody else's problem. Lead the way, oh great sniffer." However, Sam was not feeling lucky and a little pit of dread boiled up from her pelvis to her belly.

Chapter 91

"Welp, this sucks," Sam muttered in the darkened hallway. "Of fucking course management let the enchantments on the emergency magical lighting fixtures fail." She grouched as she gripped her wand with white knuckles. It was stupid, but she was trembling a little bit as she walked through the mostly silent apartment building.

"Not all of them." Gleipnir added with an unhelpful level of sarcasm. "There were at least three that I could see functioning on the second floor when we passed it in the stairwell."

"Yeah." A snort bubbled out of Sam despite the seemingly dire circumstances, "But there's none on *this* level." Her voice was saccharinely sweet with tender bile. "And this is where the monster 'smell' is coming from."

"Just stay behind me and I'll take care of it." Always willing to play the big brave protector, Gleipnir was eating up the fact that Sam was… not… comfortable? Yeah. Not comfortable with a monster being on her floor.

"What are the odds that the only monster in the building is on my floor?" Her grousing continued. "I mean, come on. There's six other floors in this building. Hundreds of apartments. Unless it formed up here it would have had to climb four stories to hunker down in one of these apartments." Her words were quiet but angry hisses now.

"Conversely," The pact item offered more unhelpful information, "It could be a flying creature that climbed *down* three floors." That stopped Sam. She froze in the dark processing the information. The only light she could see was the little lines of light that seeped under the doors lining the hallway. Some were weak sunlight. Others seemed like maybe there were magical lights on in some of the apartments. All were quiet.

"Nope." The worried warlock finally broke the unnatural silence.

"Nope, what?" Finally, noticing that Sam was no longer following him, Gleipnir turned and floated back toward her.

"Nope. I'm not doing it. I will yeet myself out of this building before I fight a flying monster."

"Oh. Pish posh." The floating Gleipnir patted Sam's hand with his ribbon. "It's an enclosed space. You'll have the advantage."

"I'm a magic technician, Gleip, not a battle mage." Sam hissed with just the slightest, okay more than slightest, bit of terror in her voice."

"It's fine. It's positively tiny compared to what we took on the other day. Now, come along. We're almost there and you'll never believe where I think it is." The morbid excitement in Gleipnir's conspiratorial tone only made the cold dread in her belly roil all the harder.

"Really?" It was dry, without any humor, because Sam just did not have any more shits to give at the moment. So, instead, she held up her wand like a flashlight and murmured a light spell. "Kynda." A pure white and yellow light like a small dim sun formed at the tip of her wand already properly adjusted to a brightness that wouldn't hurt her eyes. Still, Sam blinked several times as her vision adjusted to the new light source.

"Yes, yes." Came the distractedly happy reply, "You can spark a light now. I'm sure it isn't in the hallway, so you being able to see won't let it know we're coming." Now her pact item was downright bubbly with anticipation. "You know, I've come to realize that I kind of like fighting monsters... Sometimes... okay, no I hated fighting the big monster. That was... traumatizing. But maybe I'll like fighting this smaller one." As he babbled, Gleipnir's tone became less and less sure and Sam found herself tilting her head quizzically while she listened.

"You sound a bit uncertain about that." They paused in the hall outside their apartment, and she looked keenly at her best-friend-slash-pact-item-slash-roommate.

"Ugh. Okay. You're right. I hate fighting monsters. I just thought that if you thought I liked it then we could get this over with faster so we could just go home and not have to worry about monsters anymore. But... hmmm..." He stopped talking as he examined the door to their apartment intently glancing back and forth between theirs and their neighbor. "I was not expecting that. Because who would? I mean the odds against it were... Because who even *has* luck *that bad?*" His glances between the doors became even more intense as he sniffed at first one then the other.

"Let me guess," The weary Sam interrupted before Gleip could get distracted again, "We do. We have luck this bad. It's in our apartment, isn't it?"

"Ha, haaahh." He drew out the second 'hah' or a beat before agreeing with a defeated sigh. "Yeah. It's in our apartment."

"Alright then." Pulling up the sleeves of her warlock's robe, she reluctantly pulled out her keys and unlocked the door. "On three. You go high. I go low."

"Right. Just like Mom taught us." There was no rhyme or reason to it, but Sam smiled. She couldn't help it. It always made her a little bit happy when Gleipnir, a millennia old magical being, referred to her mom as *their* mom. Because as old as Gleipnir was, his life hadn't really begun until the day he became her pact item. Scared, lonely, drowning in eons of guilt and self-loathing for what he'd been a part of, but so full of life and with so much love to give and terrified that he'd never been seen as anything other than what he'd been made to do.

"Right." Sam agreed softly. "Just like mom taught us. One, two," Sam caught her breath and steadied her nerves for a second pausing longer than she should have in the middle of a count. "Three!"

They threw the door open, and Sam flooded the room with light from her wand, throwing the spell she'd been holding onto up against the ceiling where it would do the most good. But they saw nothing. Or more correctly, they saw... their living room. It was just as they had left it with no major changes. Sam's cold coffee was still sitting on the coffee table. Gleipnir's workout equipment was strewn around the floor instead of tidily packed away in the corner of the room that was his dedicated gym.

Like always.

"Well, this is ominous." Gleip chimed enthusiastically.

Chapter 92

"Damnit." Sam's heart had sunk through the floor when she realized the living room, and by extension the kitchen – because she could see clearly into it from right fucking there at the door – were clear of monsters. "You know this means that it's either in the bedroom or the bathroom." She kicked at the floor in frustration.

But just to be sure she cleared the kitchen anyways. Yeah. Nothing there. It was quiet and – relatively – clean. Even the dishes she hadn't done the last time she was home were still in the sink and the trash, yep, smelled like regular trash. She opened and closed the lid hopefully. No monsters in there. Then just for good measure she checked the fridge, freezer, and all the kitchen cabinets.

"You hoping it's really small and hiding in here?" Gleipnir supplied as he followed her around the room closing cabinet doors behind her.

"Because I don't want to have to deal with the financial destruction of there being a monster in my bedroom."

"How would –?" Gleip began before Sam cut him off angrily.

"All my clothes and expensive stuff are in there."

"Ohhhh…" After a second of silent reflection, he started speaking again. "But shouldn't our renters insurance cover that? And anything that's really irreplaceable is at your parents' house."

"Huh!?" Straightening from the floor where she'd been checking the inside of the oven, Sam relaxed a bit as she contemplated the suggestion. "Renter's insurance might indeed cover that. That would rock. Let's go kill a monster." Suddenly, much more jovial about the whole situation, Sam led the way to the hall with the bathroom and bedroom beyond.

"Ohhhhshhhiiittt!" Sam and Gleipnir hopped back against the wall of the hallway as a tongue, or something, lashed at them through the bathroom door. It splashed messily on either side of the bathroom doorframe leaving running trails of what must have been saliva streaking down the off-white walls in multi-colored bubbly rivers. "Gross. Ahhh." The tongue came lashing out of the door again and Sam hopped out of its way while Gleipnir dodged in the air.

"Is that the shower curtain?" Astonishment rang in his voice. "Our *shower* is the monster? This is just some unbelievable hogwash."

"Okay." Sam edged further from the open bathroom door that she had just carelessly barreled past in her rush to see what damage, if any, was in her bedroom. "How do we kill a showe – are those my toiletries? No! That's hundreds of dollars' worth of shampoo, conditioner, and bodywashes. Ahhhh, man." But her disappointment only grew with her pact item's next words.

"It's your new alchemical moisturizer," He sniffed loudly in the direction of the rainbow smear. "…and facial cleanser set also from the smell of it."

"For fucks sake" Sam screeched up at the heavens with an inquiring gesture. "Is nothing sacred? Really?"

"I don't think now's really the time to be beseeching the Gods, Sammy." But the look that Sam threw his way had him backpedaling in an instant. "Or I could be wrong about that. Clearly, very wrong."

"Let's just kill it and be done with it." She pointed her wand into the dark bathroom and prepared to summon a spell.

"How? We can't burn it?"

"Why not?" Because that had been exactly what Sam had been planning on, a nice tightly woven fireball or fire thread spell.

"Because it's literally part of the building, made out of metal with a clay or enamel coating, and any heat strong enough to kill it will also set the building on fire." Well, when he put it that way.

"Fine. Ice? I can't just stab it. Or can I?" The thoughts started turning over in her head and she wondered at how quiet the bathroom monster was when it wasn't actively trying to eat someone. "Creepy how it inherently seems to have made itself into an ambush predator."

"Yes," The thoughtful way Gleipnir spoke caught Sam's attention and she turned back to find him wearing his googly eyes and stroking his 'chin' with the end of his ribbon. Sparing a quick facepalm for her partner-in-everything, Sam turned a flat look on the dark bathroom before tossing another light spell in there. "Kynda."

Her aim was careless and confident, and the light flared to life near the spot in the ceiling where the bathroom light used to be. Now that area was a pulpy mass of rainbow-oozing squishy bits of falling popcorn texture. Because her apartment was last renovated by assholes who thought popcorn ceilings weren't a sanitation and allergy nightmare for tenants to deal with.

"The whole room?"

"Damn. Look at how it incorporated the design, fixtures, and supplies into a semi-coherent whole." Shooting another disgusted look at Gleipnir, Sam shook her head belatedly.

"You can't wait to tell Kyle all about this, can you?" Because her pact item was just as much of a nerd about the mysterious ways magic manifested itself as her younger brother was.

"Come on, do you really think he's seen something like this? The faucets are producing the saliva, which had to have originally come from bottles, which are now teeth. But the liquid in them is now coming out of the faucets which should be filled with water but aren't." He gushed the way he did when he was really excited about things. "Don't kill it yet. I want to get an essence imprint for my Satchel Beasts collection."

"Holy shit. I haven't even though about Satchel Beasts this whole time. I've missed so many opportunities to get monster essences for my deck." Shoulders slumping with disappointment, the warlock leaned against the wall while her pact item rummaged around her personage and produced a deck of cards from the Gods only knew where. "Don't worry, I've had my satchel on me this whole time and I've been getting essences for you as well. But you do owe me thirteen blank essence collection cards."

Though she didn't know when, or how the industrious Gleipnir had managed to do what he'd done, Sam was at least grateful.

"It's gross." Her comment was inane but felt like it needed to be said. Of course it was gross. It was an entire room which had become a mouth. Vibrant colored saliva pumping out of salivary glands shaped like the faucet fixtures they had once been. The floor and ceiling were pulsating and soft like the lining of a mouth. A little army of shampoo bottles, a hard pallet of ceramic and metal from the tub. And it was all in shades of pale grey, off-white, and silver. Except for the saliva and the toiletry bottle teeth. The teeth were floppy and multicolored because they had come from plastic.

"So, gross." Gleipnir replied as he activated the enchantment on his satchel and captured essences of the monster for his favorite magical game. "Okay, done. Go ahead and kill it. I suggest freezing it until it can be shattered. That should do it." The satchel disappeared as he spoke into whatever mysterious pocket dimension Gleipnir kept such things in.

"Fine." Sighing, the Warlock of Frigg raised her wand and wove a spell of ice and binding and frost. "Vefa ok sauma. Kaldr ok kaldr." Weave and sew. Cold and cold. Elemental spells weren't really Sam's forte. But she'd done more than one in the last week and that was saying something. Frigg was a wonderful patron for a magitechnican. She was a goddess of creativity and making things. Mostly of weaving, most notably, wyrd.

In English, one could be tempted to say, Frigg was a weaver of fate.

But fate didn't have to be big important events. It could be small. And weaving, spinning, and other fiber related art concepts could be nudged, twisted, and manipulated. Like fate, one could spin, weave, and sew other materials. Or things that didn't have a physical form. Like cold. There was more a Warlock of Frigg could do, but Sam didn't need more. Just enough to follow her passions.

From her wand cold grew. It flowed into the gaping maw filling it with frost and terror. The monster knew it was dying. It could sense and feel in its twisted and warped existence. So, it knew it hurt, it was feeling a sensation that it disliked, and which hurt it. It started thrashing, the walls and ceiling spasming as its tongue lashed out again seeking the only thing it knew, food to satiate its unending hunger.

"Come on." Gleipnir nudged Sam in the direction of her bedroom. "Let's get some stuff to take home or over to Kyle's for a bit. You don't have to watch this." He nuzzled along her side and wrapped his ribbon protectively around her, guiding her to their bedroom and wiping at the tears running down her face as they went.

"I've gotten good at killing, haven't I?"

"You are a child of a long and great line of warlocks," Gleipnir chided her softly, "you were all meant for grander fates than you chose."

Chapter 93

The drive to Kyle's was morose and silent. Not for lack of effort on Gleipnir's part. He'd tried making jokes and blinking his googly eyes at Sam in the way that she found so irritatingly endearing. It did not work. Sam just gave him a few flat stares as if she was too angry or upset, or emotional to even communicate with him.

Which he was pretty sure was somehow his fault too, yet he'd be damned if he could figure out what he'd said wrong. Gleipnir's comment about her being fated for greatness was supposed to have been reassuring. A reminder that she was not, in fact, doing as much fighting as she could be if she had chosen a militaristically traditional path. Instead, she'd been angry about it.

"Am I supposed to be grateful for that fate?" Sam had snapped waspishly at him. "Am I supposed to have wanted it?"

"No." He'd reassured her with very wide googly eyes. "Never. We've just been incredibly lucky to have lived peacefully so far. I hope it continues…" Then she'd collapsed on her pink bedsheets and sobbed into her maroon satin pillowcase while her bathroom convulsed through its death throes. Gleipnir had no words to help his warlock. He was still somewhat emotionally stunted from his centuries as a magical prison warden who accidentally developed sentience.

What he did know was that they had both seen things that were nightmare-inducing in the last few days. Things that they both needed help processing. And Sam wasn't really thinking straight about that. She never did. If there was anything his warlock hated it was asking anyone for help. So, he cuddled up against her reassuringly and patted her awkwardly on her back while elongating his ribbon-tail to pack a few extra things into an overnight bag.

"Call your dad." Gleipnir gently urged Sam as she sat up to take the box of tissues he offered her. "See if he's home yet and if not, we'll head over to Kyle's since you've got a spare key, and the resident parking garage is magically insulated along with the rest of the building and you won't have to worry about maybe losing your car if the arcanes spike again." Sam blew her nose then sniffed, tears still running down her face.

But she didn't smile. There was something behind her eyes, yet it was definitely not a smile. The pact item knew that Sam needed help. A psychiatric intervention as soon as possible. She'd *seen* things in that monster. Done… it didn't matter what she'd done. What mattered was that she couldn't help any of them. She couldn't save any of the people who'd been sucked into the thing that had risen from the corpse of the dragon.

Wordlessly, she pulled her phone out of a jacket pocket with bleak pain-filled eyes. Then she dialed and Gleipnir waited with bated breath as he listened to the sound of the ringing through the speaker. One. Two. Three… six. The call went to voicemail. She hung up and inhaled sharply.

"Why didn't you leave a message?" he asked with a little bit of confusion.

"Do you really think he's going to call me back?" It was half-shout and Gleipnir felt himself recoil slightly at the venom in it.

"Well," he stammered hesitantly, "well, you can't be certain that he's…"

"He's what?" she prompted as he paused, looking for a way to phrase it delicately. "Even if he isn't dead, Gleip, what are the odds that he will look at his phone, check his messages, and actually call me back? I'm pretty sure he doesn't even know *how* to check his voicemail. Not because he's incapable of it, but because he just doesn't care enough about what anyone else has to say to him. You really think the man-child who never learned how to cook, asked his son to leave work and pick up his youngest daughter, and then abandoned said daughter in a life-or-death crisis, will fucking bother talking to me if it's the least bit inconvenient for him? And considering the current state of emergency, it's probably pretty fucking inconvenient for him even if he is completely safe. I'm sure whatever was so important he had to bail on Anna is still keeping him occupied since Mom's not around to get his attention."

Sam was furious, scared, traumatized, and holding on to functionality by a thread. Which Gleipnir was aware of, and he was about to point out that maybe she was being a bit harsh on Dad. And then... Gleipnir thought of Sam's parents as kind of his parents too. After all, they had raised his burgeoning sentience right alongside their four children despite the difficulties it would bring.

To him, their father had always been a bit of a loveable doofus-savant. Brilliant, but immature. Self-aware of his general incompetence with mechanisms to compensate for his shortcomings. This time, though...

"You're right," he sighed, hugging Sam tighter for a moment before wrapping his ribbon around her hand and tugging her to her feet. Then the ride, in mostly silence. He'd eventually given up trying to cheer Sam up and taken to sighing heavily as he stared out the window at the scenery passing by.

"There's a lot of damage." He hadn't been expecting a reply to the inane comment, but it seemed that was what finally pulled her out of her funk.

"I'm sure the big companies are already putting together their bids for the government contracts." Her mood was darkly sardonic, and it showed in her voice. Gleipnir chuckled his agreement.

"Those asshats are racing to get themselves a piece of those sweet, sweet, FEMA funds, and don't even get me started on the war research and development companies are going to wage over all the monster parts." He added to the griping.

"Oh, Gods. You know what that means!" Sam's derogatory tone of voice could only be reserved for one entity, the entity abhorred by magic users and sellers throughout the country.

"Mmmmkaay."

"Mmmmkaay." They exclaimed simultaneously as they drove through the devastated streets and chuckled together before Sam continued.

"For realz, the Magical Materials Control Agency are going to be all over New York." Breaking as she approached Central Park, Sam pulled onto the street leading towards the museum's employee housing. "It's the kind of disaster they've been waiting for to push for harsher restrictions on all magical materials." Gleipnir snorted in disdain for the government agency which often tried to overstep its boundaries and whom nobody at all respected.

"Like that's going to work. The big military contracted R and D firms will never stand for it. And big money – holy moly hot tamales!" They'd reached the driveway entrance to employee housing and had to stop when a rank of golems blocked their path. Defensive enchantments were active and…

"Sam. Hold up." Gleipnir's voice was stern and commanding.

"I see it Gleip. Their offensive enchantments are hot, they've fired off mass attacks in the last day at least. I didn't realize that there had been that kind of manifestation so close to the museum." The pair glanced at each other before eyeing the silent sentries between them and a nice monster-free apartment. Sam, like Gleipnir, could see the flows of magic and as a magic technician had a fairly good grasp of what the golems were actually programmed to do. "Maybe…" Sam started before Gleipnir cut her off.

"Go slowly. We should be fine. There's nothing in the enchantments that indicates they should view us as a threat." He added in a high tight voice as he thoughtfully examined the golems. "Let me get our F.B.I. ID cards out just in case."

"Really? You think that will help?"

"Yeah. Yeah, I think that will help."

Chapter 94

Having their identification cards out did, surprisingly, help. Samantha and Gleipnir pulled slowly through the gate as the golems that had stopped them turned aside to let them pass. The pair stole nervous glances at one another as they proceeded with caution.

"Huh," was the only comment Gleipnir made until they had left the perimeter guard behind.

"That was terrifying." Finally, Samantha let out a sigh of relief when the key code Kyle had given her allowed access to the double-gated, magically sealed parking facility below the employee housing complex.

"Ohhohohoho yeah!" A heartfelt chuckle came from Gleipnir and Sam gave him a wry affectionate smile. "Some kind of shit went down not too long ago." He was keeping an alert lookout while Sam pulled into Kyle's dimly lit, empty parking spot. It was empty because her little brother hadn't managed to save up enough to buy any of the magic-resistant cars he wanted that were designed by the Daedalus Technology research and development company. However, after the nonsense with Anna, Kyle might have changed his mind about that.

As someone who had to have a car for commuting, Sam thought it was silly to save up for years for a special vehicle. Just get a loan and pay it off. But no, Kyle wanted to either buy his fancy car outright or have a significant downpayment ready. Gurgling came from Sam's stomach, and she clutched her middle with a grimace. Slamming the gear shift into park, she unstrapped and hopped out of her car into the pale blue emergency lighting of the garage.

"Okay. Let's go raid Kyle's fridge. Maybe he's got some ice cream that needs to be eaten while the power's out." That thought cheered Sam immensely and they headed toward the door to the residential sections of the building.

"OooOOOooo, *maybe* Kyle has some Cheasoning Mix we can put on it." Beside Sam, Gleipnir was easily carrying both the suitcase he'd packed for her, as well as a smaller 'backpack' of sorts for himself.

"That's so gross, Gleip." Making a fake retching sound to mock his strange food choices. "Cheasoning Mix is intended for *savory* foods."

"Nuh uhh," he countered. Though the stairs were wide enough for them to walk side by side, they chose to go single-file in case someone wanted to come down while they were climbing. "The packaging specifically states that Cheasoning can be used to add flavor to any meal, treat, or snack whether it be sweet or savory." The words echoed in the stairwell loudly and Sam modulated her voice to be softer when she made her reply.

"I don't care what – what it says." Her hissed response changed from a booming echo to a whisper mid-sentence when they exited the stairwell to the hallway of Kyle's floor. "People who use Cheasoning on sweets are weird." She was rummaging in her purse for her key ring only to remember that they were in her pocket when she patted herself down. "Ha, there they are." She fished them out to open the door.

"Thank you." Gleipnir laughed. "I thought you'd never notice that I'm
—" He stopped mid-sentence as they both froze in the open doorway to take in
the scene. "Huh."

There was a shirtless, very buff, smoking man sitting on the couch
covered in a frosty blanket. No, he *was not* smoking recreationally. There were
no cigarettes. It was a man, who was literally exuding smoke from his snow-
white skin. He was sipping from a healing potion bottle – also frosted over – the
contents of which was really more slush than potion at this point. There were
dozens of little sparkly ice chunk-things ranging in size from the tip of a thumb
to about a hamster-ish crawling over his body. Anna and the soldier who had
been with Kyle were busy repositioning the creepy-crawly chunks of ice.

"Are you sure that the potion will still work if it's this cold?" Anna was
protesting hesitantly while she worked. "I don't want to diminish its
effectiveness? No. Stop that. How many times do I have to tell you guys to stay
off his face." She snagged one of the crawling ice-things which had been about
to crawl from behind hot-guy's ear onto his pale, sculpted cheek. "Sorry about
that director."

"It's quite all right – oh, hello." His eyes met Sam's where she and
Gleipnir were watching. Red? No. Orange? No. Brown? No. Burnt Umber! With
dark, sleek, disheveled hair carelessly across his face which he immediately
tried to brush into some semblance of order as he began to stand.

"Oh, hey, Sam. Gleip." Anna tossed over her shoulder before Jones'
voice distracted her.

"Woah, director. Not so fast."

"Where do you think you are going? My prism babies are going to fall.
Sit back down." The teen firmly instructed, and Sam felt herself mouthing the
words 'prism babies' questioningly. One look at his warlock had Gleipnir
realizing that he was going to have to take the lead in introductions because
Sam's recent trauma must have done something to her brain.

"Hello," Gleipnir started forward, tossing his and Sam's bags in the
closet along with Sam's purse which he gently teased out of her distracted
fingers. "I'm Gleipnir, and this is my warlock, Samantha." He wrapped his
ribbon around a suddenly nervous Sam and guided her toward the trio at the
couch. He studiously ignored the annoyed look that Sam shot him for using her
full name.

"Hello, Samantha. It's a pleasure to meet you." The handsome man
smiled a broad smile with full lips revealing straight white teeth and two fangs.
He bowed slightly from his seated position. "I'm sorry that I cannot greet you
in a fashion more suited to a lady."

"Will you quit moving already?" Anna rolled her eyes at the vampire
– because Sam finally realized that's what he was – and looked to her sister for
agreement in annoyance as she made a 'can you believe this guy' gesture with
her hands before grabbing another tumbling prism and reattaching it to the
vampire at a more secure location.

Chapter 95

"Hi – hi?" Sam gulped down the lump in her throat and wondered about the strange tightness in her chest then reached out to grasp the hand extended to her in greeting. "I'm Samantha Wattkins." The very athletic and muscular looking vampire took Samantha's hand in both of his and brushed his lips against the back of it. A hot blush suffused her face.

"Enchante mademoiselle." His eyes were locked on hers, bright and earnest if maybe a bit too eager seeming to impress her. Sam was stunned and silent. Reality narrowed down to that soft touch. Maybe time stopped for a second while Adrian Arcas stared into her eyes? All she knew was that her sister, the Magicorps soldier, and the entirety of the room disappeared for a few heartbeats. Had anyone, anyone ever, kissed her hand before? She had no idea. Then *he* blushed and laughed self-deprecatingly at his own behavior before running a hand shyly through his hair. What?!

What?!

What?!

The world expanded again as the rest of the couch, the three other people in the room, and indeed, the entire room returned to normal. Time began moving again.

Samantha Wattkins giggled.

Not a normal giggle. Not a we're-buddies-having-fun kind of giggle. It was…

Anna's whole body stiffened at that, a sound because she had never heard it come from her older sister's throat. Both younger sister and Gleipnir turned to stare at the prickly warlock who had scared off most of the men who had ever been interested in her. A white-haired head and a googly-eyed pact item blinked incredulously, first at Sam, then at each other, then at the director who blushed a bright scarlet.

"I'm sorry. I must apologize. You probably shouldn't look into my eyes right now. My magic's a bit out of sorts while I'm recovering." He glanced away with a morbidly shameful expression. Closing his eyes, Adrian scrubbed a hand over his face and through his dark hair.

"Wa-What?" Sam prompted with a stutter. But Gleipnir got it.

"Vampiric mesmerism." He swooped close to Sam and wrapped his ribbon protectively around her waist. Perhaps he would have said more but at that moment, a commotion came from Kyle's room. Kyle's voice, distraught and angry, came through the walls followed by Camina's low soothing tones.

His door opened to reveal Kyle in a pair of boxers, bandaged and burned. He was pointing angrily at the director and trying to hobble past his mother. She easily restrained him.

"Will you calm down?" Camina admonished. "It's just a giggle. Sam's a grown adult. I'm sure she's fine." She forced Kyle – still grumbling about vampires – back to his bed. "You sound racist right now."

"I'm not racist, I'm a brother. She's not allowed to date. It's bad enough I have to share my older sister with Gleipnir. That rat bastard." A surprised Sam gave a short bark of laughter before stifling it at Gleipnir's protest.

"I'm not a rat bastard. And I was here first." He shook a roll of his ribbon at the closed door.

"Being older doesn't count. Gleipnir." The pact item blinked his googly eyes at Anna's correction. "Kyle was part of the family first."

"What?" He made a pair of arms out of his ribbon and threw them up in the air before shouting "Why does no one *tell* me these things?" He then stormed away from Sam only to curve around and hug Camina. "Hi, Mom."

"Hi, Gleipnir." Her low voice was indulgent and amused at her children. Them being possessive of each other was certainly better than if they all hated one another so she must have done at least something right in that department. Gleipnir blew a raspberry at Anna as their 'mom' acknowledged him as one of her children. "Now what's going on out here that made Kyle want to kick his boss out of his apartment in his fireball-and-magical-drain-induced delirium?"

"It was my fault." The tall athletic vampire rose to his feet letting the cooling blanket and herd of prism crawling over him fall. In her dismay Anna rushed to catch her 'prism babies'.

"Seriously? You are the worst patient." The teen bemoaned as she gathered her pets and began consoling them in baby talk. "Did the big mean vampire drop you? Yes, he did. He just dropped you on the ground like he forgot you were even there trying to help him cool down."

"I was lax in restraining my powers and may have um… accidentally, of course…" Camina waved impatiently at him to continue his explanation.

"Of course," she prompted drily and rolled her eyes that he was so nervous.

"Used the tiniest bit of Vampiric Mesmerism on… Samantha." He *sighed* her name and Camina's eyes narrowed and hardened.

"I see." Not being a fool, Adrian immediately sensed the sudden cold shift of Camina's mood.

"I… should… I should go." He grabbed a singed jacket and dress shirt from the coffee table. "Thank you, all. It was a pleasure meeting you ladies." He nodded at Anna and slightly longer at Samantha before ducking swiftly out the door. By the time Camina had crossed the room to lock the door, Director Adrian Arcas had disappeared from the hall. She closed it and locked it before leaning against it.

"That was interesting." Jones broke the silence. Listening from the stairwell, Adrian Arcas leaned against a wall and banged the back of his head gently into it. Stupid. Stupid. Stupid.

He had very much embarrassed himself by losing control of his powers. Worse yet, he'd come on way too strong at the same time. Which made his slip-up *seem* deliberate. But it was Samantha Wattkins. He'd had a celebrity crush on her for years, *years*.

And no, Samantha wasn't as famous as her younger sister. But she'd gotten her fair share of press time. The vampire would be lying if he didn't spend the first three months Kyle had worked for him dressing extra debonair and *hoping* the mage's older sister might drop in to visit him at work or pick him up and give Adrian the opportunity to meet someone he'd admired for a while.

Despite Kyle being his employe, Adrian had never had the chance to meet his older sister. Of course, it was going to be something like this for their first encounter. There had been no meet cute, like he'd half imagined. No chance for him to say something charming, make her laugh and invite her to lunch at the museum restaurant.

His one chance to make a good first impression and he'd well and truly fucked it up while pissing off one of his employees and The Last Line in the process. It wasn't even like he'd been caught off guard. Enhanced vampire senses had let Adrian know way back before she and Gleipnir had even started climbing up the stairs that she was on her way up. Plus, the security Golem enchantments had sent a notification to his scroll when they'd come through the gates. This was all on him.

Damnit!

Chapter 96

11:14 AM September 16th, 2026
Museum of Unnatural Science and History Employee Housing

Oh no, the golems. Kyle and Jones were surrounded. Through his blurry eyes, Kyle watched in helpless terror struggling to do something, anything, as fireballs were raining down. Like an idiot, Kyle had used the wrong spell for the situation. Not just that, he'd tried to call on his own pathetic reserves of magic. Of course, this was how he was going to die.

And his idiotic mistake was going to cost Jones his life too.

The golems were approaching, and Kyle wasn't able to move let alone fight. He hadn't channeled the ambient magic effectively and now he was paying for it. Which he really thought he hadn't done. But then Kyle had reached for help from the codex. And it was gone.

Not disappeared. He fumbled slowly with weak burned arms for the magical tome of his warlock pact and found it snugly secure in its holster. It had shifted when he collapsed and was poking his shoulder at an unpleasant angle. Oh. So, some of that pain wasn't from draining his magic and surviving artillery fireballs.

No. Focus. His codex was there. Kyle could even sense it magically. He just couldn't interface with it. No. Not that either. He could interface. The flow of magic was just throttled and... weak.

It didn't matter.

The golems were coming.

The golems were coming, and Kyle's field of vision was growing narrower and narrower. The sunny autumn morning was dim and shades of gray and red-brown to Kyle. That might have been blood, though? Something was running down his face. *Thump. Thump. Thump.*

Closer.

Closer.

Darker.

Darker.

Thump.

Thump.

Tha-thump.

Tha-thump.

Kyle groaned in pain.

Tha-thump. Tha-thump. Tha-thump.

Kyle groaned as he tried to roll over. *Everything hurt!* What? *Why? Tha-thump. Tha-thump.* His pain seemed to intensify with each thump and he realized it was like the beating of a heart. No. Idiot! Not like. It was the beating of a heart, his heart. Why was he hurting again?

Then he lay there and thought about it a bit and his scattered nightmares resolved themselves into memories. Right. The jackass golems had tried to fry his ass.

"This sucks," he moaned in self-pity. "Also, not fair. I helped save a city. I feel like I should get to skip out on being in pain for a few weeks at least."

The young warlock wasn't talking to anyone in particular. Maybe a little bit to his pact item, though it wasn't sentient like Gleipnir. Few pact items were.

Familiars on the other hand –.

No. Focus. Kyle scolded himself and he started assessing his body. Opening his eyes, he recognized the familiar flat ceiling of his bedroom. Realizing he was safe, he then decided that it was safe to return to sleep. Which was exactly when he heard the door to his bedroom open and a familiar voice called out to him.

"Who you talking to shorty? There's nobody in here. I guess I might be talking to myself also, if I got hit on the noggin as hard as you had." Was…? Could Sam just not be rude and *Sam* all the time? Like, could there be five minutes after waking up when she wasn't allowed to deliberately provoke people?

"I was complaining to myself." He groaned at his older sister. "Can I have a healing potion now?" His voice cracked from dryness, and he licked cracked and blistered lips, wincing as he did so. Sam's response was a low almost malicious chuckle.

"No can-do baby brother. Doctor's orders. You've got magic saturation poisoning." Though she was laughing her voice also had the slightest hint of empathy. Probably. Maybe. Stupid Gleipnir. It was clearly her pact item's fault in some way.

"I'll risk it," Kyle whispered as his body throbbed in time with each heartbeat.

"What did I tell you?" A second voice pipped up. Lower, more arrogant, with an assumed British accent. "You must know young man that this is exactly how you got into this situation. You're too reckless." Suddenly the throbbing pain he felt got much worse.

"Stuff it, Gleip. I'm not in the mood." Summoning his strength, Kyle managed to get his hands under his pillow and pull it around his ears mostly ineffectually.

"Says the guy who killed a dragon-monster from the inside," Sam added under her breath.

"All I'm saying," the pontificating Gleipnir continued in his characteristically tone-deaf way, "is that maybe if you were a little more cautious with your use of magic you wouldn't currently be in this state." An angry growl emanated from within Kyle's pillow taco. It was followed closely by a moan of agony.

"That's enough Gleip. Let him be." Sam, being nice? And not prickly Sam-ish? Sweet! Kyle would take old-Sam any day over post-Gleipnir Sam.

"I was just trying to educat –" But his sister blissfully cut off her pact item before he could be even more annoying.

"I said *leave it*, Gleip!" Her forceful instruction was met with some mumbled grumbling that faded off into the distance. Kyle supposed that his pseudo-nemesis had wandered off to go offend someone else. But also, the spike of pain he'd felt when Gleipnir had first entered the room subsided a bit and he uncurled from the fetal position he had unconsciously assumed.

"Thank the Gods." His voice rasped through his dry tortured throat.

362

"Eh. Yeah. Probably feels better to not have a living source of magic so close to you." Sam's voice floated closer to the bed as she approached. There was a clunk of something being set on his bedside table "I brought you some water. Adrian and Mom gave you as much first aid as they could, and Mom – in a *rare* display of motherly affection – pulled strings to get a surprisingly high-level healer to take a look at you and Jones."

"Adrian?" Cautiously, Kyle opened first one eye and then the other. He was relieved that there was only a slight blurring of his vision.

"Nobody said anything about you having a concussion. Did you forget what your boss's first name is?" Concern tinted the biting quip, which Kyle ignored as he was determinedly working on stretching a shaky hand out for the glass which was tantalizingly out of reach. Kyle paused in his efforts to fix his sister with a baleful stare.

"Not concussed. Just hating that you call him by his first name. I know your type. It will start by calling him by his first name then next thing you know Gleip, and I are commiserating at the wedding reception that my stupidly sexy boss who is followed around the museum by vampire groupies is now our brother-in-law."

"Not if I tie him to a lamp post first like I did to the last asshole who broke Sammy's heart," Gleip called from the living room. Kyle and Sam laughed at that. Then something occurred to Sam, and she stopped abruptly.

"Wait! Someone did actually tie that last prick I dated to a streetlight post. The cops thought it was the boyfriend of one of the chicks he was trying to hook up with at the bar that night." Gleipnir poked his googly-eyed 'head' around the door frame for a second and Sam narrowed her eyes at him.

"Welp, that's my queue to make myself scarce." Gleipnir skedaddled quickly out of view.

Kyle smiled and then groaned and rubbed his aching chest. That was good. At least Gleipnir was always looking out for his sis even if it meant Kyle had to share his former best friend with the pact item. Then he went back to reaching for the delicious water that was just out of reach. After a bit, his sister took pity on him and helped him get something to drink. Moments later, he had laid back down and was asleep once again.

Chapter 97

The fridge was empty. Of course, it was. Couldn't expect a single guy to keep a fridge full. Sam closed the door in disappointment, waited a few seconds, then opened the door again to see if it would magically refill itself. No luck. The shelves were still baren save for the inevitable bits of organic matter that fell off produce.

On the bottom shelf, there was a small, dried milk stain, and on the top shelf a little gooey puddle of jelly. The jar it belonged to was nowhere to be found. Frustrated and hungry – she hadn't eaten since the day before, if that – she wandered over to the cupboards and began opening and closing them in a systematic search for something tasty. There was nothing.

No. Not nothing. There were dozens of dried spices and herbs in bottles, jars, and bags. Not just the regular everyday stuff either.

"Poppyseeds? Who the heck keeps poppy seeds and cardamoms in their cabinets?" she muttered under her breath.

"What's that?" Anna called from the living room where she was playing Satchel Beasts with Gleipnir.

"Nothing." She was going to leave it at that, then had a thought. What had Anna been eating this whole time? "Hey, where's Kyle's food?" Sam's call interrupted a dispute between Anna and Gleip about whether or not their cards would be more powerful in the higher ambient magic outdoors or not. Gleip was against. Anna was for. Sam tried again. "Anna! Food!"

"Huh?" The squabbling stopped. Just in time to prevent Gleipnir and Anna from opening the living room windows to prove their positions. "Oh. In the cabinet." That wasn't helpful.

"Which cabinet?" Her frustration was evident in the question, and she threw up her hands in disgust.

"All? Of them? Ha! Take that, Gleip!" A slapping sound of a card hitting the coffee table was followed by a small roar sounding as one of the magical Satchel Beast cards summoned their creature to attack Gleipir's beasts.

"What? No fair. What even is that? It must have been eight stories tall." Stomping followed suit as all of Gleipnir's summoned beasts were squashed or eaten. "Oh, it's *on*, little girl. Gleipnir is going to lay the smackdown on you." Listening from the kitchen, Sam laughed at the two having fun together. Anna was young enough that she had grown up with Gleipnir and they were more sibling-like in their interactions than either of her brothers were with Gleipnir.

"Again. There is no food to be found in the kitchen. In neither the cabinets nor the fridge." Anna groaned in irritation, slapped her cards on the table, then stomped into the kitchen. Giving Sam a flat look, the elementalist stomped over to a cabinet, opened it up then pointed at it with both hands before exclaiming with sarcasm.

"Ta-da! Food." She stood there looking at Sam as if she expected her to be all like *'Oh! Wow! Thanks!'* But Sam just blinked at the nearly empty cupboard with a couple of unrelated items on each shelf.

"Anna. That's canned beans, collogen powder supplement, and a rack of random seasonings and spices. Literally no food." At least, no food that anyone would genuinely enjoy eating. Anna's eyes narrowed and she pursed her lips in irritation at her sister before marching over to the cabinets on the other side of the room and opened the door.

"Flour." Then she marched to the fridge, opened it up and pointed at a small jar in one of the door shelves. "Yeast." In the background more roars and devastation could be heard over Gleipnir's wild cackling as he played his next card.

"So," Sam pondered her next words carefully as she continued trying not to rudely blink in surprise. "What you are telling me is that there's *no food* and someone needs to go raid Mom and Dad's fridge?" Anna's shoulders drooped and she shot daggers at her sister with her eyes.

"You are so spoiled. Kyle was supposed to go shopping a couple of days ago, but it got postponed this week. There's nothing at home either because Mom was out of town, and you. Know. How Dad is. You'll have to go shopping if you can't eat what's here." Crossing her arms, Anna flounced off back to her game and shrieked in dismay, but Gleipnir floated into the kitchen himself.

"I doubt that there are any grocery stores open," he advised unnecessarily. Power hasn't come back on yet, the AMD is still high, and there are still lesser monsters about."

"I think there will be a few open, they'll be trying to offload product before it goes bad," Sam headed out to the living room to grab her purse and keys. "I've got some cash in my wallet so we can at the very least buy something with protein in it. At the very worst we'll get takeout from Fries 'N Shakes. They never close."

"They might have closed for this," Gleip offered his counterpoint, and Sam shook her head at him as she headed out the door and down the stairs to her car. A few minutes later they were parked in front of the local grocery store.

Closed. The grocery store was closed. Yep. Of course, it was closed.

"Fine." Almost vibrating with how upset she was that the store was closed, Sam immediately began making alternative plans, trying to remember where the nearest Fries 'N Shakes was. "This is fine. It's fine." She got back in her car, gripped the steering wheel too tightly, and did not smash her head against the headrest. Her stomach grumbled its protest. "We'll just have to hunt for food."

"Oh!" Gleipnir, who had been sulking about having to leave in the middle of his game with Anna, perked right up. "I haven't been hunting for centuries. This will be so fun. I am an excellent snare. We'll have dinner in no time."

"Uh. That's not quite what I meant." But her protests were met with deaf ears... or whatever it was Gleipnir used to hear with.

"Can we try one of those ones where if someone steps in the loop they are suspended by their foot? I've been dying to try one of those since the first time I saw it on TV. So exciting." He turned his googly eyes out the window to the changing shadows of the cityscape. "We could get a moose or caribou. Because frankly, I don't think rabbit is going to cut it. I. Am. Famished. I could probably eat a moose by myself right now. Oh, what about that?"

Turning her head, Sam was surprised to see an actual deer bounding down the surprisingly undeserted street. While the traffic wasn't bumper-to-bumper it was still flowing enough that there were other vehicles on the street. Not just the abandoned ones either. And the design of the roads with the emergency vehicle lane down the center allowed for weaving in and out of the proper lane to go around those vehicles that were abandoned in the street.

"Gleip. No. I'm not going to hunt that. It's way more food than we need. And there's no refrigeration." More focused on trying to remember where the nearest Fries 'N Shakes was, Sam didn't really take her pact item seriously. He, however, continued.

"I supposed I could just catch a rabbit." He mused, rubbing a spot about a hand's width below his googly eyes as if it were a chin and he was deep in speculative thought. "Squirrels or chipmunks are an option. Hey," he exclaimed excitedly, and he turned back to Sam. "What about a pet store? Hamsters, rabbits, guinea pigs! Guinea pigs in particular were originally bread for food. I'll teach you how to skin –"

"Stop." Somewhere in the last few seconds, Sam had figured out that Gleipnir was being serious. "No."

"But you said we had to hunt for food," he responded petulantly. "You don't like any of my suggestions? I mean, if we had to, I could probably catch some fish in a pinch."

"What? Eww. No." Flustered, Sam slowed and craned her head to check the storefronts more carefully. "Gleip. When I said 'hunt' I meant look for someplace with processed food. Chips, cookies, burgers, canned goods and stuff that doesn't need to be refrigerated or cooked to be safe. Do you really think you would want to hunt, kill, and skin a squirrel? That would devastate you. They are too cute."

"Oh. Thank the Gods. Squirrels are *way* too cute to eat." This made Sam smile, and she patted Gleipnir's ribbon affectionately.

"Glad we cleared that up."

Chapter 98

4:27 PM September 16th, 2026
Museum of Unnatural Science and History Employee Housing

Thump, thump, thump, thump.

Anna paused in her second attempt to access television with her cobbled together system of antennae, laptops, and prism-assistance. The floor was shaking slightly with each thump. They *sounded* like footsteps. Who the heck was heavy enough to gently vibrate an entire floor of a building with his footsteps down the hallway?

It couldn't be a golem. Her mom had warned Anna about them, and for sure they would be too heavy to walk up the stairs into the building. Right? Then again, the building was physically and magically reinforced to be a safe haven during magical events. So…

But the steps had originated on this floor. Down the end of the hallway where there wasn't a stairwell, so whatever it was, it had already been in the building. And it was coming closer to Kyle's door. Had some idiot left a window open? There had to be protections for that. Weren't there?

What should she do? Her mom had left – called back to D.C. Her sister was out on a pointless quest for 'real food' as if she had no idea how to scrounge filling meals out of random shit in the cupboards.

Snorting in distain, Anna blew her pale bangs out of her eyes before setting her project aside. Her older sister's behavior indicated a disturbing possibility, that perhaps her parents hadn't always been the scatter-brained home keeping incompetents which Anna dealt with on a daily basis. Like maybe, they had grown up with regular homemade meals? Hmmm.

The thought elicited a frustrated growl from the teen, and she got up to check on Kyle. Yep. Still out cold. If the thing in the hallway really was a monster, Anna's best bet was to move herself and her pets into her bedroom as far from the hallways as possible, wait for it to pass by, and hope it didn't notice her and Kyle.

On the other hand, she *was* pretty handy with her magic if Anna did say so herself. Kind of. Mostly defensive stuff. And for real, what was the likelihood that it was a monster and not something super interesting like a guest of the museum. That was it. Rummaging in Kyle's bedside table, she grabbed one of his spare wands – because an added focus would be handy in a building she cared about damaging – then headed to the living room.

When the young elementalist pressed her eye to the peephole with her heart pounding up in her throat, she blinked in surprise then frowned in disappointment.

"Boo!" She groaned. "It's just the weird neighbor. Boring." Sighing, she leaned against the door and tried to relax now that there was no exciting reward for her adrenaline-fueled anticipation.

"Sorry for being boring?" Came a muffled call from the other side of the door. Anna froze. He couldn't have heard her, could he have? Slowly she turned around and put her eye back to the peephole. Sure enough, Weird Neighbor had stopped and was looking right at the looking hole. Yep. He heard her. "Is that Anna or Sam?"

"It's Anna." Sheepishly she unlocked then opened the door to peer at the twenty-something looking guy apologetically. A toothy grin with slightly elongated and rather fat canines spread across the kindly face with a shaggy mop of dirty blonde hair. "Hey."

"I'm glad you are safe after all the crazy stuff that's been happening." The neighbor scruffed a hand through his hair causing an exposed bicep to flex impressively. Which is when Anna noticed that 'Neighbor Dude', as Anna thought of him in her head, was dressed in his typical garb of surf shorts, a tank top, and flipflops. His exposed skin was covered in hairy stubble indicating that until everyone lost power, he was probably shaving all his body hair off.

"Yeah. Kyle came and picked me up from school," she admitted trying to downplay what had happened as Anna wasn't exactly sure how much of what happened was going to be public knowledge when all was said and done. To her surprise, Neighbor Dude threw his head back and let loose a big hearty tooth-revealing guffaw. Those canines really were big. But way to thick to be a vampire. Anna shuffled further back into the apartment.

"I'm sure there's way more to it than that." He chuckled after his laughing outburst shaking a finger at her. That was when the teen noticed the bag over his shoulder.

"Um…maybe – are you going somewhere?" It wasn't the slickest of topic changes, but Neighbor Dude didn't seem to mind.

"Yeah. For sure. It's farmer's market day in the park. So…" He shrugged his muscular shoulders as if it was a given that he was going to go to the farmer's market no matter what.

"Wouldn't it have been canceled?" But Anna's question was met with a blank look.

"Why?" And that question made Anna pause, because it seemed a given to her – a literal child – that the farmer's market would have been canceled. Yet this guy didn't have any inkling.

"Because of all the stuff that's been happening and the danger of all the monsters about?" Neighbor Dude's complete and utter lack of comprehension caused Anna to doubt her answer, so she was hesitant as she said it.

"Nah, dudette." Another chuckle and a bigger smile as he gave his answer in his lackadaisical surfer-dude drawl. "It's cool, yo. This is the Central Park Farmer's Market; you really think a little bit of magic is going to stop them? The venders are hard core. They stayed open during the apocalypse back in twenty-twelve. You want to come? There's always cool stuff." Anna hesitated because she didn't know this guy all that well. There also wasn't really a reason for her to go out.

"Is it safe?"

"Absolutely, it's guarded by security golems." That actually kind of reassured Anna. It also kind of confused her because Kyle was just attacked by the security golems. "I mean, unless your brother is coming? He should stay home. The golems hate that dude." This resulted in Anna sniggering, then covering her mouth with a hand, appalled that she had laughed at her brother's misfortune.

"I think I'll stay here. Kye will probably freak out if I'm gone when he wakes up." She looked at the neighbor's shopping bag wistfully because, honestly, Anna had been indoors for days, and it was getting old.

"Suit yourself, little lady. I can't wait to get myself something tasty to eat. I'm all out of food." Anna had almost closed the door, and Neighbor Dude had turned away when his words clicked in her head. She flung the door open.

"There will be food there?" While she should probably stay home, it was also likely that Sam wasn't going to find any open stores.

"Of course, there will be food." Blue eyes sparkled with amusement as well-defined massively muscular arms spread in a wide-armed gesture. "It's a farmer's market."

"Oh. Wait here a sec." She closed the door and ran to the kitchen to leave a note for Sam and Kyle. Then she stol – borrowed – a wad of cash from Kyle's emergency cash fund before running out the door and locking it behind her. "Let's go get some food."

"Sounds good. You need a shopping bag? I've got extra." He pulled a reuseable cloth grocery bag with a museum logo out of his crossbody beach bag.

Chapter 99

5:05 PM September 16th, 2026

A random street in Queens

Sam felt like she and Gleipnir had scoured every single street on Manhattan Island. Every grocery store and fast-food joint was closed. Okay. That was not entirely accurate. The Shakes 'N Fries location on 44th Street had been stepped on by something large. Three other locations had been damaged in other ways. Half the stores had been looted. Some still had small monster issues and Magicorps, Army, and National Guard personnel were clearing the island of monsters building by building.

"Okay, this is it. I'm done." Gleipnir scowled by narrowing his googly eyes angrily after the third time they were directed to turn around at a roadblock.

"If I hear one more solder in a uniform mansplain to me why we shouldn't be driving around, I'm going to do something he will regret." Sam chimed in as, she also, was fed up. The duo were tired, hungry, and frustrated and it was showing. She had just turned a corner onto a particularly damaged street – road tore up and sidewalks buckled – to head back to Kyle's place when an oasis of calm and neon lights caught her attention.

It was a convenience store. There was a line of people outside the door waiting for their turn to enter. And the road and parking directly in front of the store was undamaged, making the untouched store an island of order and safety in the carnage of the rest of the street.

"Whaaat?" She drew the word out, her head craning to stare as they drove past while navigating around holes in the ground.

"Da fudge?" Gleipnir finished for her, and she put the brakes on then backed up to find a parking spot where she wouldn't be blocking what little traversable surface was left of the street. The spot wasn't particularly close to the store.

"Let's check it out." They locked the car and trudged down the block towards the line, picking their way carefully around obstacles. "What's up here?" Casually, Gleipnir asked the person in front of them. He was floating beside Sam and stood in line with her rather than wrapped around her waist.

"It's a line to get into the store to shop." Some random citizen provided helpfully, and Sam raised an eyebrow to nod appreciatively at the obviousness of the statement.

"Why are we waiting in line, though?" It was Gleipnir's question that managed to get the answer they were looking for.

"Oh, the store has a magical security system that only allows a certain number of customers in at a time," the same man provided. "And it was shielded so nothing turned or spoiled during the Prometheus Purple event.

"Noice." Sam and Gleipnir high-fived and waited patiently for their turn. After seventeen minutes of the line crawling forward one position at a time, the pair found themselves inside the store. At the register was a clerk who looked like they were hating life right at that minute.

"Is it just me, or is that clerk bored as fuck?" Gleipnir murmured to Sam. She glanced up from busily perusing the nearly empty shelves for some sustenance which could be considered actual food. Pretty much anything that was actually 'convenient' to eat was gone and the metal shelving gleamed dully in the bright white lights of the store.

"Mmm. Yeah?" She mumbled then returned to rummaging through the condiments because she was pretty sure there was a box of... something... hidden back there. It had fallen into the space between the shelves, and she needed to nearly crawl inside the shelf to retrieve said mystery box.

"You look like some lost children just tricked you into your oven." Chortling at his joke and Sam's butt waggling while she stretched and struggled for the elusive box, Gleipnir started wandering the isles to see if there was anything else they would want. There were condiments galore. No one had wanted those. But the actual food was mostly gone. Anything refrigerated was long gone. There were a couple of bags of pretzels, pickled habanero flavored, and some 'gourmet' coffee. "Who the hell buys whole been coffee from a convenience store. And how is it 'dark void' flavored?"

"Ah ha!" Gleipnir, along with several other shoppers glanced in Sam's direction as she crowed triumphantly. "Got you, you squirmy little box of... plain pasta? Nooooo! I wanted something tastier. Boo." She shuffled morosely around the store and over to Gleipnir.

"What did you find?" She sidled up beside the pact item who gave her a conciliatory hug.

"Beef jerky," smugly, he held up the three pound bag of 'Very Plain Meat Jerky'. It was advertised flashily on the packaging as having 'just salt and meat' as the ingredients. Sam shrugged her acceptance. "It's on sale, seventy-five percent off."

"Okay. Not bad." Then she looked closer at the bright yellow and neon pink pack with a creeping suspicion. "Wait a minute. It says, 'Meat Jerky'." Pointing an accusatory finger at the unusual wording. "What kind of meat?"

"It doesn't say," the bored clerk called over from the register as he was checking out another person. "That's why people who grab it keep changing their minds at checkout." Pausing in his processing of the order in front of him, he grabbed four bags of jerky from behind the counter and tossed them up in the air before letting them fall down to the floor without concern. Then he went back to ringing up the order in front of him. "Boss has them discounted."

"Wait, are they on sale?" The guy who was being rung up asked almost reluctantly. "How much are they?"

"They're a buck a pound normally. So, seventy-five percent off whatever that is. I don't fucking care. I would give it to you just to be rid of them but the enchantments on the store prevent me from selling product for less than it was purchased for unless it is within a week of its expiration date."

"Give me two bags then," the customer requested, still sounding reluctant. "I've got an enchanted ingredient-identifier medical device at home because of my wife's allergies."

"Up to you man." The cashier tallied up two bags of meat jerky with the order and tossed them in the grocery bag for his customer. "You ready?" All the depression, exasperation, and ennui of every public facing service worker ever oozed from his being in those two words.

Chapter 100

"You really don't want to be here, do you?" It was concern that made Sam ask because, well, he'd kind of been exuding I'm-trapped-somewhere-I-don't-want-to-be vibes.

"Eh. I'm getting paid." He shrugged it off as if he hadn't been sighing theatrically every few moments and rolling his eyes each time he called out 'next' for another customer to come in. "But would you want to be here? I haven't even had time to restock the shelves, I'm afraid they'll riot out there if I close for ten minutes to use the bathroom."

"Oooh." Gleipnir gasped as the employee's words sparked a memory. "Toilet paper. I'll grab some." He bobbed off in a floating hurry only to return a few seconds later empty ribboned. "No joy."

"Do you have more food in the back that needs to be restocked?" The idea that there might be hope for a reasonable dinner sparked in Sam as she continued chatting with the worker.

"Yeah. But like I said, I can't –"

"What if Gleipnir and I were to watch the store for you, no one in, no one out while you do that?" Then she added hastily, "If it will only take a few minutes that is?" The kid was thoughtful for a second before making his decision.

"The store enchantments won't let me if it thinks it can't trust you." He was waffling but Sam was determined to find something worth eating. Thinking about her F.B.I. badge hidden away in her robe pocket and the standard law enforcement enchantments on it, she was fairly sure things would be fine.

"Why don't you try? I'm sure it will trust me." Forty-five minutes later – twenty of which had been dedicated to the sounds of the loudest shit anyone had ever taken coming from the employee restroom – Sam was sad to say that of the restocked foodstuff, only a small box of Original Flavor Cheasoning mix looked at all appetizing. Hopefully Kyle had some popcorn at home.

She and Gleipnir were workshopping on how to spin their meager haul off as better than it was the entire ride home. Gleipnir drug his ribbon behind him dejectedly as they made their way up the flight of steps to Kyle's apartment, lamenting that they didn't 'catch' anything good. None of their ideas would have made their haul look any better. When the entered the apartment, they found Anna at the kitchen counter whistling a tune which the prisms chimed a counter point to – which was a whole different issue that Sam did not have time for right now – using a Daedalus Industries hot-cold stone intended for alchemical laboratory work as a cooktop. The girl was sauteing up a plethora of vegetables and meat in a frying pan while a steaming pot of rice cooled on the kitchen table.

"What…" A lot of possible questions ran through Sam's mind as she considered which to ask first. After a moment of hesitation, she settled on something neutral to forestall any potential arguments. "…happened… here?" Yeah. That felt, not-judgy enough and not too panicked.

"I got dinner." Anna smiled happily and went back to whistling with her choir of magical pets. In her head, Sam counted to five and wondered if her sister was deliberately being obtuse or if she just was like that. On the off chance that this was an 'Anna thing', Sam chose to believe it was not deliberate.

Tamping down the flare of anger that ignited along with the terror she felt for her sister, Sam tried again.

"I can see that. Where from?" She'd only hissed that through her clenched teeth a little bit. Anna was still unconcernedly working on the meal before her, sniffing appreciatively as she added some fresh cilantro. Which was damn good smelling and Sam had to take a second to enjoy the tantalizing scent herself. Sam had sidled over next to her sister and was in the process of trying to sneak a bite of food out of the hot pan with her unwashed fingers. Anna smacked the back of her wrist with a wooden spoon. "Ow. That hurt."

"Then you shouldn't do it." The teen scolded the elder sister with a saccharine grin. "What would grandma say?" While Anna was distracted, Gleipnir had nabbed a huge forkful out of her sight. Which he showed Sam over Anna's shoulder and they high fived behind Anna's head. "I saw that," the younger sister admonished. "I just didn't care because Gleipnir used a fork instead of dirty hands."

"Spoil sport." Gleip sulked, "But where did you get food."

"The farmer's market in the park."

"What?" Sam exclaimed; frustrated that she didn't remember that there was a market, horrified that it was still happening in spite of everything, and furious that Anna had gone on her own instead of just telling Sam to go.

"By yourself?" Gleipnir was really just concerned about Anna's safety as she was his little sister and didn't want anything to happen to her.

"Chill out." Stirring the dish, she added some kind of sauce to it and tasted a vegetable. "Hmm, too crunchy still. Needs a minute. And no. I didn't go alone. Neighbor Dude took me."

"That flaked out, stoner, bodybuilder, wannabe surfer boy?" Gleip's outrage was palpable. "He couldn't cast a defensive spell to save the one brain cell left in his drug-fried skull."

"Well, he really knows his herbs. He helped me pick out all the ingredients to make this. It's his peanut sauce recipe." Seemingly oblivious to Gleipnir and Sam's indignation that she had trusted her safety to someone whom they considered to be of questionable intelligence, Anna tasted their dinner again. "It's ready. Grab some bowls."

"Of course, he knows his herbs. It's his Gods damned specialty." Sam muttered as she followed instructions because she was terribly eager to try the food regardless of the recipe's source.

"Yes, he's familiar with all the main herb varieties; Wizard Wowie, Hangman's Hashish, the Philosopher's Stoned..." Sam snigged at Gleipnir's murmured sarcasm, which Anna ignored.

"Light some candles, will you? I'm tired of having to cast light so I can see better, the emergency lights are okay and all but –"

"But regular light is better." Sam finished for her sister with an indulgent smile.

"And you know how I am with fire." They tucked into their meal with gusto, Gleipnir helping himself to a second portion which prompted Anna to make a bowl for Kyle and hide it away in the fridge.

"Can we get the recipe?" Gleipnir grudgingly admired the dish from the guy he'd been making fun of. "This is pretty damn good."

376

"Stoner food usually is." Sam agreed.

Chapter 101

6:51 PM September 16th. 2026
Washington D.C., the White House Helipad

The landscapers had been a flurry of activity all day, Camina had heard, as they prepared for the important visitors who were on that helicopter. Not just the landscapers, all the White House staff. Tours had been canceled. It had been hot sweaty work as well because the spate of nice weather which had graced the East Coast was continuing in uncomfortably warm fashion. It made the warlock glad of her armor's environmental controls. She smirked a bit as she watched perspiration beading on the secret service agents' faces and running down their unmentionables.

Overhead. a bright and shiny new helicopter's rotors made their characteristic *whuffwhuffwhuff* as it descended onto the White House helipad through the evening haze. It had been hot in D.C. today, but the air was already cooling. Perhaps Camina would have been able to smell the scent of fresh-mown lawn if he visor had been open.

However, Camina had the foresight to close her visor so she wouldn't have to squint against the gusting downdraft created by the helicopter. Beside her, the vice president squinted and tried not to grimace as grit bombarded her eyes. She couldn't help it, Camina snorted at her. Seeing the woman's discomfort a secret service mage shouted an offer to provide a barrier spell for the vice president over the linked communications network Camina was part of. Camina offered to ship his idiot ass back to his family in boxes of confetti sized bits if he jeopardized all their lives by initiating a spell when their guests were so close.

At least, that was what she wanted to say. What she actually barked at the agents was –

"No magic. Our *guests* will sense it." And she didn't have to elaborate further. They all knew who was coming. The secret service agents also knew that *they* weren't equipped to handle this kind of threat, if the visitors chose to become a threat.

Which was why Camina had been called back to D.C. while her husband was missing and one of her children was currently in and out of consciousness from some kind of magical something-not-quite-radiation-poisoning which was probably actual magical radiation poisoning. Camina's general disgust at the fact that this meeting even had to happen had come through in her tone of voice. How *dare* the Eastern Dragons play politics right now? How fucking *dare,* they try to keep up their high and mighty pretentions when they knew damn well that their kind were responsible for hundreds – maybe thousands – of deaths and *billions* in infrastructure damage.

That was why Camina was standing beside the *vice* president. Damned Eastern Dragon delegation couldn't bear the insult it would be to lower themselves to stand among non-magical folk like the actual president of the God Damned United States of America. The fury burning Camina up on the inside was real. A white-hot inferno that left her seeing red and her breath coming in short furnace blasts from her nostrils as she clenched her jaw.

Outwardly, she was, well… Imagine there was a person who was always outwardly not just calm and stoic, but cold and hard seeming? Now imagine that person filled with the rage of a thousand suns possessed by cats trying to avoid a bath and nonchalantly standing at ease as she awaits orders wearing her techno-magical battle armor powered by divine magic and holding a holy weapon powerful enough to kill a dragon. A person who was worried about their family and the only thing preventing her from seeking vengeance on the ones who she considered responsible was the fact that her husband *might* still be alive, and her child *might* not die from magical radiation poisoning. So, she was adopting a wait-and-see-mother-fuckers approach to the whole situation.

As the helicopter's engines died down and the wind subsided, Camina opened the visor on her helmet. Glancing over when the movement drew her attention, the vice president took one look at the expression on Camina's face and shuddered slightly. Returning her attention to the delegates exiting the helicopter, she pasted on her best professional-welcome expression for the occasion. Not a smile per se, but nowhere near the veiled cold snarl of blankness on Camina's face.

One… two… three… Only three individuals exited the helicopter. And they all appeared to be security, not the actual delegates. It was supposed to be a few human representatives from the court of the Chinese Empire accompanied by the rare presence of at least one, and possibly two, Eastern Dragons. There was some kind of discussion occurring at the aircraft as one of the individuals who had exited was holding a heated discussion with the other two and those remaining within. Two of the ones who had exited seemed to be security guards dressed in ceremonial garb. Very dashing and straight out of the eighteenth century.

The discussion had become an argument and was quite heated with raised voices becoming more distinct as the helicopter engine idled lower, with much curt gesturing. Someone pointed in their general direction and half the secret service agents went for their wands or weapons.

"Stand down." Camina barked curtly into her mic and then gave her helmet a command that directed the external microphones to focus on the argument. Not surprisingly, it was in Chinese. Camina had never learned Chinese, but her suit had the ability to translate for her, something Michael had forgotten to tell her about for the first several years. So, she gave the command for that to happen and listened in with only a modicum of interest.

"They are deliberately violating protocol." Someone hissed. "Look at her. She's in full armor."

"Well, what did you expect?" The woman who'd been trying to persuade the delegation to actually participate in the meeting and leave the helicopter replied reasonably.

"She's not even supposed to be here. Our intelligence said she was deployed to New York and our ag– she was being kept distracted with busy work evacuating people." That got an eyebrow raise out of Camina and the flames of wrath she was nurturing inside of her flared with new life.

"This is clearly an ambush meant to kill one of the ancient dragons." That was where Camina had to stop listening as she didn't just snort in amusement but outright chortled, before quickly regaining her composure.

"Hear anything interesting?" the vice president inquired, giving the Magicorps soldier a side-eye.

"Oh, yeah. You called it Madam Vice President." Camina informed the woman who did smile at that.

"Pissing their pants because you're here, are they?" It was the vice president's turn to chuckle. While the resulting smile didn't touch Camina's lips this time, there was a new glint of amusement in her eyes as she responded. "Their own damn fault for refusing to be in the presence of a non-magical plebian like President Van Helsing. Or perhaps they were afraid that he had some secret dragon-killing knowledge."

"Well, now it seems they may be worried about big bad Ascalon. They fear this is an ambush." Upon hearing that, the vice president snorted her own mirth.

"Oh, the paranoia and arrogance of dragons. Perish the thought. All we need is another disaster like what's happened in New York. Like one ancient dragon is worth that kind of pain." In her head, Camina finished the vice president's sentence for her. *When we can just send you to kill them at home if we really wanted to.* There had never been a reason to before. But maybe now, now Camina might be persuaded to take on that kind of assignment. Finally, one of the human delegates that was still in the helicopter got out and huffed as un-huffily as he could toward the waiting American greeting party.

"Madam Vice President," he began in a not particularly respectful and quite accusatory tone that was trying to pretend that it was neither accusatory nor disrespectful. "We were under the impression that this was a peaceful meeting to discuss the circumstances of the tragedy in New York."

"Oh," the vice president cooed in the soft gentle tones she was known for when discussing politics. "Is there some conflict nearby of which I am not aware? This is a peaceful meeting for our two great nations and noble dragons." Her bewildered expression and her absolute surety that that 'there was nothing wrong or abnormal in this situation at all' seemed to irritate the Chinese man speaking to her.

"If this is intended to be a peaceful meeting, then why is Camina Wattkins here?" he asked loudly and clearly disgruntled. Pausing for a second, he caught his breath before almost shouting the second question, which was really more a statement of the obvious. "In full armor?"

The vice president really was hamming up her agreed upon role and showed herself to be taken aback by the insinuation of both statements. Before she could respond, Camina gestured for her to wait and stepped forward slightly, servos on her suit whirring quietly with each movement. Her advance clearly startled the foreign security agent, and he stepped back several paces with wide-eyed horror written all over his face.

"With your permission, I'll handle this question, Madam Vice President." She smiled kindly at the woman beside her who nodded permission, before Camina turned back to the man before them both. The smile she gave to *him* was anything but kind. Her lips twisted and her expression morphed into one of a hungry predator and it chilled him to his bones. The instruments on her suit told Camina his heart was racing, and his breath was coming in quick little puffs that looked like the beginning of a full-on panic attack.

"What happened in New York was an avoidable tragedy," The Last Line purred in coldly reasonable tones. "Avoidable because the dragons who died, were not on U.S. soil legally. They weren't documented. So, they could not be monitored and protected. Like U.S. laws and international treaties specify and require specifically to prevent such events from happening. Was this an act of war? Was this an attack on our sovereign soil? Was this espionage? Why were those dragons here? We wouldn't want a misunderstanding to unnecessarily escalate our response. Please, let the dragons and your superiors know that I'm here, at the request of our president, to ensure America's response to this tragedy remains… proportional."

Coming Fall 2025
Kyle the Apprentice Warlock
Volume 2

Chapter 1

12:29 AM September 17th 2026
The National Museum of Unnatural Science and History

Kyle's neighbor was at work. He didn't work with the artifacts because he didn't have the skill set for it. Nor did he work in the gift shop, or in the gourmet level kitchen run by the chef that always had blood stains on him. While his people skills were pretty good – he was a friendly guy after all – the young man felt that he wasn't ready to risk interaction with the kind of people who might figure out his secret.

Because it was a *doozy* of a secret.

So, he most certainly didn't work during the day when the majority of the nerdy staff were at work and could be able to figure out that he was a little different from the average mindless stoner surfer dude he came off as. A smart person, a person with vast knowledge of magic, and auras, and history – that kind of person might begin to put together the little tells that he accidentally let slip sometimes.

A person like Kyle.

So, as friendly as he was, Kyle's neighbor and fellow employee of the Nation Museum of Unnatural Science and History, avoided Kyle. He also avoided all of the other consultants and researchers. He usually also avoided Kyle's sisters, because what if they noticed something off about him that they then mentioned to Kyle? Then Kyle might figure out that the goofy lug who missed his days surfing the Southern California Coast a lifetime ago and so very far away, was maybe someone he should be looking at a little more critically.

That afternoon had been a mistake. Helping little Anna out like that and offering to take her shopping like that. But it had been a weird week. And the kid reminded him of his own sister, who he missed terribly. Sighing, he plunged his mop into the bucket again and swished it around before wringing it out. It was almost time to change the water again.

Nah. He should change it now. No point just rubbing dirty water around the floor. And off he trundled to empty the bucket on wheels.

If he was faster than the other janitorial staff, no one really commented. At least, not to his face. But he made the conscious effort to keep his movements slowed to the pace of an average human. He used two hands to lift the mop bucket to pour out the dirty water, instead of the one he actually needed. It wasn't that heavy for him. Most things weren't. Then he paused to scratch his forearm as a new itch started.

Ever since the magic had spiked his hair had been growing like crazy and his arm was looking a little furry. If it kept up at this pace he'd have to shave on his lunch break and that would be just another oddity that might get him caught out by curious coworkers. But that was a later problem. Not a right now problem. Right now, his problem was washing the bucket, and filling it with clean water and fresh cleaning solution.

The Museum of Unnatural Science and History was both the best and the worst place he could have landed a job for him to hide out with. Free housing? Definitely a bonus. Good pay. Very good pay because of the hazardous nature of the laboratory facilities that he cleaned in addition to the public display areas. But a huge chance of getting found out by the academics who worked there, or worse, the Magicorps officers who both reported to Director Arcas but also to their superiors.

And he really didn't know which would be worse. Getting caught by some academic who might want to study him, or getting abducted to some military black site for whatever they did with his kind here. That's why today had been a mistake. Because while Anna reminded him of his own kid sister, she noticed when he forgot to pretend that he was a regular non-magical human being.

She noticed the hair on his arms had grown in over the course of a few hours in his company. She noticed when he'd been able to carry all of their combined groceries without any issue. Not to mention the fact that he had been buying enough food for a family of five because his metabolism required so Gods Damned many calories. The bags were a lot of pounds and he'd forgotten to pretend that they were heavy. He'd been out, *out* of food when he left for the market, so he was grazing as he shopped. Anna had noticed how much food he'd noshed down on.

She'd also noticed when he didn't respond to his fake name. Adam. It was new to him, and he wasn't used to it. Okay. Not that new. He'd been going by it for months. But he still wasn't used to it. Not only that, but he wasn't even sure if he wanted to keep going by that name. It was just the first thing he'd come up with because he for damned sure knew when he ended up in New York that he couldn't go by his real name in case the people who'd been after him happened to be here too.

Lost morosely in his thoughts, the man who wasn't really named Adam, didn't at first notice the faint sounds his enhanced hearing caught. A scritching, scuffing sound and an unfamiliar scent mixed lightly with blood coming from inside the secure lab with four Magicorps soldiers stationed outside it. It wasn't until he looked up and nodded at the night shift guards on his way past, that he realized there was noise within. The guards weren't responding to it, so it must have been okay. The director was probably having a snack while he worked and they might have brought in another expert - or a high ranking military person – to review their work on the artifact that caused the disaster.

"Is Kyle or the director working late?" He nodded at the door with his chin, implying there was someone in the room beyond. The casual question earned him confused looks from the soldiers before one spoke up.

"No one's working, the lab's empty."

That... that confused the janitor as he was absolutely certain that he heard someone inside the sealed lab. But maybe he just wasn't supposed to know. That must be it. There were a lot of sealed rooms that staff weren't supposed to go in, that weird sound came from if you could hear in certain frequencies. Rooms that were locked, and warded, and that the keys had been thrown away because the museum was the only place with enough magic to hold them. Not even to start about the miles of artifact storage that extended beneath the entirety of Central Park.

"Sorry. I thought I heard someone in there. My mistake. I must be on edge because of all the stuff that's happened this week. Got me jumpy." He smiled disarmingly, winked and taped the side of his nose. "My ears and nose are playing tricks on me." He continued on his way about to round a corner when the soldier who'd spoken earlier called out.

"Hey, Adam." Adam hid his sigh and plastered on his friendly smile before turning to respond.

"Yeah?" he grinned in a friendly manner while trying not to draw attention to his large canines which were too thick to be vampire fangs.

"What made you think someone was in the lab? What did you smell that made you ask if it was the director or Kyle in there?" Adam, who much preferred his real name but didn't use it here, kept his self-deprecating smile on his face as he responded.

"Oh. I just thought I heard someone in there. And blood. I thought I smelled blood. And since the director eats blood, I assumed he was what I was hearing. But also, Kyle got injured today, so maybe it was him. But I don't – I don't know. Just nerves I guess." He finished lamely and then waved a sheepish goodbye before hurrying off to continue mopping the floor. There was a lot of floor left to clean and he'd almost said he didn't recognize the scent but then there would be questions about how well he could smell and why he was able to smell that well.

Instead, he kept quiet and once he had rounded the corner and was no longer visible to the soldiers, hurried down the hall at a pace far faster than an average human could match. So, Adam, who used to have a different name, didn't notice the group of soldiers conferring about whether or not they should risk unlocking the lab to check on it. He did, however, hear the loud booming as the door to the lab was blown open from the inside and boom echoingly against the wall opposite. Half the building heard it.

Magical alarms began to whoop as automated audio messages instructed civilians to evacuate any combat zones and get prone on the ground as soon as they safely could so that the security would not target them as a threat. Following those instructions to remove himself from possible danger was exactly what Not-Really-Adam had intended to do even as additional Magicorps soldiers intercepted him.

"ID. ID. Show your identification card." One shouted while they squad of four held him at wand point. With trembling hands, Not-Really-Adam, did show them his identification card. But, he was a big guy, he made people nervous on a normal day. This had not been a normal week. The soldiers verified his identity as a museum employee by reading the enchantments on the card and verifying them against Adam's aura. "Good. Okay. You two, with me. You, stay with Adam unless we call."

Though he'd rushed to remove himself from the vicinity of the lab after embarrassing himself with questions he shouldn't have been asking, he was still close enough that maybe fighting could come his way. And that made him nervous. Because something like that could reveal his secret.

"Don't worry, Adam." The Magicorps soldier glanced at his ID card that he was still holding up with shaking hands to get his name. She was one of the new transfers and apparently hadn't memorized everyone's names yet. "They've got this." Adam nodded and lowered his hand to his chest, still clutching the card in nervous fingers while they listened to the sound of combat. Shouted spells, alchemy rounds were accompanied by flashes of light that they saw coloring the hallway intersection.

More soldiers ran past the pair and another group hurried into the hallway intersection, using the corner of the hall, Adam was on as cover. It was a loud fight. Yet with his enhanced hearing, 'Adam' could tell that the only ones making noise were the soldiers. And their voices were becoming fewer. A shout came around the corner and the so the woman guarding him gave him a reassuring glance.

"I've got to go help. You get out of here. Get to safety." She urged him as she ran off, wand at the ready and a gun in her other hand. Where safety was, he wasn't sure because the museum should have gone into lockdown. Which meant that they were all trapped in the building with whoever the soldiers were fighting. But he was damned well willing to try. That was until the fighting went silent and a strangled shriek came from behind him.

Turning, the man now called Adam saw the kind soldier who had been guarding him held a lot by her throat. He probably hadn't been meant to see it in the dim emergency lights. But his eyes were just as good as his ears. Maybe better. There they were. Two of them. One crushing the soldier's throat and grinning evilly as he did so. And the other, holding an artifact retrieval case. Behind them, bodies were strewn along the floor.

"Fight or flight." The one currently murdering a woman before Adam's eyes laughed the question at him. "Run and die or fight and die." Adam's eyes narrowed in anger, and he felt the primal instincts that were a part of his secret and which he usually fought so hard to hide, rushing to the surface. Instead of fighting them, this time he welcomed them.

Other Books From Warlocks In Space Publishing

Lines of Inheritance by K. R. Dalley

<u>Coming 2025</u>
Kyle the Apprentice Warlock Volume 2 by M. J. Okawa
Shadow Hound by K. R. Dalley

<u>Coming at a future date</u>
Kyle the Apprentice Warlock Book 3 by M. J. Okawa
Inheritance by K. R. Dalley

www.ingramcontent.com/pod-product-compliance
Lightning Source LLC
Chambersburg PA
CBHW070201120726
47909CB00001B/197